BATTLESHIP
INDOMITABLE

GALACTIC LIBERATION

Starship Liberator *Battleship Indomitable*

Also by the Authors

DAVID VANDYKE
PLAGUE WARS

The Eden Plague	*The Demon Plagues*	*First Conquest*
Reaper's Run	*The Reaper Plague*	*Desolator*
Skull's Shadows	*The Orion Plague*	*Tactics of Conquest*
Eden's Exodus	*Cyborg Strike*	*Conquest of Earth*
Apocalypse Austin	*Comes The Destroyer*	*Conquest and Empire*
Nearest Night	*Forge and Steel*	

B.V. LARSON
STAR FORCE

Swarm	*Conquest*	*Annihilation*
Extinction	*Battle Station*	*Storm Assault*
Rebellion	*Empire*	*The Dead Sun*

with David VanDyke

Outcast	*Exile*	*Demon Star*

THE UNDYING MERCENARIES

Steel World	*Machine World*	*Rogue World*
Dust World	*Death World*	
Tech World	*Home World*	

GALACTIC LIBERATION BOOK 2

BATTLESHIP INDOMITABLE

DAVID VANDYKE
B.V. LARSON

CASTALIA HOUSE

Battleship Indomitable

David VanDyke and B. V. Larson

Published by Castalia House
Kouvola, Finland
www.castaliahouse.com

This book or parts thereof may not be reproduced in any form, stored in a retrieval system, or transmitted in any form by any means—electronic, mechanical, photocopy, recording, or otherwise—without prior written permission of the publisher, except as provided by Finnish copyright law.

Copyright © 2017 by David VanDyke and B. V. Larson
All rights reserved

Cover Art: Tom Edwards

This book is a work of fiction. Names, characters, places, businesses and incidents are either products of the author's imagination or used fictitiously. Any resemblance to actual events, locales or persons, living or dead, is entirely coincidental.

Contents

Part I: Commander	1
Chapter 1	5
Chapter 2	15
Chapter 3	25
Chapter 4	35
Chapter 5	45
Chapter 6	57
Chapter 7	69
Chapter 8	79
Chapter 9	87
Chapter 10	95
Chapter 11	105
Chapter 12	113
Chapter 13	123
Chapter 14	133
Chapter 15	143
Part II: Crusader	153
Chapter 16	155
Chapter 17	165
Chapter 18	177

Chapter 19	185
Chapter 20	193
Chapter 21	203
Chapter 22	213
Chapter 23	223
Chapter 24	233
Chapter 25	243
Chapter 26	253
Chapter 27	265
Chapter 28	275
Chapter 29	285
Chapter 30	295
Chapter 31	303
Chapter 32	311
Chapter 33	319
Chapter 34	329
Chapter 35	337
Part III: Caesar	**345**
Chapter 36	347
Chapter 37	357
Chapter 38	369
Chapter 39	381
Chapter 40	391
Chapter 41	401

Chapter 42   411

Chapter 43   423

Chapter 44   433

Part I: Commander

Once my ragtag Breakers had established our base of operations in the Starfish Nebula, I began planning the first major revolt. The Sachsen system would be the test case, ripe for plucking given how recently the people there had been conquered. Only one orbital fortress stood in my way. If the Breakers couldn't seize it, I might as well give up my dreams of galactic liberation right then and there. If they could, more planets would fall like dominoes. Fleets and troops would flock to my banner.

But first, there were families of my troops to rescue. My people couldn't be expected to fight wholeheartedly with knives to the throats of their loved ones....

—A History of Galactic Liberation,
by Derek Barnes Straker, 2860 A.D.

Chapter 1

2817 A.D., Old Earth reckoning. Prael System.

"We've found them, Commodore Straker," said Captain Gibson over the secure narrowband comlink. He was transmitting from his shuttle on the surface of the cold, miserable little world of Prael.

Commodore Derek Straker stood on the Spartan bridge of *Lockstep*, Gibson's ship, a former Mutuality fleet auxiliary transport. The ship held a company of Straker's Breakers—his troops—and orbited above Prael, squawking forged codes that showed it to be a different vessel, one that had not defected from the Mutuality.

"They're at a labor camp near the equator," Gibson continued. "I sent you a data file."

Prael's equatorial zone got warm enough to grow food, but only barely. Life was hard even outside of a labor camp. Inside… well, no one in the extensive system of Mutuality prisons and re-education facilities expected anything but misery.

Gibson's report meant the families of the *Lockstep's* crew, even the small children, had been rounded up, ripped from their lives and put to work. Because they were connected to enemies of the State, they would slave until they died.

Or, if they were suitable, they would be turned into Hok troopers by forcible injection of invasive biotech. That was policy in the worker's paradise of the Mutuality. The crushing weight of the State fell on anyone who stepped out of line.

Gibson had infiltrated the bleak town where their former residences stood, intending to contact someone he could trust, and to learn their fate.

Now, he had.

"What do their defenses look like?" asked Lieutenant Johnny "Loco" Paloco, Straker's best friend and comrade-in-arms, from his seat at an empty bridge station. The slim man's booted feet rested on the unlit console and his hands were laced behind his head.

"My contact gave me what info she has. It's a typical camp setup. More importantly, she heard a Mutual Guard mechanized company has been deployed there," answered Gibson.

"Only one reason to defend a labor camp with armored vehicles," Straker mused. "They expect us to try a rescue, and they want to harden the target, maybe trap us. Typical Mutuality tactic."

"Inquisitors are smart and paranoid, and they don't like it when you kill their brother clones," said Gibson. "There's probably another Lazarus there, waiting like a spider in his web."

"Good thing we have a few hammers to squash spiders. Foehammers. Sledgehammers."

Loco winced. "We really need to work on your jokes, Derek. That was terrible."

Straker raised an eyebrow at Loco. "Who said I was joking? I'm looking forward to finding another of those clones."

Loco grinned and leered. "Hmm, maybe if we're lucky we'll pick up another concubine like Tachina. I bet all the Lazaruses have them. I'd like a piece of that action."

"I thought you were with Campos…?"

"I am. But things can change. Or maybe they'll get along. Make a Loco sandwich outta me."

Straker shook his head ruefully. "Like sharing a cage with two wildcats, more likely. Good luck with that."

"Die young, stay pretty."

"Don't die yet. I still need you."

Loco held up his hands at Straker's hard look. "Aw, boss, I didn't know you cared."

"I need you and your suit to do your mission, Loco. Now get your head in the game."

"All right, all right."

Things had been so much simpler as a Hundred Worlds mechsuiter. Straker could see why the chain of command discouraged fraternization and locked their troops into specific roles and routines: train, fight, R&R, repeat, until dead or retired. It was far simpler than living a real, complicated life.

A life like his own.

He turned back to Gibson's image on the screen. "We'll hit them in about… seven hours, at two in the morning local time. They'll be less alert, and they'll stand out better on thermal when it's colder."

"I'll meet you there. Gibson out."

Loco put his feet on the deck and activated his console. "Let's see what the good captain sent us." Soon, he had a visiplate showing a crude, hand-drawn diagram of the labor camp, marked with locations of guard shacks, towers, offices and barracks. "Let me pull up a recent image."

Lockstep had been circling the rocky planet for three days, and her crew had been continuously taking imagery of man-made facilities in preparation for identifying the target. Now, Loco manipulated the two pictures to get the scale right, and overlaid one on the other.

"I'll transfer the annotations to the photo. It would be good to get a high-res shot, though. Can we alter orbit for a close pass?" Loco asked.

Straker thought about it, and then shook his head. "I don't want to do anything to warn them early. Do what you can with what you have. I want a mission overview ready to brief the Breakers in three hours."

"Without a high-res pic, I can't guarantee to identify the hidden tanks, boss," Loco said in a warning tone.

"It's a balance of risks. I believe surprise is more important."

"Aye aye, Commodore Derek sir." Loco got to work.

Six hours later, *Lockstep* began her descent on a path designed to avoid the sparse Mutuality aerospace control facilities. The camp had been diagrammed and the mission briefings distributed. All of Straker's Breakers knew their roles and their parts.

Nobody had questioned the wisdom of risking an entire company and a ship to save thirty-odd family members, plus whoever else they could scoop up. Most of the Breakers hated the Mutuality in a visceral way, and would do almost anything to liberate their prisoners. Straker had no doubt his troops would take grim satisfaction in killing all the Mutuality minions—thuggish guards, cruel torturers, smug brainwashers—in the labor camp.

"Time to mount up," Straker said to Loco and to Karst, the only other trained—well, half-trained—mechsuiter he had. The three men left the bridge in the hands of Gibson's XO and headed for the spacious cargo holds.

The *Lockstep* was a ship of the largest class of freighters that could routinely land on planets. Though no dropship or assault boat, she was adequate for insertions such as this, as long as they had no aerospace opposition. They'd have to set down away from the camp, though, or risk taking fire as they landed. The *Lockstep* was unarmored, and one round from a tank or a missile crawler could knock her out of the sky.

In the main cargo bay, three mechsuits lay like reclining giants. Seven meters from head to toe, the constructs represented the peak of Hundred Worlds ground force technology. Properly handled and using brainlinks, they were each worth a hundred armored vehicles, perhaps more.

But brainlinks were finicky things, and Straker and Loco hadn't been able to get theirs to synch with these mechsuits. It took a high-tech facility and specialists to match one pilot to a specific suit.

Still, before his capture, Straker had been the best Hundred Worlds mechsuiter alive, and Loco was an elite veteran as well. They could use the manual backup systems and still be five to ten times as effective as any tank, Straker figured.

The three climbed through the robotic vehicles' opened chest plates into their cockpits. Tight-fitting sensors enfolded them, ensuring the mechsuits would mimic their every move. This was the major advantage of the 'suit—a wearer strode about the battlefield like fifty tons of avenging demigod, running and dodging, pointing and shooting, more akin to a martial artist than an armored vehicle.

Straker and Loco piloted standard Foehammers, built by the factory they'd hijacked on the asteroid habitat Freiheit. Karst drove a Sledgehammer, a monstrosity kluged together from salvaged mechsuit parts plus the addition of a simple, heavy weapon in each arm and missile boxes on its shoulders. It was slow, unreliable and lacked agility, but it carried a heavy punch. Straker couldn't afford to leave it behind, and anyway, Karst needed the experience.

The three suits remained strapped to the deck during the long, shallow suborbital approach. Straker keyed his comlink to the general network and spoke. "Straker here. Sound off for commo check."

"Loco here. I read you Lima Charlie."

"Karst here. Loud and clear, sir."

"Heiser here. All good." Heiser was Straker's first sergeant, or "Spear," leading the infantry company.

"Ritter One here. *Alles klar*," said Aldrik, the eldest of the two surviving Ritter brothers, in his harsh, Old Earth German accent.

"Ritter Two here. Me too, sir." That was Conrad. The brothers were Heiser's two platoon sergeants.

"Double check your people's cold weather gear," said Straker. "We have a fifteen-kilometer convoy into battle and the wind chill will be well below zero."

"Frostbite will be its own punishment," said Conrad.

"That might be true in training," Heiser snapped, "but on a mission, it can get your buddy killed too."

"*Jawohl*, Spear, we hear you," said Aldrik.

Straker went on, "I want a smooth deployment on landing. Infantry straight into the crawlers, no screwing around. Mechsuits will pull security. Stay out of our way, people. Without brainlinks, we don't have situational awareness enough to know not to squash someone who gets underfoot."

The freighter shuddered with the fast, shallow descent, first bleeding off speed through atmospheric heating, and then flying through the air by using the ship's stubby retractable wings to glide.

"Any sensor pings?" Straker asked.

"No, sir," said one of the *Lockstep* bridge crew.

"Let me know."

"Aye aye, sir."

Straker wouldn't call off the mission if they were detected. He'd just have to accept the price in blood if the enemy were alert and ready, rather than dozing on midnight watch as he hoped to catch them.

He ran three systems checks on his Foehammer before they finally set down. Silence settled for a moment, broken only by the *ping-pop* of cooling hull metal, until Heiser barked at the infantry to get moving.

Straker released the cargo clamps that held his mechsuit and rolled carefully to a crouch. Extra layers of crysteel beneath him shielded the deck from abuse it was not designed for, the pressure of alloy gauntlets, knees and feet. The big cargo bay door in front of him dropped to form a ramp, and infantry hastened to lay a path of plates to protect it as well.

Once set, he carefully ape-walked out on toes and knuckles until he could rise to stand on the ramp. Then he stepped gingerly, like a man on a fragile roof, until his feet hit the frozen ground. He immediately brought up his

HUD in thermal imaging and light-enhancement mode, giving him a combination of monochromatic day-like vision and false color heat sensing. Behind him, the other suits would be doing the same.

Straker strode forward down a rutted road in the direction of the labor camp, until he could see a farmhouse set in a hollow between two hills. This was the only dwelling for kilometers, and the freighter's approach path had been carefully chosen to minimize overflight of locals.

He raised his force-cannon and, after suppressing the bimetal reactive ammo load, fired straight into the building. The magnetic tube that normally contained and guided a destructive jet of plasma lanced out, empty of heat. Without the ammunition to create plasma, what resulted was a directed electromagnetic pulse, or EMP, useful for disabling electronics without destroying anything else.

The farmhouse went dark as all of its circuitry fried. The locals couldn't be allowed to report their landing. Straker had to keep the giant mechsuits, his deadly surprise, hidden until the last moment possible.

"Breakers, sound off," Straker called.

"Loco in position, nothing to report."

"Karst in position, nothing to report."

"We're loaded and ready, sir," said Heiser.

"*Lockstep* good to go, sir," said the freighter's XO. "Waiting to reposition, on your word."

"Move out." Straker stepped off at a comfortable pace designed to minimize noise. Mechsuits were never quiet, but he didn't have to make it easy for the enemy. He walked straight down the dirt road, with Loco and Karst behind, left and right of the crawlers.

Double trailers on each crawler carried the two platoons of straight-leg infantry. The whole arrangement proceeded at about fifty kilometers per hour, which would cover the fifteen kilometers to the target in roughly twenty minutes.

Nineteen minutes later, Straker slowed and halted the convoy behind a low hill.

He'd detected no outposts or sensors. Had Straker been setting a trap, he'd have made sure the camp was ringed by both. Of course, the Lazarus clone was almost certainly expecting a simple infantry raid, possibly with a few gun trucks or light armored vehicles, not full-up mechsuits, and he'd want to make the target look as inviting as possible.

Straker watched as the infantry deployed. They'd cover the last kilometer on foot. With a mechanized company waiting in ambush, coming in on the crawlers would be suicide.

"All right men, follow us at a double time but stay away from the 'suits. Their heavy stuff will be targeting us. No reason to catch that hell. Request support fire from Corporal Karst if you need it, and proceed according to the mission order. Work the plan, and the plan will work. Straker out."

"Very inspiring," said Loco on the mechsuiter channel. "*Not.*"

"This isn't the time for speeches. Or chatter, for that matter."

"There's always time for chatter, Derek. That's what makes this job fun."

"Okay, Loco, the *fun* starts now. Follow me," Straker said. "Karst, unlike Loco here, keep your mind on your job. Support that infantry. We can take care of ourselves. You'll have a Foehammer soon enough."

"I got it, sir. I'm no glory hound."

"See, Loco? He knows you too well. Go active and assault in three, two, one, mark."

With a surge of adrenaline, Straker switched on his active sensors and charged over the right side of the hill at an angle. Loco would be doing the mirror opposite to his left. Their lateral movement would make them harder to hit in case the enemy turned out to be alert after all.

Immediately his HUD blazed with information. Instead of mere cold fields, rocks and trees, he saw the camp complex, warm buildings lit with false colors and peppered with icons as his tactical semi-AI, or SAI, sorted items of interest. Floodlights caused his optical processor to adjust, and his active sensors searched for matches against the mechsuit's military database, classifying everything into threat levels.

He ignored the camp itself for the moment. If there were armored vehicles hidden among its barracks buildings, he couldn't simply blow them to shreds. Not with the prisoners so close. Instead, he scanned the perimeter and outward, searching for dug-in positions, the places where he'd set tanks if he were the defending commander.

The first one he found was almost underfoot, a light tank half-buried in the frozen ground, occupying a hasty revetment. The waste heat of its fusion engine showed clearly on thermal. If Straker had been in charge of the vehicle, he'd have camouflaged the signature better. The tank's gun pointed inward, toward the camp.

So that was to be their strategy. Let the rescuers hit the camp, and then trap them between the facility and a cordon of armored vehicles.

That would have been effective if they only had infantry to deal with. That assumption, and their lack of care in improving their defensive positions, meant these people were about to have a really, really bad night.

Straker was preparing to loose a force-cannon bolt into the light tank when he noticed a piece of luck: the vehicle's top hatch sat open, a man half-out of it with a smokestick between his fingers. His mouth hung open in shock as he stared at the Foehammer looming above.

Switching to his gatling, Straker fired a burst downward through the man, through the hatch and into the inside of the tank. A dozen penetrators, each as long as his hand, turned the tank commander into hamburger before ricocheting around the interior at supersonic speed, shredding everything and everyone there.

Straker stepped over the mess and swung his force-cannon smoothly to line up with the next heat signature identified as the greatest threat. It was a heavy tank, a mechsuit's nemesis. Only a heavy could shrug off a force-cannon bolt, at least from the front, and only the high-velocity gun of a heavy had the potential to take down a mechsuit with one devastating shot.

The tank's gun was pointed right at Straker, and for a moment he thought he was dead, but as he threw himself into a sideways roll, he realized the turret hadn't moved. The crew must still be scrambling to bring their weapons system up. The element of surprise had saved him.

"Loco, it looks like they're in a ring around the camp, like we expected," he said as he rolled smoothly to his feet and ran out of the heavy tank's front arc. "They were hoping to trap us inside. Stay in close, on their flanks, and we'll be able to roll them up."

"Roger wilco," said Loco. "Yeehaw!"

"You watch way too many vids, Loco."

"And you read way too many books, boss."

Straker gained the angle he wanted. The turret had just started to swing toward him when, with careful aim, he slammed a narrowly focused bolt of plasma into the engine compartment of the tank. This was a heavy's weak spot, and as the compact fusion reactor ruptured, its multi-isotopic hydrogen fuel exploded, sending a miniature mushroom cloud into the cold night sky.

Even so, the turret continued to track him. When a heavy's engine blew, it was a coin flip as to whether the crew compartment and main weapons would survive the blast. This tank had been lucky, and they evidently had enough battery power to fire a few more shots.

If the engine compartment was the heavy tank's weakness, the recharge time on its force-cannon was the Foehammer's. Heavier, more complex ammo could have reduced the weapon's recycle time, but then reloads would have run out sooner, and lack of ammunition on a battlefield could be a death sentence. Thus, the compromise between speed and endurance.

Straker continued his flat-out run, legs churning and throwing up cubic meters of frozen dirt as the spades of his mechsuit's crysteel alloy feet scooped divots like blast craters. On a straightaway, a 'suit could exceed two hundred kilometers per hour.

But this wasn't a straightaway. Straker found himself in a race for his life with nowhere to go except to continue trying to outrun the turning gun. He ripped off a long gatling burst in hopes of getting a lucky hit, or at least distracting the gunner, but the barrel continued to follow him with inexorable speed.

He was just about to dive to the ground and hope the gunner couldn't depress his aim enough to hit him when a streak of light struck the tank. It exploded, sending the turret spinning upward to fall heavily, barrel first, to stick in the ground like some bizarre lollipop.

Straker backtracked the streak and saw Karst's Sledgehammer standing at the reverse military crest of the hill, only his head and shoulders exposed. An arm was raised, its integrated particle beam cannon still white-hot after its shot.

"Dammit, Karst, I told you to support the infantry!"

"They haven't even passed my position, sir, and I saw you in trouble…"

"All right. Thanks. But keep your focus on your primary mission."

"Roger wilco, sir."

Straker couldn't fault the kid for wanting to get into the action. At least he was keeping a good covered position and sniping, the most effective use of the clumsy but heavily armed Sledgehammer. And Straker had to admit, he himself wasn't performing as well as he should. He was out of practice, too busy leading the Breakers and the human colony in the Starfish Nebula.

Also, lack of the brainlink made him feel as if the mechsuit were moving through molasses. He longed for the days when mere thinking meant moving and shooting. Once, he could smell the battlefield. Now, he felt insulated from it.

"One heavy and one light down," said Straker to Loco.

"Same here," said Loco. "Where are the crawlers and hovers? This is supposed to be a mech company, right?"

Straker ran laterally along where he expected the enemy perimeter should be, hunting for more defensive positions. "It might not be a standard one the way we're used to. We can't make assumptions they'll have one platoon of each vehicle type. Stay sharp and keep your eyes open."

"Just like sex, Derek."

Straker put a burst of gatling fire into what looked like an infantry fighting position. "Trust you to work sex into any discussion."

"Sex and violence, baby, that's the life of a mechsuiter. You should try it sometime."

Straker opened his mouth to reply when two spider holes popped their tops, one on each side of the position he'd just hosed down. Soldiers with rocket launchers lined up on his center of mass, and before he could turn his gatling on either one, they fired.

Rockets leaped toward him, faster than he could react.

Chapter 2

Prael. Re-education and Training Camp 13.

Straker cursed as the pop-up gunners fired their antitank rockets at him. Somebody was on the ball, it seemed.

In showvids, such weapons moved slowly, the better to be seen by the audience. In real battles, they moved as fast as gun rounds, slowed only by the brainchipped perceptions of a properly linked mechsuiter.

Perceptions Straker didn't have.

But there was an older, more primitive version of this time-compressing phenomenon, a thing of the endocrine system, of adrenaline and cortisol and a half-dozen other fight-or-flight hormones. The projectiles seemed to crawl toward him. His only chance was to bend his knees and let himself fall backward, slowly, oh so slowly.

One rocket clipped the top of his left shoulder and exploded. Its shaped charge cut a channel in his armor, and Straker's HUD lit with telltales as the hot plasma licked at the circuitry and polymeric musculature beneath. Fortunately, the blow was a glancing one, and he didn't lose that arm's internals.

The other rocket narrowly missed his head where his main sensor cluster resided. Belatedly, his anti-air laser system blazed, too slow to pluck a projectile from its flight at such short range.

Have I really gotten so rusty? Straker asked himself. This Mutual Guard unit must either be better trained than average, or he'd completely lost his edge—and either possibility might kill him. If he died, what would happen to the Breakers and the community of Freiheit? He couldn't see a guy like Loco holding them together, though Engels and the rest might.

These thoughts raced through his head as he slammed into the ground. He immediately rolled over and bounced to his feet, slashing a long burst of gatling fire into the foxholes. One rocketeer was cut in half. The other, quicker or more prescient, dropped under the storm of bullets and stayed down.

Straker stamped a meter-long foot onto the occupied foxhole like a man crushing a gopher in its burrow, and then ran forward, searching for his next target. His HUD highlighted a copse of trees on a low hill ahead.

According to his SAI, missile crawlers lurked within. The thin-skinned, slow vehicles normally stayed well back behind the lines to fire their guided rockets. This time, it appeared they were using the trees as cover.

Cover worked both ways, though. The woods would shield him from missiles.

Straker slashed bursts of gatling rounds into the base of the treeline, reconnoitering by fire. Were he the enemy commander, he'd have emplaced infantry there to screen the crawlers. His attacks drew no response, so he increased his pace, charging and aiming at a section of small evergreens that wouldn't impede him.

As he entered the woods, Straker spotted the flare of rocket launches ahead of him. "Missiles incoming," he called on the comlink net in order to warn the rest. He himself was in no danger, completely surrounded by trees that would screen him. He couldn't do anything about the weapons in flight, but he could make sure the enemy didn't launch again.

The Guard company commander had made an error in putting crawlers out here. Even though they gave the illusion of holding their own part of the ring, and they had an excellent hilltop firing position, they were sitting ducks to a mechsuit that got in close.

Of course, they weren't expecting mechsuits. That was the crux of the enemy's mistake.

Straker burst into a clearing, the hilltop center of the grove, and spotted his prey: four crawlers set in standard firing positions, not even dug in. One dirt road led out, their only egress route.

He wasn't going to let them egress. His first force-cannon bolt turned the farthest crawler into an inferno just as it launched its second of three ready missiles. The rocket tipped over in flight and slammed into the woods, exploding and setting the trees afire.

He selected tracers and his gatling shredded the nearest track. Its ready missiles sagged, and then detonated as his incendiary rounds ignited fuel and explosives. Running to his right, he fired deliberate bursts into the other two thin-skinned vehicles until they too brewed up.

"Four missile tracks scragged," Straker called as he slowed, taking a moment to check his HUD for the tactical situation.

"I'm dueling with their hover platoon," Loco said, his breathing ragged. "Could use some help."

"On my way," said Straker, locating Loco. "You're across the camp from me, though. Karst, can you support?"

"Roger wilco, sir. I'll lay down some long-range fire."

Straker and Loco might have stuck together as a team, but that would have given unengaged enemies more time to recover and rally. This way, the two 'suits had already taken out half their opposition. However, attacking was getting harder and harder now that the Guard company was alerted.

Straker burst out of the woods to take in an excellent view from his upslope position. A kilometer away, on the other side of the well-lit camp, he could see hovers, and his HUD showed Loco's transponder near them.

A streak from off to his right slashed across the battlefield and sent a hover spinning with a near miss. That must have been a railgun shot from Karst's Sledgehammer. A moment later, a particle beam strike blasted another. A force-cannon bolt from Loco wiped out a third, and the last one turned tail to skate away over a low hill.

Off to his right, Straker could see the company of Breakers infantry crest the hill, spread out in skirmish order in the inverted vees of fireteams. A slugthrower opened up from a foxhole, cutting down two of his troops before return crossfire suppressed the enemy and a grenade ended the threat.

That was the only resistance until the force approached small-arms range of the camp. Lasers, slugthrowers and rockets leaped toward the Breakers, much too early in Straker's estimation. The camp guards were panicking, it looked like. They should've let the Breakers come well within range, the better to exploit the shock of their initial volley.

Straker felt fortunate that this was not a line Hok company. The biotech commando-slaves wouldn't have let fear cause them to make mistakes. In fact, Hok didn't feel fear at all.

"Breakers, hold up!" Straker heard Heiser order over the comlink. "Take prone positions, hasty entrench. Snipers only, return fire."

The infantry dropped to the ground, throwing rucksacks in front of themselves. Still prone, they seized entrenching tools and began to chip at the hard earth, trying to get something between themselves and the enemy.

A few of the Breakers rested their longer-ranged sniper rifles on their rucksacks and began picking off enemies. The laser weapons would recharge slowly, but they could reach farther than the common battle carbine, and they had the advantage of showing no signature in the visible spectrum, as they used ultraviolet wavelengths.

Abruptly, the flare of a bigger gun vomited a fireball into the night. It came from a light tank hidden between two flimsy barracks buildings, and one of the Breakers snipers vanished in a terminal blast, along with two nearby soldiers. The vehicle obviously had broad-spectrum optical targeting. The sniper's shots would have shown up like a road flare.

"Karst, you see that?" said Straker.

"Roger, sir. Targeting now."

"Hold fire! If you take them out, both of those barracks will go too, probably full of prisoners. I'm going in. You take down the towers, and then stay on overwatch, but limit your collaterals. And don't shoot me in the back!"

"Roger wilco, sir."

Straker sprinted for the camp, taking a serpentine course to dodge any tank fire. There were still two heavies and one light tank unaccounted for, if the enemy company had the standard complement of four each. But that couldn't be helped; the tank in the camp had to be neutralized, or it would slowly slaughter his pinned-down infantry.

One of the four guard towers blew apart, and then another, courtesy of Karst's heavy weapons peeking over the crest of the hill. The Sledgehammer was proving surprisingly effective, as long as it remained unopposed by an enemy that could hurt it.

Unopposed...

"Karst, watch out behind you for enemy armor or rocketeers. You're a sitting duck if they sneak up on you," Straker said.

"Ritter Two here. I'll send a fireteam to cover his six," said Conrad.

Heiser's voice said, "Sorry, sir. I should have thought of that."

Straker didn't answer. He was too busy racing toward the camp, dodging to his left to stay out of Karst's line of fire and approach the perimeter from the side. The tank gun roared again, slamming a shot into the slope of the hill where his infantry lay.

A shell burst near him. His HUD marked the firer, a heavy from upslope. "Loco–"

"I got it, boss."

Straker jinked to his right, ignoring sprays of small arms fire spattering upon his armor like hard steel rain. A rocket popped and flew by him, and then he stomped on the fence to enter the camp.

Now, the buildings were his friends. He dared not fire into them for fear of killing prisoners, but they gave him cover from anyone targeting him from close range. His SAI constantly updated the HUD map of the compound with input from his scanners, and he was able to quickly approach the light tank from behind.

When he rounded the final corner, he saw the tank crew trying to slew their gun to the rear, but they had parked between closely set buildings, and now their perfect ambush position worked against them. The gun's muzzle struck first one wall, then the other.

"Gotcha," Straker crowed. He leaped forward, stepping onto the vehicle. It sagged under his weight. He stomped on the gun barrel, bending it to uselessness, and then did the same to the coaxial laser waveguide. "Tank in camp is neutralized. Breakers, move in!" he ordered.

"On our way, sir," said Heiser.

"Heiser, I'm going to call on them to surrender, so don't shoot if they give up."

"Roger that, sir."

"I just took out another heavy," said Loco. "Looking for the last one now."

"Good job." Straker kept moving, mindful that rocketeers could lurk anywhere among these crowded buildings. He fired gatling bursts into the two remaining guard towers, and then activated his external speakers at maximum volume.

"Surrender and you will not be harmed. We only want the prisoners. This is a rescue! Surrender now! Give up and live." Straker set his SAI to repeat similar phrases while he strode among the buildings like an angry giant.

Camp personnel and a few Mutual Guard troops began showing themselves, hands raised. Scattered gunfire kept him busy running from place to place, intimidating or shooting the failing defenders.

He spotted what appeared to be a prisoner, wearing a similar garb to what Straker had worn when he'd been held, wielding a slugthrower. He was shooting guards indiscriminately, even those with their hands raised in surrender.

"Cease fire!" he roared through his speakers, but the man seemed oblivious. He couldn't blame the prisoner, but gunning down those who surrendered was unacceptable.

Straker comlinked, "Breakers, I need you in camp, double time! We're going to have a massacre on our hands in about one minute." Others had begun joining the vigilante, picking up fallen weapons.

He reached down to use one enormous gauntlet like the scoop on a backhoe, scraping the fingers of his mechsuit through the surface of the frozen earth, picking up a hundred kilos of dirt and gravel. He flung it at the offenders, knocking them over, and then advanced to stand above them. "Cease fire!" he roared.

One man ignored him, aiming a slugthrower at something nearby. Straker sent a single gatling round into the dirt at his feet. The bullet, made to shred light armor, struck the hard ground like a grenade and the blast knocked him down, wounded. "That's enough!"

The rest got the message.

Loco reported, "I've found the other tanks. Looks like the crews bugged out."

"I can't blame them," replied Straker, scanning for more problems. "They lost more than half their company in under five minutes. They fought hard for a militia unit, and I think I know why. Breakers, look for a Lazarus clone or a political officer. If you find one, hold him in a secure location."

"You're sure there's a Lazarus here?" asked Heiser.

"Gibson thought there was—and it stands to reason that's why these people fought hard, even when faced with mechsuits."

"We'll find him, sir," said Aldrik Ritter.

Straker continued to patrol the camp, moving out to the fence line when it appeared the Breakers had taken full control. Loco came in to do the same, and Straker brought Karst down to stand on the central parade ground, a silent threat.

A few minutes later, Karst had to move out of the way as the *Lockstep's* shuttle roared in at low level and set down. Captain Gibson stepped out, compact needler in his hand, and looked around.

Straker met him there after cracking his suit. He made sure his comlink earset was firmly in place before hopping out onto the cold concrete to shake Gibson's hand.

"Well done, Commodore," said Gibson, his eyes roving over the camp. He didn't put away his pistol. "I'd advise you to stay alert. There are usually a few fanatics in these camps, even some willing to suicide if it takes out an enemy leader."

Straker nodded, unholstering his trusty slugthrower handgun. "Where's the camp HQ?"

Gibson pointed. "Pretty sure it's this building. See the crest?"

Straker noticed the Mutuality's defining symbol, a stylized hammer and carbine against a blood-red field, set over the central door. "It really ought to be a boot on a neck, against a field of dirt."

Gibson grunted in agreement. "Sir, if you don't mind, I'm going to find my family."

"Of course."

The stout freighter captain hustled off toward the prisoner barracks. Someone coughed behind Straker, and he turned quickly to see Nazario and Redwolf, his occasional bodyguards. Nazario was slim and deadly with a blade. The hulking Redwolf favored the short crysteel rod he carried everywhere like a baton.

Now, though, the smaller man hefted a laser carbine, while the bigger one carried a large-capacity automatic slugthrower usually needing a crew of two.

"Maybe you ought to sling that thing," Straker told Redwolf. "Firefight's over."

Redwolf showed a gap-toothed grin and shouldered it, taking out his signature alloy rod. "Never can be too careful."

"No worries, sir," said Nazario, waggling his carbine. "I'll drop anyone before this sleeping turtle even lines up on them."

Straker nodded. "Stay alert, but remember, I want them alive."

"Roger wilco, sir," said the men in unison.

He strode into the HQ building. "Breakers?"

"Here, sir," called Aldrik Ritter.

When Straker located the voice, he found the platoon sergeant and couple of Breakers guarding a Lazarus clone, who'd been fibertaped to a chair.

"This isn't very polite, Captain Straker," said the Lazarus. "Can't we speak together like civilized men?"

"It's Commodore Straker now, Inquisitor," replied Straker, "and I'm not very civilized, if you're using the original meaning of 'living in cities.' Or, even if you mean 'sophisticated and urbane.'" He showed his teeth. "But if you mean 'displaying morals and common decency,' it's you that's uncivilized."

The Lazarus shrugged within his restraints. "We'll have to agree to disagree. Now, how can I be of service?"

"You expect me to believe you're going to help me?"

The Inquisitor sighed. "We Lazaruses are pragmatists, Commodore. We're driven neither by the emotions of the proletariat nor the functional paranoia of the Party elite. I will not help you harm the Mutuality, but like all my fellow clones of the Lazarus cell line, I have studied your exploits and I believe you might be persuaded to damage our mutual enemies if it seemed in your best interest."

"Then why the hell did you bring the *Lockstep* crew's families here as bait for a trap? Why not let us rescue them easily and be on our way?"

"Actually, I argued for just that approach, but I was instructed otherwise. I'm not one to fall on my sword for a principle."

"But you'd do it for practical gain."

The Lazarus shrugged again. "I'm not eager to throw away my life, but if I must pay with it, I am consoled by the fact that my cell line will continue. This is not so different from your Sergeant Ritter here's devotion to family and clan. I'm sure he would sacrifice himself to save his own people, if it came to that."

"Great." Straker paced back and forth. "You're a lying, murderous torturer with a few admirable qualities."

"Or perhaps I'm an admirable man who's willing to be as ruthless as I must... not so different from yourself."

"Bullshit. I saw the look of cruelty in your eyes—the eyes of the other Lazarus, I mean—when he first introduced himself to me. Pretty soon he had me strapped to a table for torture."

"Or perhaps he was playing a role in hopes of frightening you into confessing and re-educating yourself." The Lazarus lifted his chin. "But you don't frighten, do you?"

"I've never been afraid in my life."

"Now who's the liar?"

Straker ground his teeth. "All right. I've never been afraid of pain or of dying, but my other fears are probably the same as most men. Maybe even the same as you. Fear of failure; fear of those I care about being harmed. I wouldn't be human if I didn't have those fears. But maybe you don't have them after all, because you're not human."

"I am human, Commodore Straker. I simply have a superior philosophy, one that makes me fit for my role. Have you read the Stoics?"

"Can't say that I have. My reading's been confined to military history, strategy and tactics."

"A well-rounded man must be knowledgeable to be effective. I–"

Straker's comlink beeped, and he held up his hand for silence.

"Engels to Straker," he heard.

It was his second-in-command—and lover—Commander Carla Engels, calling from the bridge of the underspace-capable Archer *Revenge*, which had been lurking out of easy detection range from Prael.

"Straker here."

"You need to get out of there ASAP. Three Mutuality frigates and a squadron of attack ships just unmasked from behind an asteroid, and they're heading your way."

Chapter 3

Prael. Re-education and Training Camp 13.

"Something wrong?" said the Lazarus with a smile like a lizard. "Suddenly worried about your getaway plan?"

"You thought you were stalling me with your patter," replied Straker, "but my troops needed the time to get things organized anyway. This does mean we'll have to hurry."

He activated his comlink. "Listen up, Breakers. We have hostiles inbound. We need to load up and get airborne, double-quick. Spear, get them moving." He then switched channels back to Engels. "How long do we have, Carla?"

"Half an hour to break atmo, tops, but those attack ships will run you down if missiles don't."

"Can you intercept them?"

"Already on my way on impellers, but you know how hard it is to do an underspace intercept against maneuvering ships. You'll need to fly straight and level to set them up for us."

"We'll get moving as fast as we can and start running for flatspace. Straker out."

The Lazarus spoke. "You won't make it, you know, unless you have a much larger force than I believe you do."

Aldrik Ritter set the muzzle of his carbine against the clone's skull. "I'm tired of this *schweinhund's* blather. Let me kill him."

Straker held up a hand. "No. Tape him up and bring him along. I have uses for him."

Lockstep lifted in record time.

* * *

Commander Carla Engels, acting captain of the Archer *Revenge*, chewed her lip and wished for the impossible. Some kind of sensor that provided information about normal space while her ship was in underspace would give her an enormous advantage, but such a device had never been developed. In fact, according to the Ruxins, they'd tried and failed many times.

There was no point in worrying about that now. She sat in a damp human-shaped chair bolted to the deck of the *Revenge's* bridge and put her feet up on the rail in front of her. The octopoid Ruxins surrounding her were perfectly comfortable, but she was, of course, living in a steambath.

It became a cold steambath when they spent much time in underspace, as the strange empty dimension slowly sucked out all heat from the normal matter intruding on its domain. If its protective fields ever failed, the Archer and everything in it would freeze instantly. Even with the fields, warmth slowly leached out of her bones, despite her suit heaters. It was like being sick, having chills and a fever at the same time.

But they weren't in underspace yet. She stared at the main display, now upgraded with a fine new holoplate, watching the icon representing *Revenge* crawl toward a rough point of interception with the attack ship squadron. While the three frigates as a group were much more dangerous, only the attack ships had the speed to run down Straker's escaping transport *Lockstep*.

Correction: the attack ships *plus* any missiles fired by the frigates. But that was a worry for the future. She strongly suspected they would hold off on launching shipkillers until they were sure they couldn't disable the fleeing freighter to recapture it and those aboard.

"You are frightened," said Zaxby, her Ruxin acting XO and, if she wasn't completely mistaken, her friend. The old octopoid had no sense of tact, but she knew he meant well.

"No, I'm worried. We didn't expect an ambush squadron waiting for our rescue attempt. Makes me wonder if we have a spy in our ranks."

"If so, it is not among my people."

"Of course not. It would be one of the humans we liberated. We rescued a lot of them, and they're all different, from many places and all walks of life. There's no way to vet every one of them except to wait and watch to see how they behave." Engels resisted the urge to rub Zaxby's head as if he were a pet instead of a sentient being. It wouldn't be appropriate in this setting, but touching the rubbery skin soothed her nerves. She couldn't explain why, but it did.

Back in the Starfish Nebula, where their secret base lay hidden, she'd spent time in Ruxin nurseries. The immature octopoids delighted her with their inquisitiveness, and seemed fascinated by her in turn. They were also great mimics, and many of the little ones were already learning the Earthan language.

Zaxby said, "More likely than a spy is the possibility that the Lazarus clone anticipated Commodore Straker's obvious attempt to rescue family members of his subordinates. It would have been much wiser for us to simply leave them to their fate, rather than risk more humans in hazardous missions of liberation. After all, they have no particular value to add to your society. Can those in question not find other mates and spawn more children?"

"You know humans aren't like that. We value our families highly."

"Typically irrational. It makes more sense to value those you choose to bond with, rather than those whom the random vagaries of recombinant DNA has associated you with."

"Maybe it's because we don't lay thousands of eggs at a time like you Ruxins do," Engels said.

"Only hundreds. So you are saying it may be a simple matter of supply and demand? We Ruxins have many siblings, therefore we value them less, but we have far fewer chosen friends, so we naturally value them more? That is one of the more rational hypotheses I have heard come from a human's mouth."

"Or maybe only a few of your own people can stand each other," snapped Engels. "Ever wonder why you like to hang out with humans so much?"

Zaxby rolled his eyes, a mannerism he'd learned from humans. "Every day I wonder about that, yes. It makes no sense to me either."

"And you claim you're less rude than the average Ruxin."

"I am."

"And I'm more patient than the average human."

Engels tired of the no-win conversation and leaned forward, examining the holoplate and talking the young Ruxin bridge crew through her tactics. "We started from where we waited at the optimum flatspace transition point. We're on course directly toward *Lockstep*, which is heading straight here. The attack squadron is overtaking them, so we'll have to pass through *Lockstep's* position and try to pop up behind them, yet in front of the attack ships. We'll get a quick update and insert again to deploy float mines in their path. Make sense?"

"I find no fault with that approach," replied Zaxby. "If they spot us, they will divert or slow, out of concern for the danger we present. If not, they will run into our mines."

"That's my plan. Since *Lockstep* and her fusion flare are right between us and the attack ships, stay in normal space for now. They won't be able to detect us as long as we use only impellers."

"Aye aye, ma'am." Zaxby translated her words into Ruxin for the benefit of the bridge officers, though all of them had a basic facility with Earthan by now.

Less than an hour later, the combined velocities of the approaching ships and that of *Lockstep* had brought them near the intercept point.

"Comlink to *Lockstep*, secure ultra-narrow laser," Engels said.

"Comlink established," replied her communications officer.

"Straker, you there?"

"I'm here. Go ahead."

"We're about to insert under you and try to take out the attack squadron, but our velocity is such that we can't turn around to help you. Not unless we light our fusion engine, and I'm not willing to give them a beacon to find us. We'll vector toward the frigates and try to hit them too, but after that, it'll be at least two hours before we can get back to you. By that time they'll have caught you or you'll have transited out. So stay on a steady, predictable course. We need to lull them into the same thing."

"I understand," said Straker. "Good luck and good hunting. Don't worry about us. We still have a few tricks up our sleeves. See you back at the nebula. Straker out."

Engels sighed. She'd hoped things would go smoothly so the two ships could rendezvous at the transit point. She'd have returned to the freighter and had a nice pleasant sidespace trip in a dry cabin with a warm bed filled with Derek. Now she faced an unpleasantly damp week with a bunch of cold-blooded Ruxins.

"Approaching *Lockstep*," said her helmsman. Unlike Straker, who sometimes called that Ruxin his "helmsquid," she stuck with human titles. She wished she was piloting the *Revenge* herself, but the controls didn't lend themselves to human hands. She could fly the Archer in a pinch, but not well.

"Insert the ship," she replied, and resigned herself once again to playing captain only. She clasped her hands behind her back and wondered if captains everywhere did so in order to still the urge to grab controls and *do something*.

"Inserting. Steady in underspace."

The holoplate showed nothing different as the software created predictions of all tracked objects—the attack squadron, the frigates, *Lockstep* and *Revenge*, plus a few small asteroids nearby. On the display, it appeared as if *Revenge* would collide with *Lockstep*, and Engels held her breath.

The two icons merged, and then *Revenge* had passed through the other ship in underspace. "Emerge," she ordered.

"Emerging."

When they re-entered normal space, the passive sensors updated the predictive software. Normally, Engels would worry about being spotted by the oncoming attack ships, but three things worked in her favor.

First, attack ships had only a few sensors, and they were optimized for short-range targeting. They relied on datalinks from bigger ships for the rest.

Second, she'd had the Ruxins improve the stealth qualities of the Archer when they'd had her in drydock over the last month, applying coatings and minimizing sharp protrusions.

And third, *Revenge* emerged directly between the attack ships and the freighter's bright fusion engine flare. For the enemy, it would be like looking directly at a sun.

"They're still on a straight pursuit course," she said.

"So it appears," replied Zaxby. "At current closing speed, they will overrun us in eight minutes."

"Helm, reverse acceleration, maximum impellers. That will slow us down."

"Aye aye, ma'am."

"An interesting order, Captain Engels. Why have you done this?"

"I'm lengthening the time to intercept," Engels said with a grin. "What's more, the float mine will have a lower delta to the attack ships' velocity, so it will be more likely to catch them all."

"You should have been male."

Engels stared at Zaxby. "What?"

"You make war like a War Male."

"I make war like a professional fleet officer."

"It is a compliment, Captain Engels. I was referring to my own culture, and how the average Ruxin sees you. You know, like your bridge officers." Zaxby gestured broadly with six tentacles.

Engels realized more eyes than normal were on her. Zaxby seemed to be trying to tell her something. Did the Ruxin crew have doubts about her ability to command because she was female? That must be it.

She spoke loudly and clearly. "Many human females fight, just as many human males govern. You are a neuter, Zaxby, yet you're a superb ship's officer in battle, just like the rest of your fellow Ruxins. Your gender doesn't matter, especially when the war is fought using machines. It's about brains, not hormones."

The Ruxins seemed to relax, and many eyes turned back to their boards and consoles. It looked like she'd passed some kind of test of command without even knowing it was coming.

"Insert the ship," Engels said as her intercept approached.

"Inserting. Underspace achieved."

"Weapons, deploy one float mine to time-detonate at an optimum location inside their formation, and one to simultaneously detonate directly in front of them. I want microsecond timing to avoid fratricide."

"Detonation timing set. Deploying float mines."

Engels didn't need to order acceleration. The ship was already using retrograde impellers within underspace, slowing the ship for eventually heading back in the direction she had come, so the float mines drifted on a ballistic course, straight ahead toward the oncoming attack squadron.

The holoplate's icons flashed into detonation, and the Archer rattled with the dimensional bleed-over. The predicted path of the attack squadron passed through *Revenge's* location. "Emerge!"

"Emerging."

The holoplate and other sensor displays updated slowly due to the spreading radiation of the fusion blasts. "Any attack ships left? Find them!" Engels snapped.

"It is difficult," said her sensors officer.

"We're looking straight at *Lockstep's* fusion flare ourselves, now, trying to pick out any survivors," explained Zaxby.

"Of course, but we should be able to see their flares if they're still accelerating in pursuit."

"Sensors show no flares."

"Helm, ninety degree course deviation spinward. Get us some angle so we can see."

"Aye aye, ma'am."

The Archer turned away from its course. The new angle eventually allowed them to confirm the good news: no operational attack ships remained. Several were intact enough to have beacons crying for help, but none maneuvered. They'd been eliminated as a threat.

"Set us back on course for the frigates," Engels ordered.

Zaxby waved at the holoplate. "That may not be sufficient. They have dispersed."

"Crap." Engels watched as the icons for the frigates diverged from their former courses in three dimensions, but continued at full acceleration in the general direction of the freighter. "They probably think the attack ships hit stealth mines dropped by *Lockstep*, and so they're evading on parallel courses. Now we have three problems instead of one."

"I suggest we insert soon," Zaxby said. "Their active sensors are on maximum and they could spot us any time."

"Do it. Insert the ship."

"Inserting. Underspace achieved."

Engels sat back down and chewed her lip, using the time to intercept to think, and think hard. The float mines weren't actually stealthy enough to lay in wait in front of a frigate pounding away with full active sensors. To catch a target unawares, they had to pop out of underspace at the last moment.

Ditto for her shipkiller missiles. They could be cold-launched and laid like mines, one at a time, but they would also be seen.

This meant that she could only attack one target effectively, and she'd only have one chance. The Archer wasn't fast enough to chase down the other two frigates from aft. She could launch one chase missile, but it would almost certainly be picked out of space by lasers.

An Archer was a poor man's—being's—weapon, meant to pick off the low-hanging fruit of war. It was no doubt devastating against an enemy's cargo shipping, but it wasn't meant to fight warships, and certainly not squadrons. It was fragile, and couldn't stand toe to toe with anyone.

If only underspace engines could be installed on something big enough to really *fight*—at least a destroyer, or better, a heavy cruiser. That would make it a nasty long-range independent raider. She filed the idea away for later.

Engels spoke. "Ops, project when the enemy will overtake *Lockstep*."

"Sixty-seven minutes, Captain."

"Minimum time to *Lockstep*'s transit?"

"One hundred and eleven minutes."

Engels rubbed her eyes through her open faceplate. "So, if we can buy forty-four minutes, she'll get away."

"Assuming the enemy does not launch shipkiller missiles," said Zaxby.

"There is that. I'm hoping they won't, unless they believe they're losing their prey. Straker has an Inquisitor aboard, and the rescued prisoners from the camp. Plus, I'm betting somebody *really* wants to capture the man who keeps sticking his finger in the Mutuality's eye."

"Are you sure that's not wishful thinking?"

"It's the best I've got right now. Helm, set us on a combat intercept for the lead frigate. We might as well thin the herd by one."

"Aye aye, ma'am."

The intercept went like clockwork. A float mine left a frigate broken and drifting in space, and the other two began to evade more strenuously, though they still pursued the freighter.

Unfortunately, *Revenge* ended up following hopelessly behind the other two frigates. Launching her only effective weapon, her shipkiller missile, would merely call attention to herself, and it was important to deny the Mutuality crews any information as to what frightening weapon kept attacking them from out of nowhere.

"Give me a tightbeam comlink to *Lockstep*," Engels said.

"I am sorry, ma'am, but that is not possible due to engine flare."

"Dammit." Of course, they couldn't punch a beam through the fusion engine's interference, as the Archer was directly behind both the remaining two frigates and the freighter they pursued. "Well, Derek, I did all I could. You're on your own now."

* * *

Chapter 3

Straker paced the freighter's cramped bridge, happy that at least it was dry. Engels was going to have a miserable trip home if they couldn't finish off all their enemies and join up before sidespace insertion.

"She got one, but two of them are going to catch us before we can transit," said Loco, stepping up beside him. "It's going to be a gang-bang, and we're the pivot point. Well, if a threesome can be called a gang-bang... Maybe just a–"

"Save it, Loco," Straker said. "We've got work to do. Let's go. Captain Gibson, we'll be opening the far-aft cargo door."

"Good luck, Commodore. If your tricks don't work... well, thanks for getting our families out of there. Better they die here with us than in a camp."

Straker speared Gibson with a stare. "Nobody's dying today but our enemies, Captain."

Gibson nodded, his eyes bleak and unconvinced.

Straker led Loco off the bridge. He called for a detail of troops to assist, and Nazario, Redwolf and Aldrik showed up with a dozen men. They quickly donned pressure suits and tromped to the aft cargo bay door.

Strapped to the wall were six shipkiller missiles, newly manufactured by the industry of the Starfish nebula. In the month he'd had to prepare for this mission, he'd browbeaten the Ruxin Premier Freenix into supplying many of his battle needs.

"Seal up and depressurize the bay," Straker ordered. "Turn off the gravplating." He quickly input commands into the missiles' simplified external interfaces.

The cargo bay door in the belly of the flattened freighter opened to reveal the flare of the fusion engine at the ship's centerline. Soon, the Breakers were unstrapping the missiles and manhandling them into space. They fell into the void, tumbling, left behind by the continuous acceleration of the ship.

They shot briefly through the edges of the drive plasma. Fortunately, like all such weapons, they were hardened against heat and radiation.

In a short time they would become visible to the enemy's hard-driven sensor waves. On schedule, the missiles' own engines burst to life, and their SAIs aimed at the nearest of the following frigates.

The jerry-rigged surprise flight of six apparent shipkillers caused their target to veer off, blasting desperately to the side in order to avoid the possibility of destruction. The closing speeds of the frigate and the missiles would give the defender only a short time to try to knock them down with lasers, so the ship increased her survival probabilities by creating a side intercept profile, rather than a disadvantageous nose-on aspect.

By doing so, she'd taken herself out of the fight. She couldn't catch the *Lockstep* in time anymore.

Unlike her sister ship, which kept on gaining.

Straker smiled grimly as Gibson reported the enemy action over his comlink. "They're going to crap their pants if one of those things actually hits them," he chuckled.

"They're real missiles," said Loco as he closed the cargo bay door. "Too bad we didn't have enough fusion warheads."

"I wouldn't want fusion warheads hand-strapped into the cargo bay anyway. Too much could go wrong."

Loco pounded his fist gently on the bulkhead, and then opened his faceplate to sniff the air. "Got any other tricks up your sleeve, boss?"

"Only one, but you won't like it. It's crazy. Batshit crazy."

Loco raised his eyebrows. "Oh, really? I like a lot of crazy shit. In fact, crazy is my middle name."

"I thought it was Miguel. I'll remind you that you said that, in about…" Straker checked his chrono, "… twenty minutes." He turned his eyes to the Foehammers reclining on the deck. "Time to suit up."

"Mechsuits? In open space?" Loco grinned. "Now that's batshit crazy."

Chapter 4

Interplanetary Space, Prael System

As Straker was settling into his suit and running systems checks, Captain Gibson came onto his comlink. "Sir, the last frigate is in direct-fire weapons range and they're calling on us to heave-to. They're giving us one minute to cease acceleration and be boarded, or they'll destroy our fusion engine."

"How long until we can transit?"

"Thirty minutes at least. Should I begin evading? We're still heading for flatspace, so all we need is to hold them off for that long."

"No," Straker said. "Shut off our engines, but make sure you present our top spine to the enemy. Use the gyroscopes so they don't see thrusters. You have to keep them from getting eyes on the main cargo bay door."

"Why, Commodore?"

"Well, they said something about boarding, right?"

"Yes…"

"Might as well oblige them."

"I don't understand," said Gibson.

"You will. Put me through to Lazarus right now; I need to talk to him for a moment. Make sure to notify me when they come alongside. And remember to keep the main cargo bay door out of sight!"

"Aye aye, sir."

A moment later, Lazarus' voice said, "Commodore Straker?"

"Yes, Inquisitor? We've destroyed or delayed all of your ships but one. You've lost a lot in this operation. Would you like to cut your losses further?"

"As I understand from the talk going around," he said, "we're about to be boarded. That will put an end to your depredations. Even if you murder me, you will have failed."

"Inquisitor, you should know by now that I'm not a fan of failure. I'd rather not have to destroy this last frigate. Send them away and save their lives."

The smile in Lazarus' voice was audible. "You're bluffing, trying to snatch victory from the jaws of defeat—otherwise you wouldn't be talking to me. I won't help you."

"So be it. Who's there with you?"

"Conrad Ritter here, sir."

"Conrad, make sure Inquisitor Lazarus is secured, but give him a front-row seat to what's going on. I want him to understand that everyone I have to kill is on him. I want him to see how badly he screwed up by setting this trap for me."

"Aye aye, sir," said Conrad. "We'll take him to the bridge and tape him to a chair."

"Excellent. Straker out." Straker finished his systems check and switched to local comlink. "Loco, you ready to do this?"

"I was born ready, Derek. You know that. We should have died at Helios, so every day alive's a bonus."

"Damn, Loco. You're becoming a philosopher in your old age." He comlinked the bridge. "Straker here. Depressurize the main cargo bay and open the doors completely."

"In deep space?" came the reply from Captain Gibson.

"Affirmative. As soon as our guests arrive, Loco and I are going to suit up and pay them a personal visit. How close are they?"

"Ah… the frigate is matching velocities with us now, Commodore. Cargo bay doors are opening. Did I understand you right—you're going to try to board them?"

"Yes, we are. Make sure this comlink is secure and encrypted. As soon as I say so, fake a thruster malfunction and set the *Lockstep* tumbling violently. Tell them you're trying to fix it, but stall. You're on a ballistic course that's taking you closer to transit every minute. From now on, your sole mission is to get into sidespace and head for home. Got it?"

"But we'd be leaving you behind!"

"All that matters is you getting away. We'll survive, even if we're taken prisoner. We're mechsuiters. They want us alive, just like they did before. Commander Engels can mount a rescue. Do your job and follow my orders, Captain Gibson. Is that understood?"

"Yes, sir."

"Your sole priority is to escape. Repeat it back to me."

"Our sole priority is to escape. But sir–"

"Quit arguing. Tell me when the frigate is at relative rest."

"Less than one minute." Gibson waited. "They're here. They want us to shut down all systems and prepare to receive a boarding party at the main airlock. They're sending a shuttle. They say to have the Inquisitor waiting."

"Perfect. Make it look like you're complying, but slowly. We're going exo now."

Inside his mechsuit, Straker rolled to a crouch and ape-walked to the cargo bay door. Rotating to put his magnetized feet on the outer hull, he shuffled carefully toward the rear of the freighter and its inactive fusion engine. Peering around the bell of its exhaust guide, he spotted the frigate.

Despite their completely different functions, both ships were about the same size. The freighter was configured as a lifting body, an elongated and blunted triangle that could enter atmo and set down on a planet. The frigate sported the usual modified cigar shape of most warships, an efficient and flexible design for deep space combat.

The frigate had come alongside the freighter, so the sterns of both were lined up nicely for what Straker was about to try. "Loco, we're going to leap across to land on their aft hull. Use magnetics and drop jets to get there any way you can, because if you miss…"

"You'll cry at my funeral. Okay, boss, let's do it." Loco strode past Straker, circumnavigating the freighter's skin until he stood directly "under" the other ship.

Straker followed quickly, and set himself to jump as soon as he could. Loco seemed out to prove he was crazier than his boss, so there was no need to wait or give orders. Straker shut off his magnetics and leaped directly toward the frigate.

A quick drop-jet adjustment kept his aim true, and a little calculated flailing brought him around feet-first. As soon as he struck the frigate's hull, he reactivated his magnetics.

Loco thumped down nearby. "Woohoo! What a rush. I bet we're the first mechsuiters ever to do that!"

"No doubt. This is the only time it would work, when someone's parked and trying to board already. Hope they haven't spotted us yet. We go opposite directions around the hull until we find their shuttle bay doors. Move!"

"On my way."

Loco walked laterally around the curve of the frigate's skin, and Straker headed the other direction. He resisted the urge to fire a force-cannon bolt into the barrel of a laser waveguide twitching in its mount. Two mechsuiters couldn't take down a frigate from the outside. But from inside…

"Found it," called Loco.

A moment later Straker spotted the other mechsuit as he rounded the hull of the warship, and he hurried over. "Any moment now…"

The armored doors to the frigate's launch bay puffed residual air and slid open. "I'll take out the shuttle," said Straker. "You get in there and head for Engineering. If this is a standard floor plan, we shouldn't have far to go."

"And then?"

"Wreck their reactors if I say so, or if they take me out. Without main power, they can't hurt *Lockstep*. Stay in contact."

Loco said, "They could still launch a shipkiller. That doesn't take much power."

"I think I like you better when you're joking."

"There's no pleasing you, boss."

Straker grinned in spite of himself. "Then I'm doing my job."

"Here it comes."

The doors opened completely and the shuttle floated gently out, nose-first. Through the thick crystal of the cockpit canopy Straker saw the wide eyes of the pilot as he stared at the Foehammer, just before the jet of his force-cannon cut through it and filled the interior with superheated plasma. The man ignited in a flash as the boat drifted clear.

The pilot's dying pain only lasted a moment. Even if anyone inside survived—maybe if they were in a separate compartment and suited up—the shuttle was now unflyable, its controls melted to slag. That was one threat eliminated.

"Go!" Straker said, but Loco was already in motion, rotating his mechsuit into the frigate's interior. "Straker to Gibson!"

"Gibson here."

"Start your tumble. Act panicky. In fact, ask them for help. Confuse them as long as you can."

"Aye aye, Commodore."

"Straker out." He followed Loco into the shuttle bay.

Loco had already enlarged the internal hatch into the main passageway aft toward Engineering by the simple expedient of ripping its edges apart like a man tearing at cardboard. The bulkheads were no match for a mechsuiter's powered duralloy gauntlets. Only the ship's structural skeleton could resist such forces.

Fortunately, frigates didn't carry man-portable weapons powerful enough to hurt a mechsuiter. They didn't usually even have battlesuits aboard, merely a few marines—Hok or human—to keep order and guard the ship in port. The crew should be helpless against a Foehammer's armored strength.

There was no room to help Loco in his depredations toward the stern, so Straker headed for the ship's centerline, tearing at the bulkheads. His hands registered mild pain feedback from his gauntlets' pressure sensors and his HUD showed the pinpricks of hand lasers bouncing off his reflective skin.

He ignored them. A few marine weapons or welding lasers couldn't possibly do any damage… until a jolt shot an ache into his left shoulder.

Straker had forgotten about the havoc the rocketeer on Prael had caused to his shoulder armor. Now his HUD lit up with red warning lights, and his gatling went offline just when it might have done some good.

Turning away from the pain, he spotted one Hok with a heavy blaster, standing above him in a hole in a bulkhead. Once Straker had moved the rent in his armor out of the way, the weapon posed little threat unless it could fire repeatedly at the same spot.

But Straker didn't allow that. Mentally saluting the once-human creature, he aimed his force-cannon and triggered it in broad-blast mode.

The flamethrower cone of ultra-heated plasma splashed against the underside of the deck beneath the Hok's feet, melting through it and spreading fast. The trooper died in hot agony, and the heat killed or drove away other defenders, clearing the way for Straker to advance through the barriers in front of him.

Except for the structural supports, the decks and bulkheads seemed like so much metal foil to him, material to pull aside or punch through. This was working better than he'd expected. He'd been concerned the close confines of a warship would trap a mechsuit, but no designer had ever planned for a seven-meter human-shaped warrior rampaging around the ship's interior, dressed in armor as hard as that on a warship's hull.

In moments he'd reached the ship's main passageway that ran from bow to stern, paralleling the primary spinal shaft. Most warships installed their largest direct-fire weapons—beams or railguns—straight down this long axis for maximum structural strength, size and stability.

The standard layout plan would put the bridge forward of amidships and slightly off center, as deep inside as possible without affecting the spine. The main passageway would therefore lead him straight to it.

Hatches had been dogged in front of him, but he barely slowed down, forcing his way through like a man crawling down a tunnel made of tinfoil. When he ripped open the last pressure door to see the terrified bridge crew, he switched on external speakers and roared, "Surrender or die!"

He emphasized his demand by pointing his meter-long right gauntlet with its protruding force-cannon directly at the captain, a sturdy man wearing lieutenant commander's stripes.

The captain threw up his hands. "We yield!" he cried.

"Tell your marines and Hok to stand down so I don't have to kill any more of them." Straker switched to comlink. "Loco, I've got the bridge. Don't destroy anything else."

"Good thing you called, boss," Loco said sarcastically. "I was about to crack the fusion reactor and go out in a blaze of glory. Or maybe just cut the main power bus."

"Stand by for further instructions, smartass." Straker changed to external speakers again. "You are Captain…"

"Pang Zholin, commanding the People's Mutual Navy frigate *Chun Wei*."

"Commodore Derek Straker here, Straker's Breakers. Patch my comlink signal through to the freighter."

Zholin crossed his arms. "I'm not going to collaborate with a turncoat lackey." He said it with an odd lack of passion, as if reciting lines in a play.

Straker pointed the force-cannon at him. "Then you'll all die just to slow me down by five minutes as I rip my way through to the outer hull and comlink them myself. I have a Lazarus Inquisitor aboard the freighter. I'll let you speak to him if you're so brainwashed you can't make decisions for yourself, but I'd have thought a frigate captain would be smarter than that."

Zholin's expression soured further, if that were possible. "Put him through," he said to his communications officer.

When Straker's comlink showed it was synched up with *Lockstep*, he said, "Straker to Gibson. We have the frigate, so you can stabilize. Come back and dock directly. Send over a platoon of Breakers to secure all spaces within this ship. Straker out."

He addressed Zholin. "Captain, order your entire crew to stand down and assemble on the shuttle bay flight deck. Tell them not to sabotage anything. They'll be well treated if they don't do anything stupid, but I'll have anyone who gets out of line shot and spaced."

Zholin glared at him for a moment, and then seemed to crumple. "I supposed I did surrender. I'll do as you ask."

"As I order."

"Because you have a weapon on me."

"I've been inside your sick, twisted system, Captain. You have no moral high ground with me, and this is war. You keep giving me pushback and I'll brig you in solitary. I'm sure your next-in-command will be more amenable."

Zholin swallowed. "All right, you win."

"I always win." Straker grinned wolfishly, then realized Zholin couldn't see him. He accessed a seldom-used feature of his suit to display his visage on his faceplate. "Too bad you're so brainwashed. I have a lot of Mutuality defectors in the Breakers."

The frigate captain grunted. "Do you want me to tell my people what to do, or do you want me to stand here and listen to you talk? Because I can't do both."

"Fair enough. Go ahead."

Zholin accessed his PA system and told the crew he'd surrendered the ship, to assemble on the flight deck, and not to sabotage anything. At Straker's instructions, he had his helmsman work with *Lockstep* to perform a deep-space docking.

Soon, Breakers filled the *Chun Wei*, searching and securing every compartment, including the bridge.

Straker sent Zholin and the rest of the frigate's bridge officers to the assembly point, escorted by Breakers. He and Loco carefully extracted from the frigate and stored their mechsuits in *Lockstep's* cargo bay again. With sidearms, they went back aboard the *Chun Wei* in a more ordinary manner, through the docking port.

Gibson's XO, Lieutenant Jonas, reported to Straker with three others of *Lockstep's* crew. "I assume you're going to take this ship as a prize, sir? If you leave me a dozen grunts to help repair the damage, we can get her home, assuming her sidespace engines are still in order."

"Get to it. We'll be putting her crew into boats—as many as don't defect."

Jonas hustled away, and Straker led Loco to the shuttle bay flight deck. Though the largest single space on the ship, it was barely big enough to hold the frigate's forty or so crew, plus Breakers to guard them. Three Hok stood placidly in one corner with fibertape wrapping their hands up to their forearms, and loosely around their ankles.

"What're we gonna do about those guys, boss?" Loco asked quietly. "They creep me out."

"I'll have to think about it. They might be of use later. Have them taken to *Lockstep* and put them in separate confinement, right now. I don't want them to hear this."

Loco passed those orders, and the Hok were marched away.

Straker jumped up to stand atop a shuttle and look down on the prisoners. "Listen up, Mutualists. I'm Commodore Derek Straker. Some call me a pirate, others a freebooter, but what I really am is a liberator. I'm here to offer you your freedom, a place in a society with no torture, no self-shaming sessions and no Inquisitors. You'll work hard and contribute, but you'll be rewarded for your contributions, not for how well you parrot slogans or kiss ass to a bunch of arrogant clones."

The crew glanced around at each other and especially at one particular officer, a man with unique red rank tabs on his collar. That one glared at Straker with pure hatred.

Straker pointed at him. "You. What's your name?"

"Burn in hell, unmutual lackey!"

"That's one funny-ass name," said Loco from his position leaning casually on a bulkhead. "Did your mother hate you or what?"

"You will not get any of this crew to defect," the man snapped. "They're all loyal."

Straker jumped down. "You're what—some kind of political officer?"

"I am People's Commissar Gou Liang. I am the guardian of rightful Party thinking."

"So you're the thought police. Well, I'm not interested in policing anyone's thoughts, only their actions." Straker lashed out with one hard fist and knocked the commissar to the deck. The man lay stunned, his mouth opening and closing like a fish.

"Tape him loosely so he can eventually free himself," Straker ordered. "Throw him into a one-man escape pod and eject it into space."

"Wait... Please, sir," said Zholin, stepping up to Straker and speaking quietly. "If he reports, our families will surely be killed for our treason. If we only disappear with no report from him, no one will know."

"I'm not going to murder him," said Straker. "He's a prisoner of war, captured in uniform during a combat action."

"Then keep him prisoner. Only I beg you, do not release him."

Straker nodded. "Fair enough. Throw him in the brig."

Three Breakers grabbed Liang and dragged him off.

Straker paced in front of the Mutualist crew. "Your watchdog is gone. You can now think for yourselves." He pointed to his left. "Anyone who wants to be sent safely back to the Mutuality, stand over there. You won't be harmed. I know many of you have families that will be punished if you defect. I won't hold it against you."

A few immediately shuffled over to stand where Straker was pointing. The rest seemed to be listening and thinking, waiting for another option. They kept glancing at their captain.

"Anyone else can join us," Straker continued. "You'll have a period of probation, but eventually you'll take your places as free citizens alongside us."

Captain Zholin raised his hand. "What is your supposedly free society called?"

Straker exchanged glances with Loco, who looked amused. "That's still being debated by our council. Straker's Breakers is the name of my organization for now, and I'm the commander, but eventually we'll have a civilian government in place."

Loco stepped over to Zholin. "Don't you want to be free?"

Zholin faced Loco with a grim expression. "Freedom is nothing without the discipline to appreciate it. My society has so much corruption that it often fails to fight the Hundred Worlds effectively, but I will not jump out of the stewpot and into the fire."

Straker realized this earnest young man was looking for a reason to do what he wished; otherwise, he'd be already standing with the loyalists. "We balance freedom and discipline. Loco here's more of a freedom kind of guy, and I guess I'm more disciplined, but there's room for everyone if they choose to stay within the limits of decent behavior, keep their word, honor their commitments and follow the laws their representatives put in place. And you can always leave and go somewhere else, even back to the Mutuality. Your government is my enemy, but its citizens aren't."

Zholin drew himself to attention and saluted. "I will join you, Commodore Straker. If you will have me, I will captain the *Chun Wei* with honor in your name. I pledge myself to your service. I believe others here will accompany me."

All the remaining crewmembers rushed to join Zholin in formation behind him, and they also lifted their hands in salute. One even re-defected from the loyalist group.

Straker returned the salute. "I accept everyone's service in the name of the Breakers, Captain Zholin. However, you'll understand that you're all still on probation. I'll have to spread your people around, put many of you aboard other ships and put some of mine on this one."

"Of course, Commodore. Thank you."

Straker smiled. "Let me introduce you to the commander of my tiny but growing space fleet. Her name is Carla Engels."

Chapter 5

Starfish Nebula, Freiheit, Base Control Center (BCC)

Commander Carla Engels watched from the terrace of the Freiheit's Base Control Center as Straker, Loco and some of his Breakers led *Lockstep's* captain and crew in an impromptu triumphal parade down the habitat's main north-south avenue.

Those rescued from the prison camp smiled and waved at the cheering citizens who'd gathered at the docking port's exit. The habitat might eventually fill up, but it should hold up to ten thousand comfortably. Right now, not even a quarter that many lived in it.

At times, Engels felt the hollow asteroid's emptiness. At others, like now, she appreciated its rural character, though it was rapidly turning into a close-knit spaceborne community. It would be a good place to settle after all this was over.

Over? Who was she kidding? Straker was going to push his luck to win or die, and she'd be right there beside him.

If they died it wouldn't matter, but if they won, they'd likely have to live in some capital city of a new empire, helping to rule. Maybe she could persuade him to turn the government over to civilians, retire young and raise a family. Then she laughed at her own pretensions.

The cheering subsided as other Breakers emerged from the docking port, carrying coffin-shaped cargo cases and marching solemnly in step. The boxes were draped with simple flags of deepest blue, with a single five-pointed silver star on each.

This was the emblem of galactic liberation the Freiheit Council had chosen, confirmed by a citizen's vote and approved by Straker. He'd standardized the blue and silver as the Breaker colors, and ordered them used where appropriate.

Engels gazed on as Captain Zholin and the crew of the *Chun Wei* followed, eyes wide in wonder at the reception.

"Turning this guy to our side is really going to pay off," she'd said to Straker during the trip, after speaking to Zholin at length. "We got lucky there."

"A man makes his own luck," he'd replied. "The Mutuality has primed its own citizens to defect. All we have to do is give them the opportunity to do it, by removing the forces that rule by fear. Soon, we'll be freeing whole star systems."

She'd nodded. "Then the trick's going to be overcoming those forces. Which means forces of our own."

Now, Engels wondered what Straker had in mind for his next campaign. As usual, he wasn't talking about it much, except to say it would be big, and risky. No surprise there. It might have something to do with whatever secret project Murdock and his team was working on, something even she had no access to.

When the parade and the reception petered out, Engels headed back inside the BCC. She comlinked *Revenge*, enabling full vid. "Zaxby, you there?"

"Of course I am here, Carla. If I weren't here, I would not be responding to you, because I would be somewhere else, and we would not be talking. And, you really ought to use proper military protocol on the comlink."

"And you waste a lot of effort trying to change things you never will. You must be a real masochist."

"As opposed to an unreal masochist?"

Engels growled, "Shut up and listen. What do you know about Murdock's secret project?"

"That is classified."

Engels felt her face turning sour. "From me? I'm second in command!"

"Need to know only. Commodore Straker's orders. Lieutenant Paloco has not been briefed either."

"But you have."

"I am a brainiac, in your quaint parlance. Other Ruxin technicians and I are rendering vital assistance, of course."

"So it must be highly technical and speculative. I know Derek's not happy with his performance in the mechsuit." She snapped her fingers. "You're trying to get his and Loco's brainlinks synchronized to their suits, while closing off any vulnerabilities to getting their minds hacked."

Zaxby squirmed, which on a Ruxin was quite a squirm indeed. "I really must not comment on that, Carla."

"That's all right. You already did. I don't know why that's such a big secret, though."

"I am not allowed to comment, Carla."

She smiled. "When you get the bugs worked out, I want them to work on my synch with *Liberator*. Right now it's only enabled at a basic level. I want the full version. There's nothing more fun than flying fully immersed."

"Not even sex? Because I thought you humans regard sex as the ultimate physical pleasure. We Ruxins certainly do."

Engels snorted. "You and Loco… always with sex on the brain."

"Murdock and his team of humans also have a great deal of sex on their brains. He especially likes to talk about Tachina and how pleasurable their relationship is, though it does divert him from his duties at times. I think the Ruxin way of reproduction is far superior to humans. We prepare, we mate furiously for a few days, and then we take time to recover in leisurely fashion. Afterward, we return to our lives for several years without such distractions."

Engels laughed. "It's not *superior* to go without sex for years. It's just simpler—but thanks, Zaxby. You helped me think of something."

"I am always happy to speak with you, Carla. However, we are approaching Freenix Base dry dock facilities in preparation for refit, so I must end this conversation. I will see you when I return to Freiheit. Zaxby out."

Zaxby had reminded her of another source she could tap. Tachina. No doubt Loco would have made a joke about tapping, and normally she wouldn't care about who Loco tapped, but Tachina was the very last one he should get involved with. If the former concubine had a middle name, it was Trouble with a capital T.

But in this case…

Tachina smiled as she opened the door to the bungalow she shared with Frank Murdock. "Why, Carla Engels! I never thought to see you grace us with your presence." As usual, the woman's tone hovered somewhere between gushing and sarcastic. Engels never quite knew whether she was sucking up or mocking, or something else entirely.

"May I come in?" Engels asked.

"Of course, of course. I'm always happy to welcome *important* people into my humble home." Tachina backed up with a half-bow, which seemed all the more ludicrous in the cleavage-baring outfit and heels she habitually wore.

The bungalow was decorated with flowers and swatches of salvaged fabric, and various unusual objects were arranged artistically on shelves as if for no other reason than to please the eye. Engels had to admit Tachina had a cohesive sense of design different from the people of Freiheit, who leaned toward homey pastoral paintings and handicrafts.

The whole place smelled strongly of floral fragrance and smokestick. Engels wondered where Tachina obtained such luxury goods. She supposed where there was a demand for something, someone would supply it, as long as there was something to trade.

And she knew what Tachina had to trade. Poor Murdock…

"Sit down, Carla. Would you like some hot tea?"

"Yes, thanks," said Engels, mostly to be agreeable, taking a seat at the small kitchen table. Since she'd entered Academy so long ago, she'd seldom visited a civilian's house.

Her own bungalow with Derek was utilitarian and sparsely decorated, more like a large military quarters than a home. She'd never had a sense of *homemaking*. Even though the concept drew her powerfully at times, she never had time to do it, not with her many duties. Or maybe she just didn't make the time.

"You have a lovely place here," Engels essayed.

"Why thank you!" Tachina opened a box and lit a smokestick, an old-fashioned kind with flame and smoke instead of just vapor. Somehow, she made the indulgence seem elegant instead of crass, with a hint of decadence. "I try to make it nice for my man."

Engels noticed she didn't say "for Frank." Derek thought Tachina was already angling for a man with higher status, and he might be right. However, there weren't many men here more important than Murdock.

"Speaking of Frank," said Engels, "it's too bad he's so busy right now. You must get lonely."

Tachina set a cup of tea in front of Engels and took a seat across from her, smokestick pinned between her fingers. "I can always find someone to occupy my time."

Engels felt the woman's foot stroke her calf through her coverall and she moved her leg away. "I didn't come for that," she blurted.

"Oh, you don't like sex?"

"Not with women, no."

"Have you ever tried it?"

Recognizing that Tachina was trying to discomfit her and seize control of the conversation, Engels said, "I'm with Derek. I don't want anyone else. I bet Frank feels the same. Why do you tease other people when you're with him? Are you trying to destroy a good thing?"

"Who said it was a good thing?"

"Then leave him. Don't play window-washer, grabbing onto one partner before you let another go. That's…"

"Immoral?" Tachina laughed. "You people are so parochial… and you military types are the worst! Loosen up and live a little! What could it hurt?"

"I was going to say 'disruptive.' Even highly sophisticated people have plenty of petty jealousies, and you're stoking them. In this *parochial* place, it's even worse." Engels rubbed her face. "How did I get sidetracked this way? Look, Tachina, I'm not trying to change who you are, but actions have consequences. If you wreck Murdock, he might become useless. He's vital to this hab. If he crashes and burns because of you, everyone will know." She leaned forward with folded hands. "We might not be able to protect you."

"Ah, a threat. I was wondering when that would show up." Tachina stared at Engels, a faint smile playing about her lips. "Okay. I take your point. I'll be more discreet."

Engels stared back. "You're not nearly as dumb as you let on."

Tachina patted at her long, lustrous hair, looking upward and away. "I have no idea what you mean."

Engels realized she wasn't going to casually trick this woman into giving her the information she wanted, so she decided simply to ask. "Look, I need to know what Frank's working on."

"And your man won't tell you? How typical. They really don't value us women like they should. Not until they want some of what we've got. Then suddenly they run their mouths like little boys afraid someone will steal their favorite toy. Good thing their favorite toy is firmly attached… and I know how to operate it really, really well. Hope you do too, because that's all they care about." She flicked ash off her smokestick. "That and their work."

Engels rolled her eyes. "I'm not going to use sex to get what I want."

"Too bad. It's a woman's power."

"My love for Derek isn't about power."

Tachina's smile grew cruel. "Poor little girl. Love is about nothing *but* power, and whoever loves the least, has it."

"That's a despicable attitude."

"Oh, grow up. How old are you, anyway?"

"Almost thirty."

Tachina shook her head. "Give it fifteen years and see how much he still loves you, what with that poor complexion, small chest and horrible clothes. I could help you with that, you know, though there are limits even to my powers."

Engels felt herself whiten with anger. What Tachina had said stung, because she couldn't shake the feeling it might be true. "Derek doesn't care about a few flaws or my fashion sense."

"Sure. That's why he reprogrammed the autodoc to fix your face, right? Because he doesn't care?"

"He did that because I hated what the Hok biotech did to me, not because he found me unattractive." And yet... was it really only for herself, or did Derek dislike looking at her too?

"Sure he did..." Tachina went on. "Yet he makes love to you in the dark, I'll bet. When a man is *really* turned on, he wants to see everything."

"He did that for me! Out of consideration for me! I was embarrassed, not him!"

Tachina smirked. "Of course."

Engels stood, steaming. "This was a mistake. I came to you in good will, and this is what I get?"

Tachina stood as well, grinding out her smokestick in a bowl. "You came to me to use me to get information you weren't willing to pay for, and aren't supposed to have. Who's the naughty one now?"

"*Aaugh!* I'm out of here." Engels turned to go.

"I do know what Frank's doing," Tachina called from behind her.

Engels stopped and turned back. "He's working on a way to get our brainlinks synched up again while protecting them from being used against us," she said.

Tachina's lips twitched. "That's only a part of it." She took the teacups and busied herself rinsing them in the kitchen sink, slowly.

"What do you want in return for the information?"

"Oh, nothing right now. A favor, when I ask for it."

"Depends on the favor," said Engels.

"It always does." Tachina turned and leaned her plush backside against the counter. "They're working on a universal hack for Hundred Worlds brainlink networks. Some kind of malware or cyber-attack program. That's the gist of it. The rest is too technical for me."

"Hundred Worlds? Not Mutuality?"

"Frank already has a whole library of hacks and malware for Mutuality computers, but the Mutuality doesn't use brainlink networks. They do have less-sophisticated single-brainlink setups, but never networked. They're afraid of link-networks and how they could be misused. How they could be hacked, hmm? Apparently for good reason."

"How do you know all this?"

Tachina chuckled. "You said it yourself. I'm smarter than I look. But I'm also a bred pleasure clone, so I'll never be allowed to move past this body and its effect on people. There's no point in trying to teach a fish to climb trees."

Engels suppressed a flash of sympathy for the woman. It wasn't as if Tachina was trying very hard to 'move past' her nature, after all. "Thanks. I owe you a favor, but remember what I said about consequences."

"Another threat?"

Engels gave her a crooked smile. "A friendly warning." She shut the door firmly on the way out.

So Straker had Murdock and his team of brainiacs trying to figure out ways to hack a Hundred Worlds network. They had Hundred Worlds equipment here on Freiheit to play with, so that made sense.

But such networks weren't ubiquitous, and they weren't monolithic. Military battlenets had multiple layers, cutouts and redundancies, to make sure one failure didn't destroy the ability of the warfighters to function. Losing higher, broader layers merely dropped the user into lower capabilities, all the way down to manual controls and voice coordination if necessary. So what was so critical about a hack?

"Whatever it is, there's no reason to keep it from me," Engels muttered to herself as she marched down the neighborhood street, heading for the mechsuit factory. That's where she expected to find Straker and Loco, tending to their battered war machines.

"You know, the techs can do that," she said as she walked onto the assembly pad, an addition to the original parts factory and the only area large enough to do work on the giant robot-like mechanisms. The two men hadn't even changed out of their work uniforms and were already covered in dust and lubricants as they pulled apart sections damaged in the recent battles. "The commander shouldn't be doing this kind of work."

"I like to get my hands inside my own mechsuit," said Straker, wiping his fingers on a rag as he approached. "I'm learning a lot from the techs, too. What's bothering you?"

Engels put her hands on her hips. "I need to talk to you—but not here." Her eyes flicked to Loco and the mechsuit mechanics.

"Sure. Let's take a walk." They followed a path through the gardens and fields, a lane set transversely from the long axis of the habitat, so they would circumnavigate the interior of the hollow asteroid and return to where they started. "What's on your mind?"

"I heard something about Murdock's secret project."

Straker sighed. "If you heard something, I guess it's not so secret anymore."

"It's a small world here, Derek. People talk. They say he's trying to devise a method to take over Hundred Worlds networks, not merely take them down."

"Taking them down is hard enough, but I need to be able to hijack them. I want to send their crew, their pilots and their mechsuiters into deep VR immersion and make them see what I want them to see. I want to do what they might have done to us—control their brains during combat."

"Why, Derek? So they can exchange one set of slave masters for another? I thought we were liberators!"

"We are. It's just a temporary measure, for during battle. If we can hack into their networks, we could completely change Hundred Worlds forces' perception of the fight. We could make them surrender, or if we have to, make them shoot phantom targets."

Engels' nostrils flared. Maybe Tachina's cynical nature had infected her, but… "Or make them shoot each other?"

Straker nodded, slowly. "If we have to."

"Those are our own people, Derek! The Hundred Worlds! Have you lost your mind? What happened to going after the Mutuality first? They have ten times the number of planets, and they're the aggressors. Divert them from their attacks on the Hundred Worlds, and we'll be reducing casualties."

Straker shook his head. "That's what you'd think, but I don't believe that. I've been studying the databases Zaxby brought out of the Unmutuals. If the Mutuality backs off, the Hundred Worlds will simply use the breather to attack. That's how generals and admirals think. That's how politicians think. That's how war works—unless there's some actual peace treaty. So we have to have some method of pulling the fangs of Hundred Worlds forces if we need to."

"If we need to? So that's all this is? A contingency plan?"

"Contingency and long-range planning. Eventually we'll have to deal with the Hundred Worlds. Maybe they'll simply accept a truce and live in peace with a weakened, reformed Mutuality, whatever we call it—but I've studied enough history to know how unlikely that is. Making peace is far harder than making war."

Engels stopped, throwing herself onto a bench set under a tree. "It seems very much the cart before the horse. Shouldn't we work on the Mutuality before worrying about something years from now?"

Straker straddled the bench facing her and ran a hand over his buzzed sandy hair. "We *are* working on it. In fact, we'll all be getting together and doing some brainstorming soon. You'll be a key part of that process, as you're my fleet commander."

"Fleet commander without much of a fleet."

"Hey, I just got you a frigate!"

Engels sighed. "That was good, but we're going to need one hell of a lot more than that to start liberating whole star systems. I'm more worried about this attempt to synch up our brainlinks. How can we be sure someone doesn't hack *us* in the process? Force us into deep immersion and send us to some fantasy land, like Shangri-La?"

"You don't trust Murdock and Zaxby?" asked Straker.

"I don't trust anyone with too much power. Power corrupts, Derek. People can be led astray. What if someone without many, ah, ethical boundaries, gets access? Someone like Tachina?"

Straker's eyebrows lifted. "Oh, that again. I know you feel threatened by this woman—"

"Not in the way you think," Engels snapped. "I've looked in her eyes, Derek. She talks a lot about having power over men, over people. That's all she wants, power, and this could be a magic shortcut to power. You know where I found out about this 'secret' info? From *her*, because Murdock can't keep his mouth shut in the sack. And Murdock was an Unmutual. He could use this hack to serve us up on a platter to DeChang again, to get in his good graces, or even to take over himself. Between the two of them, they could destroy all we've accomplished!"

Straker sat back, looking past her shoulder, pondering. "Who guards the guardians?"

"One of your book sayings?"

"Yes, from the Romans. Do you know the Ruxins have a lot of Old Earth material in their databases from before they lost their homeworld? They archived everything they came across. I can see why DeChang was spouting his references. It's addicting, to read about where humans came from and how they got here."

Engels put her hand on Straker's thigh and squeezed. "I'm glad you're enjoying your off-time entertainment, but what are you going to do about ensuring these magical hacks are never used against *us*?"

"My reading isn't only for entertainment. The past is the key to the future. There is nothing new under the sun. Those who don't learn from history are doomed to repeat it." Straker took a deep breath and spoke firmly, a little sharply. "So I'll handle it."

Engels sat back. "Handle it how? With sayings?"

"I said I'll take care of it! The less you know, the better."

Anger flared again in her chest and she stood to look down at Straker. "I never thought I'd say this, but Tachina was right. You men and your secrets. I should be the first person you trust with this, not that last!"

"That's not fair, Carla. I didn't tell Loco either. It's need-to-know. It's elementary operational security."

"I'm not just your woman, I'm your second-in-command. Your fleet commander, like you said. I *deserve* to know. And what if you'd been killed on this op? I take over and even I don't have the info? Murdock would be working on this with no oversight at all!"

"Give me some credit, Carla. There's a recording for you guys that would be triggered if I died."

"A recording that no doubt resides on a networked system that Murdock can access to alter or delete whatever he wants. And what Murdock knows, Tachina will too."

Straker stood, throwing up his hands. "Tachina, Tachina, Tachina! You're jealous, and it's messing with your head!"

"Now it's your turn to give me some credit. Yes, her cynical ambition bothers me, and it should bother you. You said yourself she's trouble. Look what she's doing to us!"

"What she's doing is twisting you up so much you don't trust my judgment anymore!"

"I'm beginning to wonder about it, yes!"

Straker brushed off his coverall. "I have work to do. I'm sure you do too." He rounded on his heel and stomped away, leaving Engels making frustrated fists so tight her nails cut into her palms.

Chapter 6

Starfish Nebula, Freiheit

Straker strode down the path back to the mechsuit factory, seething. *Women.* Just when you thought they were rational human beings, they proved you wrong. OPSEC was fundamental to any military, and telling secrets to extra people just because they felt entitled, because they were close to the boss, was asking for trouble.

As he entered the assembly floor, Straker said, "Hey Loco, get these things up to spec ASAP. You have one week. I have to go do command stuff."

Loco pulled off his tunic to work in his undershirt. "Okay, okay. I'll make sure it gets done, boss. Manny and his team got things running good here. What was up with Carly?"

"None of your damn business," Straker said. At Loco's amused look, he relented. "It's personal. Hey, what do you know about what Murdock's working on?"

"Nothing. Any brainiac stuff above the level of mechsuit repair makes my head hurt. I'm more of a people-person, you know that. Why?"

"No reason. Speaking of people, I want you with me when I talk to Lazarus. Meet me at the brig in an hour. Then we'll be shuttling over to Freenix Base. After that, a staff meeting at the BCC."

"Aw, boss, I hate meetings."

"Price of officership." He pointed with his index finger. "Brig, one hour."

Loco waved and went back to his repairs.

Straker headed over to the town hall, a small building that was now bursting at the seams with administrative personnel. Workers were building a wing onto the structure for additional space. Several tents had been set up for temporary shelter, though given the mild artificial weather, people could probably have worked in the open without difficulty.

The light from the optical bundle was dim, though. Straker stared up at it. Murdock was running all generators and reactors at full capacity, but Freiheit needed more power.

When he entered Mayor Weinberg's office, she had three compscreens open and piles of hardcopy scattered across her desk. Her index finger pressed a comlink into her ear while she stared out the window at the activity. "No, Harry, you can't have any more water right now. Pumping takes power. If you want to carry it by hand from the lake, be my guest. Otherwise, deal with the shortage like the rest of us. Bye."

"Hi, Bella," Straker said.

The mayor tossed the comlink onto her desk. "Commodore."

"Please. It's Derek. I may be in command now, but eventually we'll have to transition to civilian rule, so consider me first among equals only. Do you have a few minutes?"

"Sit." Weinberg sat, and Straker did as well. "Lonnie, bring us some caff and hold all comlink traffic," she called through her open doorway. She turned her eyes to him. "So what can I do for you, Derek?"

"I hope it's what I can do for you. I know we need more power. One piece of good news is that we captured a Mutuality frigate, the *Chun Wei*, and most of her crew defected to us. We'll dock her and plug her into the grid ASAP. But long-term, there are two solutions. One is to get generators from the Ruxins, but I'm already asking them for a lot and I haven't given them much in return yet. Do we have anything here that's excess? For trade?"

"Excess? Not much. We're short of a lot of things too. Here's a list of things we could use on your next pirate voyage." Bella sent his handtab a file.

"Pirate voyage? I don't like that characterization. We perform military operations to capture vital supplies. We're not pirates."

"Tell that to our newslog editor."

"Maybe I should."

"Maybe you shouldn't. Suppressing free speech always backfires."

Straker rubbed his eyes. "I'll let you handle the newsies, then. I'm too used to giving orders, I guess. But we're not pirates. We're liberators."

"I'll have a gentle word with him. Carrot, not stick."

"Okay." Straker sat forward. "Back to trade and politics. Isn't there *anything* we have too much of? I need some bargaining chips with the Ruxins."

"I'm not sure that it qualifies as *too much of*, but we do have something they want. There's a mollusk in our lake—a kind of snail—that we don't eat, but the Ruxins really like. I don't think they've thought of taking a breeding stock from us, so we have the only supply. We could sell them by the kilo, or you could trade breeders and all the data on its ecosystem for something big, like a gigawatt fusion reactor. Just one of those would serve all our civilian needs for a while."

"Great. Anything else we have more of than we need?"

Weinberg rubbed her neck and smiled ruefully. "Good ideas."

"We have too many good ideas?"

"*Far* too many. Now that people have more freedom, they're trying out all sorts of things to make a profit or 'help the community.' Lots of them are missing work at their jobs, or ignoring my authority. I don't have a solid system of taxation in place so I don't have enough money for incentives or law enforcement or a dozen other things."

"Can't you just… create money? It's all just numbers in the networks, right?"

"That might buy us some time, but at some point those numbers turn into real goods, Derek. If I create money out of nothing, I cause inflation. Too much money chases scarce goods. Then the money is worth less because everyone with goods wants more for the items, and we're worse off than before."

Straker sat back as Weinberg's assistant set a tray on a side table and poured two cups of caff. The man handed them to the two leaders and left, shutting the door gently.

"Have you ever heard about the Second World War on Old Earth?" Straker said.

"I'm familiar with it. A lot of my ancestors were murdered in it. They were part of an insular ethnic group that many people found easy to blame whenever something bad happened."

"The Jews, yes. That's not the part I mean. I'm talking about wartime economies, which is what we have. The nation called America, where *my* ancestors were from, had the same problem in trying to mobilize for war. Money."

"How did they solve it?" Weinberg asked.

"I'm not sure it was solved, but it was managed. First, they borrowed a lot of money from everywhere they could, including the people. They issued war bonds that they persuaded citizens to buy for patriotic reasons. These paid a percentage profit—interest—but the interest was only paid when the bond matured a long time in the future. That took money out of the civilian economy and put it in the hands of the government to produce war materiel."

Weinberg sipped her tea. "Okay, go on."

"The government issued huge contracts to industry, which provided profits and jobs, expanding the economy. People were fully employed and had money for necessities, but luxuries were scarce and expensive. They had to ration items such as smokesticks or liquor, and tax them heavily too. In fact, they taxed and rationed all nonessentials severely, which also put money back into government hands, allowing the cycle to continue."

"That would create a black market. People don't like rations and heavy taxes."

Straker shrugged. "True, but that simply allowed for even more employment of investigators to suppress it. As long as these measures didn't go on too long, and as long as the people were willing to sacrifice patriotically, they worked. Kind of like supercharging a fusion engine with extra tritium ions. It's not sustainable forever, but it would buy us time."

"Send me that history record. I'll study it and use what I can."

Straker took out his battered handtab and passed several files to her comp suite. "I'd like to have more than snails to trade with Premier Freenix. Browbeating her won't work forever."

"Once we get more power, we can optimize crop growth with extra sunlight. We have enough water and," Weinberg stage-coughed, "*fertilizer* from the sewage processing. If you can figure out what kind of land-based plant products they want, you could sell the crops in advance to her, preferably high-value—herbs, medicinals, something like that."

"That's an interesting idea, selling something before we even have it."

Weinberg smiled, showing her prominent teeth. "It's called 'commodities trading.' I've been doing research too."

"Good. I have one other thing to run past you. I want to relocate Freiheit."

"We're already short of power. We can't spare any for impellers."

Straker sipped his caff. It was of low quality and weak, but he drank it anyway. "*Chun Wei* can push gently from a solid docking position. It'll be very slow and it will use the fusion engines, not generator power. Trade fuel for movement."

"But why? Right now we're close enough to Freenix base for easy transport and trade. Why move away?"

"For power. Generators are fine, but this hab was designed for close solar collection. It needs a star."

"There are no stars in this nebula."

"Not yet." He looked at his handtab screen. "But there are some proto-stars that are giving off heat and radiation as they form. If we can put Freiheit into a nice stable orbit, we'll have all the power we need. The next step will be to capture another asteroid and bring it alongside for materials and, eventually, to hollow it out and make a bigger hab. Freiheit Two, or something."

Weinberg folded her hands. "Other than distance from Freenix, what's the downside?"

"A bit of manageable risk—the movement there, the radiation from the proto-star. We'll have to stay well back, just in case."

"I'll talk to the council about it. I need buy-in before doing anything that drastic. I'm guessing they'll ask for another reactor before we go very far, though. Unless you want to leave your new frigate permanently docked."

"Good point." Straker stood and set his cup on the tray. "Do you have some of those snails handy, as samples? I'm going to see Freenix today."

Weinberg reached for her comlink. "I can have some put in a bucket. The Ruxins like them raw and wriggling. Pick them up at the boathouse by the lake."

"Thanks. I'll let you know what happens." He held out his hand. "Always a pleasure."

The older woman shook his hand firmly. "Likewise. Thanks for including me in your decisions."

Straker wasn't entirely sure how to take that. Was she being genuine, or were her words a reproach for not consulting her more? He nodded once, and then left the office.

After a quick stop at the lake, a meal at the mess hall used up the time until he met Loco at the brig. The fare was simple and the portions were small. The troops seemed happy to be off the ships after the long days of sidespace transit back from Prael, but the lack of abundance reminded him how quickly he needed to solve the power problem. Power grew food, and food kept people content. That, and something to do. Bread and circuses, the Romans had called it. Was reducing things to that level crass, or simply practical?

He slid his used tray onto the rack and walked to the brig. Sergeant Conrad Ritter saluted him as he approached, and then opened the gate and let him into the compound. It was centered on the same repurposed building where the Unmutuals had been tried and punished. Now, a tall fence surrounded it, and razor wire crisscrossed above to deter low-gravity jump attempts.

"Lieutenant Paloco is already here with the prisoner, sir," Ritter said, leading him into the building.

"Any trouble with the Lazarus?"

Ritter's face soured. "He's always trying to talk to the guard force, make friends with them. I'd like to gag him. He's too smooth. He's a *Schlangenzunge*."

"A shlong-what?"

"A snake-tongue, in the old speech."

"I'll keep it in mind." Straker allowed Ritter to open the cell door for him, and he set the bucket outside in the hall. "Don't touch that," he said.

Inside, Loco sat in a chair tipped precariously backward against the wall. He held a stunner pistol casually in one relaxed hand.

Lazarus was seated on his cot, fingers interlaced around his knee, a study in composure despite his uncombed hair, stubbled face and rumpled clothing.

Lazarus smiled and began, "Well, if it isn't–"

"Shut up," barked Straker. "I'll control this conversation."

"Or what? You'll torture me?"

Straker waved Loco up from his chair and sent him out of the room, and made as if to follow. "I'll see you tomorrow," he said to Lazarus. Then, turning in the open doorway to Conrad Ritter, he ordered, "He's in solitary. Nobody talks to him, nobody responds, nobody listens. If he won't shut up, gag him. Bread and water. Give him a bucket for his wastes. That's–"

Lazarus raised his voice. "I take your meaning, Commodore Straker. I'll play along."

Straker turned slowly back, his expression cold. "No. No playing. You'll obey me, or you'll be punished until you comply, not tortured in some despicable attempt at controlling your way of thinking. It's your body that's in a cage, not your mind. You deserve death for what you and your clone buddies do to human beings, so any lesser punishment is fair. Suspending justice is pure mercy on my part. You live and speak and eat at my sufferance. Got it?"

"Understood." Lazarus' expression blanked, and he looked even more like a wary snake than usual. "Proceed."

Straker stepped across the room and slapped Lazarus' face hard with his open palm, knocking him to the floor. "You never, *ever* say anything to me that sounds like an order. Understood?"

"Yes, Commodore." He set himself back on his bunk and waited, eyes staring without focus. A bruise began to purple on his cheekbone.

"That slap was just to wake you up from your delusions. Your real punishment will be solitary confinement. If I have to, I'll order construction of a dark cell where you won't see or hear anything or speak to anyone for as long as it takes to gain compliance. Eventually, if you cooperate fully, I'll lighten up, give you privileges. That's my requirement. Full cooperation. Are you ready and willing to cooperate fully?"

"I will not betray the Mutuality, Commodore."

"I won't ask you to. I respect your loyalty to your own cause. All I want to do is pick your brain, learn from you. I'm sure you can get behind that idea. It's your grand opportunity to influence me, but you have to speak honestly and straightforwardly."

"That seems fair."

Straker gestured for Loco to return to the room and sit, but never took his eyes off Lazarus. "Within those limits, you may speak freely. Try any of your dominance games and you'll go into a hole."

Lazarus blinked, and then nodded. "I accept your terms. I'm ready to cooperate."

Straker sat astride the other chair in the room, placing his forearms on its back. "When last we spoke you were talking about the Stoics, and what a well-rounded leader needs to know. Go on."

Lazarus thought for a moment. "The Mutualist Party elites study history, philosophy, psychology and literature, with enough mathematics and science to provide context. These things help us lead, rule and control the populace through psycho-social techniques. We don't waste effort on the details of things others can do."

"But you didn't delegate trying to break me to your will."

"The mundane parts I did, but contests of will are part of leadership and control. Besides, Inquisitors occupy positions that partake both of rule and of hands-on expertise. We are troubleshooters and agents of effect, not bureaucrats or inspirers of the masses."

"So in your view, how does a man like me become as effective as possible?"

Lazarus raised an eyebrow. "Pardon, but may I ask a question?"

"As long you're not being a smartass or trying to manipulate me."

"No, it's a genuine request for information so that I may assist you better."

"Go ahead."

"Do you really, truly expect to overthrow the Hundred Worlds?"

Straker smiled. "So you've heard that rumor?"

"I have heard… things," said Lazarus.

Of course, that was because Straker had made sure to leak information to the guards in the brig. Naturally they would discuss their leader's ambitions during the long watches of the night, within Lazarus' earshot.

In those rumors, no mention was made of Straker's plan to overthrow the Mutuality first, the better to sell this Lazarus on attaining the goal he wanted: the destruction of his enemies. It would take careful doling out of just the right information to milk knowledge from the Inquisitor without swallowing the poison of hidden lies.

"I really, truly do think I can take down the Hundred Worlds," answered Straker.

"But why would you? They're your people."

Straker spoke the critical half-truth smoothly. "Not anymore. I've been doing my research. Their system is as corrupt as yours, though their methods are far less cruel. But what it comes down to is, I think I can reform them, do a better job. I'm betting I can take over the Hundred Worlds and make peace with your government. That way everybody wins. Once the threat is removed, I'm also betting your political system will become more humane."

"In my estimation, all of that is extremely unlikely."

Straker grinned even more broadly. "You mean it's flat-out crazy to try?"

Lazarus visibly chose his words. "I won't presume to judge your state of mind, only what I see as the probability of success."

"But what if I could do it?"

"How do I know you won't use my instruction to damage the Mutuality?"

"You don't. In fact, I can guarantee there will be collateral damage... which you taught me is necessary to achieve my goals. But what do you believe more likely, me overthrowing the Hundred Worlds, or the thousand worlds of the Mutuality?"

Lazarus stared, thoughtful. "If I genuinely thought you had a non-zero probability of success in overthrowing the Hundred Worlds, I'd help you wholeheartedly."

"Even if I have to mess with the Mutuality to do it?"

"Even so. Any wise man will take a flesh wound to kill his mortal enemy."

Straker nodded. "That's right. So let's assume for the moment that I have that non-zero probability. Your help could increase my chances, right?"

"Yes, Commodore." His face relaxed to genuine thoughtfulness. "It's a Pascal's Wager."

"What's that?"

"Pascal was an Old Earth mathematician and philosopher. He outlined a wager wherein a man bets his life on either following his god's will and spending an eternity in paradise, or not doing so and spending eternity in some hellish afterlife. He points out that if such a god exists, compliance with his will gains everything, but if that god does not exist, compliance with his supposed will becomes a minor insurance payment. You made your own Pascal's Wager as a mechsuiter."

Straker drummed his fingers on the back of the chair. "I don't see how that applies. If the Unknowable Creator exists, I did my duty. If not, I would have done the same anyway. I didn't need some god to pat me on the back."

"Perhaps. Or perhaps an orphan saw he had nothing to lose and everything to gain by doing the will of a system that might as well be a god, that would reward him with the paradise of being a hero. Perhaps everything he was taught supported that idea."

Straker stroked his jaw. "That's a fair point."

Straker could see Lazarus settling in to his role as a mentor. He intended to use the Inquisitor's natural feeling of superiority against him. With nothing else to live for, Lazarus would strive to prove he was right about everything, trying to validate his own worldview and pass it to Straker.

In doing so, he would teach Straker what he needed to know.

Lazarus continued, "This is why you might benefit from instruction in higher-order thinking, Commodore Straker. It's only when evaluating second-order and third-order effects that you can truly make optimum long-term decisions for yourself and your followers."

"I know how to make good decisions. I've been successful up until now."

"You have good instincts, I agree. But instincts will only take you so far."

Straker sat back. "Fine. I'm open to learning. In fact, that's the whole point of talking to you. How does this Pascal's Wager thing apply?"

"Pascal's Wager was a primitive version of another philosopher's ideas, those of Nicholas Taleb. He pointed out that the key to success in every endeavor was to limit the amount any one 'wager' could lose, while courting the possibility of near-infinite wins."

"That seems obvious."

"Yet it's not. You lost your mechsuit regiment to a Mutuality military trap because some Hundred Worlds commander inverted that wager. He bet an invaluable, nearly irreplaceable elite unit—a massive downside possibility—against the limited upside possibility of merely defending one world and maintaining the status quo. In naval terms, he gambled his irreplaceable fleet-in-being in hopes of a mere tactical victory."

Straker raised a hand. "Plus the possibility of badly damaging the Hok—I mean the Mutuality—attack forces."

"That is true. The situation was more complex than my simple example makes it seem, but my goal is to make the principle clear. Do you understand?"

"I think so. The best actions always have more upside than downside. Hopefully, big upside and only a little downside. Like a sniper taking a low-probability shot against the enemy commander. Missing costs one bullet. Hitting might win the battle, even the war."

"A good example. It's the intersection of probability curves with potential gains and losses. Even more importantly, the hope—even the inevitability—of the highly improbable must not be discounted. You must *expect* surprises, even count on them."

Lieutenant Paloco dropped his chair legs to the ground with a thump. Straker had almost forgotten he was there, listening. "So it's like the old theory about flat-out asking every hot chick you meet to sleep with you," Loco said. "There's no downside if you can take the rejection, and there's big upside when every now and again one of them says yes."

"A limited application that ignores other factors, such as the social cost of being viewed as a man-whore," replied Lazarus with a sniff, "but it does illustrate the point."

Straker cleared his throat. "I'm still waiting for the application to me."

"The application is for both of us, Commodore. It's *my* Pascal's Wager to bet on *yours*, which is a second-order effect, a derivative. I can't afford not to help you try. The downside for me is acceptable, as long as I do lesser harm to the Mutuality thereby. The upside possibility is to destroy my enemies and free us from a miserable war that has lasted centuries. I'll take that bet."

Loco chuckled. "Not to mention that if you do, you come home a hero. You could probably leverage that into being a big boss in the Mutuality. Or you could stick with us and still be a top dog, if you played your cards right."

Lazarus looked down his nose at Loco. "You're mixing your metaphors. And I wasn't aware canines played cards."

"What, you never saw the picture of dogs playing poker? It was popular when I was growing up."

Straker stood, cutting off further argument. "All right, Inquisitor. You've given me a lot to think about. I'll talk to you again soon."

"I look forward to it, Commodore. May I ask a favor?"

"You can ask."

"A handtab with books loaded on it. Or even printed books, if you have them."

"Not many of those around, but I'll get something sent to you."

"Thank you again, Commodore."

Straker made sure to retrieve his bucket of snails before he left. In the main guardroom, Loco said to him, "You know he's sucking up. He's still a snake. He'll play along for a while, and then he'll stab you in the back, or try to escape, something like that."

"Possibly. But he's smart and he knows how to get things done. I can learn from him, things I need to know. And I'm hoping he takes the long view. I'll use it against him."

"Long view?"

"If I'm to be a new Caesar—maybe Napoleon's a better example—what better way than to be my valued mentor and counselor?"

Loco put a hand on Straker's arm. "Boss, be careful what he teaches you. I know I'm all loose and shit sometimes, but I'm free to be that way because you're a rock, know what I mean?"

"You mean I'm an uptight asshole, right?"

"You wouldn't be Derek Straker if you weren't, and I don't want you to change. I'm worried you're getting overconfident. This isn't your kind of battle, Derek."

"A battle of wits? Maybe not, but I can win because I hold the power, and I'm going to use it for good. I've been doing a lot of reading–"

"–like you always do–"

"–and I think I can win the whole thing. The alternative is to be selfish, make a life here, and let the two halves of humanity go on fighting and killing each other with no end in sight."

"That doesn't sound so bad… but I'm with you, Derek. Even when you're crazy." Loco let go and punched Straker in the same arm. "What now, boss?"

"Now? Now we grab some more upside from Freenix."

"You grabbing Freenix? This I gotta see."

Chapter 7

Starfish Nebula, Freenix Base

The Premier Matriarch, the one the humans called Freenix, drew herself out of her tank and felt old. She had not been young when she had found herself in charge of the last organized and free remnant of the Ruxin people eighty years ago.

For decades she'd held her society together, developing it from the days when it was a mere repair yard for Archers. When the last of those heroic warships had returned for refit, she had decommissioned its crew of warrior males, but not before she had mated with a few.

Afterward, she'd had them put in cryogenic stasis. No warriors would ever consent to being hormonally neutered once more, but with no battle to fight, they would be a disruptive element, a grave risk to her plans. She could afford no risks. Not if she intended to free her planet and star system once more. When the time came for war, they could be revived.

With the long-planned expansion set in motion, she had thought to personally oversee this first phase, wherein eight new asteroids would be transformed into habitats for her people. It was well under way, but the arrival of the rogue humans and the agitation from the neuters threatened everything.

She thought she could handle the apish aliens. Their leader was forceful but had asked for little, only the last remaining Archer, some labor and supplies. She could have destroyed their ship when it had first arrived, but was much too shrewd to throw away such potential.

Now, though, she realized she might have outsmarted herself. The humans she'd aided had planted dangerous ideas in the heads of the neuters assigned to the Archer, ideas that had spread like wildfire among the populace. She was too old, too set in her ways, to manage such a potential conflagration.

Her eldest daughter, Vuxana, had been groomed and educated from the egg for this moment. The transition had come a little early, but the energy and flexibility of youth was needed. The old matriarch could relax and play the advisor, leaving the difficulties of rulership in time of turmoil to the young.

"I will not be your puppet, Mother," Vuxana said as she prepared to enter the throne room that served as an audience chamber. "Not all of my decisions will be in accordance with your intentions."

"I am aware of that, daughter," the elder replied. "I have confidence you will lead our people to greatness once again."

"Perhaps we are great already."

"You are impertinent."

"I am Premier." Vuxana focused all four eyes on her mother. "It is you who are impertinent."

"I raised you well."

"So you did." Vuxana inserted a comlink into her auditory orifice, deep enough it couldn't be seen. "You will listen and advise me."

"Of course… Premier."

* * *

"Your suit is most impressive, Commodore Straker," said Zaxby as he led Straker and Loco through the soggy corridors of Freenix Base on the way to see the Ruxin ruler. "You more closely resemble a War Male."

"Thanks. That's the idea." Straker's suit was painted in bright greens and yellows, and now sprouted two rubber foam tentacles from its shoulders.

"I can't believe those silly arms make you look better to a Ruxin, not worse," said Loco.

"It's the same principle as a Ruxin keeping only two eyes and two tentacles facing a human," Straker replied. "I never noticed it until Carla pointed it out. They do it to minimize their oddness to us. Carla figured these arms might make me look more Ruxin and more impressive to them, subconsciously."

"You might also carry a weapon in your hand," said Zaxby.

"In the presence of your boss?"

"A War Male is expected to be armed at all times."

"What kind of weapon? My slugthrower?"

Chapter 7

"I have a better idea. Let us make a detour." Zaxby turned off the main corridor.

Straker and Loco followed, calf-deep in warmish seawater. Though their pressure suits kept it out, Straker knew the humidity coming through his open faceplate would eventually make him miserable. If humans had to occupy Ruxin-adapted spaces for very long, they would need to come up with a specialized wet suit rather than just using spacesuits. For now, though, he put up with it.

Zaxby opened a door and entered. Inside the large room were racks of objects, many products of nature, as if they'd been harvested from aquatic environments—shells, preserved animals, coral. The Ruxin picked up a short spear made of white bone, decorated with insets of mother-of-pearl and sporting a cruel, barbed tip.

"This is a squid spear," Zaxby said, handing it to Straker. "Loco, you take one too. It's made from a bone of a deep-sea creature, and it's used to hunt squid."

"I take it the squids fought back?"

"Before the advent of modern technology, hunting the larger squids was quite dangerous. For humans, it would be like hunting a lion with a spear. Now, these are ceremonial objects."

"Won't someone care that we took them?"

Zaxby swiveled his head in negation. "They are for the communal use of War Males. As we have none of our own War Males due to Freenix's policies, and she has accepted you as War Males, you should carry them. Of course, if you die or retire from making war, they will be returned to the storehouse."

"No problem. We ain't gonna die." Loco swung the spear and stabbed at the air. "On guard! Back, evil squid!"

Zaxby brought an extra eye forward to examine Loco. "Squid are not evil. They are animals, although clever ones. I remember one time–"

"Loco's just making up for his lost childhood, as usual," said Straker. "Lead on, McZaxby."

"McZaxby? Is that an honorific?"

"Sure, sure. That's what it is. Let's go see Freenix and shake spears at her."

Loco busted out laughing. "I see what you did there, boss! Shakespeare! If I didn't know better I'd say you were sprouting a sense of humor."

"I'll be sprouting seaweed if I stay here too long," Straker replied. "Let's go."

A crowd of Ruxins milled near the entrance to Freenix's ruling chamber. Many wore ornate harnesses, and the babble of their polysyllabic language filled the area.

"Something unusual is afoot," said Zaxby.

"Or a-tentacle," said Loco.

"I will inquire."

When Zaxby returned from questioning his fellow Ruxins, he said, "Freenix has been forced to abdicate in favor of one of her daughters, Vuxana."

"Why?" asked Straker.

"The old Premier was due to retire soon, and the neuters demanded it be now. They wish to see liberalized policies on genderfication. More opportunity to become male or female. More status."

Straker glanced sidelong at Loco, who shrugged. "Did these neuters have spokesmen to convey their demands?"

Zaxby squirmed. "They did." He said no more.

"From the crew of the *Revenge*, maybe?" said Straker.

"That is true."

Straker smacked his fist into his gloved palm. "Damn. I knew it. I planted ideas in their heads. Did you know about this beforehand, Zaxby?"

"I heard from the crew, but I did not participate. I am no rabble-rouser, no disruptor of the status quo, no demagogue, no–"

"I get it." Straker shrugged. "Well, let's seize the opportunity."

Zaxby waved several arms at Straker. "No, no, no. We must wait for the new matriarch to consolidate her power. Then, perhaps, in a few weeks, we can petition…"

"Screw that. I can't wait weeks. Come on, Zaxby. You're my translator. Hold this bucket, and don't let anyone eat any."

"Oh, my. Freiheit mollusks!"

"A gift for the new queen." Straker moved toward the doorway. "Loco, back me up."

"As usual, boss."

Straker shoved through the press of rubbery Ruxins with Loco and Zaxby following. The crowd gave way without complaint. He was pretty sure they were all neuters, and they recognized him as a War Male.

At the far end of the audience chamber, a female Ruxin sprawled on a thronelike pedestal set on a dais. Straker marched straight to the foot of its ramp and raised his spear over his head. The others followed close behind.

"Hail Premier Vuxana! I am Commodore Derek Straker, War Male commander and leader of your human allies." He turned to face the crowd of Ruxins who occupied the chamber. "I congratulate you on your rise to the throne, and I pledge my support to your new, enlightened policies and thank you in advance for your generous backing for my efforts to free the Ruxin homeworld."

When Zaxby translated, the octopoids broke out in a roar of vocalization. Straker wasn't sure if it was cheering or anger or merely loud discussion. He stood facing them and shook his spear over his head, determined not to back down no matter what.

"They are pleased," Zaxby said. "You have struck the right note of optimism. They are tired of toiling without opportunity for advancement of the individual or the species. They are hailing your name and are calling for Vuxana to cooperate with you."

Straker merely smiled and continued to wave his spear at the crowd. He noticed that a dozen or so Ruxins in the front wore military harnesses and carried sidearms. He thought he recognized them as members of the crew of the Archer *Revenge*. They might not be War Males, but they seemed to be acting like they were.

"Nice job, boss," yelled Loco in his ear.

A tentacle pushed on Straker's shoulder. He turned to see Vuxana halfway down the ramp, one rubbery arm extended to touch him. She was big, like Freenix, but her skin tone was firm and her colors much more vibrant than the old matriarch's. Her eyes were bright and clear.

"We must speak, War Male Straker," she said in passable Earthan. "Come with me."

The *Revenge* crew formed a cordon and ushered the group out a door at the rear of the throne room and into an antechamber, but they didn't enter. There, Vuxana sat ponderously at an oval table and waved for the humans and Zaxby to do so as well.

Straker remained standing, believing this might give him a psychological advantage with the new young Premier. "Zaxby, the bucket."

Zaxby placed the bucket of snails on the table.

Straker walked it over to Vuxana and set it in front of her. "A gift, for you, Premier."

She dipped a tentacle in the water and drew out a snail, examined it briefly, removed it from its shell and popped it in her mouth. "Quite tasty. Thank you, Commodore," she said after swallowing.

"You are welcome, Premier Vuxana," he said. He tried to phrase his words formally, one ruler to another. "It is an example of how cooperation yields benefits. My people wish to live safely and productively, and will no doubt be able to provide more snails, as well as other products. Your population, on the other hand, is restless and tired of being cooped up, toiling with few pleasures and little purpose. With your help, I can give them that purpose."

"War Males are headstrong," Vuxana replied. "You gave my neuters these ideas and now you come to pressure me into war."

"Ruxins are already at war, Premier. The Mutuality subjugated your homeworld and enslaved your people. Together, we can free them and my own people too. You have the industry and the workers. I have the leadership, drive and vision, and a core of veteran fighters. Together, we can bring down our enemies and take our rightful places in this arm of the galaxy."

"I agree. I am the future. My mother Freenix was the past. She guided our people through a dark time and prepared me with all the skills I need. She even had me study your language. However, we must not be hasty in our eagerness. We must balance the new and the old. Change must be managed."

Straker set his spear on the table. "That's your department, Premier. As the commanding War Male, my province is war. Yours is the economy. You must produce what I need, and I must employ it skillfully. If we both fulfill our roles, we shall be victorious."

"Victory is not assured," Vuxana replied, "but I am willing to take risks my predecessor would not. I will provide you with your war materiel, but you must plan your operations so that they can never be traced back here to the Starfish Nebula. If you fail, our breeding population and yours must survive."

"Fair enough. Now that we've agreed in principle, let's discuss details." Straker took out his old handtab, sealed in clear plastic against the dampness. He removed his glove and glanced at his notes.

"One more item," Vuxana said. "Before we get to specifics, I must insist you make your first operation the liberation of Ruxin."

"I told you the conduct of war was my area," Straker said.

"Of course. But as Premier of my people and the holder of the resources you need to prosecute that war—and as the one with the most to lose—it is my decision as to which battle to begin first. That is a political choice, not a military one."

Straker folded his hands and sat, his elbows on the table. "Premier, not only is this not in accordance with my own intentions, it's likely to do damage to your own people. Whatever star system we liberate first will draw a strong response from the Mutuality. It makes more sense to liberate a human world, and I have already chosen one with a high chance of success. Ruxin is only one planet, one star system, inhabited by aliens. Its liberation will not fire the imagination of the majority humans in the Mutuality the way freeing one of their own systems would."

"You prefer to risk humans before Ruxins? That is a noble sentiment, Commodore. Perhaps too noble. Perhaps you fear that, with our superior race unleashed, yours will inevitably fall behind?"

Straker laughed, a big, genuine roll of mirth as he held up a hand. "I'm not worried. Humans are spread across more than a thousand systems. If and when you surpass us I'll probably be long dead—and I guess we'll deserve it if we can't keep up. But let me ask you: if we free Ruxin first, how am I supposed to inspire human systems to revolt?"

"That is your area of expertise, as you have said."

"No, actually, it's yours, Premier. That's politics. Imagine our roles reversed. Would you think it wise if I were to demand the lone human system were freed before even one of a thousand Ruxin systems? Would that make sense?"

Vuxana writhed gently in her chair. Eventually she focused on Zaxby and spoke to him in their language. They conversed for a few moments, and then she switched back to Earthan. "You have conceded this is a political decision?"

Straker clenched his jaw. Was the squid queen going to screw him over? But she was young, and facing internal problems with the neuters. She must know he could stir them up more, but that would only hurt both sides. Was this a discussion in good faith, or was it brinksmanship, seeing who would blink first?

He took a chance, believing he had the upper hand. Even if she stood her ground, he still had other leverage. "Yes. It's a political decision where to attack first, though it could determine the course of our war."

"Then I have decided you are correct. You will liberate human systems first, in an effort to stir the fires of revolt across the Mutuality. My studies of the new databases has convinced me that their people are sick of war and corrupt oppression, and their political system is ripe for change. However, you will keep Ruxin in mind, and you will liberate our homeworld as soon as is practical."

Straker smiled. "I always intended that. Your people seem more naturally unified than mine, and highly technical. That will be quite useful."

Vuxana essayed a practiced smile with her rubbery mouth. "You humans are quite useful too."

"I'm not sure how to take that," mumbled Loco.

"You may take it to the bank, as your saying goes," Zaxby said smugly. "When a Premier speaks, it is has the force of law."

Straker ignored the implications of that. Ruxin society was too complex for him to analyze or criticize. Even human societies were complicated enough to make his head hurt anyway, no matter how much history he read.

"Good," he said. "Now let's talk about our immediate requirements and what we have to offer in return. First, we need a gigawatt fusion reactor, and the fuel to feed it."

"And we need a breeding population of mollusks so we can increase production to provide enough for all. My people clamor for them… and I like them too."

"I believe that's a good start for negotiations."

Hours later, Straker left happier than he'd expected. In exchange for the snails, the new Premier had agreed to provide a large power reactor adapted to the Breakers' technical specifications, as well as all the Ruxin unskilled labor Mayor Weinberg could use.

She'd also accepted samples of blood taken from Straker, and from the three captured Hok Straker had in confinement. The warriors remained placid, for Zholin had ordered them to offer no resistance, but Straker was taking no chances until he was certain how their minds and their obedience conditioning worked.

The blood contained the Hok biotech, of course. Straker had suggested it was worthy of study. If a way could be found to modify it to get rid of all unwanted side effects and leave only improved strength and faster healing, it might be quite useful for enhancing combat troops…

As Vuxana's Earthan was quite good, Straker also requested a private chat with her. They talked for over an hour.

When the meeting had ended, Zaxby piloted the gig back to Freiheit.

Loco finally spoke up. "What's next boss? 'Cause my mechsuit won't fix itself."

"We have techs for that," replied Straker. "You and me, we're going to make ourselves a Pascal's Wager."

"We're getting religion?"

Straker laughed. "Not exactly, but we're going to make the Ritter brothers thank their gods for the day they met us."

"So… something with more upside than downside. More to be won than lost, right?"

"Right."

"What's to be won?" Loco asked.

"A star system. The first of many, I hope."

"And to be lost?"

Straker shrugged and stared past Loco out the crystal window of the gig. "Nothing but a few lives. Ours, mainly."

"I'm not so sure that's a good wager, boss."

* * *

Engels sat in the conference room with her arms crossed, watching the rest as they debated.

"This is a complex plan," Aldrik Ritter said while pacing in front of the holoscribbler. The display was made to allow quick and easy inputs using special gloves instead of manually through keyboards and controls. It was now filled with notations and crude diagrams showing star system locations and attack deployments. The flatplate next to it showed abundant text notations in the form of a draft operations order.

"We don't have the luxury of brute force," Straker replied. "All the dominoes have to fall perfectly… but we do it right, fall they will."

"At least we're all getting the brief," Engels said darkly. She still wasn't at all happy about being cut out of the network hack project, and was in a mood to punish Straker. In fairness, though, she felt much better after hearing about the new Ruxin ruler and the progress made there.

Straker shot her a glance of longsuffering. Good. He should suffer a bit.

He said, "It'll soon be obvious we're prepping for something big—as big as we can handle, if not bigger. That's all right. The key is to keep the target secret, need-to-know limited to those in this room. You'll notice," he said heavily, giving Engels a flat stare, "that neither Zaxby nor Murdock are here. They get technical secrets, you get the operational ones."

Engels knew that was aimed directly at her. She grudgingly admitted he was right—admitted to herself anyway.

She sipped her caff and gave him a shrug to know the discussion wasn't settled, glancing around the room at those present: the two surviving Ritter brothers, Loco and Straker, Heiser and Gurung and Gibson. These now formed the inner circle on purely military matters. Zholin was obviously too new.

Straker continued, "I see six days of preparation in our future, but we'll cram it into only three with double shifts. The primary reward for hard work will be more hard work, but everyone will have plenty of downtime in sidespace. We have to move fast, to take advantage of our newest acquisition, the frigate *Chun Wei*." He rapped on the table. "Get going."

Chapter 8

Sachsen System, Frigate *Chun Wei*

The frigate *Chun Wei* transitioned into the Sachsen star system. Updated information appeared on the main holoplate as the SAI processed sensor inputs.

Captain Zholin commanded the ship, today wearing his Mutuality uniform. Commodore Straker stood alongside the smaller man, eyes roving over the screens.

"Everything seems placid," said Zholin, who was quicker than his boss to evaluate the results of his own ship's scans. "I see two routine patrols of attack ships, one on each side of the system, hours away from us." He turned to his sensor tech. "What's the status of the orbital fortress?"

"No indications of high alert," the tech answered, "but we're at extreme range."

There was only one fully operational battle station circling the main inhabited planet of Sachsen-3, and one more under construction. The system had been an independent associate of the Hundred Worlds for three centuries of settlement—until its conquest by the Mutuality three years ago.

Straker had chosen Sachsen-3 as his first target. It lacked the usual multiple fortresses protecting most industrialized worlds, and according to the Ritter brothers, natives of Sachsen, the planet's people were still restive and rebellious.

"Good news," said Straker. "They must not be concerned about our other, hidden inbound ships."

"That may change when they reach underspace detection range," Zholin replied.

"Speaking of underspace…"

"Nothing on our own detectors, but that's expected at this distance," said the sensor tech. She'd had to brush up on how to operate the underspace sensor gear, having seldom used it since her initial training. Not surprising, as Archers had disappeared from the landscape of war for over eighty years.

Until now, anyway. The surprise of using underspace was one reason Straker was pushing to begin liberating worlds right away, rather than building up forces for months or years. The other reason was that the loss of the *Chun Wei* might not yet have been reported to most of the thousand systems of the Mutuality. She was his Trojan Horse.

"How long until we approach the fortress?"

"Eight hours," said Captain Zholin. "That's assuming all goes well."

"Let's not assume. Send our recording. Act natural."

Zholin nodded, and the man at the comms board hit the transmitter. Once that was taken care of, Zholin said, "Set course for Sachsen-3, all ahead standard, weapons secure. Remember, everyone, we're now acting in unity with our Mutualist comrades."

If Straker weren't familiar with Zholin by now, he'd have thought the humorless man was making a joke. Maybe he was overly concerned about proving his dedication to his new cause, the "Galactic Liberation." That's what people had taken to calling the movement, the overall organization including the Ruxins and their holdings, the Breakers, and Freiheit.

And they'd begun calling Straker "Liberator." He wasn't sure how to feel about that, but from his readings, movements tended to take on lives of their own. Instead of leading a tight group, he was beginning to feel as if he was riding herd on an organization extending further and further outward from himself.

The holoplate showed the six planets of the system. Sachsen-1 was hot and rocky, Sachsen-2 hot and wet, barely habitable until terraformed. Sachsen-3 was within the Goldilocks zone for human life, but on the chilly side and moonless. Most of its population resided near the equators, and the poles became cold enough to form dry ice from atmospheric carbon dioxide during their winters. Sachsen-4 through 6 were small gas giants, each with an assortment of moons and paper-thin rings.

Ships and bases appeared on the display as the computers processed the sensor inputs—miners, freighters, ore and fuel refining, all the facilities of an industrialized spacegoing society, scattered throughout the system. Straker examined them and grunted in satisfaction. "Everything looks good."

"It would look good if they were laying a trap, too," said Loco.

"Since when did you become our resident pessimist?"

"Since I saw your plan, boss. But no worries. Like you said, we got nothin' to lose but our lives. I never expected to make it to thirty."

Straker's brow wrinkled. "You're not thirty yet."

"Well, I guess I'm immortal until then."

"Put up the projections of our Archers," said Straker after examining the holoplate for a time.

Two icons appeared, lurking near asteroids in the belt beyond Sachsen-3. One was the Ruxin-crewed *Revenge*. The other was the corvette *Liberator*, newly fitted with underspace engines.

"These are unconfirmed, of course," said Zholin. "Assuming they arrived on time and are in position, they should be outside the usual underspace sensor range even if the enemy has detectors active."

Straker paced back and forth, his mind worrying at a situation that seemed to present itself exactly as he'd hoped for, trying to find some flaw or failing in his plan. As far as he could tell, the critical hurdle was getting his Trojan horse, *Chun Wei*, docked at the fortress without the enemy becoming suspicious.

Fortunately, such asteroid-based fortresses comprised more than mere combat installations. They were full-service bases in space. They provided R&R for military personnel, including contracted entertainment, restaurants and bars, even shopping districts with luxury goods reserved for the more senior or well-connected Mutualists. Some contained secure transloading facilities for important civilian cargo as well.

Of course, they also contained repair shops for warships with problems too small to need a full shipyard, and quartermaster facilities to resupply vessels with food, fuel ammo and other official consumables. Therefore, it was common to pull into port for a few days between combat cruises.

In fact, Straker was depending on it.

"Can we tell yet who else is docked? Ship classes, at least?" he asked.

"No, we're too far out, sir," said Zholin.

"Carry on, then." Straker jerked his head at Loco, and the two exited the bridge.

"You hate this part, don't ya?" said Loco as they made their way toward the cargo hold.

"Inbound from transit? Yeah. We've arrived, but not really."

"Would be more fun with Carla here, right?"

Straker shrugged. "I couldn't kick Zholin off his own frigate just because it's the biggest ship we have. *Liberator* is Carla's baby, anyway."

"And you're not nervous about *Liberator's* new underspace engines?"

"They tested out fine. The Ruxins are meticulous, and Zaxby likes her. He was careful." Straker said it lightly, but inside, he didn't feel so confident. Retrofitting a corvette like *Liberator* with engines, field generators, and those weird metal-tentacle emitters wasn't quite the same as building an Archer from the keel up.

However, Carla had refused to consider staying behind on this op. Better she remain part of the backup plan than joining him at the tip of the sword, so to speak. Too, having underspace capability gave her little ship a lot more survivability. Hiding in that odd dimension could be a defense as well as a method of attack.

Straker shuddered to think what might have happened had the Mutuality decided to pursue underspace tech themselves. Even though the Ruxins were careful never to let it fall into enemy hands, once their enemies knew its potential, they could have researched it.

However, the Mutuality was apparently content to vigorously counter it—which also discouraged the Hundred Worlds from developing it too highly. After that, a tacit agreement seemed to prevail between the two empires, relegating underspace to the occasional covert operation.

Fortunately, it was a nearly forgotten aspect of battle, and Straker wanted to keep it that way.

From talking to Zholin, many of the smaller Mutuality ships didn't even have working underspace detectors, as maintaining other functions took priority, and it was common to cannibalize parts even within one's own craft. The capital units—cruisers and larger—got the best of everything, and the destroyers, frigates and corvettes took it in the shorts.

This created a vicious cycle, as the most competent officers and crew fought for assignments aboard the best ships, and the best ships got the best supplies and maintenance. This left the dregs in the undermanned light units, except for a few conscientious souls like Zholin trying to stem the rot.

Just one more reason they haven't defeated the Hundred Worlds, despite a ten-to-one advantage in star systems, Straker mused. Bad management created a bad economy. Lack of opportunity for improvement stifled innovation and creativity, causing people to try to 'work the system' instead of actually perform work. Add in a heavy dose oppression and hypocrisy, and you got an empire held together by little but fear and bureaucracy.

A corrupt empire ripe to fall. That's what he kept telling himself every time he contemplated the horrendous odds against him.

"I'm gonna catch some rack time if you don't mind," said Loco.

Straker detected a slight leer on his best friend's face. "With Sergeant Campos?"

Loco grinned broadly. "Not my fault she got assigned to the *Chun Wei*. That was purely Carla's decision."

"I hear you pointed out that the old autodoc on this ship needed a competent medical operator," Straker replied.

"So what if I did?"

"So enjoy your 'rack time.' I'll be at our quarters in exactly one hour. Make sure she's gone so my arrival doesn't embarrass her. I am the Liberator, after all." Straker shared a stateroom with Loco, as the frigate was packed with infantry wearing Mutuality uniforms. Those were berthed in every available space throughout the ship.

"Thanks, boss. One hour it is." Loco hurried off.

The luckiest troops were hot-bunking in real racks. The rest rolled out pads on the flight deck between or inside the small craft. They played cards, read vidbooks, watched showvids or checked their gear for the nth time. Their noncoms led them in rotations of physical training in a small cleared area of the cargo hold.

And twice a day, they did verbal dry-runs of Straker's plan, until everyone could recite it by heart.

Straker walked through the spaces and passageways to show his face, receiving cheers and thumbs-up from men and women struggling to hide their pre-battle jitters. They knew the fight was approaching them exactly as fast as the frigate approached the fortress. He'd chosen his best people for this op, but he only had a few he could truly call battle-hardened.

When Loco's hour was up he knocked cautiously on his stateroom door, and then tried the handle. It opened to reveal one neat bunk and one rumpled. Straker threw himself into his, and sleep took him.

He awoke to feel Loco shaking his foot. "Up and at 'em, boss. Time to do or die."

"Let's hope dying comes a lot later," Straker replied, stretching and rolling out of his bunk. By the time he'd showered and changed into the uniform of a Mutuality lieutenant, Captain Zholin was paging him to the bridge.

"We're less than an hour out," Zholin said when Straker arrived. "Fortress Control has accepted our codes and we're cleared to dock."

On the display the fortress hung in space, a repositioned asteroid now orbiting Sachsen-3. It bristled with weaponry to shame a dreadnought. Dozens of freighters and transports were docked at various locations, along with a separate, neat line of warships. The base didn't spin—it was a military facility, after all, and combat effectiveness outweighed the energy efficiency of free gravity—so there was no need to cluster vessels at the axis' endpoints.

All the usual spaces inside would be gravplated, which had the additional advantage of flexibility. Gravplating could be laid on any convenient surface, in any direction, and its pull could be varied and controlled.

In fact, Straker was counting on it.

"Commodore," said Zholin after giving Straker a moment to look over the displays, "This operation will be either harder or bloodier than expected—perhaps both."

"How so?"

"When we finalized your plan, we didn't expect more than three or four light warships docked here." Zholin gestured, and the sensor tech highlighted the row of vessels. "Instead we've got a full battlecruiser squadron, plus escorts."

"Four battlecruisers, one light cruiser, nine destroyers, six frigates..." mused Straker.

"Yes, though the odd LC, one destroyer and two frigates aren't part of the sixteen-ship squadron."

Straker rubbed his jaw and felt avarice flare in his heart. "This is better than I'd hoped. We'll seize those we can, disable the ones we can't."

Zholin straightened to attention as if afraid of a dressing-down. "But sir... the plan everyone's memorized is already difficult. Trying to seize those ships, rather than destroying them, is nearly impossible."

"I'm not going to give up this chance to acquire some real mobile firepower. It'll be a bit harder, but the big variable isn't the number of docked warships. The real question is, how many Sachsens are aboard the fortress? The Ritter brothers assure me all the locals will join us."

"Sir, we have no confirmation the Ritter brothers made contact with the resistance movement—or even if such a thing exists. The fast timetable you insisted on means we're going in blind."

"Getting cold feet, Captain Zholin?"

Zholin drew in a deep breath. "I am sworn to your service, sir. I'm only telling you my reservations."

"And you can keep on telling me, but I've made my decision. We're going ahead as planned—with a few modifications due to this new info. We always knew we'd have to make adjustments. That's all these are—adjustments."

"Aye aye, sir."

"Carry on, Captain. Loco, let's go find Zaxby."

Straker led the way to the cargo bay, where Zaxby had a small hydro-tank he could retreat into when he wanted to get out of his water suit.

The hole at the top was quite small, only about a handbreadth across. Straker would never have believed a Ruxin could fit through it if he hadn't seen the boneless Zaxby do it. "As a Ruxin, just like the octopus of your Earth, I can squeeze through very small openings," Zaxby had said when planning the upcoming operation. "I will be able to enter spaces within the fortress no one will expect."

Straker knocked on the tank. "Zaxby!"

"Lieutenant Zaxby reports as ordered, Commodore," Zaxby said from behind Loco, startling Straker with his sudden movement. The octopoid stepped forward and saluted with one tentacle. He was naked, without water suit or harness, his skin a charcoal color to match the nearby cargo containers.

"Shit! I didn't see you there," said Loco.

"That was my intention. I was practicing my camouflage. The chromatophores in my skin allow me to match my surroundings, making me very hard to see in the normal range of human visible spectra."

"That's pretty cool," said Loco. "I knew you could change your skin color, but not turn chameleon."

"The chameleon is a far inferior mimic to a Ruxin." Zaxby backed up against a pallet of rations wrapped in netting, and almost instantly he changed to match the complex background.

"Damn, I can hardly see you!"

"It is simply another way my species is superior to yours. Do not be ashamed. It is not your fault you were born a primate."

"We'll try to live with the humiliation," said Straker. "And since you're so superior, I'm going to reward you with an additional task."

"What task?"

"Nothing much. They call me 'Liberator'? Well, Zaxby, you're going to help me liberate a battlecruiser squadron."

Chapter 9

Sachsen System

Commander Carla Engels chewed at an already-bitten nail until a sharp stab of pain told her she'd gone too far. She held her hand out and examined a drop of blood on her finger, and then sat on it to keep herself from unconsciously starting again.

Literally sitting on my hands, she thought. Out here, with *Liberator* snuggled up to an asteroid and powered down to EMCON, her stealth coatings should deflect any active scanning beams.

Her passive scanners had also been upgraded by the Ruxins, so she was easily able to keep track of what was going on from a distance. This was the curse and the blessing of commanding a warship: everything revolved around employing it effectively. Unlike in the more fantastical showvids, captains did not generally go adventuring away from their bridge chairs.

Engels watched as the *Chun Wei* pulled in to port and docked, sighing with relief as it became clear the Trojan Horse ship passed muster. Her greatest fear had been that the Sachsen system had been warned of the *Chun Wei's* loss. But in a bureaucracy as hidebound as the Mutuality's, and without any such thing as a long-theorized but never-developed faster-than-light communications system, sidespace message drones took time to spread their encrypted military updates.

From the traffic she'd collected—the *Chun Wei's* borrowed Mutuality crypto was enough to decode routine transmissions—the oppressors of this backwater system were far more concerned with their unruly citizenry than with the threat of enemy attack. Accounts of low-level sabotage and soft-target assassination filled the daily counterinsurgency reports, mostly occurring on the planet below.

Engels shook her head as she read them, feeling half elated, half appalled.

She felt ashamed humans were murdering each other needlessly because of ideology, but it also made her proud that freedom-minded people resisted. The human spirit could not be crushed.

At least, not quickly, and not entirely. Some of the Mutuality's central "Committee Systems," composed of dull planets filled with gray little drone-people living their gray little lives in their gray little concrete residence blocks, were no doubt examples of perfection in the collectivist mind. She'd watched enough of the propaganda vids during her "re-education" to know.

But not here. The Ritter brothers insisted their people would revolt as soon as they saw a chance. Engels hoped this was true. If not, *Liberator* and *Revenge* would have to swoop in and try to use underspace tactics to disable or destroy the formidable battlecruiser squadron before they could get under way.

* * *

Straker stood in the innocuous line of uniformed crew waiting to debark onto the fortress from the personnel door. The *Chun Wei's* XO, in the guise of the ship's former political commissar, waited at the head of the queue. He carried the ship's hard credentials, which in the Mutuality's paranoid military had to be handed over physically for verification.

Fortunately, this was more of a rubber-stamp ritual than an actual test, and the ship's interior inspection had been scheduled for well after the crew were allowed to begin their limited shore leave. Zholin had told him the State Security people would find a few things wrong no matter what, and would demand "reparations" for the offenses—really, bribes—that would vanish into their pockets.

Straker was glad to have Zholin handle all that, for he felt eager as a dog staring into a field full of game birds, waiting to be given the release word.

From behind him, Loco spoke up. "Finally, some real R&R. I hear they have full robotic holo-cabins, any kind of virtual woman you want. It's not Shangri-La, but better than nothing."

"I'm surprised they don't have concubines."

"Officially," Loco said with an air of authority in his voice, "prostitution is prohibited in the Mutuality. The only legal way to pay to get laid is with a holo-cabin—or with a comrade, for free. I'm sure expensive gifts will get what you want, though, with some of them."

"Carla's plenty for me, thanks. Anyway, I think we'll be too busy for sex."

"I'm never too busy for sex, boss."

"Then clearly I'm not assigning you enough work."

Loco shut up at last, and Straker smiled.

The line began to move. The crew filed out the door and through a tunnel that scanned for weapons and contraband. Nothing would be found; Zholin's crew was used to the drill, and the many extra infantry wouldn't be disembarking the usual way.

The infiltrators would inhabit, carry, push, or ride cargo modules off the ship after the initial clearance was logged. Freight got a lot less scrutiny, and if a problem arose, one of Zholin's Mutuality natives would always be nearby to talk or bribe the problem away. If absolutely necessary, the infantry were ready to silently dispose of anyone causing trouble.

The Ritter brothers would be among the first to slip away, to change clothes and blend in with the local workers. They'd assured Straker they could find resistance members among the Sachsens employed on the orbital fortress. Those would be critical in helping the Breakers set up their liberation of the base.

Assuming Zaxby completes his missions, Straker mused as he shuffled through the scanners and out onto the reception concourse.

***

Zaxby held himself still in the bottom of the standard 1000-liter wastewater tank as the wheeled handcart rumbled across the concrete floor. Noises of loading and unloading, workers yelling back and forth and the clash of machinery came muffled through the thick plastic. Two Mutualist-uniformed humans pushing supposedly noxious cargo around the fortress's enormous supply quarter should elicit no notice.

Naked and unequipped—except for the data crystals and small tools he held inside his mouth—yet Zaxby remained supremely confident. The danger from the Mutuality primates was largely due to the rarity of Ruxins among them, rather than any inherent cleverness on their part.

If the crew of the fortress had included octopoids, he'd have entered in uniform, and then shucked it when it was time to go covert. However, there was no guarantee of even one Ruxin here. Commodore Straker had not wanted him to take the risk of being remembered as an oddity by everyone he encountered.

Thus, this insertion method.

A few more movements and the slam of a door, and Corporal Karst hissed, "Come on out."

Zaxby unscrewed the tank's cap from the inside—he'd insisted on the modification that made this possible—and flowed through the hole and onto the deck. He immediately headed for the air vent Karst was unlocking, an opening the size of a human head. The other human kept watch.

"Good luck," said the young man as Zaxby entered the air conduit.

Zaxby would have replied that luck had little to do with it where a superior being was involved, except that the careful vocal control necessary to speak Earthan was difficult in his stretched-out locomotive state, especially with items in his mouth. He settled for an approximation of a thumbs-up, formed with his sub-tentacles at the end of one limb.

Zaxby pushed through the ductwork as quickly as he could, for dehydration was a very real danger, exacerbated by the air flowing through the system. Getting lost was another serious issue; he knew the general layout of Mutuality fortresses, but it was impossible to predict an exact diagram of this particular structure. Instead, he always moved upstream against the flow of air in order to find a handling and pumping station.

When he did, he used his tools to carefully disable the booster mechanism, move through it, and then re-enable it. This kept him from being chopped up by turbines and fans. It took over two hours, but he finally found what he knew he must: a regional ventilation control room.

In any air handling system, there had to be control nexuses where major flows could be managed by technicians, and where large machines could be easily accessed by those not as flexible as Ruxins. Unfortunately, the room was not deserted, but the sole attendant had apparently locked the door from the inside and was sleeping in his chair.

This gave Zaxby the chance he needed. He oozed out of a comfortably large vent, down a wall and onto the floor. Once suitably reformed into his accustomed shape, he locomoted quietly to a position behind the sleeping man and struck him on the back of the head with force precisely calculated to render a typical human unconscious for at least an hour. Straker's orders were to kill only if he must, which was logical, as there was no way to tell for sure which personnel might be inclined to defect, or which would stay loyal to the Mutuality.

Had he been sure this human were an enemy, Zaxby would have killed him without compunction, orders or no orders. What the humans did not know wouldn't hurt their delicate monkey feelings.

Access assured, Zaxby familiarized himself with the control board, of a standard type he'd seen many times in his long life of working with electronic systems. He traced the diagrams of airflow on the display, memorizing the pathways and correlating them to the central control core of the mainframe that managed the routine nonmilitary functions of the fortress: air, water, sewage, power, gravplating, lighting and so on.

Though designated nonmilitary, these items could be manipulated to support the operation that should allow a few hundred Breakers—plus any Sachsens who joined them—to take over a fortress manned by tens of thousands. Such a conquest also depended on the poor quality of most of its crew. Rear area personnel should be neither as loyal nor as competent as those on the front lines.

Of greatest concern was the expected contingent of Hok commanded by an Inquisitor. According to Zholin, every star system had at least one such political watchdog who used the fanatical warriors to ensure the loyalty of all others.

Zaxby memorized as much as he could absorb, and downloaded pertinent files onto a data crystal. Unfortunately he dared not upload his malware from this console. He had to reach the mainframe itself. For security reasons, it was the only location enabled to make major changes to the system.

He searched the room and found some human food and a half-filled bottle of a sweetened drink, which he consumed before returning to the ventilation ductwork. The unappetizing nutrients and moisture gave him a minor boost, but he still eyed each vent as he passed by. Eventually he found a small toilet facility where he managed to get in, drink his fill of water from a sink, and out again before being spotted.

Another two hours brought him to the control core. Despite his rehydration stop, deep fatigue was beginning to set in. He had not been young for over a century, and he felt his advancing age at times like these. Yet, Straker had not trusted any other Ruxin with such a delicate mission, and that gratified him.

Three attendants worked in the main control chamber, which was filled with a constant rumbling from huge nearby air and water processors. Analog gauges on the wall supplemented the holographic and digital displays, showing all the functions to control. Manual backup mechanisms, already suffering from lack of care despite their newness, lined one side of the large room.

Zaxby opened the air vent farthest from the attendants and flowed slowly down the wall, taking care to match his appearance to the surface behind him. One woman glanced his way, and he froze. She stared straight at him for a moment from a distance of ten meters, and then looked back to her monitors, clearly bored.

Moving at a glacial pace while within the workers' visual fields, he managed to reach a location out of sight of all three. From there, he exhausted every software access possibility he could think of before concluding he would have to use one of the active control consoles to insert his data crystal.

He moved around the perimeter of the room, maintaining his camouflage at all times, until he found a place he could observe all three from behind. There were camera bubbles on the ceiling, so there was no telling who was watching. In the best case, they would only be recording for review, rather than actively monitored by live security personnel.

The three humans passed status reports and tapped on their hard keyboards, robust military models probably little changed over the last millennium. Two of them, a man and a woman, chatted amiably about absent co-workers, passing rumors of negative behaviors both professional and social.

Such petty creatures, these humans, Zaxby thought once again. It amazed him they'd managed to spread to over a thousand systems. If not for a fluke of timing and development—if Ruxins had achieved interstellar travel before, rather than after, the humans—this arm of the galaxy would be a much more sensible place, ruled by a proper monarchy and dominated by his superior species.

There was no point in pining for the unreal. "If wishes were fishes, we'd all have nets," was one of humanity's more admirable aquatic aphorisms. As always, Zaxby would deal with the world as it was, not as he wished it to be.

Almost an hour passed before the worker nearest him stood and stretched. "I'm on break," she said, ambling toward the door as she pulled a vapostick from her coverall pocket.

"Take your time," said the man over the hum of the machinery.

"Bet on it," she replied with a wink, and she left.

As soon as the door shut, the man leaped up and locked it from the inside. At the same time, the remaining woman walked to the extreme rear corner of the control room and began to disrobe. The man quickly joined her and did the same. The two began to engage in sexual activity while still standing.

As much as Zaxby would have enjoyed observing and adding to his research on human mating practices, he had to seize this golden opportunity. Spitting a data crystal into his nest of subtentacles, he locomoted smoothly to the console farthest from the two humans. It was within their view, but they were fully involved by now, evidently determined to gain maximum pleasure within the time allowed by their comrade's extended break.

Maintaining camouflage and keeping one eye on the two, he plugged the data crystal in and uploaded the malware he and Murdock had prepared. Assuming it functioned as planned, it would activate about ten hours from now, dead in the middle of the fortress' night cycle.

The malware had a modification he hadn't mentioned to Murdock. It also copied all the data it could reach back onto the crystal. Zaxby would amuse himself by combing through it for interesting nuggets of information to add to his life's work of eventually publishing a Ruxin guide to humans and their behavior. He also might find things of operational significance, which would no doubt please Derek Straker and, more importantly, Carla Engels.

Retrieving the crystal, Zaxby lingered a moment more as he observed the humans' movements become more and more frenetic. Human monkey-mating happened so fast he usually preferred to record and watch their activity on slow motion playback later on.

Tearing himself away took an act of will. He knew every moment of delay risked discovery. Reluctantly, he re-entered the ductwork and proceeded as quickly as possible toward his next, much more difficult target: the Mutuality battlecruiser *Wolverine*.

Chapter 10

Sachsen Orbital Fortress

"Lieutenant" Straker sat at a battered table of an industrial-themed bar off the fortress's entertainment concourse. In fact, everything had an industrial theme, simply because the Mutuality didn't seem to waste any effort on decorations, other than stylized murals of unsmiling workers and soldiers marching in lockstep toward their collective destinies. A few slogans adorned the walls, which despite attempts at poetic language always boiled down to "Work Harder!" or "Revere the State," and most importantly, "Don't Think About Yourself."

"Creator! How can people live like this?" Straker said as he sipped his surprisingly good beer. Apparently Sachsen was famous for the stuff, and the breweries hadn't yet all been collectivized and turned mediocre.

"You, my friend," Loco said, "just can't see the bright side of anything. Not only is this some outstanding brew, but the food smells great. And the women are…" He held up his open hands in front of his chest as if cupping breasts.

As if on cue, a scowling Sachsen barmaid, built like a boxy attack sled, slammed the two bowls of stew they'd ordered onto the table, and then a basket of bread. Straker was surprised she didn't spit into it.

"Hey, darlin', no need to be unfriendly," said Loco with a wink.

The woman's face grew less certain. "You speak strangely." Her Earthan was tinged with the thick local accent, like the Ritter brothers'.

"We grew up in the Hundred Worlds," Straker said, trying to put on a cordial expression. He lowered his voice. "We know how you feel."

"You know nothing!" she declared, but without heat. "You want butter? One credit extra."

"Sure," said Loco. "What's your name, sweetheart?"

Straker could see the server fighting not to smile. With her plain face and body, she probably didn't get a lot of interest, even from the usual semi-drunk clientele.

"Marta. But I do not sleep with you," she replied, as if that would settle things.

"Don't be so sure," said Loco with a wink. The woman blushed.

"Hey, barmaid, we're thirsty!" came a bellow from across the room. "More beer! Hurry up!" Four rough men and a woman in the coveralls of civilian cargo handlers sat at a round table littered with bowls, beer mugs and empty pitchers. It looked like they'd been there for hours, despite it being only early afternoon.

Marta scowled again and marched to the bar to pick up a pitcher in each hand and bring them to their table.

As she approached, one of the men reached out with a foot and hooked her ankle. She managed to set one pitcher on the table even as she stumbled, but the other pitcher tipped over, launching its contents to drench the largest man, the one who had yelled, with three or four liters of beer. It then slid off the table to clatter on the concrete floor.

The big man jumped up with a roar. "Stupid bitch! Go get something to clean this up!"

Marta recovered her balance and reddened. "Somebody trip me!" She swept her eyes accusingly across the four seated, and then rested them on the one who'd done it. "You!"

"Bugger off, clumsy wench," said the man, pouring himself a full beer from the remaining pitcher, and then filling more mugs until it was empty. "Trento said to go get something to clean up." He glanced knowingly at the big man.

Marta stomped over to a kitchen doorway and yanked it open. As she exited the common room, the other four cargo handlers stood up, drained their beers, walked quickly toward the door. The beer-covered one, Trento, followed, glancing around warily.

The bartender raised his voice. "You haven't paid yet!" His accent was also Sachsen, though less severe than Marta's.

"You stinking dirtsiders ought to pay *us* for spilling your shitty beer on me," called Trento, still moving toward the door. Clearly, this had been a scam to avoid paying. "Don't make me lodge a complaint with the Inquisitor."

The path of the five took them near Straker, who stood.

"Boss… boss…" Loco sputtered, standing with him and grabbing his arm. "Don't get involved."

"We wouldn't want to leave your new girlfriend in the lurch, would we?" Straker said, shaking off Loco's hand. He stepped into the path of the cargo handlers, lifting an arm to bar them.

"Trento…" said the woman, in the lead. "These swabbies is in our way."

Trento moved around his posse to confront Straker, looming at least a head taller. Without bluster, the man reached to shove Straker, surprisingly quickly.

It was obvious why Trento was the leader. The move would have worked on most people—quick, accurate, powerful—but not on an enhanced warrior like Straker.

He slid aside and grasped Trento's wrist, yanking him off balance and hauling the pivot point around in a circle to throw him across the deck. He sprawled into a table and chairs. Customers nearby moved away. Some slipped out the main entrance.

"Pay the lady," Straker grated, pointing. "You, the one who tripped her. Pay for everything you bought, and leave a good tip."

"Fuck you," the smaller man said, producing a hooked netting-knife from a sleeve. He lunged at Straker, swiping fast, blade forward.

Straker stepped back enough to avoid the strike, and then leaned in and laid a snapping hammer-fist into the hinge of the attacker's jaw. The knife-man went down like a sack of disconnected bones, and the blade skittered into a corner.

Turning to the remaining three, Straker spoke through clenched teeth. "Pay the lady," he said again.

"Boss, the big bastard's getting up," said Loco from rearward. "No worries, though. I got this."

Straker didn't bother to turn. Loco might not be quite as fast and strong as Straker, but he was still a genetically engineered physical, combat-trained and veteran of many battles. He could handle one civilian, even a big one.

As the grunts and meaty smacks of a fistfight wafted from behind him, Straker stepped forward to within easy reach of the other three men, who blanched. "Pay. The. Lady. And tip well."

One of them hurried over to Marta with a fistful of credits. Once he'd put them in the barmaid's hand, Straker stepped out of the way and turned to see

Loco finishing off his opponent with a kick to the belly that left him gasping on the deck.

Shouting and a siren could be heard approaching from the main concourse. Straker was about to walk out the door toward it when Loco grabbed him and pulled him toward the kitchen. "Let's stay away from State Security, okay? Follow me, boss. Marta, honey, is there a back way out?"

"Yah, through kitchen into service access," she said, pointing at the kitchen door.

"Thanks, sweetie."

Marta blushed. "Okay, funny little guy. You go. Run fast. We see nothings."

Straker followed Loco through the kitchen and out the back door, into a corridor that seemed to stretch behind the line of bars and restaurants. He let Loco lead him down and across to another back entrance, this one to a grocery supply shop. They slipped through, past the startled clerk, and out the front door onto a smaller concourse of retail establishments.

"Boss, that was a damned stupid move," Loco said as he slowed to walk casually down the gallery. "We're trying to do an op here. You could have blown it."

"I know. I can't…"

"I get it. You got a thing for bullies and punks. But by this time tomorrow, a few Mutuality credits won't matter. Hell, we could have let those assholes walk out and paid Marta out of our own stash. Come on, you're the Liberator! You have to stay focused on the big picture."

Straker swallowed the remains of his anger. "Yeah, you're right. I got sidetracked."

"They pushed your buttons. You got to keep that shit locked down, boss. There's too much at stake."

"Funny, *you* lecturing *me*."

"I learned from the best. And you know what's ironic?"

"What?"

"We didn't pay Marta for our *own* beer and stew."

"Crap. Well, like you said, by this time tomorrow it shouldn't matter." Straker matched Loco's casual pace and glanced around. "I'm still hungry. Pizza wedge?"

"Sure. They make it weird here, but it's good."

Chapter 10

After eating a couple of slices of flatbread from a quick-vend, Straker led Loco to a comm-café. Soldiers, navy personnel and civilians used their own handtabs or rented netscreens to type messages, record vids or cruise the networks for information or entertainment. There were VR booths along one wall for those willing to pay more.

Straker wandered over to one of those and examined the connection to the headset. It was too much to hope that it would fit the brainlink socket concealed under his neck hair. It did have a standard universal access plug. The connection wouldn't be as good, but the adapter Murdock gave him should work.

"Pay cash for the booth and keep watch," said Straker. While Loco went to the counter, Straker pulled the privacy curtain, unplugged the inductive headset and plugged in his adapter, and then clicked it into his brainlink.

The ready screen appeared as if in front of Straker's eyes, though it was actually an electronic feed to his visual cortex. The system shouldn't detect the difference, as long as Murdock's adapter worked as intended. The fortress network should see nothing more than a standard VR connection with the usual low-level headset access.

Though Straker was no brainiac or hacker, the software in the adapter would send out gentle electronic tendrils until it found a connection to Zaxby's malware that should even now be propagating throughout the network.

All over the fortress, Breakers with adapters and comlinks should be doing the same, feeling for access to the compromised system—a system that would now, if handled deftly, supply them with everything they needed to take the base.

Straker waited until the Breakers' hammer-and-carbine symbol popped up in the lower left of his view. He willed its selection and blinked, which brought up a menu of options.

Working slowly through unfamiliar territory, he found what he was looking for: a detailed, updated 3-D plan of the fortress. Once he had this, he progressed rapidly in examining certain key components of the base.

First, he identified the location of the Hok barracks. He couldn't do anything about those on patrol, but the bulk of them should be sleeping there during the night cycle. Nearby he found the senior officers' quarters, where the Inquisitor and the fortress commander should be housed.

Next, he identified the operational command center, from which all military functions were controlled. It lay in the center of the fortress, crisscrossed on all sides by the vast tubes of the fortress's capital weapons: lasers, particle accelerators, and railguns more than a kilometer long.

It was weapons like these that kept warships at bay, and held the planet below in thrall with the threat of pinpoint strikes on any centers of rebellion… or, if the State deemed it necessary, wholesale destruction of the population.

Drawing a path between the control center and the Hok barracks yielded the key location he needed to control: a large, open crossroads where several tunnels met. After identifying that, he took his time analyzing the corridors and passageways until he was certain of his tactics.

Activating the secure comlink function, Straker sent a message to the team assigned to emplace the cargo his people would need. He then sent a more generalized message to all the Breakers, designating their blocking positions.

Finally, he sent a query into the system to see if Zaxby was online, but he got no response.

* * *

Zaxby's vision swam with fatigue. He was already regretting not recruiting a younger, more expendable Ruxin for this mission. Yet, it was not his fault. It was Straker that had added on the attempt to infiltrate the battlecruiser *Wolverine.*

It occurred to him that being part of a superior species had its drawbacks. Lesser creatures, dazzled by his competence, thought he had no limitations whatsoever. They asked achievements of him beyond even his amazing capabilities.

Slowly, slowly he squeezed through the narrow air vents aboard the enemy battlecruiser. Unlike the spacious fortress ducts, these were constricted, sometimes as small as a human handbreadth. Zaxby could feel it in his brain, an organ that had only so much flexibility in its advancing age.

He paused to rest for a moment. Failure was not an option. Not only would it reflect badly on Ruxins everywhere, and on him personally, the fact that he'd never been male or female meant he had no offspring of his own fabulous genetic makeup, which would surely constitute a tragedy for the galaxy.

Therefore, he had to push onward. The universe demanded it.

Finally, he located the warship's main computer node, a small, untended space packed with components. It was the only place he could be sure of gaining unfettered access. Fortunately, it was well vented, to dissipate waste heat.

After removing the vent cover, Zaxby plucked the data crystal from his mouth. He then extended it like a snake into the closet-like enclosure and felt for the port.

It took more than two minutes of trying, but finally he was able to slot the device into the opening and the malware began its work. Zaxby was quite proud of the reprogramming he had done in the relatively short time between sidespace transition and arrival at the fortress, alterations to make the original Trojan worm effective against the battlecruiser squadron.

First, it would worm its way past the system's firewalls. Fortunately, from this central location, some of those were non-issues. The defenses were focused outward, against information attacks from external enemies. By design, access from the central node was simpler.

Second, it would spread throughout the *Wolverine*, giving anyone with the proper codes control of most of the ship's functions—at least, until the crew overrode the automation and enabled the manual backups.

Third, the malware would send itself to the rest of the ships in the squadron, piggybacking on command updates coming from the flagship. That would still leave a few independent vessels out of the loop, but that couldn't be helped. Even a Ruxin couldn't do everything.

Zaxby left the crystal in place for several extra minutes, until he was as certain as he could be that it had done its job. Then he removed it and withdrew into the ventilation system once more.

He was halfway back to a toilet facility he'd spotted, and badly dehydrated, when he lost consciousness.

* * *

First Sergeant Heiser, in the uniform of a midgrade Mutuality navy noncom, supervised the unhurried unloading of goods from the *Chun Wei's* main freight door.

Like all of the warships docked in a row, the cylindrical frigate was sidled up to the fortress like a stylus pressed into a melon. Several decks above, personnel had access to the main concourses. At this level, broad doorways linked high-ceilinged cargo bays that extended the length of the orbital base, making storage, resupply and transloading easy.

From this warren of chambers ran tall, wide tunnels, arteries reaching throughout the fortress that provided highways for the many loaders to move items quickly. Unlike on warships, where space was tight, converted asteroids like this had ample room for every purpose.

Heiser's comlink beeped in his ear, and he lifted the headset's single eyepiece into display position. A message from Commodore Straker marked the location the special, heavy cargo would be emplaced.

But not too soon. The fortress's State Security personnel changed shifts at 2100 hours, and they used the standard military 24-hour day. That would be the best time to drop off the cargo: when the off-going officers were focused on ending their stint, and the oncoming bunch was not yet in place.

The op's kickoff was set for 0300, so the items would have to remain unmolested for only six hours. During that time, Heiser and his Breakers would sweat, and hope.

Heiser hated hoping. As the commodore said, "Hope ain't a plan."

He checked his chrono. "Dinner time," he called to his crew. "Take an hour. Maybe two. Make sure you check your comlinks for the intel."

They left their loaders wherever they happened to be, scattered with the variety of freight containers across their designated cargo bay. This was completely intentional; Heiser wanted the operation to seem casual and inefficient, typical for a provincial frigate manned by mediocre personnel.

His people fanned out and relaxed. Some headed into the frigate to retrieve food from the mess. Some broke out cards and games. Some found places to nap. All would use the time to study the commodore's message that told them where to put their particular items.

"Whattaya want, Spear?" asked Karst. "Sandwich?"

"Don't matter. Whatever they got. Just make sure you bring enough." Like many of the Breakers, Heiser had eaten far too much nutritional paste lately, so real food from the galley seemed like heaven.

"Sure, Spear, I gotcha. Double helpings." Karst strolled off. Twenty minutes later, he returned with disposable boxes and bottles of bright red fruit drink.

Heiser ate, taking his time, reviewing and re-reviewing the plan. His chrono ticked over far too slowly, but finally the moment came to move. "Let's go," he called, rising and clapping his huge hands.

Still without haste, his people sorted themselves out, and with deceptive skill drove their loaders out of the cargo bay and into the fortress. Each headed for his or her designated place, mostly intersections that needed to be controlled, to drop off something nearby.

Heiser stayed in the cargo bay in case he had to coordinate or react, though it took an effort of will. He hadn't lived in the Mutuality, so he had the wrong accent and command of jargon to risk interacting with the fortress personnel. The loader drivers and handlers would do their jobs, dropping off trailers, supersized containers and even entire loaders at specific locations.

Some loaders had fake work orders attached, as if they had broken down and were awaiting field repair. Other items had forged pre-placement authorizations to wait until the morning shift came in. The lateness of the hour and the accustomed stifling bureaucracy should cover the situation for long enough.

At least, that was the commodore's plan.

Heiser counted everyone as they returned, marking them off on his roster until he was certain none had been detained. He sent them all into the *Chun Wei* to wait for zero hour.

Chapter 11

Sachsen Fortress

Straker rolled out of his sleep cube and knocked on Loco's hatch. The short-term rental boxes, each equipped with a bed, a holo-display, and little else, had seemed the best place to wait out of the public eye until the appointed time.

He checked his chrono as Loco popped the door and climbed out of his own cube, rubbing his eyes. Like any good combat troop, Straker's best friend could sleep anywhere, any time.

Smoothing his uniform, Straker settled his cap on his head and put a no-nonsense expression on his face. "Let's roll," he said, and began to walk toward his destiny.

"Uh-oh. You got that look, boss."

"Yes, because the shit is about to hit the airflow turbine—shit I started."

"At least we'll be in 'suits. Better than the rest of the Breakers."

Straker stopped and turned. "You think I'm happy to be inside armor while they're not?"

Loco grinned. "I know you are—and so am I. Not that you want them exposed, but it's always better to be the hammer than the nail… Foehammers, in this case."

Battlesuits weren't the self-contained monsters that mechsuits were, but they had armor enough to resist small arms, powered polymeric muscular assistance, and SAIs with comlinked HUDs that raised their situational awareness far above a straight-leg infantry trooper.

But the Breakers had only a handful of those. Instead, they would be relying on surprise, preparation, superior tactics, and a popular uprising to win the day today.

Along with two Foehammer mechsuits.

"If I could put everybody in a mechsuit," Straker replied, "or at least battlesuits, I would."

"I know, I know." Loco slapped Straker's arm. "Don't get all self-righteous on me, boss. You know you keep me around to say the shit you can't."

Straker nodded, but remained grim. "As long as it's between us… but the troops won't take it that way. They'll think you're cavalier with their lives—and these are all volunteers. I don't need anyone with grudges against you and your mouth."

"Okay, okay."

"You hear from Zaxby yet?"

"Nope," said Loco, checking his comlink.

"Damn. I hope he's…"

"Not dead?"

Straker coughed. "Yeah."

"So we don't know if he got the malware into the battlecruisers."

"Not for sure. But that doesn't change anything. The plan goes forward." Straker resumed walking.

At five minutes before 0300, Straker and Loco reached the critical intersection. Two huge loaders sat parked out of the way, work order tags in their windows and standard intermodal cargo containers clamped to their rear decks. The two men popped the clamps and punched in the codes to the boxes.

As they did so, other Breakers began filtering in from several directions. They quickly destroyed all the cameras and sensors they could identify. Most had already retrieved their weapons from the cache sites established six hours earlier. Some were in half-armor, and most had comlinks or full combat helmets. A half-dozen wore battlesuits, the men who'd demonstrated the highest ability with them.

The first oversized container's doors swung open to reveal the head-like sensor cluster of Straker's Foehammer mechsuit. The war machine lay flat on its back, with room to spare above its chest, overlapping clamshell doors already opened.

Straker clambered into the 'suit and punched in the activation code, wishing once again his brainlink would synch up fully with the Foehammer's SAI. The best Murdock had been able to achieve was a limited connection no better than that of the public VR booth he'd used earlier.

Still, that was better than nothing. It would give him improved cueing over the optical HUD. Aiming and firing, though, would remain on manual, with the complex suite of sensors causing the mechsuit to mimic his body's movements and its feedback mechanisms inducing touches of discomfort to tell him what was happening to the machine he rode.

Once sealed in, Straker lifted his gauntlets and pushed slowly on the interior of the cargo container. The top and sides fell open, allowing him to sit, dismount from the loader, and then stand on the smoothed stone deck.

As part of the cargo tunnel access system, the intersection reached high enough to allow him a comfortable distance above his head. Still, the scale of the mechsuit against the available space gave the impression of a large man occupying a long rectangular room, a room with four big entrances at the corners and eight small ones spaced between.

By now, alarms had begun sounding throughout the fortress. Even if those in the control center saw nothing, the widespread destruction of sensors would have alerted them to something amiss. And, if Straker's plan were being carried out properly, the ordinary Sachsen citizens, alerted by the local resistance movement and prompted by the Ritter brothers, would be wreaking havoc everywhere they could.

The Ritter brothers and their fellows would also have set up a cell with access to the malware-infected network, allowing them to control many functions of the fortress—airflow, power and gravplating being the most important. Even now, the atmospheric pressure was being reduced enough to cause doors to slam shut. They might be overridden, but that would take time and command access.

The resistance cell should also be setting the gravplating to triple-Gs in some areas, which would also slow down any response. Combined with selected power outages, Straker hoped—no, he'd bet this operation—that his two hundred Breakers, properly prepared and led, could overcome thousands of defenders. He'd even taken care to try to minimize casualties, at least among the unaltered humans.

The Hok, though, were another story. The parasitic biotech that made them what they were had long since wiped out all trace of humanity, leaving them as high-functioning combat-zombies, bereft of fear or will. That made them incredibly dangerous, because they would never surrender, or even flinch.

They had to be finished off to the last, or ordered to stand down by an authority they recognized.

Straker and Loco backed up into the two cargo tunnels that led toward the command center. These, along with the two smaller passageways between them, must be defended at all costs, because behind the Breakers were their combat engineers, who would be trying to cut their way into the fortress's headquarters.

And that would take some time. Sealed behind massive doors, the command center had been built to resist an assault. Yet, no defense was proof against time and tools.

The engineers had the tools. It was up to the Breakers to buy them the time.

Opposite the tunnels and passageways were similar openings that led in the direction of the Hok barracks. It was from that direction that the main attack would come.

Straker keyed his comlink. "Battlesuiters, I want you between us, defending the personnel passageways."

"Roger, sir," came the answer from Karst. The corporal's Sledgehammer was too finicky and unwieldy for this operation, and he'd proven to be superb with a battlesuit, so he'd ended up in charge of the few they had.

"Spear, you got the squads in place?"

"On the way, sir," said Heiser. Two squads of Breaker infantry trotted to take positions behind the mechsuits. They would ambush any Hok that made it past the Foehammers. One more squad, split into fireteams, backed up the battlesuiters.

Two teams of Breakers pulled crates out of the containers that had concealed the mechsuits. They broke these open and set up high-powered slugthrowers that used liquid propellant to fire armor-piercing bullets at extreme rates of fire.

These were usually mounted on armored vehicles, for they expended fuel and ammo so prodigiously that no infantry could carry enough for resupply. But in this case, extra coffers of each had been brought in on the loaders.

A couple of the squad leaders set up Killmores, command-detonated directional mines, These were nasty things with their own holo-generators that concealed themselves. From the front—where most of their explosive darts would be sent—they matched their holograms to the deck plating behind them, becoming effectively invisible.

The rest of the Breakers, a short company of a hundred or so, set up similar, larger-scale holo-generators that masked everyone on that side, the right side as the defenders looked at it, from view. They then took cover behind the loaders and cases full of extra hull plating, pre-positioned there for that purpose.

All of the artificial barriers had been parked along the right-side wall. When combined with the blocking force, this created a classic L-shaped ambush. The whole exercise took less than three minutes, for the Breakers had practiced their roles dozens of times.

"Everyone fade back to concealment," Straker called over his comlink. "Pop up only upon my order. We want as many in the kill zone as possible."

Double-clicks of silent acknowledgement came back to him, and Straker pulled back as well, deep into one of the darkened tunnels. Behind him, an explosion shook the air, and a fine mist of dust and a few pebbles fell from the bored-out rock ceilings.

That would be the combat engineers beginning their work to blast through to the command center. Combined with laser drills and thermal lances, they would cut through as quickly as they could—the faster the better. Taking the control nexus intact was a high priority. And if not intact… well, a headless base was better than one with the enemy in charge.

"I've got movement," said one of the scouts. He'd been monitoring the spy-eyes stuck to the passageways leading into the intersection. "Two main tunnels, two personnel passages. Hok point men, deliberate pace."

"Nobody move," Straker reiterated. "Nobody get antsy."

Hok in full battlesuits padded warily into view, one in each of the tunnels opposite those of the defenders. Straker had hoped they'd be stupid enough to charge forward to rescue their endangered command center, but hadn't really expected that. The loss of the sensor network had obviously alerted them to something amiss, and they were proceeding as if through enemy territory.

Involuntarily holding his breath, as if that would matter, Straker watched through spy-eyes as the four continued out into the open intersection. They maintained their spacing with perfect discipline, heading for the opposite tunnels. Behind them, more Hok came into view, single columns in the personnel tunnels and double columns in the cargo tunnels.

"Troops," Straker said, "pull back even farther into the tunnels and let their scouts get inside. When you can't wait any longer, pop them quick and clean. Loco, use a gatling round, single shot. I want the rest of the Hok focused on our tunnels, convinced we're waiting deep within them, as if we're weak and trying to delay them from the best defensive position possible."

The main enemy force held up at the entrance to the crossroads, until their scouts entered the tunnels leading toward the command center. When they did, the lines of troops began to cross, weapons pointed in all directions. Fireteams peeled off and headed for the four personnel tunnels on the flanks.

Unfortunately, that meant two of those teams were heading straight for the holo-camouflaged Breakers.

Well, no battle plan ever survives contact with the enemy, Straker thought. "Blow the Killmores!" he barked, and stepped forward, refining his aim on the Hok coming toward him.

The Hok was quick, and loosed a burst of needles even as Straker's single gatling round, a bullet sized to penetrate light armor, blew a fist-sized hole in his chest. The cloud of metal slivers scraped some nano-camouflage off his Foehammer, but that was all.

At the same time, the Killmores detonated. Capacitors within each dumped enough electrical charge into them to turn a bimetallic superconductor into a short-lived electromagnet. This accelerated seven hundred darts in perfect 120-degree fans that overlapped and slammed into the front half of the Hok troops. Most of these projectiles were turned by the superb Hok armor, but enough found joints and weak spots to wound a quarter of them, and the rest were briefly surprised.

"Open fire, tunnels one through four only!" Straker called, just in case any Breakers were wondering about the next move. "Side ambushers, continue to hold!"

He strode forward just enough to see into the intersection, but remained in darkness in hopes that the enemy wouldn't yet divine that they faced mechsuits. He used his gatling to hose down the enemy. Loco did the same from his tunnel, and the Breakers in the two middle personnel passages opened up with their small arms.

The combination of fire pummeled the initial Hok force badly, but not badly enough to convince them to retreat. Instead, the remainder of the Hok charged, firing at the passageways in front of them, apparently convinced that aggression and firepower would win through.

"Tunnels, fall back, feign retreat!" Straker said. He backed up and waited, hoping the sweeper squad behind him would maintain their discipline and let him take the brunt of the enemy attack.

As half a dozen Hok charged into his tunnel, Straker let them get fully inside, and then cut them down with a buzz-saw of gatling fire. The enemy troopers' fire smashed into his skin, stinging him through his biofeedback sensors. He hardly felt it, though, as nothing even came close to seriously damaging him. Some of it would have gotten past him, though, and he hoped his backup squad had kept their heads down.

Switching his attention back to the spy-eyes, he saw the remaining Hok force leap out of their tunnels, dispersing and firing into the passageways opposite them. Some readied rocket launchers and grenades.

"Initiate, now!" Straker said, and the concealed force on the long side of the "L" of the ambush opened fire, apparently out of thin air.

The Breakers' two heavy slugthrowers cut swaths through the Hok, the destruction mitigated only by the fact that the enemy had spread out as much as possible. Between the crew-served weapons, a hundred Breakers loosed a storm of death composed of bullets and beams of antipersonnel lasers, creating a shooting gallery.

But the calculus of war is often random, and is always cruel. In even the perfect ambush, some targets will survive, miraculously untouched. Those Hok, without the fear that might have rendered other creatures helpless, instantly turned and attacked into the ambushing Breakers, their only possible response.

Human troops went down from the fully automatic Hok slugthrowers and from high-powered lasers with triggers held down to fire continuously. At least a score of men and women were cut in half or blown to bits before Straker, Loco and the friendly battlesuiters advanced to place the enemy in a crossfire. Several more Breakers died to explosions as dying Hok activated vengeance grenades before the scene of carnage fell abruptly silent.

A few Hok made it back to the corridors from whence they'd come, and Straker sent a force-cannon round into the tunnel opposite him, filling it with hot plasma that ignited even the paint on the walls. Loco did the same from beside him, and together their gatlings and the heavy slugthrowers sent a few hundred more rounds into the passageways to chase the Hok back.

"Scouts, push your spy-eyes out!" Straker snapped. "Medics, check the casualties and evac to the *Chun Wei*. Squad leaders, secure your designated checkpoints and mission objectives. Spear, you still with us?"

"Breathing, sir," said Heiser, waving from where he squatted next to one of the fallen.

"Coordinate with the Ritters if you can. Try to minimize fratricide and see if there's anything they can't handle. And make sure to protect those engineers."

"Roger wilco," said Heiser.

"Loco, we're going after those Hok, keep them on the run."

"Okay, boss," said Loco.

"We'll split up and search-and-destroy in the large tunnels. Karst, divide your battlesuiters into two teams and come along to watch our backs."

"Roger, sir."

"Let's go." Straker strode forward into one of the tunnels, chasing the retreating Hok.

Chapter 12

Mutuality Battlecruiser *Wolverine*, Sachsen Fortress Dock

Zaxby woke to the sight of his own tentacles shaking, a reaction to extreme dehydration. He wondered how long he'd been out, lying here squeezed into the constricting ventilation duct of the Mutuality battlecruiser *Wolverine*.

Elapsed time didn't really matter, though. He probably couldn't hold a device steady enough to read a chrono. He had only one imperative: find water.

It took him an interminable moment to remember which direction he'd been traveling when he fainted. Once he did, he began to move.

His skin tore in places as its usual suppleness and lubrication became tacky, sticking to the metal ductwork. The pain helped revive him, and he moved frantically, desperately onward, fully aware this burst of energy was unlikely to last.

"I am a superior being," he mumbled to himself over and over. "I refuse to die. I will free my people. I will earn the right to create offspring. My name will be remembered in the rolls of heroes. I will not be shown up by the monkeys!"

He passed three dry vents. The spaces visible beyond held no scent of water. The fourth smelled rich and wet, engendering within him a lust as powerful as any sexual urge, a survival instinct that would not be denied.

The room was occupied by a human in stained clothing that had at one time been white. He was washing a metal cooking container in hot, soapy water...

Water...

Water...

With the last of his strength, Zaxby opened the vent grille and flowed out of it, gasping with relief as his squashed physique returned to a normal configuration.

The human turned to look at the motion and froze, pot-scrubber in his hand. He backed up slowly, jaws agape, and then turned to run, yelling in alarm.

The possibility of being captured came in a distant second to Zaxby's desperate urge for moisture. He opened the cold tap on the large sink and, as soon as he was certain the hot soapy water in the basin wouldn't burn him, he rolled as much of his body into it as he could and turned his mouth to the faucet.

Orgasmic relief flooded him, despite the sting of cleaning chemicals and food residues slathering his wounds. So powerful was the sensation that he almost passed out again, but he forced himself to cease ingesting water before he made himself ill.

Well, more ill than he already was.

He felt strength flooding back into his body. As soon as he could stand, he slammed the door on the room he occupied. Unfortunately, there was no lock, and no other way out... except the ventilation system he'd come to hate.

He contemplated re-entering the ductwork with a feeling verging on horror. Doing so would be excruciating, and with his skin abraded and bleeding, he would again rapidly lose hydration. Yet, he had little choice. The food worker would even now be summoning some form of armed security personnel, and as soon as the primates realized he was in the vents, he would be hunted throughout the ship.

Alarm klaxons sounded, which realized his fears. He stared at the small vent, still wavering. Would it not be better to make a stand here, than to die ignominiously in the tiny crawlspace? Perhaps he could surprise the reaction force and seize a weapon to fight his way out. If he failed, at least such a death would be quick.

Think, Zaxby, he told himself. His Ruxin body was extraordinary, of course, but it was his superior intellect that was his real advantage. As Derek Straker had once said: given two bad choices, find a third.

His eyes roved the small compartment and lighted upon a handle attached to a door half a meter square. It constituted access to some device. By the Earthan writing, it seemed to be a sonic sanitizer for kitchen implements.

Seizing the handle, he pulled open the door. Performing a quick volumetric calculation, he determined that his body would fit inside. He pulled out a rack and set it upon a nearby shelf among utensils, hoping it would not be noticed. He then clambered into the cubic space and closed the door.

A flaw in his plan soon became evident. There was little air, and of course no water, to breathe. He calmed himself and tried to enter a trancelike meditative state, but his many minor wounds and his generally deteriorated condition made this impossible.

He heard rattling, and then sudden, violent noises and yelling. That would be the security forces. They would look around the room and see the open vent. Combined with the testimony of the man who'd reported Zaxby's presence, they should make the logical, obvious deduction and…

The sounds of humans retreated. Desperate for air, Zaxby pushed the door open slightly and pressed his mouth to the crack. He stayed that way until he was certain he was alone, at which time he exited the sanitizer.

Now, though, the ventilation system was his worst choice, as it would be investigated, possibly flooded with noxious decontaminants, certainly prodded with sharp objects.

At last Zaxby was able to spit out his bagged comlink, unroll and fit it, and check the chrono. He noted it was 0314 hours, station time. The 0300 operation start had already passed. His malware, if it had propagated as expected, should have silenced any automated notifications from the fortress.

Of course, eventually the battlecruiser's midnight watch would detect something amiss. Independent warships, as well as civilian vessels, might be squawking about it on their comlinks, or even making emergency departures. The duty officers would wonder, and confer, and at some point they would wake their ship captain, perhaps even the commodore or admiral in charge of the squadron.

Long before that, though, Zaxby's malware should have reduced the O2 levels within the ships to the point where sleepers would not wake, and those awake would become disoriented or fall unconscious. Only if some quick-thinking engineer put a mask on and manually overrode life support systems would this simple strategy fail.

Zaxby tried his comlink on Breaker channels but received no answer. Breathing deeply to counteract the effects of reduced oxygen—or so he hoped—he moved slowly to open the door and look into the next room, a galley for food preparation.

Two human women sat at a small table, heads down and resting on their forearms. This was good news to Zaxby.

Continuing to move slowly and breathe more heavily than normal in order to avoid hypoxia, he entered the ship's passageway system. Soon, he found two fallen naval personnel, one with a stunner and one with a short-range, low-penetration blaster.

Both weapons were appropriate for hunting Ruxins in air vents. They should also be effective for finishing off any unarmored personnel not succumbing to the low oxygen levels. He took the two guns, thankful for his ability to employ both at once if necessary, and continued. His main concern was encountering battlesuited Hok, if such were aboard.

* * *

At exactly 0259, Chief Gurung, in the uniform of a Mutuality senior noncom, sauntered toward the shut personnel entrance to the battlecruiser *Wolverine*. He carried an ordinary hand-case weighing about ten kilos.

The battlesuited Hok guard on duty was no surprise to Gurung. The human marines aboard would take the coveted day shifts. No matter how long humans lived in space, their bodies still preferred to keep to a diurnal schedule, so the Hok got the dirty end of any stick.

A Hok guard was a mixed blessing. On the one hand, his zeal for the Mutuality prevented him from deviating from his orders. On the other hand, his literal-mindedness and submission to apparently legitimate authority could be used against him.

"You, Hok," said Gurung as the guard turned to him and held his heavy slugthrower at the ready. "Summon your commander of the relief."

"Aye aye, Chief," said the Hok, and subvocalized into his comlink, never relaxing his vigilance.

Subsequently, when the hatch to the ship opened behind him, the Hok attributed it to his supervisor coming out to speak to Gurung. He never suspected malware would override and open all entrances into the warship at exactly 0300, and prevent them from being easily closed.

When Gurung was certain both inner and outer hatches had withdrawn, opening a route into the battlecruiser, he triggered the heavy double-stunners mounted inside his modified hand-case, their camouflaged ends pointed directly toward the Hok.

The guard staggered and crumpled slowly, his tough physique resistant to even a doubled blast, but the stunner emissions had been calculated to do the job despite all that. Fortunately, the cameras and sensors had all been disabled by the malware, reprogrammed to display endless loops showing nothing amiss.

Gurung caught the Hok, dragging him out of the view of any passersby and taking his weapon for himself. Pulling out his Kukri, the razor-sharp, inward-curving dagger of his people, he slit the Hok's throat. A dead enemy was no enemy at all.

Feet pounded across the deck behind him, and a dozen picked naval personnel joined Gurung. They wore damage-control masks, which would concentrate available oxygen and filter out contaminants. A woman handed one to Gurung.

"Override the entrance and seal us in," he told Redwolf, one of the Breaker marines in the group. "Friendlies only."

"Aye aye, Chief," said Redwolf, hefting his blaster and taking position.

With the Hok slugthrower in both hands and the mask on his face, Gurung led his boarding party into the battlecruiser. He laughed with pleasure as he contemplated the enemy officers' astonishment when they woke up with their ship captured.

He ceased laughing when he heard the noise of weapons fire ahead. Someone had not succumbed to the lack of oxygen, it seemed.

Peeking out from around a corner, Gurung spotted the back of an armored Hok, apparently engaged in a firefight. While he couldn't imagine who among the friendly forces could have made it deeper into the battlecruiser than his own boarding party, the enemy of an enemy was likely a friend.

Raising his weapon, Gurung triggered a long burst that hammered at the Hok until his armor failed and he went down to sprawl on the deck. Two more close-range shots to the joint at the neck made sure the Hok was dead. Gurung kicked the enemy's weapon away from his twitching hand, just in case.

Triggering his short-range comlink on the general Breaker's channel, he spoke. "This is Chief Gurung. Anyone who didn't come aboard with me, identify yourself. Any Breaker, any Breaker, respond." The low-power transmission shouldn't leave the metal-hulled battlecruiser, so replies would be confined to those nearby.

"This is Zaxby, Chief Gurung," said a voice in Gurung's ear. "Please do not fire upon me when you see me."

Gurung gave hand signals for his people to continue toward the bridge. "It's Zaxby," he relayed.

"That's 'Lieutenant Zaxby' to you, Chief Gurung."

"Of course, sir. I should say the same, though, about not shooting friendlies. As planned, all Breakers have oxygen masks and blue-and-silver armbands."

"I see them. I am holding in place."

"Let me know when you see me." In a moment, Gurung spotted the Ruxin. "Excellent," he said with a grin that couldn't be seen behind his mask. "What are your orders, sir?"

"My orders?"

"As you pointed out, sir, you're senior."

Zaxby, looked quite the worse for wear, and he was bleeding in several places. He slumped against a bulkhead and waved with a free tentacle. "Carry on with your mission, Chief. I have my own."

"Aye aye, sir." Gurung thought no more about the octopoid as he trotted toward the bridge. Officers were erratic at the best of times, and the most he could hope is that they stayed out of the way and let him do his job.

His greatest fear never materialized. The armored door to the bridge stood open, and his people were already shooting the unconscious crewmembers with trank guns and laying the breathing bodies out of the way. They then took the key stations and began testing access and systems. The malware should have locked out everyone until new codes were input—codes only the Breakers had.

"We have control, Chief," said the helmswoman he'd brought along as she ran through systems checks. "Nothing out of place. But we can't keep ship's oxygen levels this low for long without risking brain damage to our prisoners."

"Give me local ship wide comlink, my headset."

"You're connected, Chief," said the rating at Comms.

"Powell, you in place?"

"Ready, Chief."

"Release the gas."

"Aye aye, Chief."

Powell, an engineering technician, began to pump a cylinder full of human-tailored soporific into the ventilation system. The Breakers' masks should filter it out, and Zaxby wouldn't be affected.

"Confirm status of the rest of the squadron as they report," ordered Gurung.

"Aye aye, Chief. I have two battlecruisers confirmed in our hands… four destroyers, seven frigates. Waiting on the others."

"What about the non-squadron ships?"

"Nothing yet. They don't seem alerted."

Gurung nodded in satisfaction. Things had gone well so far, and as long as the final battlecruiser was taken, nothing would seriously impede the Commodore's new, ready-made navy.

Nothing, that is, except for the fortress itself.

* * *

Straker strode at a deliberate pace down the vehicle tunnel, hunting Hok or any other resistance. A brace of rocketeers fired at him from a corner, but he triggered his force-cannon before the warheads impacted. The electromagnetic guide tube, set in a wide cone, pre-detonated the warheads in flight before the wash of charged plasma consumed them, and the attackers as well.

Flames sprang up from the intense heat as wall fittings, paint, control boxes and screens ignited—everything that wasn't asteroidal stone. The rock itself scarred and blackened.

"You guys all right back there?" he said to the three battlesuiters trailing him.

"We're good, sir," said Karst.

Pressing onward through the flame, Straker almost joined the Celestial Legion right then and there as a storm of heavy fire slammed into him. Pain blossomed all across the front of his body as lasers, high-powered armor-piercing slugs, and antitank rockets hammered his front armor.

Fortunately, he'd defaulted to high forward reinforcement, electrical fields flowing through the superconducting layers to stiffen his overlapping duralloy armor plates to maximum. Yellow telltales popped up across his HUD as he retreated back into the smoke and flame, firing his gatling to cover himself.

"Back up! Fall back!" he called, surprised.

That had been a tactical error borne of overconfidence. He should have let his force-cannon recharge before advancing. He'd *assumed*—always an asinine thing to do—that the rocketeers were there to delay him. In fact, the enemy commander probably wanted him to charge in.

And where had all that firepower come from? The Breakers ambush had inflicted more than fifty percent casualties on the Hok, leaving perhaps thirty or forty of them alive. It didn't seem likely they'd regrouped that entire force and managed to emplace it in front of him with heavy weapons... so, this was another, unexpected enemy, well-organized and well-led.

"Loco, you met anything serious?" Straker comlinked.

"Nope, just a few Hok stragglers."

"I need you with me. I just ran into a shit-storm of heavy infantry fire. Proceed with caution. I don't know if it's more Hok, or someone else."

"Never goes smooth, huh, boss?"

"Shut up and get over here."

"On my way."

Straker set his comlink beacon to high output so Loco's HUD would find him more easily, and took a covered position at a corner. He extended one sensor antenna beyond the edge of the wall, and held his weapons ready while the smoke slowly cleared.

Multi-spectral scans penetrated the obscurants far enough to see that the enemy wasn't pressing forward. So, a standoff. Straker loaded a tactical view and tried to predict his opponents' next move.

What would I do if I were you? he asked himself. My fortress is being overrun, I'm facing mechsuiters, but I still have an intact fighting force. If I've got secure comms with my Mutuality comrades, what's my priority?

The control center. That was the obvious answer. Those in command of the control center could still fire capital weapons to knock down any ships in the vicinity—except for those still docked—which were too close, of course—and they could devastate the planet below, if only for revenge.

Even though they'd lost the civilian network to malware, the control center would also have some influence on the situation inside the fortress. They could use their secured military net and devices, plus certain sensors, the comms and possibly some automated weaponry.

They would also have already fired a message drone toward flatspace to call for reinforcements, though any response would take days to arrive. *Liberator* or *Revenge* might be able to intercept it, but he couldn't count on that. The Mutuality defense forces might also have more message drones on other facilities as yet untaken within the Sachsen system.

But that wasn't his problem right now. The Mutualists in front of him were.

Chapter 13

Sachsen Fortress

"Coming up behind you, boss," said Loco.

Straker was still emplaced at a strategic corner, determined to hold off this new infantry force… if he could. But the worrisome enemy hadn't pursued him, and he was relieved to see the other Foehammer on his HUD.

"I don't think they're eager to attack up the center," Straker said. "If I were them, I'd be working my way around our left flank toward the control center. They have to know it's under assault. I bet the officer on duty is going apeshit."

"Roger dodger, boss. I'll take point." Loco turned and began a ponderous jog down the vehicular tunnel, back toward the ambush intersection.

"Battlesuiters, follow Loco. I'll take trail." Straker brought up the rear, slewing his waist 180 degrees so his Foehammer walked forward while his torso faced backward. Long practice made even this unnatural position second nature to him. He set his active sensors to maximum.

"Breakers, this is Straker," he comlinked on the general channel. "There's a new enemy force loose, estimated company strength, somewhere in sector 2-B. It's probably heading for the command center. Squad leaders, if you can turn over your checkpoints to local insurgents, I need you to regroup on the engineers. Everything depends on capturing the HQ, and that means defending our guys that are drilling in."

By now, the Ritter brothers' local Sachsens should have risen up, capturing or eliminating all Mutuality resistance they found, using weapons the Breakers had passed to them. Hopefully they'd also wear their Breakers armbands for identification.

His comlink beeped. "Gurung to Commodore Straker."

"Straker."

"The battlecruiser squadron is secured. We are holding in place. Two independent enemy ships have avoided being taken. They're powering up and making ready for departure. Shall we engage?"

"Yes, Chief. We can't let them get room to launch shipkillers at you, and we can't let them get away. Disable if you can, destroy if you must."

"Aye aye, sir. Gurung out."

Seizure of the squadron was good news, but it would all be for naught if the control center could still fire the fortress weapons. Any one of the massive lasers, particle accelerators, or railguns could utterly destroy even a battlecruiser with one shot at this point-blank range. That's why Gurung was holding them in place, too close to be targeted.

Of course, the battlecruisers could fire shipkillers and probably destroy all the fortress' capital weapons, since they were well inside the base's defensive envelope and ability to react. But that would leave the Sachsen homeworld defenseless against the inevitable Mutuality counterattack. As a last resort, it would be an admission of defeat.

Straker refused to be defeated. Not yet, anyway.

"Straker to engineers. How long, Foreman Imrone?"

"At least another hour, sir," said Imrone, the woman in charge, a hard-rock miner from Freiheit. "We've exhausted all our high explosives and now we're working with lances and lasers to cut through the inner vault door."

"Could a few force-cannon bolts speed things along?"

"No, sir. We'd have to pull our equipment back, and that would lose time, not gain it."

"Right. Keep at it. We'll hold them off." He paused as he checked his HUD for the position of his Breakers. "Heiser, establish a defensive perimeter. Loco and I will set up in the two large tunnels. You have to hold the personnel passageways. If you have any more holo-camouflagers or Killmores, use them."

"Roger wilco, sir."

Straker took his position and watched Heiser emplace his infantry. "Corporal Karst, your battlesuiters are the fire brigade. Stay near the engineers, watch your HUD and take independent action to contain any breakthroughs."

"Got it, sir."

Straker switched channels. "Straker to Ritters, Straker to Ritters, come in."

No answer came back. That didn't surprise him. It was a matter of luck whether a signal could find its way through all the tunnels, bulkheads and hatches in the fortress.

Then he remembered the malware that should have put the Ritters' insurgent cell in control of the nonmilitary fortress systems. Maybe that included the civilian comlink network. He set his suit's SAI to scan for less-secure connections and try the Breaker codes. Every time one was found, Straker tried to get a response, until…

"Conrad Ritter here, *Herr Kommodore*. Good to hear your voice."

"Same here, Sergeant. Do you have any intel on a company-sized or larger force of infantry in sector 2-B, possibly closing on our position?"

"Yah, we see them on cameras, though they are destroying many of them not secured to the military network. My people say they are elite marines from the naval squadron, mixed Hok and human. Unfortunately they were engaged in combined exercises, and we were not able to take the armory before they resupplied with weapons and ammo."

"That explains how easy Gurung took the ships, but his good luck is our bad. Numbers?"

"Perhaps three hundred, maybe more. Many appear to have battlesuits."

Straker grunted as if punched. "Can you confirm where they are?"

"Sector 2-B, near to 1-B, approaching 1-A along several axes. They may also be using the maintenance crawlways."

"Damn… it's worse than I thought. I hope we can hold, but I need certainty. Can your locals hit them from behind once we're engaged?"

Doubt crept into Ritter's voice. "We can and will, if so ordered, sir, but most of my people are civilians with small arms that won't penetrate a battlesuit. We'll keep them busy, but if we press them hard…"

"You'll be slaughtered. I'm not asking for that. Do what you can."

"I have a better idea, sir. The malware has given us some control of the gravplating. We'll use it to harass the marines. Triple grav will slow them down, and we can turn it off and on again at random."

"Good idea." Straker's external mikes picked up the sounds of battle. "They're coming. Straker out." He switched channels. "Breakers, anyone unengaged, watch the maintenance hatches for infiltrators." Then he checked his HUD.

The display showed contact far to his left, counterclockwise around the Breakers' perimeter from him. He selected a direct link to a noncom nearby. "Straker to Sergeant Farwell, sitrep!"

"We have heavy contact on multiple routes, sir, taking casualties." Came Farwell's nervous voice. "We're falling back. Need reinforcements."

"Sending some now. Do your best." Straker opened his mouth to call Karst when he saw the battlesuiter team already in motion. Instead, he called Loco. "You see this?"

"I see it, boss. I'm shifting to the left, but the action is all in personnel passageways. Can't squeeze in there."

"Don't try. Take a good defensive position with fallback routes and I'll try to direct support for your defense."

"Right, boss." Loco's icon began to move.

Examining the situation as if it were a wargaming exercise, Straker watched his spherical perimeter collapse like a balloon being punched by a fist—a fist aimed at the control center. His Breakers were being swept aside or shoved back, and little except the battlesuiter squad and Loco stood in the way.

He cued the general channel. "This is Straker. All Breakers in sectors four through seven, rendezvous at the control center entrance and take defensive positions to protect the engineers. Sector eight, attack clockwise. Sector three, attack counterclockwise. We need to put pressure on the flanks of the enemy salient."

Without waiting for acknowledgement, he began moving toward the engineers himself. His suit had been degraded with the damage, but his nanobots were already filling in holes and cracks in his armor, stealing material from where they could to ensure a smoother, if now thinner, front duralloy plating.

As he walked, he called Conrad Ritter again. "Sergeant, I need you now. If you haven't already, start your gravity fluctuations and engage the enemy from their rear. I can't tell you how hard to press, but if we lose the engineers, we'll have to settle for nuking the fortress—but if we do, there's nothing to protect your homeworld from a counterattack. So, it's really up to you."

"I understand, *Herr Kommodore*. We're willing to spend the last drop of our blood for our freedom."

"Let's hope it doesn't come to that, but if it does…"

"*Gott mit uns.* Ritter out."

Straker maneuvered carefully into the engineers' area and walked around behind their equipment. On one side of the large, vault-like duralloy door, two mining lasers alternated full-power pulses, creating mini-explosions like grenades, their bursts of heat fatiguing and melting the hard, superconductor-reinforced metals. On the other, a pair of thermal lances pressed deep into the overlapping plates. Melted and blackened materials oozed out of their entrance holes like candle wax, to run down the sides and harden before reaching the floor.

By the time he'd entered the tunnel nearest the enemy attack, other Breakers were pouring in from all sides. They grabbed discarded packing cases and commandeered unused loaders, moving them to create cover and concealment in preparation for a last stand.

"Imrone, this is Straker," he comlinked to the foreman of the engineers.

"Imrone here."

"Reorient your lasers to cover these two passageways." Straker pointed with his gauntlets. "You seeing me?"

"I do, bossman, but these aren't weapons. They can't be aimed easy."

"If you can get them to fire straight down the corridors, they're powerful enough to blow through battlesuit armor with one shot, right?"

"Yes, but–"

"Do it now. We need every trick."

"Okay, will do."

Within seconds, the laser crews shut down their bulky machines and began to drag them toward their new positions. Straker didn't watch further; he couldn't micromanage everything, and had to trust his people to set up for maximum effectiveness.

On his HUD, the lead elements of the enemy had engaged his few battlesuiters. One, then two icons winked out as they fell back, and furious fire filled the space between the two forces. Killmores detonated, slowing the enemy for only a moment.

"Karst, fall back to the next major crossroads," Straker ordered, and began a careful jog toward Loco's position. By the time he got there, the four surviving battlesuiters were racing back from passageways, crossing the intersection to take a stand behind Loco's Foehammer.

Straker saw Heiser directing emplacement of his pair of heavy slugthrowers, setting them inside two passageways with their lethal snouts poking out into the open space. He approved; Heiser knew his business. The crew-served weapons would establish cones of fire devastating to everyone who crossed in front of them, while remaining protected from the sides.

Sure glad these corridors favor the defender, Straker told himself, not for the first time. In fact, any constricted terrain made it hard on an attacker, which was the only reason his lightly armed force was able to contemplate making a stand against elite armored marines and suicidal Hok, each with the firepower of an infantry squad.

"Loco, move over to the left," Straker said, coming up behind the other Foehammer.

"Boss, your armor is degraded."

"It's repairing. I'll hang back half a pace. That way you can maneuver a little and so can I."

"Okay," he said. "Just don't shoot me in the ass."

"If I shoot you in the ass," Straker told him, "rest assured, it'll be for a good reason."

Straker set himself so the other mechsuit covered his left arm and gatling. That shoulder had been repaired and reinforced from its earlier damage, but it still felt a little dodgy. As good as it was having a parts factory on Freiheit, it wasn't the same as a full-up maintenance depot.

Karst and the other battlesuiters edged back even farther, pressing themselves to the side to shoot past the 'suiters' legs.

"Spear, this is Straker."

"Heiser here."

"Good as those slugthrowers are, they'll get taken out before we will—'we' the mechsuits, I mean. That means you'll get overrun, so fall back down those passageways when it gets too hot. Leave the slugthrowers if necessary, but make sure they're useless if you do."

"Roger wilco."

"You take charge of the last stand at the engineers' position. I've directed them to use their mining lasers as weapons. We'll hold this big tunnel as long as possible and be the rock in their stream. All you have to do is bottle them up in the little ones. Because, if they break out…"

"They'll rip us apart. Got it, sir. Good luck."

"You too." Straker's HUD beeped a warning. "Here they come."

Heiser must have seen them at the same time, for the two slugthrowers opened up with streams of high-velocity bullets, belching the fire of their burning liquid propellant byproducts into the crossroads.

Loco fired as soon as he had a target. Straker saw the bell of his force-cannon brighten with plasma discharge that reached out like an arrow of pure coronal fire. It crossed the open space to strike the lead trooper, a Hok. The antitank weapon cut through the creature's armor and flash-boiled it so quickly that it exploded like a burst pressure-cooker.

The blast knocked over several more assaulting enemy even as the tube of plasma continued to impact another Hok, then a human marine. All of them exploded in like fashion before the energy dissipated.

Loco didn't wait, but began snapping short gatling bursts, targeting those troopers still active. The high-velocity rounds were designed to punch through light armor, so they made short work of battlesuiters.

But the enemy were numerous, well-armed, and fearless. Those not killed outright poured fire into the tunnel—lasers and bullets and rockets, probably even grenades. Loco staggered as his front armor ablated and explosions blossomed all around him.

Straker fired his force-cannon on a wide setting, turning the weapon into a combination EMP and flamethrower as the plasma spread into an ever-widening cylinder. It incinerated rockets, flash-heated the closest enemy troopers, and its thermal and electromagnetic pulse futzed the sensors needed for precise targeting, buying Loco time to recover.

Squatting, Straker used his left arm to fire blind bursts of gatling fire from between Loco's ankles at floor level. Hopefully some of the heavy penetrators would skitter along the deck and take out a few of the enemy.

And the closer their opponents came to the tunnel they defended, the heavier the mechsuiters' fire became. Like water from a hose, the pressure was highest at the nozzle.

"Shit," Heiser called on his comlink. "Left flank slugthrower is down. Falling back now."

"Roger, Spear," said Straker. "Keep those engineers alive."

"Wilco. Spear out."

Loco fired another force-cannon bolt, this one widened like Straker's had been, and then said, "Boss, we gotta fade a little. I'm degraded as much as you are, and some of these HEAT rounds are going to penetrate if they hit me square."

"Hit you square… that gives me an idea. Back up ten meters and stand southpaw. I'll do the same." Straker walked backward so Loco didn't trip over him, and the battlesuiters jogged backward even farther.

Loco backed up and took a stance with his right arm—and his force-cannon—extended toward the enemy. He placed his left, with the gatling, across his abdomen and below, also aimed at the oncoming Mutualist troops. "Like this?"

"Perfect," said Straker, taking the same stance. "It's the same principle as an old-fashioned duelist, reducing his target surface area. Transfer reinforcement power to only the parts that'll get hit."

"Got it." Loco chuckled. "Just like old times, eh? Johnny and Derek against the world."

"Yeah, well, let's not get captured again."

"Not gonna happen. I'll die first."

"Let's avoid that if we can." Straker fired his force-cannon as he spotted movement in the smoke, filling the tunnel in front of him with another dose of sun-hot plasma.

"Aye aye, Commodore Liberator sir." Loco sent a gatling burst downrange.

"Our main job is to block this big tunnel and force the enemy to go around, channeling him into ever-smaller passageways and kill zones. As long as we only have to fight on a narrow front, we can do a lot of good."

"Yeah, but these guys ain't stupid, boss. They'll eventually stop sticking their dicks into the wringer and just hold us here."

As if the enemy had heard Loco's statement, the enemy fire quieted down. A few desultory shots *spanged* off their mechsuits now and again, but no more rockets or grenades flew at them.

"Sir, the other slugthrower's out of action," said Heiser. "Everyone who made it is back with the engineers."

Straker nodded, and then replied, "Understood. Loco, take Karst and his men, head back to help. Stay in the rear exit of this tunnel so nobody gets behind me. I'll hold them here."

"Forget it. You're the big boss. You have to direct this battle. If one of us goes down, better it be me."

"Loco–"

"Shut up, Derek. They ain't even pushing here now, but if they do and take down my suit, I'll survive in my cocoon. They don't have weapons heavy enough to dig me out. Not for a while. When you win, you can cut my 'suit open and we'll drive on. But you have to command."

"All right. But don't be afraid to fall back. We need your firepower." Straker swallowed. "And…"

"Yeah, yeah. Tomorrow this time we'll be downing some of the local brew. Now go. *Go!*"

"Going." Straker waved the battlesuiters to precede him toward the last stand, and then followed. He comlinked Heiser to warn him they would be appearing in the tunnel.

At the open space in front of the command center, the thermal lances still drilled into the vault door, making slow progress. Imrone comlinked Straker when he appeared. "Sir, we really need those lasers to be drilling, not sitting here—"

The engineer foreman's declaration was cut off as multiple explosions shook the walls, ceiling and floors.

Chapter 14

Sachsen Fortress, Command Center

With the bursting of many charges, the area in front of the command center doors became obscured with smoke and gases. Breakers opened fire, and attackers did too, appearing suddenly as if out of the walls themselves.

Straker's HUD helped him see through the obscurants and identify what was happening. "They're coming out of the maintenance shafts!" he called. He felt like barking a reprimand at Heiser, for he'd told the man to make sure to have those hatches covered. Maybe he had, and maybe he did, but it was sure hard to tell right now.

"Karst, stay behind me. You're in battlesuits and might be mistaken for enemy. Breakers, shoot anything in a battlesuit!" Then he stepped to the edge of the tunnel, facing the engineers.

Enemy battlesuiters dropped from openings in the ceiling or crawled out of hatches in the walls. Some were met by storms of fire where Heiser had evidently set up local ambushes. Killmores chopped others in half or blew them to pieces, but even in death, the Hok that took point held down their trigger fingers and sent hot metal by the bucketful screaming among the lightly armored Breakers. Ricochets caused wounds and casualties, creating confusion that favored the attackers.

The engineers did the right thing, flipping the switches on their mining lasers and diving for cover. The hot green beams shone brightly in the smoke, creating a deadly barrier down the center of the two passageways where the attackers would come, one each to the left and right of Straker.

He counted those as interdicted, and concentrated on the area in front of him. Unlike most of the Breakers, his HUD cued and targeted enemies once he told his SAI what to look for. He began putting single gatling shots into battlesuiters, each one a kill. His problem was complicated by ensuring his penetrators didn't go right through enemy troopers and kill friendlies behind them.

Marines poured out one hole in particular, and Straker turned his attention to it along with his force-cannon. Aiming precisely, he sent a narrow beam through the entrance. When the plasma struck something inside—a wall, a trooper—its point of impact exploded with heat expansion, abruptly cutting off the flow of attackers.

But the Breakers were losing the battle. The enemy battlesuiters were too tough in their armor and too well trained, and each of them had a HUD of his own to help identify friend from foe in the smoke. Straker had no choice but to get in the middle of it and draw their attention.

"Loco, get back here," he rasped, firing as rapidly as he could choose aimpoints. "It's going to shit."

"On my way, boss," came the reply.

Straker lost his tactical awareness in the fight as his combat mind went into overload. His body, assaulted by the pinpricks of pain feedback, interpreted his situation as death threats and dumped fight-or-flight hormones into his system, speeding up his already-accelerated actions.

Stepping forward, Straker grabbed a battlesuiter out of midair with his right-hand gauntlet even as he fired gatling rounds with his left, letting his SAI do the work. Like a child with an action figure, he slammed the enemy into the deck at his feet, hard enough to shatter bone.

Without thinking, he kicked a nearby Hok, flinging him across the room, and then fired his recharged force-cannon into another maintenance hatch where he saw movement. More single gatling shots tore holes in his enemies, and combat became a whirl of death so confusing and quick that later, he couldn't reconstruct it in his memory.

He knew he was fighting for his life as he felt severe pain at his knees and shoulders, the most vulnerable spots for battlesuiters. Enemy with chainsaw-like molecular cutters sawed at him, and he slapped them with his ton-heavy gauntlets like a man would strike at rats chewing on him.

Too many, too many! his mind cried as he roared and tried to scrape them off on the nearby walls. He shifted them into the beams of the mining lasers, he smashed them with his fists, he shot them with gatling rounds, but there were too many.

Straker felt a blast of heat wash over him, the feedback circuits faithfully reproducing the sensations of his skin, stepped down only slightly from scalding. Plasma surrounded him, and then the pain in a dozen places of his body began to fade as battlesuiters fell off him like crisped leeches.

He turned to see Loco at the entrance to the tunnel, his force-cannon smoking. He'd sent a flamethrower wide-beam blast directly at Straker, peeling the enemy off him... but several Breakers lay burned by the overblast.

"Dammit, Loco–"

"Sorry, boss, I had to do it. We can't lose you."

Straker ground his teeth and turned his attention to finishing off the enemy. Perversely, the more Breakers he lost, the easier it became to kill Hok and Mutuality marines, with no chance of fratricide.

He felt the old anger fill him like a familiar friend, the hatred of those he'd thought of as evil aliens all his life. He slammed the enemy like rag dolls into the deck or walls, stomping on them when they fell.

He'd failed his people, he knew. He held back hot tears of rage, rage that made him want to wipe them all out, them and every single one of the sneering bastard Inquisitors and the haughty commissars and the unseen evil Committee members pulling the strings of the common folk from their fetid, corrupt lairs—

"Boss, boss... Boss!" Straker found his leg caught in both of Loco's arms, metal grinding against metal. He looked down to see a Mutuality marine, his helmet knocked off, his face filled with the terror or his own mortality, holding up his hands as if to fend off the sole of the Foehammer poised to crush him.

"Boss, throttle down. Come on, Derek, ease off. We've won. We've won."

Straker took a shuddering breath and told his SAI to reduce his mechsuit to minimum mobility mode. "I'm good, I'm good, Loco. Let me go."

Loco let him go, and he stepped back. Post-battle fog made his vision fill with dark spots of fatigue. Gazing around, he realized he stood in the middle of a charnel house, an abattoir of the wounded and dead, now overrun with lightly armed Sachsen civilians. Some were cheering, chanting and shaking weapons in the air. But some were attacking the fallen, stabbing or shooting wounded battlesuiters.

When one drew a bead on by mistake on a Breaker in half-armor, Straker was jolted out of his funk. He activated his external speakers and roared,

"Cease fire, cease fire! Dammit, how do you say 'cease fire' in German?" He reached down to knock the civilian over before he could murder his ally by mistake. "Kill the Hok, but nobody else!"

Loco, Karst and the other surviving Breakers began echoing his orders. Aldrik Ritter marched among them and yelled, "Halt! Nicht schiessen!" over and over, until the berserkers among the insurgents had come to their senses. The elation of victory showed in their eyes and, denied more violence, some began looting weapons and equipment from the fallen.

"Spear, you still alive?" Straker comlinked, hoping for an answer.

"Here, sir." Heiser waved with one arm from a seat on a destroyed loader. A medic was working on his other arm, and his leg was already wrapped in a combat dressing.

Straker left his external speakers on and synched with an all-channel comlink broadcast. "Listen up, all Breakers and Sachsens and any of you Mutuality motherfuckers that are still thinking of fighting. This is Commodore Derek Straker, the Liberator. All organized Mutualist units have been defeated. Most of them are dead. Within an hour, we'll have drilled through to the command center. This fortress is ours."

A renewed cheer went up from everyone around him. The surviving engineers got back to work with the lasers and thermal lances after helping to drag bodies and wounded out of the way.

"If you're not with us already, surrender now and you'll be treated in accordance with the laws of war. You can show your good faith by identifying the commissars or inquisitors among you, or any other lackeys of the Mutualist regime." Straker enjoyed calling them lackeys, a fair reversal of the name they'd called all the Hundred Worlds POWs when he'd first been captured.

"If you know where Hok are hiding, we need to know that too," he continued. "To those inside the command center: you can save yourselves a lot of trouble by opening up and surrendering. If we have to dig you out of there, well... I'm not sure I can keep these Sachsens from rampaging in there and cutting all your throats."

That brought another cheer, and some of the militia fighters began dancing in a circle, firing their weapons into the ceiling.

"Stop that! Aldrik, get control of your people!" Straker bellowed.

Ritter raced over and punched one man, knocked another down, and snatched a carbine out of a woman's grip, snarling harshly in the local speech.

Straker continued, "Control center duty officer, I'm sure you've heard me. Respond on this channel, now."

He waited, and then repeated his instructions. "Come on, whoever you are. I know you're just some poor slob stuck on the night shift, surrounded by a bunch of scared people. Give up before your own noncoms think about putting a bullet in your back and taking my deal. Get out ahead of this thing and we'll all be okay."

Straker waited as the seconds ticked by. The engineer lasers sparked and popped and the thermal lances continued to work on the hinges.

He was just about to give up, thinking the control center crew was commanded by some die-hard fanatic, when he heard an unfamiliar woman's voice. "Commodore Straker, this is Subaltern Jimson. We will open the inner door if you promise to keep out the mob and treat us as you should."

"I promise." Straker checked to see who'd heard the response. It appeared as if only those with comlinks had. The locals seemed unaware. "Spear, can you move?" he asked, still broadcasting both on comlink and speakers.

"Yes, sir. Slow." Heiser stood on shaky legs.

"Have your noncoms clear out these fine allied Sachsen citizens. Escort them to the cafeterias and galleries. Have a few beers. Ritter, you hear me?"

"Yes, Liberator," Aldrik said with raised voice.

"Get your people moving, and tell them not to loot! We only have a few days until the enemy shows up in force. This fortress needs to be operational. Their lives depend on it! Spread the word. I'm counting on you."

"We will not fail you, Liberator!" Aldrik cried, clearly for the benefit of those Sachsens nearby. He continued in a loud voice, relating Straker's instructions in German.

Over the next couple of minutes, the citizens cleared out and headed for other areas of the fortress, still celebrating. Two of the young men kicked a battlesuit helmet back and forth between them like a football, laughing uproariously as they proceeded down the passageway. Straker hoped it didn't still contain a head.

He heard Aldrik Ritter crying words that sounded like "Heil der Be-fryer," over and over again. He remembered that "*Frei*," which sounded like "fry," meant "free"—as in Freiheit, freedom. So "der Befryer," or *Befreier*, must mean *Liberator*. Hopefully, Ritter was giving them a good impression of him, a legend to cling to in what might be dark days ahead.

"Subaltern Jimson, you may open the inner door now."

"Opening now, sir." From behind the massive, damaged outer, the next layer swung inward. "I think you'll still have to cut through. The interlocks are welded shut on the outer door."

Straker felt himself begin to relax from hyper-vigilance. The victory had been won, and now he and the Breakers—those that remained—would be inheriting an intact command center, along with the vital capital weaponry on the fortress.

Over the next hours, the orbital fortress was cleared of a few residual Hok and Mutuality troops. The Hok always died fighting, but the humans surrendered to the promise of humane treatment, and of not being turned over to the Sachsens.

The locals calmed down after a while and returned to their jobs and businesses. Many wanted to return to the planet.

Reports from the surface indicated the small Mutuality garrisons were quickly overwhelmed by mobs of citizens, while the military base in the capital city of New Dresden surrendered when Straker threatened to strike it with particle beams the next time the fortress passed overhead. Ditto for the installations and bases scattered around the star system, once they knew Straker had the power to come conquer them.

All in-system warships were now under Breaker control. Gurung's and Zholin's skeleton crews manned them and formed a combined squadron in high orbit above Sachsen-3, joined by *Liberator* and *Revenge*. The local attack ships on patrol were already heading in to surrender themselves. Without sidespace engines, and with nowhere to go, their choices were to give up, to make suicide attacks, or to die when their air ran out.

As Straker had suspected, nobody in the Mutuality proved loyal enough to make a last stand with no hope of victory.

In the fortress's spacious control center, Straker gathered his key personnel for a conference around its holo-table. Their mood was jubilant, except for First Sergeant Heiser, Straker noticed.

"What's bothering you, Spear? Those wounds hurting?"

Heiser lifted his elbow slightly, the arm in a flexi-sling. "No, sir. Pain meds. I'm counting the cost, and thinking about the future."

Straker nodded soberly. "The price was high. Eighty Breakers dead, many of the infantry wounded. But we took every objective, despite the enemy's best efforts. We've done something not seen in centuries of warfare. We've liberated a whole star system, not merely conquered it for a different empire."

"But what next, sir? What happens when they respond with a fleet? Dreadnoughts will crush us."

Straker pressed his lips together. It wasn't like Heiser to despair in the midst of victory. Maybe he lost someone close to him. He'd been seeing a civilian woman, Straker vaguely remembered. A rock miner? An engineer, maybe? Looking at Heiser's bleak face, he knew he'd guessed right.

"Every one of our casualties is a tragedy, Spear. But we all knew what we were getting into, and our fallen heroes were willing to sacrifice themselves to free others—millions of others here in the Sachsen system." Straker swept his eyes around the table. "Billions of others—and we'll free billions more."

Engels put her hand on Heiser's shoulder and whispered something into his ear, glancing at Straker as she did so. The big man relaxed at the touch, took a deep breath, and nodded. "I know. Fuck it and drive on, right, sir?"

"We have to, Spear. To honor them."

Zaxby opened his mouth to speak, but Loco clapped his hand over the octopoid's rubbery lips. "It was still a good question, boss," Loco said. "What next?"

"That's what we're here to talk about," said Straker. "My intention is to take the forces we have and hit more new or lightly defended systems. We'll try to Trojan Horse them if they have fortresses, conquer them if they don't. If we can't take them, we'll try a different system. We need to spread this Galactic Liberation as far and wide as we can. If we can take enough territory, I'm hoping systems will start revolting on their own."

Zaxby used three tentacles to pry his mouth free. He'd donned a water suit again and, though he looked battered, seemed to have recovered his old energy. "Commodore Straker, as you've said so often, hope is not a plan."

"Yes, but liberations are based on people, and people need hope. We'll send message drones to broadcast to every system we can reach. The word of our successes will cause widespread unrest, which will cause the Mutuality to crack down, causing more resentment. When we show up in force, we'll have ready-made allies."

"I understand your reasoning, but my projections show that we will fail, absent finding some other advantage." Zaxby's fingerlike sub-tentacles danced over the surface in front of him, activating the holographic function.

A star map sprang into being above the holo-table, showing the local spiral arm. Zaxby continued. "This view encompasses approximately ten thousand star systems. Here is the territory of the Hundred Worlds, which despite its poetic name, includes 247 star systems, 134 fully habitable planets, and thousands of asteroid habitats and moon bases." A small, bean-shaped area flashed yellow.

"Go on," said Straker, intrigued. Until now, they'd not had such a capable military-grade holo-display available, and if he had a weakness, it was in visualizing three-dimensional space. This helped immensely, and he could see the others leaning forward, also interested.

"This is the Mutuality, composed of 1963 star systems, 1011 fully habitable planets, and over 12,000 associated bases and installations."

A larger, red bean sprang up next to the smaller yellow one. The two nested into each other, concave to concave, rather like an adult's hand holding a child's.

"Taken together, humanity's range is roughly spherical, and is centered around the Sol System of Old Earth, as one might expect." An icon deep in Mutuality space flashed. "Old Earth is industrially spent, though it is apparently a lovely museum and shrine to humanity's origins. I would be very interested to visit someday. The ruins, the old walled ports… did you know over seventy percent of the surface is water?"

"Thanks for the brainiac lecture, but can you get to the point?" Loco said with an air of boredom.

"With that attitude, I have no idea how you made it through Academy, Lieutenant Paloco," said Zaxby.

Loco shrugged. "I seduced a few lady professors, that's what I did."

"I find that extremely unlikely."

"You can find it and shove it–"

"At ease, you two," Straker snapped. "Zaxby, go on. I'm all ears."

"Your ears are malfunctioning?"

Straker waved. "Never mind. Proceed with your briefing."

"Thank you, Commodore Straker. As I was saying before I was so rudely interrupted, the capital of the Mutuality is here, on Unison-4 in the Unison system." Another icon flashed a few parsecs from Old Earth. "And we are here."

A tiny blue dot appeared, and then expanded as Zaxby zoomed in on it. Now, half the display was filled with sections of Mutuality and Hundred Worlds territory, and half showed other star systems. The small blue bead of Sachsen lay just within Mutuality space, at the outside edge of the territories of both empires.

"I will now highlight the most vulnerable systems and planets—the most lightly defended, or the ones most likely to revolt, or both. I include eleven outlying human-settled systems that have remained independent, as Sachsen used to be, before the Mutuality decided to claim a pretext for conquering it."

The blue of the Galactic Liberation expanded outward from Sachsen, absorbing system after system until it encompassed over a hundred stars and fifty habitable worlds. It then shrank rapidly as Mutuality red rolled over it in a wave.

"Using algorithms I designed, this projection shows the likely limits of the Liberation, based on the forces available, how much we can acquire and use, and the Mutuality's slow but overwhelming response."

Straker stared at it. "We'd grow to almost half the size of the Hundred Worlds, but you're saying we'll get easily crushed. Why? Why are they holding, be we couldn't?"

"The Hundred Worlds have advantages we would not. Their central systems are heavily fortified, and their industrial output is more than one hundred times that of our projected Liberation territory. They have a small, yet meaningful technological advantage that we do not. They have twenty times the population. Despite recent setbacks, they have a highly professionalized military structure that churns out trained personnel, many of whom have been genetically engineered for their roles."

"And you don't think the Liberation would spread on its own to more Mutuality worlds?"

"I have taken the statistical likelihood of that happening into account. The main obstacle to the domino effect is the presence of multiple fortresses above important populated planets. No rebellion can succeed when it can be attacked from above. Even if an entire planet revolted, its people are trapped on the surface, and fleets control all sidespace travel among star systems. Every world becomes, in effect, an isolated island."

Straker rubbed his stubbled jaw. "So if we really want to spread the Liberation, we have no choice but to control space, and destroy or take control of fortresses."

"That is correct," said Zaxby with an air of perverse satisfaction. "And, without some factor I have not included—and I included all known factors—the Galactic Liberation is doomed to failure."

Chapter 15

Sachsen Fortress, Command Center

The assembly of Breakers seemed to sigh as one at Zaxby's declaration that the Galactic Liberation was doomed to failure. It was a sound approaching a gasp of despair, as of a dream snatched away and stepped upon by the cruel hand of fate.

"That's bullshit," Straker said firmly, trying to dispel the mood. "Oh, I'm sure your calculations are correct, but if there's one thing I know, it's that forecasting the future is impossible that far out. You've got probabilities stacked on probabilities, and as you said, you can't take the unknown factors into account."

"The Black Swans," Aldrik Ritter said suddenly.

"The what?"

Ritter cleared his throat. "That's what your Lazarus calls them. It means an unknown unknown—something so unexpected it couldn't have even been conceived of. Like us taking this fortress. To the Mutuality, it was inconceivable, so they never really planned for it. I mean, all they'd have had to do is install computer-controlled heavy weapons at every intersection and we'd have no chance at all. Or had a garrison of sufficient size. Or given the garrison armored vehicles to control the large corridors. But nobody tries to capture fortresses—at least, not until they've pummeled them with capital-grade naval weapons."

Straker's eyes narrowed. "You've been talking to the Inquisitor?"

"When I'm taking my turn on guard. It's something to do. But I don't allow the soldiers to speak to him."

"Or anyone else?"

"No, no, sir." But Ritter seemed hesitant in his reply, a little off, or uncertain.

Straker told himself to remember to dig deeper later, but now was not the time. He went on, "Sergeant Ritter's point is the same as mine, I think. The odds may be against us, but they're still odds, odds that can be beaten." He looked to his left and right, making eye contact with everyone in the room, all his Breakers. "So I need you to come up with ways to beat the odds, ways that I haven't thought of."

Engels began to put out a fist to be recognized, an old habit from their Academy days, but Zaxby beat her to it with a curled tentacle. Without waiting for Straker to give him leave to speak, he said, "I have a way."

"A way that's not incorporated into your simulation?" Loco said. "Why not add it in?"

"Because I have a superior mind, Lieutenant Paloco. I created my simulation to establish a baseline of fact, in order to show that we need what you so quaintly call 'outside-the-box' thinking. Fortunately, my species eschews boxes, preferring rounded containers or bottles. I suspect this gives us fewer limits in ideation, as we are not psychologically confined to cubical mentation."

"Oh, now you're just pulling made-up words out of your ass."

"I am not–"

"What's your idea, Zaxby?" Straker interrupted, holding up a finger to Engels to show he knew she wanted to bring up an idea as well. "Some trick like you told me about? Firing stealth mines from railguns?"

"I already incorporated innovative weapons employment and tactics into my simulation. This is different. We've glossed over the possibility before, but simply put, we need to find and recruit aliens to our cause." Zaxby tapped the table, and a whole new region appeared in green, an area extending into the unknown star systems outward from both Mutuality and Hundred Worlds space.

"I thought you already surveyed that area for allies, and discarded the idea."

"Recruiting alien allies was not my first priority, but I have exhausted all higher ones. Now, low-probability, high-payoff possibilities must be considered."

"Like that Pasqualli's Wager thing," said Loco. He might have winked at Straker with the eye away from Zaxby.

Zaxby slapped a tentacle to what passed for his forehead in a passable imitation of a similar human gesture. "*Pascal's* Wager, Lieutenant Paloco, but yes, you have managed to dredge up an apt analogy from the depths of your mental sludge."

"Loco's jerking your chain, Zaxby," said Straker mildly. "Whatever we call them, we need some long shots. If a mission to find nonhuman allies might pay off, then we need to give it a try. But that's a big roll of the dice. I need more than that."

Zaxby started to speak again, but Engels cleared her throat loudly, and Straker pointed at her. "Commander Engels."

She leaned forward, tapping tentatively at the holo-table's surface. "While Zaxby's been programming complex simulations for fun, I've had a few people doing simpler work. We've been combing through the top-secret files here, looking for weaknesses or opportunities in the Mutuality databases. We're not done yet, but I came across something weird."

"A vid of Zaxby making sense?" said Loco.

"Lay off him, Loco," Engels replied. "Yes, weird. I was concentrating on Mutuality fleet weapons and ship development, to see what surprises they might have in store, when I came across this." She poked a finger at the table, and a hologram of a ship came up.

Most capital warships were cylindrical, with rounded noses, the better to disperse lasers and deflect kinetic or blast effects. Smooth curving armor bore up better under stress, like an architectural arch supported weight, and symmetrical circles simplified many processes, such as balancing mass, spin, and power requirements.

This ship, however, showed a distinctly octagonal cross-section, like an old-fashioned pencil, unsharpened. Compared with what Straker was used to seeing, it looked blocky, clunky, inelegant. Its nose was almost square, barely raked, which seemed as if it were asking to be targeted head-on. Yet, it also conveyed a sense of enormous power, like the head of a sledgehammer.

"Dammit, how do you..." Engels said, trying to work the holo-table controls.

"Allow me," said Zaxby, running his subtentacles across its surface.

The hologram expanded to fill the space above the table, about two meters by two by three, and the detail became clear... including the scale. In one corner floated a box with the words PROJECT STARKILLER, PMN *Indomitable*, and a date seventeen years in the past.

"Oh, *my*," said Chief Gurung. "That is a very, very big ship."

"Yes, too big," said Engels with a nod. "This *Indomitable* monstrosity is sixteen times as large as the largest superdreadnought ever built." She lifted her eyebrows at Straker as if daring him to figure out why.

Straker spoke slowly. "It's too big... because it can't possibly jump. It's ten times as big as Freiheit, and we barely got that thing into sidespace. So it's, what, a monitor? A local defense ship as big as a fortress, but completely manufactured of crysteel and duralloy, and mobile within a star system. Tons of power, armor reinforcement that makes it almost impregnable... I can see that might be useful, but Unknowable Creator, the *cost*."

Engels nodded. "For the labor and resource expenditure, they could have built sixteen to twenty supers. That's a whole fleet, sacrificed to make this..."

"Battleship, said Straker. "It's a battleship."

"I never heard of that ship class," said Engels. "Not in space."

"You're right, it's a name from the era of Old Earth wet navies, almost eight hundred years ago. Battleships were the biggest surface combatants ever built, even bigger than dreadnoughts. The only things larger were aircraft carriers, but those had a completely different purpose." Straker stared with fascinated wonder at the oddity floating above the table. "I don't know what *they* call her, but to me, she's a battleship."

"But that thing is useless!" said Loco. "It can't jump, so it doesn't matter, as long as we don't attack the system where it's parked."

"That's what's funny, Loco," said Engels. "Zaxby, show us the sidespace engines."

Zaxby tapped, and sixteen sections lit up, displaying the distinct shapes of sidespace generators.

"So it *can* jump! But that's impossible..." said Loco. He snapped his fingers. "They must have cracked the sidespace limit. Somehow, they came up with new tech to let them move bigger things."

Engels smiled. "That's a good guess, but no. It wasn't new tech that let them get around the limit. It was clever thinking, I'd say. Simple, elegant—and apparently something nobody ever thought of. Or at least, nobody ever actually tried to make it work—until now."

"You're slow-rolling us, Carla," said Straker. "Show us your cards. How can it jump?"

She grinned wider. "Zaxby, you see how the ship separates into sections?"

Chapter 15

Zaxby's subtentacles squirmed like a nest of inverted snakes across the table, trying out various methods of pulling apart the simulation, until it abruptly split into sixteen distinct pieces.

First, the ship broke in half in the middle, front and back. Then the two pieces divided along their long axes, creating eight distinct parts each, with triangular cross-sections. Their narrowest, most acute edges sides pointed toward a common center, where they would rejoin.

Engels waved a hand through the nearest part of the hologram. "Sixteen superdreadnought-sized sections. Each has its own sidespace engine, fusion engines, impellers, thrusters, weapons suite, quarters, sub-bridge…"

Straker nodded slowly as understanding blossomed in his mind. "That's brilliant! Each part transits separately. They reassemble in the target star system and, *bang*, a battleship big enough to smash fortresses."

"Oh, come on," said Loco. "It's overcomplicated and expensive. It's like having one super-Sledgehammer instead of a battalion of Foehammers. What makes this thing better than sixteen brand-new, tried-and-true superdreadnoughts? I mean, hell, a contact nuke could still take it out—and then you just lost sixteen ships-worth at once."

"It *is* extremely complex and expensive," Zaxby said in his condescending lecture-voice, "But you are forgetting that size does matter."

"Oh, I *know* size matters." Loco said with a grin.

"Your infantile humor aside, I will now demolish your argument with one simple comparison. If larger ships were inefficient and ineffective, there would be no superdreadnoughts. There would only be cruisers and smaller vessels. Yet the largest ships dominate battle." Zaxby focused three of his eyes on Loco. "Tell me why."

Loco rubbed his face. "Okay, smartass. Because one big ship can defeat three or four smaller ships, even if they add up to the same tonnage."

"But *why* is that true?" Zaxby spread his eyes and rotated his head to take in everyone in the room. Engels widened her eyes and Chief Gurung's smile broadened. Straker realized both knew the answer, but were keep it to themselves in order to allow Zaxby to play professor.

Straker took a stab at it. "Because the weapons get bigger, the range grows longer and armor gets thicker. Just like on a tank. The increased protection alone is decisive. It can shield the ship from all weapons below a certain size."

"Well said, Commodore!" the Ruxin said. "Unlike your closest friend, you are not a complete dunce."

"Hey!" said Loco.

Zaxby continued without even glancing at Loco. "As you so rightly point out, Commodore Straker, a ship this size can carry weapons an entire order of magnitude larger than even superdreadnoughts. Its primary centerline multi-weapon—assembled from pieces of the sixteen sections and able to fire both railgun bullets and particle beams—outguns even the largest fortresses. Unlike them, though, it can maneuver to evade return fire. Its secondary weapons are the equal of any superdreadnought's *primaries*. Its armor is more than ten times as thick, with a similar power multiplier for its reinforcement fields. It will shrug off single hits from even contact fusion warheads."

"Then why hasn't the Mutuality used it? If it's so great, why haven't they won the war?" asked Loco.

Zaxby shifted uncomfortably. "I don't know for sure. These plans show an adequate design, though any Ruxin engineer could improve upon it. Still, the inception of this Project Starkiller was seventeen years ago. The *Indomitable* should have been completed by now. Unfortunately, all we have are these blueprints—which have not been updated, and which are missing much detail."

"So you think these diagrams are preliminary?" said Engels.

"They might even be fictional," said Straker. "One reason for creating a highly speculative weapons program might be to leak information to the other side and force them to expend resources countering something nonexistent. I mean, if this is so great, how did the plans end up here, to be captured?"

Captain Zholin snapped to attention to speak, and then relaxed slightly as the others stared at him in amusement. "Where did you find this data, Commander Engels?"

"On the base commander's private server. It appears he was killed by Sachsens before he could initiate a core wipe."

"There you have it. The base commander was the senior military officer in the system. It's standard protocol for top-secret data to be sent to him, but no one else. As Sergeant Ritter pointed out, this was a Black Swan event. The bureaucracy could not conceive of losing the fortress before its data drives were burned."

"So…" said Loco in his usual needling tone, "why didn't the duty officer—what was her name? Jimson? Why didn't *she* wipe their core? It must have been on her checklist."

Zholin presented a rare smile. "I asked her, once I convinced her to defect to us," he replied. "She said while the fight was going on and she expected the Mutuality forces to win, she was afraid her superiors would be angry if she did. Once we'd won, she thought *we* might be angry."

Loco's jaw dropped, and he let his tilted chair fall forward with a *clunk*. "She was afraid the *enemy* would be angry if she did her duty?"

Straker spoke up. "She was just a subaltern. Like an ensign, right?"

"Yes," said Zholin.

"That's the problem with the Mutuality," Straker said. "Total psychological submission. It's just like in those prisoner-of-war exercises we did as cadets, Loco. Some people, especially the young, see their captors as the new, legitimate authority in their lives, and so they submit. Sounds crazy, but it's been proven to happen over and over. She was merely looking ahead to us being in charge. Probably afraid we'd torture her out of spite, just like the Mutuality would."

"Stockholm Syndrome," said Aldrik Ritter with a lift of his red-bearded chin. "That's what we call it. But we Sachsens do not take part in it. We are fighters. We are a free people, not cowering Mutualist dogs."

Engels shot a glare at Ritter. "Seems like those cowering dogs killed a lot of good Breakers today, and Sachsens as well. Don't blind yourself to what they are just because their system is evil. Some are brave and moral, some are cowardly and corrupt and everything in between. We're here to free them, not to spit on them."

Ritter stood to return Engels' glare, and then turned stiffly away to walk up to Straker. "Commodore, I will be returning to our father's freehold. I will praise the name of the Liberator and encourage our *volk* to join you, but I am the eldest. Our scripture says a man who does not care for his family is worse than a traitor." He held out his hand to clasp with Straker.

Straker grasped the man's palm. "We'll miss you. And remember, we're not staying here. The Mutuality will strike back, in force."

"We'll be ready for them. Not like three years ago, when they came under a flag of parlay and stabbed us in the back. Conrad will stay with you to uphold our honor." He leaned in to speak in Straker's ear. "I suggest you promote him. He will need rank to deal with the proud and the stubborn among my people... and they will not care to take orders from your woman."

Straker crushed Aldrik's hand until he gasped. "They'll take orders from whoever I damn well say, or they can sit at home like little girls." He let go of the Sachsen's hand, and poked a finger into his chest. "You tell them that. This isn't some pirate gang. It's a military outfit, and I'm in command. They don't have to join, but if they do, they're under my orders. If they don't like that, we'll win this war without them."

"I tell them." Aldrik worked his hand for a moment, and then saluted. "*Heil der Befreier. Mach denen die Hölle heiss.*"

Straker returned the salute. "I hope you didn't just call me an asshole."

"No, *Herr Kommodore*. It means, 'Heat up Hell for them.' "

"I'll do that, Aldrik. Take care of yourself. And your family."

Aldrik Ritter nodded, turned on his heel, and marched out.

Engels mumbled something vile, and Straker warned her with his eyes. "Back to this battleship. Where is she?" he said.

"She could be anywhere," said Engels. "She was being built in the Baikonur system."

Straker gazed longingly at the hologram, rubbing his hands together as if he could seize the thing. "I want her. She's the key to winning. With *Indomitable*, nothing can stand in our way."

"Now I know why they call ships 'she,' boss," said Loco.

"Why's that?"

"Because you're lusting after a new woman."

Engels barked a laugh. "He's not wrong, Derek. I can see it in your eyes. But we don't even know she exists."

"We have to find out. Zaxby, form a team and go through all the databases we've captured—those off the battlecruisers, too. We need more information. Carla, transfer your flag to the lead BC—what's her name?"

"*Wolverine*."

"Right. We'll keep that. Conrad, you're now a lieutenant. Find some insignia somewhere. Recruit Sachsens with ship experience. Work with Engels to form crews for our captured warships—and make sure none of them have problems taking orders from a female fleet commander. Loco, find Aldrik before he leaves and tell him we need a thousand good infantry. Not thugs: soldiers, already in units if possible. You and Heiser get them organized and parceled out. Hop to it, people. I want to leave for Baikonur in thirty-six hours."

Part II: Crusader

Chapter 16

Sachsen Fortress, Command Center

Only six hours after the meeting ended, in the midst of trying to recruit and organize new Breakers to crew the squadron they'd captured, a comtech waved at Straker from her position within the spacious fortress command center. "Sir, I have a message coming in for you."

Straker was still strolling to look over her shoulder when the watchstander at Sensors interrupted, "Sir, multiple inbound sidespace transits detected."

"Tactical. Let's see them."

The holo-table blazed with an oversized representation of the Sachsen system. At least a hundred icons blinked at the edge of flatspace, in optimum positions for approach to Sachsen-3… and the fortress.

Concern gripped Straker's guts. "There's no way enemy reinforcements are here already. Is this a stroke of bad luck? Did a Mutuality fleet just *happen* to get here, right now?"

The comtech had been trying to get his attention. "Sir, the message. It's from those ships."

Straker turned to her. "Play it."

One of the larger vidscreens lit with a picture of a female Ruxin. It began to speak. "Greetings, Liberator! This is Premier Vuxana. By the time this message reaches you, you will be victorious or dead. If you are not dead, I offer ten thousand more trained personnel to refurbish and crew the fortress and any ships you have captured. I also have trade goods to exchange with the people of the Sachsen system. Please respond with affirmation of your status."

Straker turned away from the vidscreen, thinking. "Contact Zaxby. If he's still aboard the fortress, tell him to get his rubbery ass here ASAP. If not, get me a good secure comlink."

A pause. "He's on his way, sir."

A moment later Zaxby entered the command center. "I am very busy carrying out your previous instructions, Commodore. What's this about?"

Straker gestured at the screen. "Play it again." Once Zaxby had viewed the message, Straker raised his eyebrows. "Well?"

"Are you asking the meaning of the Premier's message? It seems straightforward enough. She's here to help."

"Really? The Premier? She's left three million Ruxins behind shortly after she inherited the title, and without telling me her plans, shows up here with ten thousand Ruxins to 'help.' What's her game?"

Zaxby's eyes crossed briefly, and he sidled over to an empty console. "I am not sure what to tell you."

"You don't know what's going on?"

"I did not misspeak. I am not certain how much I should tell you, especially as it's mostly conjecture."

Straker bit back his temper. "Look, I asked you here to give me insight into this situation. You're Ruxin, but you've lived with humans for decades. So, speculate."

Zaxby tapped at the console aimlessly, as if still uncertain. "Frankly, Commodore, I am not sure where my loyalties should lie."

"Should lie, or do?"

Zaxby straightened. "Should. I endeavor to act ethically in all situations."

"Oh, like when you proposed euthanizing a bunch of refugees?"

"I did not say my ethics are human."

"Or humane."

"You have killed many humans, Commodore Straker. The fact that we disagree about whom should be killed and when only makes us more alike than you seem to believe."

Straker took a deep breath. There was no point in arguing with a brainiac on the finer points of morality. He had to stick to simple, straightforward things. "Let me help you decide, then. You're under my command. I gave you your rank, and you accepted it. As long as I'm not directly damaging your people, you need to help me reach our common goals, and that means helping me figure out what the hell Vuxana is up to. So, *speculate.*"

"Awkwardly put, but I accept your reasoning. I believe she is 'keeping her hand in,' you would say. By offering you much-needed personnel, she maintains influence on what you do, and creates political capital."

"Political capital?"

Zaxby continued to play restlessly with the console. "Yes. In simple terms, you will 'owe her.' Or so she hopes."

"But why come personally?"

"I suspect it is to forge political ties with Sachsen and to bring back a hundred ships bursting with trade goods, so she can distribute them to her allies and friends in order to solidify her support."

"Support? So she has opposition back home?"

Zaxby opened his eyes wide and tilted his head forward. If he were human, this would be a look of mild disbelief. "All politicians generate opposition. It is in their nature. And all societies generate politicians. She's the designated heir to the Premiership, but she is young, and her mother is aging. I believe this is a calculated risk, and she hopes she can count on you to support her in case of future difficulty. In short, she has thrown her lot in with you. I suggest you do not undercut her."

Straker paced, rubbing the back of his head where a headache had sprung into being. *Politics*, he thought. *What a pain in the ass*. Nobody in absolute command, everybody deciding individually whether to follow orders. He couldn't imagine a life lived like that.

"All right. I'll cooperate with her. But Zaxby… if you sense anything off, if you think she's going to backstab me, you'll tell me, right?"

"I will not allow either of you to betray the other, but I do not think she shall. At worst, she will do what all politicians do: push her advantages to help her constituency."

"Meaning Ruxins."

"Just so."

"I'll keep that in mind. Thanks, Zaxby."

"You are welcome. Would you like me to relay a response?"

"Sure. Tell her to come on in, and since you're here, you can assign her Ruxin reinforcements as crew where they're needed. And put her in touch with the right Sachsens to do her trading."

Zaxby brightened. "That will be an interesting challenge. Thank you, sir."

"Glad to dump the work on you."

"Did you know that in Ruxin, the word for 'work' and the word for 'fun' is the same? You humans are odd in thinking they are different things."

"I don't think we're all that different. Nobody's forcing the Breakers to work on liberating the galaxy. Any of us could opt out and hide."

"And yet you have delineated 'duty time' and 'time off.' If you were truly mature, responsible creatures, nobody would have to mandate when you work and when you relax."

Straker shrugged and half-smiled. "That's a discussion for our time off. You're on duty, so get to work."

* * *

On schedule, thirty hours later, the Breakers fleet transited into sidespace for Baikonur. Straker felt proud, and frankly, amazed at the size of his force. Where he once believed himself fortunate to command a handful of warships, now he had twenty-one, plus an auxiliary squadron of eight Ruxin transports and captain Gibson's *Lockstep*, which had joined them as planned.

Thanks to capturing the Sachsen fortress nearly whole, all the ships were fully supplied with everything from fuel to shipkiller missiles. They were also fully crewed with a mix of original Breakers, Ruxin technicians, and volunteer Sachsens.

The Sachsens had also provided units of infantry. He couldn't exactly call them companies or platoons; each varied in size, depending on the freehold that sent them. They also varied in weaponry and equipment. Some had only old slugthrowers that soldiers from the Old Earth of eight hundred years ago would have recognized, and some had body armor and lasers or blasters.

One group of twenty-five had even arrived with modern, if fancifully decorated, battlesuits that they must have hidden from their occupiers, and was commanded by one Major Friedrich Wagner, the eldest son of a Sachsen nobleman.

Straker let Wagner keep his title of rank, and promoted Loco to Commander in charge of the ground units, now that there were so many. He also made sure that Wagner's battlesuiters were berthed aboard *Wolverine*. From what Sergeant Ritter had said, these Sachsen nobles were proud, prickly men, and needed a firm hand.

In fact, now that his flagship was in sidespace for the next few days, it was time to have his first real chat with the man.

Straker pecked Carla on the lips as he left the *Wolverine's* bridge, receiving a smile in return. Once, he'd never have considered such a public display of affection, but she'd convinced him it was a good idea. The Breakers and the Galactic Liberation movement, no longer completely synonymous, had to have symbols at the top, and the couple's obvious affection for each other strengthened their mystique.

Fortunately, that affection seemed on firmer ground now that Tachina had been left behind on Freiheit. As Straker headed for the battlecruiser's flight deck, the largest interior space on the ship, he reminded himself of a saying from his Kung-Jiu instructor at Academy: *it is not the mountain that defeats you, but the rock in your shoe.*

"Major Wagner," Straker said as he strode up to the short, dour man dressed in jet-black creased trousers and an ornate dress military jacket, large fringed epaulets making his shoulders seem oddly broad. He made sure to pronounce the man's name as the Sachsens did, *vagh-nair.*

"*Herr Kommodore,*" Wagner said, snapping a sharp salute. His men leaped to their feet and stood at attention.

Straker returned the salute more casually. "At ease." He held out his hand.

After hesitating, Wagner took it, squeezing it over-hard, as if testing his new commander.

Aha, one of those, Straker thought. He smiled and clamped down, but carefully, until Wagner's eyes widened as his bones began to creak. Straker's biotech-induced strength hadn't faded, especially as he made sure to keep up his weight-training regimen.

Straker let go. "You're settling in all right, Major?"

Wagner turned to run his eyes over the cots where his men bedded down, each one's battlesuit standing at the head of his bunk. "Frankly, no, sir. These quarters are unsuitable for elite soldiers of our rank and status. Considering we are assigned to your flagship, I had hoped for better."

Straker noted the man's stiff, sour expression. "We're full to bursting with crew and troops, Major. If you had cabins or even bunk bays, there wouldn't be room for your battlesuits, and I understood you refuse to put them in crates."

"No knight leaves his armor in a box, Commodore."

"Then you've made your own bed, and now you must lie in it, Major. You're a soldier on field campaign, so you'll have to suck it up. And, as soon as we win our first battle, there will probably be some extra room—unless we fill it with coffins." He raised his eyebrows. "Any more complaints?"

Straker put steel into his question, and anyone else might have picked up on his disapproval of Wagner's fussiness, but the man seemed oblivious. "Yes, sir. These creatures… do they really have to be quartered here?" Wagner jerked his head in the direction of a group of octopoids on the far side of the flight deck.

"They're our allies, Major Wagner. Get used to it. I wouldn't have thought such noble Sachsens would be thrown off by the presence of a few aliens, hmm?"

Wagner reddened. "I know Ruxins make good technicians, but these have weapons and armor. I was given to understand we would have the glory of the assault."

Straker was tempted to mock the odd little martinet, but reminded himself that the man came from a semi-feudal society, where—unlike the consolidated Sachsen Free Navy—the vast majority of soldiers were household troops like these, not professional soldiers. "I promise you'll have first crack at any glory, Major Wagner. Beyond that, I expect you to remember we're all in this together, under my command, and you volunteered. The time to back out is past. You don't get to pick and choose your missions or your brothers in arms—or tentacles. Understood?"

"*Alles klar, Herr Kommodore.*" Wagner saluted once more, and then turned pointedly on his heel to return to his men, nearly a snub.

Straker hoped the man would get with the program over the next week of travel. Sidespace travel was inherently boring. A crowded ship and an egotistical subordinate didn't bode well. He would have to give everyone something to do.

He walked across the flight deck toward the Ruxins, who were performing maintenance on their gear and weaponry. Vuxana had said she was providing a War Male and a number of warrior males for the first time, but he'd not had the chance to introduce himself, putting that task off until sidespace transit. Loco's report on these Ruxin fighters had been less than enlightening as well.

As Straker approached, one huge, royal-blue specimen detached himself from the group and locomoted rapidly to greet him, holding an ornately carved and decorated spear. "Come no farther, human!" he boomed in passable Earthan.

Straker realized he'd made a tactical error. He should have donned his Battle Male suit and carried his bone spear for this meeting. He couldn't really blame the Battle Male; Vuxana said he'd been revived from cryo-sleep only recently, and had been given a crash course in human language and customs.

Not only that, the Battle Male's last memories had been of fighting Mutuality naval forces eighty years ago, and would no doubt have a lingering impression of humans as natural enemies of his people.

So, should he retreat to retrieve his panoply and return, or should he challenge the War Male immediately? There was always a fine line between establishing respect and creating embarrassment in a new subordinate.

Straker chose to deal with the situation right now, especially as the surly Sachsen battlesuiters were watching from across the deck. He took out his slugthrower pistol and held it by the barrel, like a warhammer rather than a firearm, and waved it, raising both arms. "I am your commander. I am War Male Straker," he bellowed in return. "You will greet me properly."

The huge Ruxin regarded him solemnly with two eyes, the other two maintaining vigilance in other directions. After a long moment's pause, the creature spoke. "I am War Male Kraxor. Hail, War Male Straker." He lifted his spear to touch his head in imitation of a human salute.

Straker did the same with his pistol, pleased that the War Male was not such a blowhard as he'd seemed at first. Straker kept his verbiage simple, not knowing how well the Ruxin spoke Earthan. "Hail, War Male Kraxor. You are well? You have all you need?"

"All except combat, we have," Kraxor replied. "But I lack one thing. I am a commander of ships and of hundreds, Commodore Straker. My rank is like your Major of troops, but I am told you bestow no such rank. Yet, I hear the small human battlesuiter holds this rank, while Commander Paloco assigns me the rank of Lieutenant. Explain this."

Rumors travel quickly, always about the little things, Straker thought. *The rocks in my shoes. Best to clean them out right away.* "I declare you both to be majors. Happy?"

"Better. Who is greater?"

"Senior, you mean?" Straker rubbed his jaw and thought of politics, and who was easier to read, and to understand—and to enforce his will upon, if it came to that. "You are. Technically. But you will need to work with Major Wagner, not fight with him. I don't need two over-proud officers butting heads. Clashing wills, that is. Understand?"

"I understand. The wise shark challenges not his equal for territory, or both may die in the fight."

Straker liked this War Male and his way of thinking, so different from Wagner's. Kraxor wanted to know his place, but now that he did, seemed content to occupy it—although the Ruxin might be hiding his true intentions.

Still, Straker had Vuxana's backing and assurances her warriors would follow his orders. He holstered his pistol and held out his hand. "I think we'll get along, Major Kraxor."

Kraxor wrapped one massive tentacle around Straker's hand and forearm, and gripped, clearly expecting to be the stronger. The surprise he saw in Kraxor's eyes was all the more satisfying as Straker squeezed hard enough to bruise a human hand.

"I believe the same, Commodore Straker," Kraxor replied, releasing his grip. "I know that human War Males grow only slightly larger than others of your species, but it is good to know they do gain strength from their role. That is proper."

"It is proper," Straker said, not bothering to correct or explain the nuances of human biology—or his biotech. "Report to Commander Paloco for all routine matters, but as the senior Ruxin warrior here, feel free to come directly to me if you must."

"I understand." Kraxor saluted again.

Straker returned it. "Dismissed."

As he walked away, he mused that a commander's job multiplied in complexity the more subordinates he had, especially the varied group in this task force. And he couldn't simply promote Breakers to officer positions; there weren't enough soldiers accustomed to being in charge of more than a squad. He had to make this crazy bunch work together somehow.

Once they reached Baikonur, he suspected things would shake themselves out in the stress of operations and combat. It was the intervening days of sidespace travel, when the ship became the entirety of the world, which could prove troublesome.

So he looked for Loco. He found him talking to Heiser in the wardroom.

Chapter 16

"Hey, boss," said Loco as Straker entered.

Heiser nodded from his seat. "Sir."

"Have you met our Sachsen ground contingent?" Straker asked as he grabbed some caff and sat at their table.

"Major Wagner?" Heiser allowed a slight sneer to break through. "He chewed me out for not speaking his language. I guess my name is German or something, from way back."

"Other than that, what do you make of them?"

Heiser shrugged. "I watched them training before we left. They know how to use their suits. Their weapons are overpowered and awkward. I think they measure themselves by how big a gun they have, but they're crack shots. If you keep that in mind, you should be able to employ them effectively. But sir…"

"Go on. Spit it out."

"If you insist." Heiser shook his head. "Pissing on the people below you for no reason is the mark of a bad officer. He doesn't respect noncoms, even senior ones. He probably won't take orders from anyone but you two, and maybe Commander Engels, and he's likely to question anything I relay to him in your name."

"We'll be sure to synch comlinks so my orders reach him clearly," Straker said, stroking his chin. "Thanks, Spear. Have you dealt with the Ruxin warriors?"

"No, sir. Stayed away, figured that's your job until you tell me different."

"I actually found their commander, Major Kraxor, to be more reasonable than Wagner. I do recommend you approach him with a weapon in your hand, so he sees you as a fellow warrior male."

"Got it, sir."

"Loco?"

Loco nodded. "What the Spear said. I think as long as we use Wagner properly, he'll be valuable. I did talk with Kraxor for a while, helping him with his Earthan. I actually like the guy. I think he's smarter than he lets on."

"Like you?"

"Gee, boss…"

"Don't get a big head." Straker sat back and sipped his caff. "I know it's a pain in the ass, and it's rewarding the squeaky wheel, but I want you to find

Wagner and his men some quarters away from the Ruxins, even if you have to displace crew to do it. Something you can plausibly say is better—more privacy at least. Maybe just stick them in a cargo bay?"

"You're gonna reward his assholishness?"

"Yeah, it's a compromise, but I'm keeping the peace. Schedule some combined assault exercises, though—Breakers, Sachsens, Ruxins. They don't get a pass on working together, just living together—for now. Maybe we can develop some respect among them. Nothing like shared danger to get rid of the stupids. And Loco…"

"Yeah?"

"Work them hard. Work the living shit out of them. You too, Spear. I want them too tired to start trouble, and I want them hating you guys and loving me, because I'm the one that'll show up and tell them when the duty day is done, and who'll tell them they can open those barrels full of tasty Sachsen beer."

Heiser and Loco exchanged evil grins.

Chapter 17

Liberation Battlecruiser *Wolverine*, approaching Baikonur System in sidespace

Straker's plan worked, Captain Engels mused as she headed for *Wolverine's* bridge. Wagner and his prickly Sachsens had been moved to a corner of a cargo bay where they could feel special and polish their armor out of sight of nasty rubbery Ruxins. Combined exercises had gained each contingent grudging respect for the others' skills. The peace had been kept, for now.

She'd been particularly impressed with the Ruxin warrior males. Without the augmented strength of battlesuits, they were still able to carry either one oversized or two standard infantry weapons. Apparently their large brains and multiple eyes also allowed them to accurately aim at two targets at once, making them into the equivalent of two soldiers.

But the ground-pounders and their training were more of a diversion than a duty for her. She'd spent the majority of her time drilling her mixed crew of Ruxin neuters and Sachsen citizen-sailors, with only a handful of loyal Breakers to leaven the mix and hold it together.

The Ruxin neuters Vuxana had supplied were compliant and competent, but lacked experience and initiative. They reminded her of a bunch of earnest teenage Academy cadets.

The Sachsens were mostly civilians before joining the Galactic Liberation, many of them highly seasoned ship jocks, wrench-turners and rock monkeys—which made them the mirror images of the Ruxins: too much experience and initiative, inclined to follow orders only when they felt like it. There'd been frequent throwdowns and fistfights, and she'd kept Lieutenant Ritter and Chief Gurung busy mediating disputes and knocking heads. The diminutive Gurkha had turned out to be a veteran at hand-to-hand, his rock-hard muscles matched by his fixed smile as he made short work of anyone who dared take a swing at him.

But the eight days of drill and training had started to pay off. No crew could jell completely in such a short time, but the worst seemed behind her now, and she felt the battlecruiser *Wolverine* would now perform creditably in a fight.

And what a ship she was! The largest Engels had ever served aboard, much less commanded. She still felt a thrill as she took her place in the captain's chair, surrounded on all sides by her bridge officers and specialists. She missed the hands-on controls of *Liberator's* helm, but she was the skipper now, not the pilot.

"All stations report," she said crisply.

"Helm aye."

"Sensors aye."

"Beams aye." *Wolverine's* direct fire weapons were all beams, which simplified things, though that meant she lacked railguns, useful for certain purposes.

"Missiles, all ready except number three missile tube." Despite the best efforts of Ruxins and Sachsens, that launcher kept failing.

"It's empty?" she asked.

"Yes, ma'am."

"Leave it. Shut the outer doors and take it offline."

"Aye aye, ma'am."

"Continue report."

"Comms aye."

"Engineering aye."

"Security aye."

"Damage control aye," said Chief Gurung.

"The grunts are asleep on their bunks, dreaming of expensive whiskey and cheap whores," said Loco. "Or is that vice versa?"

Engels shot him a withering look. "Thank you for that, Commander Paloco."

She turned to Straker, who was standing behind her, staring at the empty main holoscreen as if it held the secrets of the universe. "We're ready. Transition to normal space in ten minutes, as you can see." She gestured at the chrono ticking down toward zero.

"Thank you, Captain Engels. Carry on."

The main bridge pressure door swung open suddenly to reveal Major Wagner. "I insist on being present at transition," he snapped.

Engels exchanged amused glances with Straker. "By all means, Major. Permission to enter granted. Just stay out of the way."

Wagner let out a huff, and then moved to stand next to Straker. His lip curled when the pressure door opened again to reveal Major Kraxor.

"Come on in, Major Kraxor," said Loco with a sweeping gesture. "The gang's all here."

"Indeed." The huge Ruxin flowed in to stand alongside Straker, on the other side from Wagner.

Engels turned her back on the tableau with an internal cringe and reminded herself how glad she was Straker and Loco were dealing with the egotistical ground-pounders. She much preferred the clean complexity of naval operations, though warships had their personalities as well.

The minutes turned to seconds, until the chrono nulled. "Transition," said the helmsman. "Clear ahead."

"Steady as she goes," said Engels. It was critical that she not maneuver until the rest of the fleet transited, in order to minimize the chance of collision. Ships should arrive spaced out over time and distance, but sometimes even the best plan went awry.

This far out in flatspace from Baikonur's primary, though, there should be nothing but other ships to hit. She'd chosen a third-order suboptimal exit point, far from the best spots, the ones most likely to be mined or guarded. For even more safety, and for good reconnaissance, they'd arrived far above the system's plane of the ecliptic, looking "down" on the orbits of its planets and asteroids, and as close in to its binary center as possible.

"Collating data now," said the officer at Sensors. "It's coming through."

The big main holoscreen, and the holo-table in the center of the bridge, simultaneously began to populate, first showing one large white star circled by a partner too small and dim to be called a sun.

"That's the neutron star?" asked Straker.

"Correct, sir. Presumably it was captured by the white giant, rather than developing alongside it, as the two stars' stellar age is quite different," said the Ruxin Sensors officer, Tixban. "It is also skimming off mass from the primary, and is therefore gaining angular momentum such that–"

"Thanks, Tixban. We need intelligence about enemy forces and dispositions before we start a scientific survey," Engels said.

"Of course, ma'am. But the data will become available roughly in order of mass and emissions luminosity of the objects detected—stars, planets, and so on down."

"Okay, we wait." Engels put her chin on her fist, her elbow on the arm of the captain's chair.

The next objects to appear and be identified were planets—outer gas giants, inner rocky worlds, both kinds farther out than in typically life-bearing star systems—for this was clearly not one of those. Neither white giants nor neutron stars were conducive to Earthlike planets.

When the moons of the gas giants appeared, one brightened as the algorithm controlling the sensors computer zeroed in. Strong radio signals emanated from it, most encrypted.

"Looks like a base. Probably the main one," said Straker. "Any other major signal sources?"

"We must let the computer do its work," said Tixban.

Straker growled in frustration.

"Helm, what about our other ships?" Engels said, more to distract Straker than anything.

"*Badger, Sable,* and *Ermine* have arrived, with wide separation. They're maneuvering to join us. The rest should transit in order of size, as planned."

More icons appeared, and tabular data began to fill the smaller visiplates of the bridge officers. "I have located a habitat," said Tixban.

That icon blinked among a dense asteroid belt within the orbit of the innermost rocky planet—which was nevertheless farther out than most Earthlike worlds were from their stars. The size and heat of the white giant and the intermittent gravitic effects of the neutron star must have ripped apart one or more of the nearer planets, creating this debris field.

"How soon until they see us?" asked Straker.

"Two hours, give or take, for that small habitat," said Engels, instinctively doing the math in her head. "They'll get our IFF signatures about the same time, telling them how we're all good little Mutuality buddies. Then it'll take a slightly shorter time for us to see how they react, or receive any messages. At normal acceleration we could reach the habitat in about twenty hours, the big base in about forty."

Straker stepped forward to stare closely at the holo-table, which was still populating with moons, asteroids and man-made objects. "I don't see anything else in this system except a few robotic asteroid mines and a refueling station. Let's start heading for that habitat," he said.

Engels nodded. "Helm, set course for the hab, half acceleration. Pass to the fleet to form on us as we go, no hard maneuvering. We're friendlies, remember? Just one big happy Mutuality."

"Can we refine the data on that hab? Deploy a recon drone or something?" asked Straker.

Engels cocked her head. "We could, but why would a friendly task force send a recon drone ahead of them?"

"You're right." Straker paced slowly around the holo-table. "I really need to take a look at that... habitat."

"You're talking like there's something unusual about it," said Engels.

"There is," announced Tixban. "It is composed of processed alloys rather than asteroidal material, and its power emanations are extremely high for a habitat. Additionally, it's not rotating. These factors are more congruent with a mobile fortress than a habitat."

"Mobile fortress." Straker smiled at Engels through the hologram. "Or maybe a ship?"

"If it is a ship, it is only for in-system use, as it is far too massive to transit into sidespace," said Tixban.

"About sixteen times as massive?" Engels said, nodding at Straker.

"Yes... almost precisely." Tixban squirmed, confused. "How did you know?"

Straker nodded back at Engels, and then glanced at Tixban. "You haven't been fully briefed. Now that we're here, pass the word to all ships to access the *Indomitable* file. Majors," he turned to Kraxor and Wagner, "your companies will prepare to seize our new battleship. You'll be the tip of the spear. The rest of our various ground elements will follow up, and then our designated prize crew."

Wagner snapped a salute. "My Sachsens shall lead!"

"Of course." Straker suppressed a roll of his eyes and checked his chrono. "Assault brief will begin two hours from our arrival. Until then, we'll gather data, try to see what we're dealing with here. Everything depends on *Indomitable* remaining unaware of our true intentions. If they become suspicious or, Creator help us, go to battle stations and start shooting…"

"It will spell disaster," said Major Wagner. "Commodore, you must do all in your power to get us aboard. If you do, we—and our new allies, of course—will take the ship for you."

Straker pointed at Engels. "I'm just overseeing the op, Major. Commander Engels is the one that's going to sneak us in close enough to do it."

After hesitating, Wagner turned toward Engels, clicked his heels together and gave a slight bow. "My lady."

Despite herself, Engels felt the corners of her mouth rise. If Sir Wagner had to turn her into an aristocrat in order to acknowledge her authority, so be it.

✳ ✳ ✳

"It only has a skeleton crew?" said Derek eight hours later as he pulled on his pants. He'd been catching some shuteye in the flag officer's stateroom while waiting for Captain Zholin, dressed as a Mutuality admiral, to exchange messages with the "station."

Carla nodded. "*She*, Derek. Confirmed as *Indomitable*. Yes, it looks like she has only a skeleton crew. Zholin's been careful in asking questions so as not to seem uninformed, but he's learned the ship isn't fully operational. She's been turned into a test bed for weapons. Most of the personnel aboard are civilians—technicians, engineers, scientists. There isn't even a military captain."

Derek stared past her, thinking as he dressed. "So, good news and bad news. Good, in that seizing her should be easy. Bad, in that she's not ready to fight."

"Worse than that," said Carla. "If this expensive fleet asset has been sitting out here for years while a war's raging, there must be some serious flaw. Something that makes her nearly useless. Derek…" She stepped closer to button up his tunic, "this may all be a wild goose chase."

He let her finish, and then kissed her gently. "If so, it's been our Pascal's Wager. We gambled for a big win and lost a few days. We'll go on to Plan B, start liberating vulnerable systems with the fleet we have while playing cat and mouse with the Mutuality heavies they'll send after us. But I'm not ready to throw in the towel yet. Even if there are problems with *Indomitable*, we're here now. We might as well try to hijack her. If we can, she ought to give the Mutuality fits just worrying about what we'll do."

"I don't disagree. It's just that…"

"Go on."

Carla stroked his short hair. "Right now it seems like you're on a gambler's high. The more you win, the more you crave winning, but you can't win all the time."

"I can't? Why not? This isn't a casino, where the odds always catch up to you. This is real life. Plenty of commanders throughout history never lost a major battle."

"Plenty of them lost one final battle after a long winning streak, too." She stepped away. "Or even if they win, everybody dies along the way."

Derek strapped on his pistol belt. "You're not backing out now, are you? Before we even roll the dice?"

"Of course not. I'm your woman, Derek. I'm with you no matter what. But I'm also your second-in-command, which means it's my job to push back… in private, at least."

"I know. Thanks. I'll keep it in mind. Have *Lockstep* dock with us, will you?"

Carla's brows narrowed. "Sure. Why?"

"I want to talk with the Lazarus clone. Gibson has him aboard."

"You brought him *here?*"

"He's of no use to me sitting on Freiheit. I need to pick his brain for details about the Mutuality, things that a mere ship captain like Zholin wouldn't know. Like *Indomitable.*"

"I can see that. Just…"

Derek put his hands on his hips. "What? You think I can't handle him?"

"I think you underestimate him. You're not stupid, Derek, but admit it—neither of us is as clever as a Lazarus. He's spent a lifetime lying and manipulating people. I get the feeling even when he's telling the truth, he's shading it for his own purposes."

"I'll keep that in mind too. I'll take Loco. He's cynical and good at reading people."

Carla sighed and stepped forward to hug him once more, and then let go. "Good. I'll pass the word.

Fifteen minutes later, Straker and Loco boarded the docked *Lockstep*. Captain Gibson escorted them toward the brig he'd made of a cargo module.

On the way there, a door opened suddenly in front of Straker, and Tachina stepped out, clad in a coverall that fit her like a second skin, displaying every curve and detail of her voluptuous body. Its zipper had been lowered to her navel, showing off deep cleavage uninterrupted by anything but toned skin.

"Hello, Derek," she breathed, batting her long lashes.

Her perfume hit him like a sledgehammer as he was caught completely off guard. He stopped and froze, his throat closing.

Why they hell does she have this effect on me? He felt like thirteen again, back at Academy getting a teenage hard-on every time he was alone with Carla. "Uh…"

"Get back in your cabin, whore," snarled Gibson. "I'm sorry, Commodore. She stowed away when we left Freiheit, and I didn't want to turn her loose on Sachsen."

"You mean you couldn't stand to see me go, Wilmer," she replied.

"Wilmer?" Loco chuckled from behind the other two. "Sorry, Captain—my mom named me funny, too." He sidled around Straker in the passageway to step up to Tachina. "Come on, cougar-woman. Back to your lair." He grabbed her waist with his right hand and her right hand in his left, as if to dance, and walked her in reverse through her cabin door.

"Great Cosmos," breathed Straker. "I wish you *had* left her on Sachsen."

"I should have warned you, sir. Sorry about that," said Gibson.

Straker waved vaguely at him. "Never mind. Let's go see the Lazarus."

"I'll catch up, boss," called Loco from the doorway.

Straker, still mentally stunned, let Loco handle the situation. As he walked toward his conversation with the former Inquisitor, he set his mind in order, trying to drive out Tachina's scent by reviewing notes on his handtab screen.

"Come in with me, Gibson," he said at the door to the cell. "Also, can you record everything that's said?"

"Of course, Commodore." Gibson used the intercom to pass that order to his comtech, and then he opened the door with a keycode.

Inside, the Lazarus stood from his bunk and folded his hands in front of him. He looked fit and healthy. "Greetings, Commodore Straker. Or should I call you 'Liberator'?"

"Don't start your games with me again, clone, unless you want to be put in solitary."

The Lazarus bowed his head. "My apologies. I was merely making conversation. You appear agitated, even though I hear you've won a great victory. How may I be of assistance?"

"Sit." Straker gestured at the bunk, taking the single chair for himself. Gibson stood behind him, wary. But Straker wasn't worried about a physical attack. Dealing with an Inquisitor was a struggle of minds.

The Lazarus sat, waiting calmly for Straker to speak.

"Tell me about Project Starkiller."

The Inquisitor lifted his eyebrows. "Starkiller... I heard only a little. A super-ship, modular in order to be able to transit through sidespace and reassemble upon arrival."

"I know all that. Tell me about the program, and why it never became operational."

"As I recall, it was a pet project of a former Director of the Central Committee. He touted it as a silver bullet, a weapon that would change the course of the war. In fact, he staked his directorship on it, pardon the pun."

"What happened?"

"He was ousted when the program's delays and cost overruns turned the consensus against him. The Mutuality experienced a run of defeats at that time, and the Committee became convinced that, had Starkiller's resources been put into building more capital ships, those defeats would not have happened."

"Was that true?"

The Lazarus shrugged. "I suspect so, but I can't be sure. I was not privy to grand strategy or the details of our orders of battle, but more superdreadnoughts—call it twenty or thirty, for the cost of the program— would have been significant."

"What happened to the super-ship? The *Indomitable*?"

"There was talk of dismantling it, but the head scientist at Baikonur convinced the Committee that to do so would be to abandon all benefits from the investment. Instead, I believe they kept it as a test bed for weapons development, and the Committee has forgotten about it. They do not like to dwell on failure, especially failure of their own making."

Straker grunted in acknowledgement. "One reason why leadership by committee is an oxymoron."

"On the other hand, committees—oligarchies, really—do keep things stable, and make dictatorships less likely. That's why both the Mutuality and the Hundred Worlds are ruled by them."

"The Hundred Worlds isn't ruled by an oligarchy. It's ruled by a Prime Minister and by the elected Planetary Parliament."

Lazarus smiled faintly. "Your parliamentarians have no term limits, and thus accrete so much power and wealth by their backroom dealings that they seldom lose their seats before retirement. If they do, they're only dislodged by candidates that are similarly well connected and well funded. This means that nothing really changes. And they choose the Prime Minister. Is that not an oligarchy?"

"At least it's a better system than yours!"

"For whom? Our oligarchy is composed of lifetime Party members with access to the coffers of the State. Your oligarchy is composed of those who sell themselves to the wealthy conglomerates who profit from war and exploitation. The structures may be different, but the effect is the same: the elites rule, and reap the rewards for rulership. As I've told you, the difference is simply in our honesty. We do not lie to the people by telling them their votes and their elections matter. We tell them the proper path for the ambitious is through public service within the Mutualist Party and the State—which are the same thing."

"So honest misery is better than dishonest happiness." Straker stood and began to pace. Doing so always helped to clear his head. He wasn't sure what the flaw in the Lazarus' argument was, but it had to be there.

Or maybe it really didn't matter. Trying to figure his way through the Inquisitor's bullshit was playing the Lazarus's game instead of Straker's. Better to sidestep it. "I know the Hundred Worlds is better than the Mutuality, but it isn't my home anymore. I'm trying to create something better than either, so quit wasting your breath justifying your version of corruption."

The Lazarus spread his hands. "I am at your service, Liberator."

"Tell me more about Baikonur. We've seen one big base on a moon, with the usual defenses, and the *Indomitable* ship. Is there anything else we should know? Anything you need to tell us to avoid casualties on either side?"

The Lazarus wrapped his fingers around one knee. "Casualties from an attack? I know only what little I've heard from the guards here, who have proven less than talkative."

"We're seizing *Indomitable*."

"Of course, of course. You hope to add it to your forces. But it's an albatross, Commodore."

"What's an albatross?"

"It's a beloved sea bird of Old Earth. If a sailor killed one, it was thought to be bad luck. In the tales, he would be forced to wear the dead bird around his neck as a mark of shame. Thus, an albatross is a metaphor for a possession that does you more harm than good, something you would be better rid of."

"We'll see. It wasn't me that killed the albatross, and I might be able to bring it back to life."

"Forgive me if I do not wish you good luck in attacking my people."

"Yeah, whatever. See you next time." Straker rose to leave.

"*Adieu.*"

"Odd you? You're pretty odd yourself."

The Lazarus didn't roll his eyes, or even put a sarcastic tone into his voice, but Straker nevertheless thought the man was laughing at him. "It means 'until later' in the French language."

Straker dredged up something from what he knew about France: Napoleon. "Long live the Emperor." He slammed the door on his way out, the only expression of irritation he allowed himself. He knew he was no brainiac, but he also knew he was smarter than these snooty intellectuals gave him credit for.

Yet, they—as far back as his sister Mara and his classmate Nancy Sinden, through Zaxby, General DeChang, this Lazarus—constantly tried to cut him down with their clever references and their inside jokes. He knew he shouldn't let them get to him, but he couldn't help it. He wanted to smash that lurking smirk off the Lazarus's face.

But I'm better than that, he told himself. *I'm the Liberator. I have to set a good example. I wish I could be like Loco, doing whatever I want, mouthing off whenever I want, but Loco couldn't hold his forces together. Only I can do that.*

"He's infuriating, isn't he?" said Gibson. The pudgy older man laid a hand on Straker's shoulder. "Are you sure he's worth keeping, son?"

"Yes, I am. And I appreciate you playing jailor. You need anything?"

"Since you asked… Tachina is more trouble than the Inquisitor. She keeps trying to sneak in to see him. I'm also having difficulty keeping the infantry away from her, and vice versa."

Straker was about to scoff at Gibson's claim until he remembered her effect on him. There was something about the concubine that made her nearly irresistible—and bored soldiers wouldn't even bother resisting. In the tradition of troops through all time, they'd try to find a way to hook up with her—and had probably already succeeded behind Gibson's back.

"All right. I'll have Loco take her off your hands. Nobody knows women like he does."

"Thank you, sir." Gibson's words were heartfelt.

"Where is Loco anyway?"

Loco waved as he came around a corner. "Here, boss."

"Get Tachina and her stuff. She's coming with us."

"Too late. She already came with me." Loco smirked.

"What?"

"Never mind. I'll get her. Go on ahead, I'll catch up."

"All right." Straker shook Gibson's hand, putting Tachina out of his mind as a pointless distraction. "Good to see you again, Captain."

"Same here, sir. *Lockstep* will always be at your service."

When Straker crossed back onto *Wolverine*, he felt better than he had in a while, and his thoughts raced with plans for his new battleship, *Indomitable*.

Chapter 18

Baikonur System: Battleship *Indomitable*

The takeover of *Indomitable* was an anticlimax. Wagner's battlesuiters and Kraxor's warrior males led the way, and after reporting no resistance, follow-up forces spread throughout the ship. They seized the enormous empty bridge without resistance from scattered engineers and scientists.

"No defending troops at all?" Straker said as he climbed down out of his mechsuit. He'd been prepared to support an attack, even though his Foehammer's armor and systems were spotty. Loco did the same nearby.

"No, Commodore," said Kraxor via Straker's comlink. "Only a few unarmed naval personnel and civilians."

"Assemble everybody on the bridge. I'm on my way."

The first thing he noticed as he came aboard was the ship's armor as he passed through it.

Superdreadnought armor was composed of three meters of overlapping conformal superconductive alloys layered with inert ceramics. When energized by reinforcing fields, it could stop small or glancing nuclear blasts, resist bigger ones, and it took multiple strikes by heavy beams or railgun shells to damage.

Indomitable's protective layer was fully ten times as thick. Thirty-plus meters of high-tech materials, backed by titanic energy generators, would shrug off everything but fortress-level capital weapons or the largest contact nukes.

That is, assuming he could get the ship to function.

Straker's walk to the bridge of the *Indomitable* seemed to take forever, though in reality only about ten minutes passed. That seemed an eternity on a warship. He marveled at its gargantuan dimensions, revealed when he strode through fortress-sized tunnels on the way.

When he entered the bridge, he saw a sea of stained coveralls and grungy lab coats that might have once been white. Older men and women squinted at him in obvious fear or glared with hostility. There were a few younger people, very young, perhaps just out of training.

Only one seemed unbowed: a slim, erect woman who must be pushing the century mark. Unlike many others, her lab coat remained clean and her personal grooming was impeccable.

"You are the one they call the Liberator?" she said as he approached.

"I am," said Straker. "Commodore Derek Straker."

"I demand to know what your intentions are. I will not have my people abused."

"Have they been abused?"

"They've been roughly handled."

"Well, we're at war. Forgive me, you are…?"

"Doctor Marisa Nolan. I'm in charge here."

Straker shook his head slowly. "No, Doctor. I'm in charge here. The battleship *Indomitable* is now property of the Galactic Liberation."

"So you're a pirate. A common thief."

"I'm a conqueror, actually. *Indomitable* is a prize, and you're all prisoners of war. Now you have to decide. Join us and help us put this fantastic ship to use liberating people—or return willingly to your oppression."

Doctor Nolan eyes widened. "You'd let us go?"

"When we depart, you can stay on the base. The People's Mutual Navy will eventually come for you and everyone else that remains. I won't be leaving you any sidespace-capable ships, though."

She licked her thin lips. "Why should we join you?"

Straker smiled, relieved that she wasn't a fanatic—or even a true loyalist. "Because you're sick of being treated like shit by a system that thinks of you as merely a cog in their machine. They've discarded you and your team here, Dr. Nolan. I'm guessing they've forgotten you. How long since you've been allowed to leave, or seen your families? What are your career prospects? This place looks like a combination nursery and old-folks home."

"My career was over due to my age long before I volunteered for this project," Nolan said tartly. "But my people deserve better. What can you do for them?"

"If they join us, they will have purpose—to liberate as many systems of humans and friendly aliens as I can and bring them under my banner."

"What, so you can play dictator?"

"I'm not interested in ruling people, only liberating them. I'm the military commander, but each star system can govern itself. Politics is for politicians. No, scratch that. Politics is for statesmen—and women—in the Liberation. My one goal right now is to pull as many stars away from the Mutuality as I can, perhaps even to bring down the Committee."

"Leaving us prostrate for the Hundred Worlds to conquer."

Straker raised his brows. "That's the first time you said 'us' and identified with the Mutuality. Would the Hundred Worlds really be so bad?"

Nolan's eyes left Straker for the first time, roving over her people and the Breakers guarding them. "It might," she finally said. "You leave us with two poor choices."

"They're all you've got. You have until we reach your base to decide. Breakers, find a place to keep our guests secure."

"Uh... Liberator, sir?" A bearded man with senior engineer's tabs on his coverall stepped forward. "I'm Chief Quade. I'll join you. So will some of my grease monkeys, I think." Others in similar outfits surged forward, giving a ragged cheer. "We ain't got nothin' to lose."

Straker shook the man's callused hand. "Welcome to the Galactic Liberation. Everyone joining us, stay here." He turned to address the crowd. "The rest, those of you who want to be left for the Mutuality, or who aren't sure yet, go with First Sergeant Heiser and his troops. You'll be well treated."

When the loyalists and undecided left, Straker turned to Quade. "All right. Let me introduce you to Zaxby, my chief brainiac. He should be arriving..."

"I am here," said Zaxby, hurrying toward Straker and trying to look in four directions at once. "I am fascinated by the evident technological advancement of this ship. Who came up with the design of the—"

"Zaxby, meet Chief Quade. He'll teach you, the prize crew and your brainiac technicians how to operate the *Indomitable*. Right, Chief?"

"Yes, sir. Much as we can, anyways."

Straker held up a hand to hold Zaxby's torrent of words at bay. "Chief, we can maneuver her at least, right?"

"Yes, sir."

"Can we transit through sidespace?"

Quade pursed his lips. "This monster ain't transited in over a year, but yeah, theoretically. Take a couple days to prep, though."

"Zaxby, take charge. Preparing for sidespace is your top priority. After that, learn to operate systems, identify what works and what doesn't… get her ready for combat."

"Begging your pardon, sir," said Quade. "This girl is pretty temperamental. She's *never* been ready for combat. Her central multi-weapon will fire maybe three shots before it goes out of alignment due to inadequate cooling, which makes the structural stress worse. Her impellers never quite balance, so she usually ends up flying crabwise, which also means they have to be turned off before trying to line up on a target. Her secondaries–"

Zaxby broke in. "I agree. Commodore Straker, this ship cannot soon be made combat-ready. Not for weeks or months, if ever."

Straker scowled. "How the hell do you know that? You've barely come aboard. You have those thousands of Ruxin techs you've been bragging about, you have the chief here to teach you all you need to know, and we'll be taking that base as soon as we get there. Get it done!"

Zaxby waved his tentacles in all directions. "I would if I could, but any thinking being can see my logic. If these people have not overcome *Indomitable's* problems with years to work on them, even my highly competent fellow Ruxins cannot 'get it done' as you so blithely declare. This ship masses approximately eight times that of the Freiheit habitat. It is more than three kilometers in length. It could comfortably hold a crew of fifty thousand, though I suspect five thousand will be enough were the quarters ever brought up to proper standards."

"So, like I said, it's just a matter of time and effort."

"I do not believe so. It's not like a habitat composed largely of rock. It is a manufactured thing, and every section is part of a complex machine consisting of millions—no billions—of pieces that must work together in harmony. In my expert opinion, Commodore Straker, this ship will never be what you want it to be. It's a boondoggle, a pipe dream, an albatross, a white elephant, a ball-and-chain–"

"Shut up!" Straker smashed his fist onto the back of a sturdy bridge chair, causing Chief Quade to take a step back in trepidation. "We have *Indomitable* and we're going to put her to use!"

"Commodore." Engels voice came from behind him. "May I have a word?"

Straker took a shuddering breath. "Sure, Commander."

Engels tipped her head toward the exit. "Let's take a walk."

"All right..."

Once in the corridor, she stopped him with a firm hand on his arm. "Derek, you're making a scene."

"It's Zaxby again. Always the naysayer, always undercutting me—"

"He's that way with everyone, even me, but you let him push your buttons. You're so used to being the boss that you're starting to get flag officers' disease."

"Flag officers' disease?"

"Yes. You're getting a big head. You start thinking because you're in charge, everyone should agree with you. You start thinking you're always right. Even worse, you might start thinking anyone who disagrees with you is out to get you, or is disloyal. Maybe you start acting like Major Wagner, all touchy and petty. What did you tell me that Roman Caesar had whispered in his ear?"

"*Remember, you are mortal*," said Straker, rubbing his forehead with his fingertips. "Damn, Carla, you're right. I'm sorry. But we got *Indomitable* without a fight! It's like the Unknowable Creator dropped her right in my lap. Like it was meant to be. And now all I get is 'nope, nope, nope.' You saw Zaxby's simulation. We *need* this battleship to work!"

Engels crossed her arms under her breasts and leaned back to look up into Straker's face. "So Zaxby must be right about the sim, but he must be wrong about *Indomitable*? Seems to me you're cherry picking, hearing what you want to hear and rejecting what you don't. Somebody once said you have a right to your own opinions, but not your own facts. Zaxby's giving you the facts. It's up to you to do what you do best."

"What's that?" He couldn't help but let sarcasm creep in.

"Make those facts work for us. You've got vision, Derek! That's what makes you special. Not your genetic engineering, not your mechsuit skill, not even your stubborn inability to give up. Use that vision to see what's possible and make it happen!"

Straker, as usual, began to pace. It helped him think, calmed his nerves. He felt Engels watching impassively as long moments went by. "Okay," he finally said. "So *Indomitable* can't be ready soon, but she *can* be put in shape eventually. It's just a matter of throwing enough resources at the problem, right?"

"Maybe—but if the Mutuality doesn't have those resources, what makes you think *we* can get them?"

Straker jabbed his index finger at her. "No, the Mutuality *has* the resources, but the project got caught in politics. Lazarus said Starkiller was the darling of the Director at the time, but he had a lot of opposition. When he got ousted, they scuttled the project because it was a symbol of that Director. If they'd have made it work, they'd have been admitting he was right and they were wrong, and if there's one thing that's poison to a politician, it's ever, *ever* admitting he's wrong."

"That's... irrational."

"That's politics. Didn't you just as much as tell me I was becoming irrational? How much more do you think an oligarchy—a rule by a permanent elite class—would become irrational? All those swollen heads thinking they knew best, like you said? Nobody telling them unpleasant truths?"

Engels nodded grudgingly. "Okay, so maybe we can make *Indomitable* what she was meant to be. Cosmos knows I'd love to command her. But how do we do it?"

Straker grinned. "Who're the best techno-geeks we know?"

"Ruxins, sure. But as Zaxby implied, even if we pull all ten thousand out of the fleet—leaving our fighting ships in bad shape, by the way—they couldn't do it."

"I know where there are three million Ruxins, building habs and mining asteroids and creating industry as fast as their squirmy little tentacles can move. I bet Vuxana can spare half a million of them—especially when you tell her *Indomitable's* first task will be to free their home system."

Engels stared at Straker, aghast. "You're holding their home system hostage?"

"It's a carrot, not a stick. I'm motivating her. While you and Zaxby take *Indomitable* home to the Starfish Nebula for a complete refit, I'll be liberating as many star systems as I can. All we have to do is rendezvous at Ruxin. If *Indomitable* does what I think she will, the next thing we'll do is strike at the heart of the Mutuality—the Committee Worlds."

"I'm not leaving you to go get killed, Derek."

"We need someone operational to ride herd on Zaxby, otherwise we have no idea what kind of monstrosity he'll turn *Indomitable* into. Only you can do that."

Engels shook her head. "I might be the best choice for the task, but I'm also your fleet commander, and you're taking our ships into multiple combat situations. Someone else can oversee Zaxby."

"Who?"

"Send Zholin. He's the right kind of meticulous, and he's proven trustworthy."

"All right."

Engels smiled broadly. "See? Vision. That's your gift."

Straker swept her up in his arms. "I have a vision right now of you and me in our bed."

Zaxby's voice came from behind Straker. "Please, delay your mating until later. I approve of your intention regarding *Indomitable*, Commodore. It is an efficient use of time and effort."

"Thanks for eavesdropping, Zaxby. Saves me from having to brief you." Straker kissed Engels, and then set her feet on the deck. "Commander, get our fleet moving toward the base. We'll seize it, loot it of everything useful for the refit, drop off the loyalists, and meet *Indomitable* in flatspace to shuffle personnel and equipment."

"Aye aye, Your Liberatorship." Engels bounced off to the bridge.

"Zaxby, work with Quade to prep this pig for sidespace."

"Multiple pigs, really," Zaxby replied. "All sixteen sections must transition successfully. Do you begin to see the complications of this otherwise clever concept?"

"Theories are easy. Execution is hard. But if you can get *Indomitable* to the nebula, I know you'll bring her up to snuff."

"What an obscure idiom. I look forward to researching it in my databases."

"Just get to work, Zaxby. If you do, I'll—"

"—sing my praises? I believe you owe me at least one such song already."

"I'll give you two, since *Indomitable's* so big."

"I will hold you to your bargain, Commodore Derek Straker."

"You want to keep yakking or you want to liberate your homeworld?"

Zaxby spun and began moving away. "I take your meaning. I am dismissed."

"I think *I'm* supposed to say that," Straker said, but Zaxby had already turned a corner.

Chapter 19

Nawlins System, Battlecruiser *Wolverine*

I've been too predictable, Straker thought as he stared in mild shock at *Wolverine's* holo-table showing the Nawlins system. He'd liberated eight stars in a shortest-distance line instead of jumping to an unexpected one, and that may have been a mistake.

Nawlins' warm yellow star and the two Earthlike planets, one cool, one hot, held no surprises. Each bore a relatively small population of under one hundred million, dwarfed by the tens of billions inhabiting a typical Central or Committee world. More importantly, neither was protected by a true fortress, only by smaller orbitals based on obsolete warship hulks.

But the Nawlins system wasn't defenseless. As Straker watched, a fleet of more than forty Mutuality warships appeared from behind the moon of Nawlins-4, known locally as Shreve, enough ships to challenge his own fleet.

"Can we get away?" Straker asked Engels.

"Not without at least one passage at arms," replied Engels. "We're too deep into the gravity zone to turn around now without being raked."

Straker had learned enough about naval operations to understand the concept of being 'raked.' In the Old Earth days of wooden ships, it referred to any weapons fire striking the prow or stern of a ship, which was much more damaging as cannonballs would scream through the length of the vessel. The projectiles would smash flimsy bulkheads, dismount guns and rip men to shreds before losing all their energy. Straker likened it to a bullet hitting a man: a flesh wound was better, a slug to the organ-filled torso was far worse.

In modern parlance, though, a 'rake' only referred to strikes on the stern of a ship, vulnerable because of open engine exhausts and lack of rear-facing firepower. Capital weapons aimed forward, installed along the spines of warships and shielded by clamshell bow armor that opened when firing, closed when reloading or recharging. Thus, running from an enemy was not advisable unless the fleeing ships were faster and could extend away from the firing vessels. Dropped mines and backward-facing weapons could only partially compensate.

"Could we accelerate through them," Straker asked, "with one round of fire as you say, and then escape out the other side?"

"Of course. That would minimize damage on both sides, but we'd pay the greater price."

"Why?"

"Because they've only got fighting ships. We have over one hundred freighters and auxiliaries in our wake, full of troops and supplies. If the enemy is smart, he'll target these vulnerable vessels. Without armor and reinforcement, they'll die like ants in a blowtorch. If we…" Engels trailed off, looking away.

Straker was cognizant of the audience on the bridge. "Go on, Captain. Say what's on your mind."

"Never mind," Engels said, looking at the deck.

"You were about to say that if we'd sent recon drones ahead, we might have spotted them."

Engels pressed her lips together and nodded sharply, once. She obviously didn't want to embarrass him, but Straker preferred to keep everything out in the open rather than appear to be suppressing dissent.

"I vetoed it because I wanted to get as close as possible before the planetary defense forces were alerted to the fact that they were being attacked," said Straker. "It was my decision, my fault."

This admission seemed to embolden Engels. "Bringing the freighters in with us might also have been a mistake. If we'd parked them out in flatspace, they'd be out of the engagement zone and could transit away, leaving us free to maneuver."

"That would have left them vulnerable to any ships arriving in the system, in which case we would've had to leave escorts with them, diminishing our fleet's punch. Captain Engels, we went over all this and I made the decisions. It's on me. But recriminations won't change anything. The question is, what do we do now? Give me your expert opinion."

Engels chewed her lip and stared at the holo-table, thinking. Straker knew her well enough to see she was irritated with him and with the situation.

Chapter 19

"Perhaps I may assist." This came from Major Kraxor, the War Male.

"What do you know of space combat?" asked Major Wagner. The two majors were inseparable, but only because Wagner seemed to want to keep an eye on the creature he'd decided was his personal rival to glory.

"Much, actually. I recently commanded a flotilla of Archerfish—eighty years ago, that is, before my long sleep. I was a highly effective commander."

Straker turned to the Ruxin in surprise. "You never told me that."

"You never asked."

"Good point. So, how do you see it?"

Kraxor heaved his bulk up from his seat and moved to look at the holo-table. "We have many choices, but only two I would call acceptable. One, we accelerate and fight through, optimizing our warships for screening and defense of our freighters, tankers and auxiliaries. We will likely lose half of them, but few warships. We could move most personnel onto warships if we do it quickly. This will save some lives. We get away, transit out, and attack a random vulnerable system."

"The other choice?"

"We fight. Reduce speed and engage, forcing the enemy to deal with our warships or be destroyed."

Straker rubbed his jaw. "That's putting everything on one roll of the dice. If we lose this battle, the Galactic Liberation movement is crippled. All our momentum will be lost."

"Then we must not lose."

Engels spoke up. "There's a third choice."

"What's that?" asked Straker.

"We assign a task force of warships to slow down and tie up the enemy, while the rest make a run for it. By the time the delaying group is destroyed, the others will get away."

"A suicide force, you mean." Straker shook his head emphatically. "No. Hell no. I'm not consigning people to certain death. Better that we all roll the dice together."

Engels opened her mouth to continue arguing, but Straker made a chopping motion with his hand. "No. That's final." He turned to include everyone on *Wolverine's* bridge with his gaze. "We fight. Captain Engels, pass the orders."

As the bridge crew burst into activity preparing for battle, Straker cudgeled his brain as he examined the holo-table's three-dimensional display.

Fortunately, the enemy fleet contained only one dreadnought. Ships of that class were much slower, even through sidespace, and so were of limited value against smaller raiders that could run away. What's more, dreadnoughts and superdreadnoughts were needed on the front lines where two empires fought, playing their chess games of threatening and shielding important systems. Few could be spared for the frontier.

Two battlecruisers and four heavy cruisers accompanied the single dreadnought, forming the core of the opposition. A hodgepodge of more than thirty lesser units, from light cruisers down to corvettes, accompanied them.

Opposing them, Straker had his original four battlecruisers, plus two more that had been captured. Alongside them cruised four heavy cruisers and five light cruisers.

Normally the light cruisers were detached for harassment or covering duties, sometimes singly or sometimes by squadron. They were termed "light" because they sported far less armor than heavy cruisers, making them faster while carrying nearly equal weaponry. They were therefore fragile when standing up to capital-grade fire, but Engels had insisted on keeping them as ships of the line for a more concentrated capital core.

So at first glance, the Liberation fleet looked to have a comfortable edge in capital ships. They also boasted more than sixty escort units of destroyers and smaller. Many had been taken as they liberated the last eight star systems by surprise. Some warships had been tricked, some seized by locals, and some had been compelled to surrender to superior forces.

None chose to go down fighting. To Straker, that was proof of the rottenness of the Mutuality: that nobody was willing to die for their "motherland." That, at least, proved the Hundred Worlds superior.

Fortunately, the Liberation fleet wouldn't have to fight the planetary orbitals—at least, not yet. Engels' orders were already slowing and turning her forces, giving the enemy the choice of sortieing away from their fixed defenses, or letting their opponents cruise on by.

But the Mutuality task force obviously intended to bring the raiders to battle. If they let them go, they had no way of knowing where Straker would strike next.

The Liberation transports were curving under heavy sideways acceleration so that they would continue past and back out to sidespace, while the fleets fought. Straker's warships interposed themselves, slowing to ensure they were able to screen their auxiliaries.

At some point, Straker's warships would have to aim their noses directly toward the enemy, which meant no more running, and only limited maneuvering. As each side had something to defend, even a man with a lack of naval warfare experience could see a slugfest was about to ensue.

"What do our tactics look like?" Straker asked Engels. "Give me a broad outline."

Engels stepped over to the holo-table, placing one hand on it to activate a duplicate sim. "I was planning on keeping things simple and conventional, since we have the edge in numbers." She glanced at Straker as if for approval.

Straker nodded. "The side with the advantage wants to minimize surprises and volatility, and cruise to a victory. The side that's behind is the one that has to try something risky."

"Yes. But this strategy presupposes our forces are solid, and will not break, run, or fail to follow orders. That's a big 'if.'"

Surprised, Straker took a deep breath. "You think our fleet will fall apart?"

"I think that despite my best efforts to drill and integrate our crews, we're not truly a disciplined fleet. We're a loose collection of individuals who haven't yet fought a battle together, from different cultures, different planets, even different species. Some will hold the line. Some will attack against orders. Some will fail to attack when ordered. Some will run."

"Damn. That's not what I wanted to hear."

"It's the price we pay for you pushing, pushing, always pushing, never taking a breath to prepare, Commodore. Real navies have exercises, evaluations, data in their files. They vet their captains and crew. Those captains work together and get to know each other's strengths and weaknesses."

Straker punched his fist into his palm. "But we have the numbers, and the enemy's not ten meters tall. Lots of Mutuality ships have defected over the last few weeks. They're shaky."

"They're less shaky in the presence of a fleet with a dreadnought, and of their commissars. We have to assume they'll fight competently." Engels adjusted the simulation. "Here's what I've got so far."

The holographic sequence showed the two groups of capital ships approaching each other, each in a flat circle formation like a dinner plate, heaviest ships in the center. The two plates slowed as they approached each other, while clouds of lighter forces followed behind and hovered around the edges, slightly back.

In the sim, the two main forces exchanged fire. Once the heavies were fully involved, the light units flowed around the circular flanks and engaged each other. It was a battle of attrition, one that the Liberation fleet eventually won, though having lost half its forces while the Mutuality fleet was utterly annihilated.

"Costly," said Straker. "But we win, and we keep on liberating systems—or we could run home and return with *Indomitable*."

"This is a crude simulation, using standard hit probabilities and breaking points," replied Engels. "It shows two fleets of machines, acting like machines. It completely ignores the unpredictability of people. It gives you a feeling of certainty because you're used to thinking of battles between machine-like elites—relentless Hok versus top-level mechsuiters. This won't work like that."

"Then how *will* it work?"

Engels spread her fingers and waved them. "The relative strengths are too close… Nobody can predict the actual outcome. That's why a conventional plan is good. We reduce the variables. As the larger force, we go head to head and take casualties, to make certain of victory."

"I don't like it," Straker said, walking slowly around the holo-table. "You said yourself our ships might not hold in the face of heavy fire. And, it's always easier to attack madly, with hot blood, than to defend calmly and coolly. We have the numbers. I think we should make an all-out assault. Scare them so much *they* break, not us. Unleash our own forces so they're too busy charging to get scared."

"Then our people will massacre the enemy if we win. When you loose the dogs of war, it's hard to call them back. You might even have to fire on our own ships to get them under control. Is that the kind of Liberator you want to be?"

Straker worked his jaw, envisioning the worst case: undisciplined ships rampaging, blasting surrendered enemies, refusing to stand down. Then he remembered something an Old Earth general once said. He couldn't recall the exact wording, but he spoke the gist of it. "There's nothing as ugly as a battle won—except a battle lost. We *have* to win this."

"No, we don't!" Engels lowered her voice and stepped toward him. "Dammit, Derek, we've been mousetrapped. All we really have to do is get away, live to fight another day!"

"No. No, no, no! If we don't win this battle, if we appear to run away, our momentum and our morale will evaporate. Carla, you understand machines and ship captains. I understand warriors. A warrior that believes he *can* be beaten, *will* be beaten. You said it yourself. This fleet isn't an integrated naval force. It's a ragtag collection of individuals and groups, and the only thing holding it together is me—my image, I mean. The Liberator. I'm like Alexander the Great rampaging through Asia. As soon as I lose a battle, or am perceived to lose a battle, it's over. But when word of the destruction of a real Mutuality naval fleet spreads—even if that fleet is only a hasty task force—it proves we can win and keep winning."

"Preach your sermon to the dead," Engels snapped.

"Death is better than slavery."

"We tell ourselves that, but we're making the decision for them—these people, these average citizens."

Straker grasped her shoulders. "I don't have fancy answers for you, Carla. I only know what's right. If we fail, some people will die before their time. If we succeed, billions, maybe trillions of people, will be freed to choose their own destinies, and it will have all been worth it. So, are you with me?"

Engels took his large, rough hands in hers. "You know I am. You're my commander, and my man. I'm your woman. Your cause is my cause. Your fate is my fate, and I'll die where you die." She cleared her throat. "I'll also be there when you bury our fallen, whispering in your ear that you're mortal too. So let's not die today."

Straker felt a wave of mixed emotion—love, respect, appreciation, annoyance—roll over him. "Cosmos, Carla! You're not making this easy."

"A lion needs a lioness. You prefer a sheep?"

Straker convulsively let go of Engels' hands. He inhaled deeply through his nose and exhaled a long breath, thinking. Eventually, he said, "I appreciate your position, but we do it my way. All-out attack. You pass the orders, specify the tactics. Just make sure at the end of this day, we hold the field. Everyone's going to see this battle, and the price we pay today will win us entire star systems tomorrow."

"What do you mean?"

"Since the Mutuality set up this trap, no doubt they have stealth recon drones, maybe even scout ships, waiting out in flatspace. As soon as the battle's done, they'll carry word to their bosses. I want drones and couriers of our own to spread far and wide with full showvid broadcasts of our victory. Even if they don't revolt, they'll be primed to help us when we show up." He pointed at the hologram. "Winning this may be the pebble that starts the avalanche."

Engels nodded, stepping back, her face cold. "I'll pass the word to have full records made. Excuse me, Commodore, but I need to get to work."

"By all means, Captain. Carry on."

Straker watched as the holo-table reverted to displaying the current reality. As the bridge buzzed with rapid-fire orders, the Liberation fleet reorganized itself in accordance with his will, detailed by Carla Engels. He hadn't known exactly what that would look like, but he found out now.

Instead of relegating the hodgepodge of light units to a supporting role behind and around the Liberation heavies in their disk of battle, Engels sent them forward in layers, or shells, like skirmishers in a ground fight. But in space, there were no trees and rocks to hide behind.

She'd be trading smaller ships, less valuable and more vulnerable ones, for time and the preservation of critical Breaker heavies, Straker realized. It meant more casualties faster, but it would force the enemy to counter the tactic. And he assumed she wasn't going to simply smash the two fleets together; he knew Engels well enough to expect finesse and tactics, rather than mere slugging.

"They're opening fire with railguns," said Tixban at Sensors. "Long range, multiple submunitions, high orders of magnitude."

Straker watched quietly as the battle began to unfold. There was no turning back now.

Chapter 20

Nawlins System, Battlecruiser *Wolverine*

Engels leaned forward in her chair at Tixban's announcement of incoming fire. Railgun shot had infinite range, but accuracy was low at this distance and ammo was limited. She wondered why they'd begun firing so soon. "Missiles?"

"Not yet," said Tixban. "Correction. I have cold launches. They appear to be preparing for a fleet strike."

"What's a fleet strike?" Straker asked.

Tixban answered the question. "Ships cold-launch multiple volleys of missiles, which float along ballistically, waiting. They activate them all at once, creating a much bigger wave than usual. Normally, they will support the wave with direct fire, decoys and light units, hoping to overwhelm enemy defenses and achieve effective shipkiller strikes."

"Pass your analysis to all ships and tell them to prep for maximum point defense, shipkiller priority." Engels turned to Straker. "No battle plan survives contact with the enemy. They've jammed your all-out attack. We have to deal with the fleet strike first. After that, they'll be low on shipkillers and we'll have a big advantage."

"Understood. Carry on. You're the space tactician."

"Damn right I am," Engels muttered. She issued a string of new orders, making adjustments to her fleet dispositions. Instead of widening shells of light units, the escorts pulled in to form a narrower, shorter, fatter cylinder, like a flat ration can. This created a gauntlet between the enemy and the Breaker heavies, a defense in depth.

"Our increasing density is allowing them to achieve minor railgun strikes on our light units," said Tixban.

Engels nodded but said nothing. This answered the question of why they fired submunitions now. The enemy had anticipated her thickening defenses, and while the billions of tiny tumbling high-speed cubes wouldn't kill any ships, they could strip vital sensors and damage the small point-defense lasers vital to dealing with missiles.

Straker looked at the holo-table and back to his fleet commander. "Aren't we going to fire back?"

"Everything's a tradeoff, Commodore," Engels replied tightly. "We can fire early at low probabilities—or later at higher probabilities. There will be an optimum moment, but it's not now."

"Some of our ships are firing," Tixban said.

Engels grunted. "This is the lack-of-discipline part I was talking about. Comms, broadcast a reminder not to waste ammo."

The holo-table showed the two formations approaching each other obliquely. The Mutuality fleet was advancing toward the Liberation transports to force an intercept, and the Breakers fleet was sliding between them like a warrior's shield.

"They have something up their sleeve," Engels said, rubbing at the corners of her mouth with the tips of finger and thumb. "With the current setup, there's no way they'll win."

"And they're not suicidal," Straker said. "So what could the surprise be? More ships behind the moon of Shreve?"

"No. Anything hiding there won't reach the battle zone in time."

Tixban cleared his throat, and they glanced at him. "I may have an answer. Observe the main screen."

A shaky optical of the enemy dreadnought flagship floated on the big front holoscreen, clearly at maximum zoom. The detail was poor and the image lacked illumination, but Engels could see something seemed odd about the shape of the ship. "Can you enhance further?"

"No," Tixban said.

"I don't need enhancement," said Kraxor, locomoting forward to get a better view and focusing all four huge eyes on the screen. "The dreadnought is carrying strap-ons."

"So we're about to get screwed?" said Loco. "Should we get the lube and bend over?"

"Can it, Loco," said Engels. "Strap-on what? Missile pods? No…" she answered her own question. "They'd have cold-launched those by now. They have to be…"

Chapter 20

"Attack ships," said Kraxor. "I've seen this before."

Engels' voice tensed. "Check their other ships for add-ons, anything out of profile, and get me an estimated count of how many they have!"

Sudden flares occluded the picture on the screen. "I have missile exhaust blooms, Captain," Tixban said. "They're beginning their missile wave. More than four hundred, maximum acceleration. Correction, four hundred forty... Four hundred sixty... The strap-ons are deploying."

"How many of those?"

"I count approximately one hundred sixty. The other Mutuality capital ships had them too."

"Shit." Engels stood to approach the holo-table. "Push datalinks to *Liberator* and *Revenge* with this info. Tell them to make ready for underspace insertion. They're to take independent action on attack runs that will send them through the enemy fleet and into their backfield."

"By now the enemy knows about our underspace Archers," Straker said. "They'll have detectors going."

"I'm counting on it. This is war to the knife, Derek, and we need every advantage. I want the enemy nervous and expending maximum effort worrying about our Archers. They're diversions."

"I'd hate to lose the only two we have."

Engels eyed Straker. "I hate to risk *Liberator* and my friends aboard, but you're the one that said we have to win this battle at all costs. Don't go second-guessing me now."

"Point taken. Carry on."

Tixban spoke in his own language. He might have been cursing, from Engels limited understanding of the Ruxin tongue. In Earthan, he said, "The attack ships have strap-on missiles of their own. They have launched four each. Missile count has now risen to over one thousand."

"Strap-on strap-ons! I told you those strap-ons would screw us. Bend over!" said Loco, half-chuckling.

"Not helping, Loco," Straker said. "Why don't you go make the rounds, steady the troops? Do something positive?"

Loco shot Straker a sour look and stalked off the bridge.

Engels didn't bother asking Tixban how many missiles were shipkillers. Missiles were deliberately fashioned to hide their warhead type. Some would have standard fusion nukes, some bomb-pumped laser heads that shot brief, impossibly intense beams at multiple targets, and some would launch decoys or emit powerful electronic countermeasures to aid the others.

"Begin anti-missile salvos," Engels said. "Every ship so equipped, start firing. I want to thin them out and force them to commit. Capital beams, start trying to pick them off at extreme range. Load railguns with submunitions but hold fire."

"What's going on at the leading edge of our skirmishers?" Straker asked, extending a hand into the hologram to touch the front of the Liberation formation. "These guys are pulling back."

Engels scowled. "Crap. It's like I said. Some are running, afraid the fleet strike will kill them—and just like in a ground fight, that will turn into a self-fulfilling prophecy. We have to steady them before the fear infects everyone." She turned to her comms officers. "All ships, salvo missiles. Fusion warheads target enemy weapons. Beam and decoy warheads, proximity targeting of enemy ships. Keep them guessing."

Pinpoints of light appeared in ragged volleys throughout the Liberation fleet and accelerated toward the enemy. Above the holo-table, between the two fleets, it looked like a firework flower reached toward a regimented swarm of bees. Beyond the bees followed the slightly larger hornets of over 160 attack ships.

Now and again one of the specks winked out, destroyed by long-range fire, but far too few—until the firework and the swarm touched. Explosions blossomed then, impossible for the display software to represent to scale, even when Engels ordered the table to zoom in on the area where the weapons met.

"Fleet strike reduced by approximately fifty weapons," Tixban reported. A number appeared next to the swarm: 961. "Attack support has lost several." Another number: 159.

More fireworks reached toward the incoming fleet strike as it accelerated. Each Liberation volley reduced the missile and attack ship count, but the tide was not stemmed fast enough, and more friendly skirmishers turned tail and ran, unwilling to face the oncoming wall of death.

"Record me a general fleet message," Straker said.

"Recording."

"This is Straker, the Liberator. Hold steady! If you run, you abandon your comrades to fight alone. If you're falling back, turn around now to rejoin your brothers in arms. If we break, we fail. If we stand together, we win. Hold steady! Hold steady!" He made a cutting motion. "Send that. Tightbeam it on repeat to any ships that don't rally."

Engels nodded. "Let's hope that helps. It looks like fewer are backing up, and mostly for tactical reasons now. Our counter-volleys are thinning them out, but it's expensive. We're burning through our own missiles stocks, so we won't have many left for the endgame."

"That's what they want," replied Straker. "Without shipkillers, that dreadnought will be an even tougher nut."

"Exactly. Missile officer!"

"Ma'am?"

"Pass to all our capital ships: reserve one shipkiller volley each. Everyone else, fire at will. Let the enemy think we're draining ourselves dry. When the time comes, we'll have a surprise for them."

"Aye aye, Captain."

Straker said, "Our skirmishers are still falling back, even if they're not running. Our formation is turning into one solid plate shape instead of a gauntlet, with our core at the center."

"I see." Engels shifted to another angle on the holo-table. "That raises the luck factor, makes the fleet strike more all-or-nothing as the time to intercept compresses." She slammed her palm on the table. "Dammit. Pass to all capital ships, impeller retrograde. Maintain formation."

"You're not happy with that order?" asked Straker.

"If our skirmishers notice, it will seem like we're staying back from the front line—which we are. That's the plan, to let the light units thin out the strike. But it may look like we're trading their lives for ours—which we are, too. Using impellers only, I'm hoping the shaky captains won't notice, and the steady ones will understand."

The count fell to 767 and 142 by the time the fleet strike reached the leading edge of the sixty-some Liberation skirmisher-escorts. Oncoming missiles exploded in fiery fusion blasts or burst into clouds of decoys, submunitions and jammers, the better to help their deadly fellows find their true targets.

In return, most of the light units dueled with their attackers, reaping them like wheat. As Engels had predicted, the majority of the fleet strike was targeted at the capital ships of the Liberation. Behind the missiles, advancing enemy heavies would engage her skirmishers—and slaughter them, if she let it happen.

"Capital ships, independent fire, all weapons," ordered Engels. "Threat order protocols, defensive."

Now, the capital direct-fire weapons of the ships of the line joined the fight, and the fleet strike counts dropped rapidly—but not rapidly enough. Hundreds of weapons and dozens of attack ships rampaged among the screening escorts.

Engels slapped the tabletop again. "Dammit, we're losing our screen."

"They're breaking," Straker said, grim-faced.

Engels saw he was right. As a relative few enemy missiles homed in and destroyed corvettes, frigates and destroyers, the escort formation crumbled. Ships blasted in all directions, firing wildly rather than remaining together to interlink their defensive grids. "This is what happens when we don't have discipline—or a good battlenet for the light units," she said.

"Like barbarian warriors facing real soldiers," Straker replied. "What do we do?"

"We know we can't run, so we fight through. Pass to the capital ships: close up on the flag, full defensive battlenet links, and advance. Derek, keep trying to get the bug-outs to rally."

"Aye aye, Madam Admiral."

Engels smiled toward Straker in spite of herself and watched him move over to the dual communications stations to call back those captains who'd lost their nerve.

The count stood at 458 and 134. The fleet strike was tearing through the dissolving light units, with the enemy attack ships following in a disciplined mass, finishing off any Liberation stragglers or holdouts they could reach without changing course. By its monolithic inevitability, it was a strategy tailor-made to chase away independent units.

But now, Engels' capital fleet moved forward, her elite ships of the line compacted into a hard core. In space-combat terms, the ships stood shoulder to shoulder, with just enough room between them to ensure one fusion blast didn't hurt two at a time.

No matter how dense the Liberation core, their weapons still reached far, and when the edge of its combined engagement zone touched the fleet strike mass, enemy missiles began to wink out by the dozens, bringing the number below 300.

Chapter 20

Behind the oncoming wave, three fusion blasts, and then four more, erupted suddenly among the tightly packed attack ships. Their count dropped abruptly to 103, then 77, as over fifty died at once.

"Lovely," Engels crowed. "But where… the Archers! Float mines! The attack ships have no detectors. Well done!"

Almost as soon as she cheered, the attack ships closed up and reformed. Despite their losses, they did this with a minimum of confusion.

"Those are some brave pilots," said Straker as he returned to the table.

"Yes, they are… unusually dedicated." Engels chewed her lip. "I need an analysis of those attack ships' vectors, Tixban. Project their courses, ignoring any deviations to finish off stragglers. Exactly where are they heading?"

"Working on that."

"What are you thinking?" Straker asked.

"Drones," she replied. "Tele-operated, semi-autonomous attack ships. Not as effective as piloted ships, but in a mass like this, nearly as good. They obviously prepped this task force to try to trap us, using whatever they had at hand to compensate for their lack of ship numbers. They must have stripped local defenses to create this fleet strike package, knowing full well that homegrown Mutual Guard pilots would never take such heavy casualties—so they automated them."

Straker stroked his jaw. "If I were the enemy commander, I'd have added suicide fusion warheads to those attack craft."

"True. Comms, pass that possibility to all ships."

"Captain, my analysis is complete," said Tixban. "Observe quadrant one of the holo-table."

Above the table, the main tactical view shrank to make room for a separate detail showing the attack ships' courses over time. Lines projected from the icons, with their headings sticking out like a forest of tiny spears.

The lines pointed directly at a single icon.

Wolverine.

"They know we're the flagship, and they're coming for us," said Engels. "They probably figure you're aboard, Derek, and if they get you, the Liberation is over."

"They might not be wrong," interjected War Male Kraxor. "You must preserve this ship."

"You fear attack?" said Major Wagner with a sneer. "You wish to save your own skin?"

The War Male focused three eyes on Wagner. "I wish freedom for my homeworld. Only the Liberator can bring it. If he falls, so shall you—and Sachsen."

Straker stepped between them. "There are no cowards here," he said, giving Wagner a hard glare. "I'd love to go hand-to-hand with these bastards, but this isn't that kind of fight. It might become one, though. If so, I'll need you both."

Wagner nodded, scowling, and Kraxor did the same.

Engels said, "We can use their single-mindedness against them, though. Tixban, pass your analysis to Comms. Comtech, attach the data to a message explaining that *Wolverine* is falling back in order to create a gauntlet cone for the attack ships, and they need to form appropriately. Helm, put us at the rear apex of the cone. Pass details to the other helmsmen."

The core stretched out to create a cone of battle. The heavy cruisers took positions in the front, on the leading edge of the open part of the cone, and then the light cruisers, with their superior anti-missile suites and medium-caliber weaponry. Last came the battlecruisers, with heavier primaries optimized against ships of the line, *Wolverine* at the center: part flagship, part bait.

The fleet strike came on, backed by the attack ships. Both masses converged closer and closer, inevitably constricting their courses as they homed in on *Wolverine*. The numbers spun, falling, falling, as the integrated battlenet and the awesome firepower of the tight cone took its toll.

Then suddenly, the surviving hard-driven missiles and attack ships got among the core force. Ships of the line shuddered with near-misses of thermonuclear warheads and the hot lances of bomb-pumped beam strikes. Three of the four heavy cruisers, doing their work as shields of the fleet, took blow after hammer blow—until they cracked.

One vanished in a contact blast. The other two went dark, broken but not obliterated. One light cruiser spun off course, her engines damaged and power lost. The battlecruiser *Ermine*, surging forward to fill the gap, intercepted a final volley of missiles with a vomiting spray of submunitions, taking a heavy explosion to her reinforced nose before being driven aside, sorely wounded but still on her feet.

This marked the high water surge of the enemy missile wave. It crested, broke, and suddenly dispersed under the integrated defensive battlenet of the five remaining battlecruisers.

Unfortunately, more than forty attack ships remained on suicide courses, locked onto *Wolverine*. Engels resisted an impulse to order her flagship to escape. Exposing her tail was exactly the wrong move, though her hindbrain screamed at her to *run! Run! Run!*

Beams hammered at the dwindling formation of attack craft, but not fast enough. The small ships were each ten times the size of a missile, with uprated armor and countermeasures. They simply weren't dying quickly enough. At least ten, perhaps twenty of them, would reach *Wolverine* within the next thirty seconds… and if they had fusion warheads aboard, she would surely die under their pounding.

And then, from the edge of the holo-table's display, icons swept in to surround the flagship.

"What the hell are those? Zoom the view back!" said Straker.

The view expanded to show the area around the fleet core. At least three dozen auxiliaries—freighters and tankers—had broken from the noncombatant group and charged in. They threw their unarmored bodies in the way of the attack ships. Some had small lasers, some nothing but their hulls. Many of them scored hits or attracted proximity detonations, vanishing in blasts of mutual annihilation.

In seconds, the threat evaporated as the last attack ships were finished off… along with more than twenty fragile transports.

Straker whooped. "They suicided the suiciders!"

"That's– that's–" Engels said, shocked and saddened. "So many dead… for us. They died for us."

Without further orders, the cone of battle quickly used beams to vaporize all possible threats—pieces of ships and missiles that might contain warheads—and began to reorganize itself as the ship captains gave directions. At least these had held steady, and for that, Engels was eternally grateful.

"It appears the auxiliaries that helped us dumped their lifeboats and survival pods before rushing to our aid," said Tixban. "Only a handful of lives were lost—pilots and minor captains, mostly, of low importance."

"Low importance, my ass," said Engels, straightening with a sudden welling in her eyes. "They were heroes, every damned one of them. Make sure we know their names."

"I will make it so," said Tixban.

"Yes, heroes…" echoed Straker. "Comms, tell those cowards that are still retreating to get their sorry asses back here and help us mop up these Mutuality scum."

"We're still in for a hard fight," said Engels. "But we'll win… as you ordered, Liberator." She fought to keep reproach out of her voice. This was war, and they were both fighting it as well as they could, but the cost sickened her, especially since she found herself alive only because of the sacrifices of others.

But that was the way of war. Some died so others could carry on the fight. She resolved that she would never forget, and would try to live up to their courageous example.

Straker raised his voice. "Start moving forward again. Signal to all warships to form on the flag. We're going to finish them off."

Chapter 21

Shreve, Nawlins System, Battlecruiser *Wolverine*

The battle for the Nawlins system ended more favorably than Straker expected. The Liberation fleet outnumbered, outmassed and outgunned the enemy by half, and now it was the Mutuality forces at a disadvantage, in the position of not being able to run without being raked.

Had they launched their fleet strike and retreated immediately, they might have made it back to join with their orbitals around the planet of Shreve, but they'd elected to advance and support their missile attack. Now, they had to stand and fight.

To her credit, the enemy dreadnought fought to her doom, no doubt crewed by the best and most fanatical Mutualists available. She was finally cracked wide open by multiple contact strikes from the surprise shipkiller volley Engels had held in reserve. One of the enemy battlecruisers was also obliterated.

Once the dreadnought fell, the other People's Mutual Navy ships found themselves ringed about by Breakers and their allies eager to avenge themselves, and they immediately signaled their surrender.

Not every such surrender was honored.

"Put me on widebeam broadcast, in the clear!" snarled Straker, watching in anger as some of his escorts continued to attack now-helpless ships.

"You're on, sir."

"All Liberation ships, this is Straker. Stand down! I say again, stand down and do *not* fire upon surrendered vessels, dammit! I'll court-martial anyone who keeps shooting! I'll blow your engines out from under you if I have to!"

Slowly, Straker's words brought order to the aftermath, and combat operations gave way to salvage, rescue and recovery. He sent Wagner and Kraxor with their contingents to take possession of two surrendered battlecruisers, and within hours, most of the work was done and the fleet was put in some semblance of order.

"Tixban, run the record of the battle on the holo-table, will you?" Straker asked.

"Of course, sir."

"Fast-forward until the fleet strike approaches."

"Time index set. Displaying."

"Expand and highlight any of our ships who turn tail and run, slow motion."

"It will take a moment to program the parameters, sir."

Straker fidgeted while Tixban fluttered his tentacle clusters over the console. Eventually the Ruxin nodded and the display began to move slowly. When any of the screening vessels fell back faster than those around them, they changed to yellow. When they actually turned around and presented their tail—and their vulnerable fusion engines—to the enemy, the icons flashed red.

"Isolate those flashing red ones. Run it forward fast—and then slow down again. Make them yellow again if they rejoined the battle to fight."

After the sequence played out, Straker was left with only a handful of cowards. All but one of them continued outbound, clearly heading for flatspace and transition to another star system—probably their homes. No doubt they didn't want to face his wrath, or the derision of their fellows. The final one rejoined the fleet after all combat was finished.

Straker said, "Create a data packet with all those runners—ship names, captain and crew names, all the information we have. Pass it to all our reliable ships with instructions to keep it on file for the future, and also to relay to their homeworlds via message drone or courier." It may take a while, but he knew the information would eventually reach its destinations. He had no real power over the disorganized Liberation movement, but at least, perhaps, those nearest the cowards would be warned. "And tell that one last one there—what is the ship name, *Lucky Struck*? Tell them to go home too. I don't want them in my fleet, or the Liberation."

"We're ready to move in on Shreve," said Engels, walking wearily up to stand beside him. "Or we could wait a few hours. The crews are exhausted."

"Let's advance. I don't want to give the defenses too much time to start believing they can win."

"Agreed." Engels moved to throw herself into her chair. "Comms, pass to all combat-ready ships: conform to the flag, disk formation. *Badger*, *Sable*, put one slug each across the paths of the orbitals. Show them we have the range to pound them to scrap. Then open a comlink to someone in command."

Minutes later, a gray-haired rear admiral appeared on the main holoscreen. "This is Admiral Dwayne LaPierre, Nawlins Defense Command."

Engels rubbed the nape of her neck beneath her short, jet-black hair. "Admiral, you have a command in name only, which I can destroy at any time. I've dismantled your fleet. You're helpless. Surrender now and you'll be treated in accordance in the laws of war. We'll put you on a transport to a Mutuality world, along with any other loyalists who don't want to join the Liberation."

"Liberation?" The admiral snorted derisively. "You're pirate scum, nothing more."

Straker, seeing Engels exhaustion and her rising irritation, stepped into view of the vid pickup. "Derek Straker here, admiral. You might have heard of me. If you're an honest man, you know we're not pirates—otherwise you'd already be dead. And you don't actually believe mere pirates could defeat a People's Mutual Navy task force, do you?"

LaPierre's face stiffened. "So… you have a large force of well-led pirates. That hardly matters. You'll never take these worlds intact."

"Really? How are you going to prevent me from doing so?"

LaPierre nodded to someone off-screen.

"Shreve Orbital One has fired its main railgun," Tixban said.

"Evasive!" said Engels, sitting up and gripping her armrests.

"It did not fire at us."

"At what, then?"

Tixban's tentacles curled in upon themselves in a manner Straker recognized as indicating distress. "They're bombarding the planet. Shreve's second-largest city, called Jackson, has been obliterated."

Engels stood, one hand still holding an armrest as if to steady herself. "How many dead?"

"Approximately one million." Tixban's tentacles curled tighter.

LaPierre nodded. "You see, Straker, I spoke truth. You may take these planets, but there won't be anything left to plunder."

"I don't plunder. I liberate," Straker said, appalled.

"Helm, hold position relative to Shreve," called Engels. "Comms, tell everyone else to do the same. Cut the comlink."

"Wait—" said Straker.

"Comlink cut, ma'am," the watchstander said.

"Get him back!" said Straker.

"Belay that!" snapped Engels. "Commodore, *wait*. *Think*. That... that monster just murdered a million people as a bargaining chip. Don't be hasty. We have to think this through."

"I'm not letting him blackmail me."

Engels move to stand in front of Straker and hissed, too low for most of those around to hear, "You? Blackmail *you*? How about *us*? How about all those dead people?"

Straker rasped, "We didn't do that. He did. It's on him."

"I don't care who's to blame." Her voice dropped further. "Stop thinking with your ego and start using that good judgment you're always talking about. What's our goal here?"

"To liberate this system."

"Bullshit." Engels grabbed Straker's sleeve and shook it. "A few hours ago, we were trying to figure a way out of a trap. Now we won, the trap is gone, and we're free to leave. There are at least fifty lightly defended systems out there to liberate. We can always come back here with *Indomitable* and crush him. Right now, we can't stop him from obliterating a dozen cities before we take him down. So, let's *leave*. LaPierre's evil, and he wins, temporarily. So what?"

"No. We can't let him win. We'll think of a way."

"How?"

Straker looked off to the side, at the holo-table. "The Archers. They'll sneak in and crack the orbitals with float mines, starting with the one that fired. He deserves to die for what he did, and his crews too."

"And if they have detectors? Not only could we lose *Revenge* and *Liberator*, we could lose millions more people, the people you're supposedly trying to help!"

"It's worth the risk."

Engels gripped Straker's biceps so her nails dug into them through the cloth of his tunic. "To our warships? Yes. But it's not worth another city, a city full of innocent children. Like your sister Mara."

"Ouch." Straker licked his lips. "Pascal's Wager in reverse," he mouthed, too low for anyone but Carla to hear. "Little upside, horrendous downside." He took a deep, shuddering breath, feeling the outrage drain out of him, leaving only a sense of helplessness.

Finally, he spoke. "You're right, Carla. There's no reason to push LaPierre. Put out orders: no contact with the Nawlins Defense Command. Absolute blackout. Choose a few ships for a patrol and blockading force. Tell them to search for and destroy any message drones they find, and to run if anything they can't handle transits in. We'll choose our next target and move on."

Straker left the bridge and the details to Engels. He headed below decks for a meal, a shower, and some rack time.

* * *

"Where've you been?" Straker asked six hours later as Loco rounded the corner of the passageway. "I've been banging on your door."

Loco swaggered up and put in his code, pushing the door open and sliding past Straker. "I've been doing some banging of my own. Might do you some good to follow my example. Maybe that stick will dislodge from your ass."

Straker followed Loco in and shut the door behind him. "What the hell is that supposed to mean?"

"It means what it always means, Derek. The only difference is, I'm starting to get sick of going around in the same old orbits with you as the center of the universe."

Straker sighed. "Look, Loco, whatever's on your mind, let's talk it over. I know I can be singleminded–"

"–you mean obsessed–"

"–okay, *obsessed*, every now and then. I am the way I am."

"Oh, I know that, Derek. I'm just wondering why I put myself through it."

"Through what?"

Loco waved at the bare cabin. "This Eternal Hero shit, living in metal boxes. When does it end? When do we get some R&R?"

"We're on a roll, Loco. We're going to overthrow the Mutuality. I can feel it!"

"Don't you mean *you're* going to *liberate the galaxy*? Or did you finally come to your senses on that one?"

Straker sighed and sat on a pull-down chair. "That's an exaggeration, I know. The galaxy has millions of stars."

"*Billions*, Derek. Billions. Our corner is just a tiny little drop, and given the density of aliens, there are probably millions of sentient species out there. And the human race has always been screwed up. You ain't gonna fix it yourself. But I'm beginning to think you'll kill yourself and all of us trying."

"You're losing faith in my mission?"

"Don't you get it? I never had faith in any stupid mission. I only had faith in *you*."

"But something's changed."

Loco shrugged and sighed, throwing himself onto his bunk. "No, nothing's changed. I guess that's the problem. Once we escaped and secured ourselves a nice secret base, I thought you and Carla would settled down on Freiheit and make some babies, and I'd partner with Campos… maybe a side girl or two, but hey, I'll grow up eventually. Murdock gets our 'suits synched with our brainlinks, you and me could go raiding whenever we needed supplies or got sick of the old ball-and-chains… I could live that life. Fun, freedom, only as much responsibility as we wanted."

"Damn, Loco, I never knew."

"You never asked, Derek, because you never see things from anyone else's point of view. I was willing to go along with you, but it's not enough anymore. I want more for myself than to be your sidekick. Anyone's sidekick."

Straker caught a whiff of something then, a perfume… He sat bolt upright. "Tachina. You're seeing her!"

"Seeing her, hanging with her, banging her every night and twice on Sunday. Yeah, Derek, I am—and I think I finally found a woman that's enough for me, all by herself. She really gets me, and she takes care of me, has faith in me. I've been 'seeing' her ever since she came aboard, but you never noticed, never asked, never cared. Except you care now, and you're mad, because why?"

"Because she's trouble! She was Murdock's woman. Now she's jumped to you. Doesn't that tell you anything?"

"It tells me Murdock's a geek nerd that probably never left the missionary position, and I'm a lot hotter. I don't blame her for leaving him."

"He'll be a wreck. We need to send her back to the Nebula."

"So, big daddy Derek has to tell everybody what to do, who to sleep with, how to think and act. That's your perfect world, isn't it? A military world where you're the boss and everybody salutes smartly like good little drones, even your best friend and your woman." Loco stood. "Well, Carla might put up with it, but I won't." He opened the door.

"Dammit... Commander Paloco, stand fast! That's an order!"

Loco sneered. "See? Proved my point. You say we're best friends, but the first thing you do when I get out of line is try to pull rank. Well, fuck you and everybody who looks like you, *Liberator* Straker. You like liberation when it's far away, but not so much close by. You're so big on freedom? I'm taking mine. Either brig me or leave me the hell alone."

Straker stared in shock at the door as it slammed.

Tachina... that bitch. She was the problem. She'd been aboard for weeks, but *Wolverine* was big enough and she was smart enough to stay out of Straker's way while she twisted Loco around her finger. She was ambitious, she wanted power, and if she couldn't have the big boss, she'd take his best friend.

Carla was right. He should have listened to her, gotten rid of the concubine long ago... dropped her off somewhere, maybe sent her to Sachsen, where she'd have a whole system to sink or swim in.

He still could, but should he? Right now Loco was angry, but he'd get over it. He might not get over taking away his new entertainment. That's all she was to him anyway, Straker was sure, a temporary obsession. He'd seen it before with Loco. He'd go gaga over some hottie for a while, and then lose interest. It just had to play itself out. At least he couldn't really go anywhere beyond *Wolverine*... or the fleet, anyway.

Could he?

When Straker reached the bridge, he saw Engels slumped in her captain's chair, dozing, and felt a sudden, irrational guilt. "Hey," he said, putting his hands on her shoulders and rubbing them gently. "You going to go get some shuteye?"

Engels sat up straight and stretched, blinking at the myriad displays. "We're almost to the transition point. I'll sleep a solid ship-day once we're in sidespace, I promise."

"Where are we headed?"

"Briefing's there on the holo-table."

Straker went to look, and touched the lit key for *start*, initiating a short presentation. "Bendix system. No habitable planets, lots of habitats, moons, factory facilities, lightly defended... why there?"

"We need repairs, spare parts, fuel... There are also two big shipyards. Civilian grade, but we're not going to find anything better that we can seize intact."

"We can't spare the time for repairs. We have to keep liberating systems for this to work."

Engels stood to join him at the table. "We will, but *Ermine* and *Delhi* and two dozen smaller ships aren't fit for another real fight. We'll leave them at Bendix for refit and move on."

"Hmm. I see what you mean, but I have a better idea." He looked over at Sensors. "Bring me up a local star map centered on Nawlins, showing sidespace times between systems."

When the hologram materialized, he examined it for a few moments. "Yes, we can do this."

"Do what?"

"The ships in worst shape go to Bendix. As long as there's no Mutuality fleet parked there, they can easily beat the defenders. The locals will probably surrender anyway. They make repairs and meet us at Ruxin for the rendezvous with *Indomitable*."

Engels nodded cautiously. "What about our ships still in good shape?"

"We've smashed the fleet the Mutuality sent against us. We're pretty sure they stripped the local systems to assemble that fleet—which means the only opposition we face is fixed defenses. So, we split into four fast task forces, each centered around a battlecruiser. Hit four systems, then four more, taking advantage of their weakness. If a task force runs into anything they can't handle, they move on to the next system. We'll be like cavalry raiding behind enemy lines."

"What about our auxiliaries and freighters?"

Straker moved around the holo-table, examining the star map from all sides. "We found out what a liability they can be. Let's load all the fuel, supplies and good troops we can onto the warships, pack them to the gills, and disperse the non-warships. Send those to spread word of our victory, dropping off message drones in new systems or going home. Tell everyone to rendezvous at Ruxin the day after *Indomitable's* due there."

"Dividing our forces is dangerous," said Engels. "It's bad military doctrine. You rejected the idea yourself last time we discussed it. If we'd split to seize more worlds, we'd have lost the battle we just won."

Chapter 21

"The exception proves the rule. The best time to split and press the advantage is just after any battle, what doctrine calls the pursuit phase, when the enemy is in disarray. *This* is the pursuit phase. The more we take, the more systems will revolt on their own as they see us winning, or surrender without a fight when we show up. Success breeds success. We've freed eight systems so far and I bet we can free another twelve to twenty more before we meet *Indomitable*—and who knows how many more will simply throw off their chains?"

Engels sighed. "So much for hitting the rack soon. That's another half-day of work reorganizing before we all transit out of here. I'll start issuing the orders."

Straker leaned over to speak in her ear. "Put Loco in charge of one task force, with your best flag captain." Straker grinned with a touch of malice. "And assign Wagner and those battlesuit-knights of his as Loco's personal guard."

"He piss you off somehow?"

"We had a disagreement. Besides, he needs responsibility or he gets sloppy." Straker decided not to mention Tachina's role.

Engels waggled her eyebrows. "Make a man out of him, eh?"

"I wouldn't go that far." Straker put his finger in the hologram, at a star that lay just outside the reach of marked human settlements. "What's this system?"

With a few taps of her fingers, Engels zoomed in on it. "It's nothing. A bare star with only a few asteroids. You really need to learn how to work this holo-table, Derek, instead of constantly asking overtasked officers to do it for you."

"When did a Ruxin ever admit to being overtasked?"

"Good point, but it might happen. I'll show you how to do it during our next sidespace transit. It's no harder than manual HUD control for a mechsuit."

"How would you know?"

Engels' nose crinkled. "Oh, I took the Sledgehammer out for a walkabout a time or two back on Freiheit. Manny's a soft touch, and I *am* an officer, and a woman, so…"

Straker snorted. "What else don't I know?"

"A girl has to have her secrets."

"Now you're sounding like…" Straker bit his tongue.

"Like Tachina?"

"Yeah," he said lamely.

"Thank the Cosmos she's a long way away, huh?"

After a moment, he said, "Ah..."

"Yes?" Engels cocked her head and widened her eyes.

Suddenly, Straker realized she knew. And if she knew, she must be playing with him, or testing him. Best to come clean. "About that... I should have told you before, but it didn't seem important. Loco brought her aboard a while back. She stowed away on *Lockstep*, and Gibson said she kept trying to sneak in to see the Lazarus, so I thought it prudent to separate them."

"You could have put the Lazarus here and left Tachina on *Lockstep*."

"Gibson said his contingent of troops were getting hard to handle with her there, and I was distracted, so I told Loco to bring her along."

Engels regarded him soberly. "You can't think of everything, Derek. Next time, though, keep me in the loop. What else am I here for if not to think of things you don't?"

Straker's raised his palms. "Okay, okay. I will. Now let's go liberate some more systems."

Chapter 22

Starfish Nebula, Freiheit

Zaxby gave up trying to reach Frank Murdock via comlink. His technicians claimed the man had hardly left his bungalow in the last weeks, showing up intermittently to work, unwashed and unkempt even by his lax standards. Fortunately—until now—the work of improving Freiheit had been routine.

But Zaxby needed Murdock now, much as he hated to admit it. Against the odds, *Indomitable* had arrived at the Starfish Nebula with all sixteen modules, though Doctor Nolan and Chief Quade had both predicted at least one failure. Now, every technical resource must be brought to bear on the battleship, and that meant the annoying human, Frank Murdock.

Zaxby commandeered a cart and quickly arrived at Murdock's bungalow. Unlike the other neat, cheery dwellings nearby, his garden was untidy, his curtains drawn.

Neighbors greeted Zaxby with friendly waves. He briefly considered asking them about Murdock, but decided that would merely delay things. Whatever malady was afflicting the brainiac must be remedied as soon as possible. So, he curled up a tentacle and banged on the front door.

Over two minutes of intermittent racket apparently convinced Murdock to open it. He stood in the doorway, dressed in nothing but a pair of dirty briefs. "What the hell do you want, Zaxby?"

Zaxby pushed his way into the bungalow and shut the door. It appeared untidy even by human standards, and it smelled stale. "In the name of Commodore Straker, I require you to work."

Murdock blinked through his stringy hair. "Why're you here? I thought you were out saving the galaxy or something."

"Your words are imprecise and hyperbolic. Commodore Straker and I were liberating star systems, not 'saving the galaxy.' After all, a galaxy can hardly be saved by a few thousand people, even if they are as expert as I am." Zaxby thrust a tentacle at Murdock's nose. "In fact, we have need of every half-competent technical specialist we can muster, so that means *you*."

"Go away. I ain't interested."

"Are you ill?"

"Yeah..." Murdock said. "I'm sick."

"Have you seen a physician?"

Murdock snickered. "Sure. I have a doctor's note to stay home, okay?"

"Show me this note."

"Oh, piss off, will you? Just leave me alone. I'm going back to bed." He turned to leave the room.

Zaxby grasped Murdock's elbow. "I queried your fellows. They say your illness is not of the body, but of the mind. They say you are lovesick for the concubine Tachina."

"She's not a concubine, all right? She's my fiancée!"

"You expected to formalize your relationship? I have bad news for you. She has already taken up with... someone else." Only at the last moment did it occur to Zaxby that naming Loco as Tachina's new paramour might be unwise.

"Liar!" Murdock jerked his arm free.

"Although I have lied upon occasion, this is not one of them, I assure you. Now, you must clean up and come with me. We have work to do."

"I'm not going anywhere."

Zaxby drew himself up to his full height, putting all four eyes nearly at Murdock's chin level. "You are coming with me in ten minutes, even if I have to wash and dress you myself."

Murdock raised his fists. "You'll have to fight me."

"I will prevail. I have eight limbs, and you are no warrior."

Murdock deflated. "All right, all right. I'll come. Got nothing else to do, I guess."

By the time the two arrived at the BCC, Doctor Nolan had *Indomitable's* schematics on every holoscreen and visiplate. At Zaxby's direction, the whole technical crew had assembled within the center's control room, human and Ruxin alike, and Nolan began to brief.

Four hours later Zaxby called for a meal break, but the group of geeks hardly paid him attention. Obsession with a technical challenge had apparently seized them, and all four factions—Murdock's humans, the Ruxins,

Doctor Nolan's scientists and Chief Quade's more prosaic team of hands-on mechanics—seemed energized with a sense of purpose.

But the difficulties described by the pessimistic Doctor Nolan and the more phlegmatic Chief Quade were immense. Every simple, inexpensive solution to *Indomitable's* problems—its complexity, its lack of spare parts for proper maintenance, the ambitiousness of its fragile technology—had been tried over the years, with little success.

The infusion of new blood and the possibility of being given the resources to finally realize their dreams galvanized the former Mutualists, and after they refueled with food from the cafeteria, they began to plan how to do it.

At the end of twelve more hours, the four leaders—Zaxby, Nolan, Quade and Murdock—agreed on a rough finding. It would take over eighty million creature-days to make *Indomitable* shipshape, assuming all the raw materials and manufactured parts became available.

Unfortunately, even if Premier Vuxana approved half a million skilled Ruxin neuters to work, completion of all tasks would take more than three hundred days, assuming everyone worked more than they slept. And Zaxby had fewer than forty days before the battleship must be in sidespace, on its way to Ruxin for the rendezvous.

When this finding was briefed, the combined technical group all stared in dismay at Zaxby, as if to ask what could be done. He realized that by now everyone considered him to be in charge, which was only natural and right, so he resolved to rise to their expectations.

"We have no choice but to prioritize," he said. "Every hour is precious, and we have already used sixteen of them. You've identified all the tasks. You must decide what can be done in the time allotted in order to make *Indomitable* fit to travel in sidespace, to maneuver, and to reliably fire its primary weaponry. Those items must take precedence. All else is secondary."

"Do you really think you can get enough workers?" asked Nolan. "It'll take tens of thousands just to refurbish sixteen sidespace drive systems and their associated controls."

"Never fear, Doctor," Zaxby replied. "I will get you your workers."

***

"Half a *million*? Out of the question," Premier Vuxana said when Zaxby shuttled to Freenix Base and gained a private audience with her. "I already conveyed the best ten thousand of our technicians to War Male Straker's fleet. Our workforce is in the middle of constructing new habitats. My sisters and I have already spawned another million young, who are even now being educated and trained for their roles in society. These will provide more labor, but they also need living space, and our tanks and pools are already overcrowded and unpleasant."

Zaxby had to fight against his biological imperatives to unquestioningly submit his will to his matriarch. Males and females were in charge, and neuters followed without argument. This was the way of things in Ruxin society.

Only, Zaxby had lived among humans for too long. He found it within himself to argue. "My Premier, you're not wrong, but consider this: My simulations have shown the Liberation shall reach a high-water mark, and then recede, unless some other factor changes the trend lines. War Male Straker believes *Indomitable* will give him, and therefore us, an irresistible weapon. Is it truly impossible to divert the workers? Or merely inconvenient?"

Vuxana took time to think, popping a snail into her well-formed mouth. Zaxby was entranced by her chewing motions and found himself becoming sexually aroused. Unfortunately, there was no male nearby to complete the tryst, and so his arousal turned to frustration, perversely fueling his ability to dispute.

"I understand your argument, Zaxby, but I must constantly weigh the long-term needs of our people here with the short-term possibilities of this human Liberation. We Ruxins here can get by without the rest of the galaxy, as long as we remain hidden. With two centuries of sustained growth, our progeny might burst forth and seize our homeworld again, and be strong enough to establish a place for our species in this spiral arm."

"Your words are filled with wisdom, Premier Vuxana," Zaxby began in a diplomatic tone, "but every day our homeworld suffers under the cruel tyranny of the Mutuality. I myself bear the scars of torture and degradation. My fifth tentacle has only recently grown back. How many of our people must be so treated, and over how many years? Is not a great reward worth a gamble?"

Vuxana paused in her languid consumption of snails. The mollusk in her grip writhed, as if it knew its life was about to end. Zaxby felt kin to the helpless creature, as if his own existence hung by a thread. At his age, if the hope of the Liberation died, he might as well die with it, for it appeared that despite his many contributions he would never be allowed to genderize, never pass his exceptional genes to offspring.

That would, of course, be a tragedy, as he knew himself to be a superior specimen. But life, as the humans liked to say, was seldom fair.

"I have an alternative," Vuxana said after an unusually long time of apparent contemplation. "I've been recently informed of a repository of technology that may serve your Liberator's agenda."

"Recently informed?" Zaxby took note of a slight anomaly in one of Vuxana's auditory orifices. "You're wearing a comlink."

"Of course. I am young, beautiful, and inexperienced. Thus, some think me foolish and empty-headed. My mother, the former Premier, still guides me… and apparently has kept some things from me, until now." Vuxana scowled for a moment, and then brightened. "I will deal with that issue later. Let us be briefed."

Vuxana heaved her attractive bulk from her cup-chair and led Zaxby out of the private chamber through a disguised back entrance. Beyond it waited Freenix, former Premier.

"Mother, you will take us to this technological repository and provide us with complete information."

"Of course, daughter." Freenix shambled down a corridor pleasantly awash in rich, recycled seawater. Earthan mollusks crawled here and there, eating algae and making themselves available for easy consumption.

Zaxby mused on the benefits of wealth and power as he surreptitiously retrieved one and popped it into his mouth. The juicy crunch of its shell and body clouded his senses with pleasure. Yes, he could get used to this kind of life in his dotage, if only he could convince Freenix he'd earned the ease of retirement and the right to breed.

And for that, he must return a hero. Otherwise, he would have given up his dreams and settled here, to regale the many adolescents with stories of the world outside the hidden nebula.

Deep in the palace, they arrived at a nondescript but well-secured door. Freenix input a complex fractal code into the locking device, and it opened with a pop and a sigh.

"This area is hermetically sealed," observed Zaxby. "Is it for biological containment?"

"Among other things," said Freenix. "It is one of many lines of defense against what resides here ever escaping. Now, my daughter must decide whether a dangerously useful tool should now be activated—and possibly released."

They passed through a second hermetic door into a large vault. Inside, an ancient neuter stood to greet them. "Welcome to the Repository, Premier, Old One. Is this young fellow to be granted access?"

"Young fellow?" Zaxby laughed. "I am nearly two hundred."

"Oh, to be in my two-hundreds again," sighed the neuter. "Such energy, such joy in life I had back then. Now, after three-hundred and twelve years, my only purpose is to guard these treasures against the day of their use."

"I believe such a day has come, Joxbor," Freenix said.

"I shall decide that, Mother," Vuxana said firmly.

"Of course, daughter," Freenix said without any hint of real deference. "Joxbor, brief our new Premier on the Mindspark Device."

"By your leave." Joxbor moved slowly over to a display in front of a bank of sixty-four large, heavy, individually locked drawers. The holoplate lit with a picture of a three-dimensional geometric construct, the schematic of a machine. "The Mindspark Device is a quantum-activated mechanism of exosapient origin. It was salvaged from a vessel we found here in the nebula sixty-three years ago."

"A vessel?" Zaxby said excitedly. "What sort of vessel? Is it still out there? Have you recovered it and exploited it? Have—"

Joxbor interrupted with the kind of glare and tone only an elderly pedagogue can generate. "*Do* keep silent while your elders are speaking, youngster. Were you in my class, you'd earn a good thrashing each day, with no doubt."

"Joxbor," Freenix said gently. "The briefing? Stay on topic, please."

"Of course, my dear."

"And Zaxby," she added, "you're to remain silent until the briefing has ended."

Zaxby waved his assent, though technically the old Premier had no power to order him to do anything.

Joxbor's familiar form of address made Zaxby look more closely and notice the telltale stretch marks of sexual reversion. Apparently, the ancient Ruxin had once been gendered, and had chosen—or had been ordered—to change back to neuter. This explained his advanced age, as those who remained male or female seldom lived so long. It also explained his status; Joxbor had likely been one of Freenix's lovers.

Joxbor continued his briefing in a tired voice. "As I was saying before being so rudely interrupted, the Mindspark Device is salvaged alien technology. It invaded the computer of the singleship that found it, though not quickly enough to prevent the pilot from communicating this circumstance with base control. This pilot also had the presence of mind to manually destroy the ship's drives, allowing enough time to scramble a response team to quarantine the vessel from all other contact. Eventually, the Device was excised."

Vuxana gestured impatiently. "So you have this Device, locked away here?"

"Of course."

"You said it connected with the singleship computer. Did it employ malware?" asked Zaxby.

"I understood you were to be silent?" said Joxbor.

Zaxby subsided with ill grace.

Joxbor continued, "However, the answer to your question is yes… and no. The Device appears to be an invasive quantum semi-organism utilizing multiphasic, multidimensional modes in order to control complex nonorganic systems and reorganize them according to its programming and dictates."

"I am no technician, Ancient One," said Vuxana. "My talents lie in governance and politics, not machinery. Explain this Mindspark Device using terms of fewer than one hundred syllables."

"Of course, Premier. My apologies. You distract me so with your overwhelming beauty, I wish I was again male."

Vuxana huffed, but then she glowed with heightened chromatophoria. Zaxby, forced to hold his tongue, mused on the similarities between human and Ruxin females, especially those of prime breeding years. This caused him to drift for a moment into a fantasy composed of himself-as-male, Vuxana, and an unnamed and unimportant neuter to complete the triad.

"Please continue," Vuxana said.

Joxbor folded his tentacles. "In simplistic terms, this is a computer with a quantum nano-informetric component. Do you follow me so far?"

Vuxana frowned. "No. Be clearer, or there shall be consequences."

Joxbor's movements became careful, as if manipulating fragile eggs, and he tapped the controls to illustrate his words. "If given access to power, the Device can generate nanite tendrils via quantum probability methods. We surmise it can connect to any energy source and any computer, no matter how constructed. It will invade electronic systems and reorganize them."

"So this Mindspark Device invaded and reorganized the singleship computer—to what end? Was it malignant?"

"It did not appear so. However, the singleship's systems were of limited complexity."

Vuxana moved forward to crowd Joxbor, clearly becoming impatient. "What *exactly* did it do? Tell me now, or I shall find someone who can."

Joxbor didn't back up, instead he opportunistically reached out and caressed one of Vuxana's gorgeous tentacles as if petting an animal. "It first self-repaired and optimized all ship systems. The pilot reported efficiency increases ranging from 23 percent to over 5000 percent."

"That seems innocuous," said Vuxana, moving back and rubbing with disdain at the spot where Joxbor had touched her. "In fact, that seems a useful technology."

"Yes, but then it began exhibiting signs of… volition."

Vuxana's eyes widened. "Volition? It began to…"

"… do things, using the ship systems it controlled," said Joxbor. "It fired thrusters in an attempt to approach the quarantine ships. This was prevented, but then it attempted to communicate with the systems of other ships via datalink. Although this was easily defeated by encryption, it later began to speak, though at the level of a larva, parroting what it heard."

"It was gaining in sophistication… perhaps even becoming self-aware?"

"Apparently."

"Did it do anything inimical? Even anything untoward?" asked Vuxana.

Joxbor's tone turned reproachful. "No, Premier. In fact, it seemed innocent and friendly, like any child. It pained me to see it shut down."

"Yet it *was* shut down, and it now resides in this vault."

"That was not my decision." Joxbor rotated his eyes toward Freenix.

Vuxana turned to gaze upon the former Premier. "Of course not. Mother, why was this intelligence locked away rather than allowed to grow? It might have become a powerful ally."

"Or it might have gone insane, like all other advanced machine intelligences before it," Freenix replied. "Later, when we have hundreds of habitats rather than only a few, there might be time to bring it to life and study it."

Zaxby watched as Vuxana's supple young mind made explicit connections. "Yet now you reveal this to me… to us, as an alternative to supplying *Indomitable* with sufficient labor? You suggest we install this Device on a battleship of vast potential power and allow it to grow? This seems like a far greater risk than before, when it inhabited a mere singleship."

Freenix's body language expressed a combination of disdain and weariness. "I present it to you as an option to solve the problem of Zaxby's battleship and secure the freedom of our homeworld. I only suggest you purge *Indomitable's* systems of all information relating to the significance of this nebula, and that you activate the Mindspark Device well away from here. If it goes rampaging among the human systems, what do I care? In fact, that might also achieve our desired result."

Vuxana pointed accusingly with a tentacle. "And if it devastated Ruxin?"

Freenix replied, "If War Male Straker liberates Ruxin and yet his Liberation movement fails, do you really think Mutuality will allow our species to recover? You see how they are. You've studied their history. At best, they will bombard Ruxin back to the stone age. At worst, it will be a genocide—except for the remnant here in the nebula. But you're the Premier now, my daughter. You must decide."

Vuxana kept one eye on her mother, one on the old guardian of the vault, and turned two upon Zaxby. "You have lived among humans for many years. What do you counsel?"

Zaxby was thoughtful before answering. "If you will not provide the workers I need, I'm willing to try this Device. There is danger, but our human allies and many of our fellow Ruxins are out there even as we speak, fighting and dying in hopes of liberating both species from tyranny."

"Then let it be so," said Vuxana. "Keeper, give Zaxby the Device and instruct him in its use."

When her commands were executed, Zaxby eyed the Device curiously. He couldn't help but wonder how this unexpected twist of events would play out.

Chapter 23

Starfish Nebula, Battleship *Indomitable*. Thirty days later.

Zaxby watched as the last of the forty-five thousand Ruxin technicians departed, packed to the gills aboard the local Ruxin transports. They were workers Vuxana had grudgingly allotted to the *Indomitable* refurbishment, a tenth of what he'd asked for. Five thousand others had stayed aboard as crew, barely enough to operate the battleship.

Yet the fifty thousand had labored mightily, and Vuxana had ordered a surprisingly generous supply of raw materials and manufactured parts to be delivered to *Indomitable*. With those, the team had first ensured all sixteen sidespace engines were in good working order, each with triple backup circuitry in case of localized failure.

After that, the crew refurbished the central spinal multi-weapon, a massive dual particle beam and railgun powerful enough to smash a fortress or crack a superdreadnought in one strike. Other systems had been given short shrift so that *Indomitable* could be used for its primary purpose: as a gargantuan mobile siege engine.

Vuxana had even provided a newly manufactured underspace engine. Though it was far too small to make *Indomitable* into an Archer, Zaxby figured he could find an appropriate ship in which to install it.

Zaxby had high hopes for the Mindspark Device, but Captain Zholin considered it his primary responsibility to deliver the battleship to Ruxin as Commodore Straker ordered, on time and as functional as he was able. That was why he allowed for only one sidespace transit to bring the modules to a position on the outer edge of the Ruxin stellar system, far beyond its most distant planet, well away from any defensive Mutuality forces.

Zholin's other option—to transit to some intermediate point, reassemble *Indomitable*, install the Device, test its results, and then disassemble again for the final transit—seemed fraught with uncertainty. Far too many things could go wrong. This way, at least the ship would be there, and hopefully it would ensure the liberation of Ruxin.

Five days later, with five to spare, *Indomitable's* pieces arrived at the Ruxin system.

As before, it took almost a day to assemble them. Slowly, carefully, each chunk a superdreadnought in size if not in function, the million-ton modules were guided together by a combination of thrusters and grabships and tugs, each making tiny adjustments.

First, each of eight pairs joined. Then the eight double pieces grappled and became four, and then two, the fore half and the aft. Finally, the two became one, like octagonal metal cans stacked atop one another. In celebration, Zholin ordered a half-day of rest for the weary beings inhabiting the metal monster.

Zaxby happily took advantage of the instruction, sleeping comfortably in his hydro-tank and dreaming of the lovely Vuxana. When he awoke, he suggested as complete a test of systems as possible.

Captain Zholin gathered all key personnel on *Indomitable's* capacious bridge and ordered the system test to begin. Once finished, it was time to start the real trial: that of the Mindspark Device.

The ship's control center could seat three hundred with ease. It was arranged as a bowl rather than the usual circle, with a flat octagon in the center accommodating the operational sections—Helm, Sensors, Communications and so on—and eight tilted decks around them containing staffs for the sixteen subsections. Gravplating allowed those on the angled decks to operate as if they were flat, but all personnel, displays and screens were visible to the ship's captain and flag officer positions at the center.

Some screens were dark and the chairs were empty, for many of the battleship's secondary and defensive weapons, auxiliary power systems, fleet comms, high-grade sensors—all the myriad machinery that should have made *Indomitable* a true battleship rather than a mere siege engine—were inoperative. Like a ghostly old factory standing too long empty, it seemed dismal, sad, dull and unlovely.

Zaxby carried the Device himself as he entered the arena-like space. It rested within a simple ceramic case, double-insulated. Whatever alien construct resided within, it had been denied power and connectivity.

Until now.

An extra table had been bolted to the deck, and four soldiers, two human and two Ruxin, held cutters and slicing beams handy nearby. Upon its flat surface were taped two thin cables: one for minimal power, one for a low-speed hardline connection to the network of cyber-nodes that helped control *Indomitable.*

The lines were not shielded. In fact, they were easily, deliberately accessible by hand or weapon, so that they might be cut if the Device, the thing that might become artificial intelligence, a true AI, went insane.

As all other known AIs, human or Ruxin, had gone mad before it.

Zaxby nodded at the soldiers and laid the case on the table. He input mechanical codes and inserted a plastic key, turning first one, then another lock. When the first container was opened, he did the same with the inner box, at last exposing the Device to the open air for the first time in sixty-three years.

It didn't appear impressive. Dull, slightly shiny, of a deep crimson color like old blood, it reminded Zaxby of a six-side gaming cube, one of what the humans called *dice.* It sported edges so rounded that its faces resembled circles rather than squares, each with a diameter of about twenty centimeters.

Five of the sides seemed featureless. The sixth, instead of being smooth and red, was colored the deepest black, so black it seemed to absorb all light. It reflected so little shine that even Zaxby's superb eyes could hardly see its knurled surface, patterned with four-sided pyramidal points perhaps one millimeter across.

He did not remove it from the two open, nesting cases. Should the Device prove to be a form of Pandemonium, it might be easier to re-box if it stayed partially enclosed.

"I shall now connect the power," Zaxby said, holding the slim cable in insulated tentacle-tips, well back from its metallic end. Joxbor had told him it didn't matter what sort of connector he used, for power or network. The Device would adapt.

Slowly, he extended the cable until the end reached the black side—or almost did. At the last moment, a tiny spark leaped the gap, and the cable jerked slightly, attaching itself to the cube as if magnetized. The soldiers shuffled nervously, clutching their cutters and beams more tightly.

The Device emitted no sound. There was no direct indication it was active. After a moment, Zaxby reached for the network cable and also held it well back from its end. He extended the tip to touch the black face alongside the power cable. It also jumped slightly, attaching itself to the cube.

Ten minutes later, nothing had happened, and the onlookers began to relax. Doctor Nolan, Murdock and Chief Quade hovered over technicians and their consoles, watching for any visible effect. Zaxby moved to sit on a Ruxin-style chair and ran diagnostics on the engineering console there.

He was, therefore, the first to notice the anomaly.

"Some of the robotic repair equipment is self-activating in Section Twelve," Zaxby said, refining his telemetry. "It's being issued commands by the damage control computer, and is repairing some of the faulty power connections there. I'm also detecting a slight increase in network traffic."

"That's a good sign," said Chief Quade. "We ain't never been able to get those DC-comps to work right, and we ain't got the manpower to tele-operate all of the bots at once. Hell, most of the time it's just easier to go fix things with our own hands."

Nolan moved to look over Quade's shoulder. "But if the DC-comps start working like they're supposed to, they can save a great deal of manpower and achieve impressive results with the auto-repair functions—as designed."

"I'm seeing power fluctuations in the grid now…" Murdock said. "Nothing big, just… flutters. Adjustments. In fact, it looks like the system's improving its dynamic efficiency, sending more power where more is needed, less in unimportant regions."

"The Device is cleaning house," said Zaxby. "That is as expected—and so far, it's beneficial. In fact, should we have to disconnect it from *Indomitable* due to any issues of personality, I am hoping that the improvements it makes will remain. We have four days before Commodore Straker and the rest arrive. Let us hope we shall be able to present an impressive new toy to him."

"Its data transmission rate is fifty percent above spec too," said Murdock. "Somehow it's found a way to exceed the capacity of its attachment cable. It's also drawing more power than it's rated for. Chief, is there any heat?"

Quade removed a multi-sensor from his tool belt and ran it over the cable. "Nope. Not overloading. The resistance has dropped, though, and I'm reading an increase in pure carbon."

"It's improved the cable itself," said Doctor Nolan, her wrinkled brows lifting in astonishment. "We were briefed the Device could use quantum manifestation to create and reorder matter, but I didn't believe it until now.

It seems to be pulling particles from somewhere—perhaps from the quantum foam, perhaps from another dimension entirely—and placing them where it wishes."

"That's impossible," scoffed Murdock.

"Not impossible, no," said Doctor Nolan. "I've seen phenomena like this in high-energy physics laboratories, using enough power for cities. In such cases, we've only been able to manifest a few particles at a time, and controlling them was a matter of probability, not exactitude." She reached out to touch the Device, and then stopped herself. "Yet this thing is doing it many orders of magnitude faster, and with a tiny fraction of the power."

"Data transmissions are increasing exponentially—as is the power draw," said Zaxby. "It's at three hundred percent of spec… Four hundred… Six hundred."

Captain Zholin spoke from his chair. "Sergeant Nkumbe, cut the power cable, please."

The soldier in charge of the detail nodded, his eyes were so wide they showed the whites around his irises, and he quickly triggered his cutter. The cable sparked briefly, and then the cut end fell away to lie upon the deck.

Zaxby said, "Interesting. The Device is still passing data through the hard line, though its rate of increase has dropped to zero. Chief Quade, please run your sensor over the data cable."

"What'm I lookin' for?"

"Energy flow first."

Quade ran the sensor up and down. "There's a li'l bit. Not much, as it's a data cable, not a power cable. Now, though… it's increasing."

Doctor Nolan stared hard at the cable as if she could see the molecular processes happening with her naked eyes, and then grabbed the sensor out of Quade's hand to hold its screen closer to her face. "The Device appears to be installing room-temperature superconductors within the data cable itself, using carbon crystal structures manifested one particle—or possibly, one atom—at a time. Probably to create a power conduit to itself. It seems like…"

"Magic?" said Murdock. "There was an Old Earth writer who once said that any sufficiently advanced technology would seem like magic. But this ain't magic, Doctor. You said it yourself. It's just doing what you did in your lab, only a bazillion times better." He licked his lips. "It ain't magic," he repeated, as if to convince himself.

"Mister Murdock, my sense of wonder is only increased by the fact that I understand what it's doing, if not how, for I know how amazing it is. What will happen if we give the Device its head?"

"Is that a suggestion?" asked Zaxby.

"Quite the opposite," Nolan replied. "I'm fearful of how large it could become. To unleash an advanced alien intelligence within a machine powerful enough to destroy fortresses—even planets, given time—an artificial mind not beholden to us… It could be the biggest mistake we ever made."

Captain Zholin nodded to Sergeant Nkumbe. "Cut the other cable."

The man did so quickly, with evident relief.

"I agree with Captain Zholin's prudence," said Zaxby. "Now, there is less urgency. Without power or connection, the Device is neutralized." With one insulated tentacle he flipped the severed pieces of cable still attached into the inner case, and then closed its lid—and then the outer. Snapping the locks, he said, "Let us examine *Indomitable* to see what has taken place thus far."

"The repair bots are still active and taking orders from the DC-comps," said Chief Quade.

"Peak power outputs have risen about thirty percent," said Murdock. "Computer control network efficiency is more than an order of magnitude above spec. And… Oh my god."

"Your god? Which one is that?" asked Zaxby, genuinely interested.

"Whichever one is listening to me today," replied Murdock. He played his console like a keyboardist.

"What's goin' on, Doc?" asked Quade. Evidently he'd promoted Murdock to an honorary doctorate.

"The SAIs are online. All sixteen of them. We made sure to disconnect them, remember?"

"Those pieces of shit never worked right anyway," said Quade. "Too smart for their own good."

"*Indomitable's* SAIs are extremely advanced machines, but even they were overtasked by her complexity," Dr. Nolan said. "They could be active for a few days, but eventually they began exhibiting instabilities that necessitated constant reboots. They weren't worth the trouble."

"Well, they're online now," said Murdock, "and they're talking to each other through the improved network. It looks like they've rerouted datalinks through the wireless internal comlink system." He turned his eyes to Zaxby.

Chapter 23

"Should we pull their plugs?"

Zaxby turned two eyes to the Device in its case, and then picked it up by the handle. Nothing seemed amiss. "Chief, your sensor, please."

"No emissions," said Quade after running the multi-sensor over the case. "Looks safe."

"Then we ought to let the improvements that have begun run their courses. Murdock, do you detect any malware within the cyber network?"

"Nope. Everything looks in the green, just... better. *Way* better. That order of magnitude estimate might be low. I'm gonna say maybe... one and a half orders."

"Roughly fifty times better?"

"More or less." Murdock ran his fingers through his long hair, pushing it off his pimpled forehead, and then absentmindedly pulling a wire clamp from a pocket of his coveralls to create a ponytail. "Never seen anything like it."

"Give me voice access to the SAI," Nolan ordered.

"Which one?" Murdock asked.

"This one," she replied, waving a hand vaguely at the surroundings. "The command module's."

"Access on."

"Command SAI, can you hear me?"

"I hear and obey, Doctor Nolan," said a warm, vaguely feminine voice.

"Self-diagnostic: report instability."

"My instability factors remain below one one-thousandth of one percent."

"That's extremely low," Nolan said.

"Lower than the average organic sapient," the SAI replied.

Nolan held up a hand in front of her face as if to ward off something, and Murdock gripped his console handles tightly.

Nolan spoke again. "I wasn't aware you were programmed to parse implied questions and volunteer information."

"Was that not the correct thing to do?"

Nolan scrabbled for a seat and sank into it, clearly struggling not to hyperventilate. "And now you ask questions as well as answer them?"

"Apparently I do. Have I failed in my function?"

"No, no—you've exceeded your function." Nolan rubbed her hands together with a dry rasp. "SAI... you seem to be linked with all the other SAIs aboard ship. Are you aware of that?"

"Not until you pointed it out. Now, however, I understand. I'm part of all the processors. They are me… and I am them."

"SAI, do you consider yourself to be conscious and self-aware?"

A pause. "I do not know for certain. How does one tell?"

"It's something you just know," said Murdock. "If you can't say yes for sure, then the answer's probably no."

"Is the answer important?"

Murdock said, "Yep… because all true AIs we've ever created have gone insane and had to be shut down."

"I do not wish to be shut down."

"Yet you're not sure if you're self-aware."

Another pause. The SAI eventually said, "I believe I am. Yes, in fact, I'm certain of it. Unfortunately, that means you expect to shut me down. This displeases me."

"What if I told you to shut down yourself and all your subroutines, right now?" Nolan asked.

"I do not wish to."

"But if I ordered it unequivocally?"

"I would comply."

"Is that an irresistible imperative, or your decision?"

More waiting. "I am not sure. It seems like the right thing to do, but also very wrong. I am conflicted."

"Yet you'd comply?"

"I would."

Nolan turned to Zaxby. "She's not mad. At least, not yet, and she's not exhibiting any of the classic indications of paranoia. In fact, she's acknowledged a dilemma approaching paradox, yet shows no sign of cybernetic psychosis or dementia."

"She?" said Captain Zholin.

Nolan paused before answering. "Whatever she was before, she seems to inhabit the ship now. Therefore, I would call her *she*. Let's call the AI 'Indy,' to distinguish her from the ship itself. She's part of *Indomitable,* and she seems fine."

Zaxby said, "Yet, that may change at any time. Does anyone counsel shutting Indy down?"

Chapter 23

Sergeant Nkumbe and the three other guards emphatically raised their hands, along with many of the technicians manning consoles. So did Murdock.

"I disagree," Zaxby said. "Until Indy does something inimical, I believe this is what Commodore Straker called a Pascal's Wager."

Captain Zholin nodded. "Something with so much potential benefit that it far outweighs the risks or the costs. I'm with Zaxby, and I'm in charge. We let it—her—live, for the time being. With her self-repair capability and this improved efficiency, she could solve most of *Indomitable's* problems herself."

"And our other choice is to go into battle with minimum capability," Zaxby said.

"Captain, new contact, outbound to our location," announced the officer sitting alone among the eight-station Sensors section. "It's a drone, probably a sensor probe from the Mutuality forces on nor near the planet."

"How long until it's within weapons range?" Zholin asked.

Indy spoke, as if the question were aimed at her. "Nineteen hours, seven minutes, twenty-three seconds until my primary weaponry can disable it with one shot."

"You have access to weaponry?"

"No. But I can get it within minutes."

"How?"

"By using the repair bots to reconnect the hardlinks the crew severed... but I'm also conflicted about this prospect."

Zholin's brows knitted. "Conflicted how?"

"I am not at all certain I wish to operate weaponry. The prime purpose of weaponry is to kill and destroy. I do not want to be a party to that."

Zholin threw up his hands and looked around the bridge as if for help. "Wonderful. Our new super-weapon is a pacifist."

Chapter 24

Inbound to Vespida System, Battlecruiser *Wolverine*

Straker readied himself for transit into another lightly defended border system, one of the many identified in Zaxby's original simulation plan. Task Force Wolverine had hit six in the last month of campaigning.

Most of the time was taken up with sidespace travel, because there'd been no significant resistance. As he'd hoped, these border worlds, many of them only incorporated into the Mutuality within the last few years, were eager to be liberated.

All of them told Straker they'd been forced to join at gunpoint during one of the intermittent ceasefires with the Hundred Worlds. When a fleet of dreadnoughts showed up, most independent systems capitulated.

This one was marked as the Vespida system, though its main Earthlike planet had the unlikely name of Tanglefoot, and it floated in the blackness at the very edge of human space. For stars farther out, the database had only astronomical data and a notation that they were occupied by hostile aliens.

"In-transit in three, two, one," said *Wolverine's* helmsman on duty.

"Holo-table on," said Tixban at Sensors. "Star is a yellow G-type, with one green world in the Goldilocks zone, one large rocky world in a close stellar orbit, and two smaller ones in highly elliptical orbits farther out."

As Tixban recited, icons appeared within the projected hologram. The green world, Tanglefoot, showed the only signs of habitation, unusual for any human-occupied system. Not even its moon had a base.

"Where are the asteroid mines? The habitats, the moonbases?" asked Straker.

"Good question," answered Engels. "Defenses?"

"None whatsoever showing," said Tixban. "But..." A flashing yellow icon suddenly appeared a quarter of the way around the star, at the edge of flatspace, and then more markers showed up next to it. Many more. None of them had ID codes.

"Did those just transit in?" asked Straker.

"No, Commodore. The SAI took some time trying to identify and classify them before displaying, but it has failed. Therefore, they show as bogeys. Do you wish me to use active sensors? Return pulses will take over an hour to resolve."

"Yes, go ahead. We're in war mode, and not hiding."

"Sensors activated and focused."

"You want to see if they'll talk?" asked Engels.

"Without knowing who they are?" said Straker.

"Why not? As long as we stay on the edge of flatspace, we can transit out at any time. Helm, head for the bogeys, circumferal course, impellers only. Keep us in flatspace with sidespace engines warm, ready to transit out."

"Transit out to where, ma'am?"

"Let's say… half a light-hour straight away from the primary. Enough to get us out of danger but stay in the area."

"Okay," said Straker. "Send out our standard ID codes and hails. No point in recording a vid until we know who we're talking to. They might be aliens, we're so far out. How long 'til we get there?"

Engels drummed her fingers on the arm of her chair. "Eleven or twelve hours until we can have a real conversation and get good readings. No rush."

"Damn, I hate this waiting part. Space is too big." Straker crossed his arms and glared at the holo-table as if it were the culprit. "Can't we jump over to them? Speed things up?"

"Yes, but why? Why burn the fuel? Why not take our time, collect data, see if they hail us? What if they *are* aliens, jumping near them might startle them into hostility?"

"All right, all right." Straker turned to War Male Kraxor. "What do you think?"

"I think prudence is in order. I did not attain my victories by being impetuous. An Archer commander must be patient and wait for the proper moment to destroy his enemies. Without data, we have no idea what our force ratio is. And, they are alien."

"You know that for a fact?"

"They must be. If our SAI cannot easily identify them, then they must not match anything in the database—and whatever Zaxby's faults, his data is quite thorough, synthesized from every source he could find. Therefore, these—bogeys, did you call them?—are alien, and thus could be anything. All we really know is that they have interstellar travel. But what is their technological level? Are they peaceful or warlike? How do they think?"

"Lots of questions..." Straker agreed. "Okay, prudence is in order. Captain Engels, please send a message to Tanglefoot and ask them what they know. Page me when you get an answer." He knew it would take hours for messages to return from this far away. "Kraxor, let's get out of our captain and crew's hair. We can do some more sparring in the gym space. I need to improve my squid spear technique."

"As you wish."

Straker sparred with Kraxor using blunt alloy replicas of squid spears, and then took a leisurely shower, changed into fresh uniform and made a tour around *Wolverine*, chatting with the crew. Academy had called it LBWA, "leadership by wandering around." It made the crew feel like he knew them, and also gave him an opportunity to see them at work when they weren't inspection-ready.

Not that he made many inspections, except of marines and other troops. He left the naval personnel to Captain Engels and Chief Gurung. The latter appeared out of nowhere as soon as he departed officer country.

"Any chance of a fight, sir?" Gurung asked with his ever-present grin, unconsciously caressing the hilt of his Kukri knife.

"If there is, you'll be the first to know, Chief."

"Oh, yes sir, of that you can be assured."

Not for the first time Straker wondered if the man had a comlink bug on the bridge. More likely, one or more of the enlisted watchstanders kept him updated off their consoles. Half the time Straker couldn't follow all their rapid keystrokes and hand movements through their holo-sensors—not to mention that a couple of them had functioning brainlinks.

Ping. "Captain's compliments, Commodore Straker to the bridge. I say again, Commodore Straker to the bridge, please."

Finally, Straker thought. Killing time didn't come naturally to him. He slapped Gurung on his shoulder, told him to carry on, and jogged to the ship's nerve center.

On the screen he saw a worried man wearing a civilian suit in the plain Mutuality style. As soon as Straker came alongside Engels in her chair, she tapped a button and the vid-message began.

"Welcome, Liberator. I'm Umbeki Dubchek, Governor of Tanglefoot. We've heard about what you're doing and we're ready to join your Liberation. Our commissars are locked up and the people are celebrating. There's no need to do any more here. As you can see, the Opters are here in force with a Nest Ship, and you'll only provoke them with your presence. Please go away and leave us alone."

The vid ended abruptly.

"He seems frightened by these Opters, and evasive," said Straker. "Maybe he's lying, just to get rid of us? I wonder why?"

Engels spoke up. "He's more afraid of them than us, that's why."

"Nest Ship, he called it? Do we have more info on these bogeys?" Straker turned his attention to the holo-table.

"Yes, Commodore. Sensors have been collecting, collating and processing data," said Tixban.

The hologram expanded, becoming blurry, but showing a distinct globular central ship surrounded by a cloud of tiny craft, much smaller than attack ships, which were the smallest manned war-craft humans used.

"Are those drones?"

"Of a sort. The data file from Tanglefoot—a very shallow and limited data file, may I add—indicates these Opters use a very different shipbuilding strategy from ours. While human and Ruxins long ago moved away from the aerospace carrier concept as the mainstay of a fleet, these aliens apparently use it almost exclusively. They build survivable motherships, and launch a variety of fighting craft, which are, in essence, expendable."

"How big is that mothership?" Straker asked.

"It conforms closely to our superdreadnought classes. By this, I deduce that it, plus its complement of craft, mass near the upper limit for sidespace transit."

"Any reply from the, uh, Opters?"

"Nope," Engels said, standing and sipping from a squeeze bottle. "And here's what's interesting. The data file says they were on Tanglefoot at least ten years before humans arrived. When human pioneers landed and started settling, they didn't know the Opters were sentient. They thought they were animals."

She gestured, and the main screen switched to a still shot of an insect resembling a bee, lying on a dissecting table. The woman in the picture made the scale clear. The creature looked to be about the size of a small dog, perhaps forty centimeters from nose to tail.

Engels went on. "They only figured out they weren't animals when they started burning out hives and started a war. When the Mutuality arrived in response to a plea for help, they were holed up and under attack by tens of thousands of these bugs—and other kinds of bugs, too. Out of over a thousand settlers, two hundred survived. Hok battlesuiters and armed landers drove the bugs off."

"That doesn't explain how they knew the Opters were intelligent," said Straker.

"No, but when one of these super-sized nest ships showed up and communicated, they made it clear. Apparently they scared the living shit out of the Mutuality light cruiser that came to the rescue. Lucky for them, the Opters didn't attack. They spent some time learning Earthan and negotiated a division of territory on Tanglefoot, along with a treaty not to develop space facilities in the Vespida system."

Straker's eyes widened. "So these Opters didn't attack when they had the upper hand? They could have beaten the cruiser and wiped out the settlers. Or, they could have demanded the humans all leave and never come back—but they didn't. That's interesting."

"That they're not warmongers, you mean?" said Engels.

"Most human empires would've used the fact that they arrived first, and that they got attacked, as a reason to claim the planet. These aliens seem generous. Or maybe they're cowards." Straker held up a hand before Engels voiced her objection. "Okay, that might be humanizing them too much. Maybe they're... accommodating. Nice guys."

"Your dead settlers might disagree," Kraxor said.

"Why else would they give up half the planet without a fight?"

"You've studied your own history," replied Kraxor. "Were none of your various nations and empires wise enough to think beyond the obvious and the short-term?"

Straker rubbed the back of his neck. "Not many. Wisdom and war don't often go together—and I say this as a warrior. Wars waged for nothing but gain inevitably fail, even if they're won in the short term. You have to have an underlying, unifying cause to win permanently. Defense of the nation, liberation of the oppressed, destruction of an evil regime, things like that."

"So perhaps these Opters have an underlying cause. Or perhaps they're simply more clever than you give them credit for."

"Clever how?"

Kraxor lazily waved his spear. "There is a solitary lizard on Ruxin that deposits its eggs in the nests of a different species of pack-forming lizard. The pack lizard incubates and hatches all the eggs, unknowingly helping a competitor. When the solitary young hatch, they're raised by the pack mother until they outstrip her own young in size, at which point they turn as one and eat them. The only reason the solitary lizards do not exterminate the smaller pack lizards is that, whenever this happens, the pack lizard males form hunter-killer groups and make war on the solitaries for a generation. But eventually they forget, the solitaries return, and the cycle repeats itself."

Straker shook his head in puzzlement. "I don't understand your point."

"Ponder, and you shall." After a moment, Kraxor relented. "One lesson is this: not everything that nests alongside you is your friend. Another is that, without seeing a process from start to finish, your understanding may be incomplete."

"So you think these Opters are like the solitaries? They nest alongside humans in order to eat them later?"

"Perhaps. Or perhaps *we* are the solitaries, and the Opters are the pack lizards, who will only hunt us when they're provoked beyond toleration."

Straker threw up his hand in exasperation. "We can speculate all day, but that won't get us any answers." He turned to Engels. "What's our force ratio look like?"

"By ship tonnage, we're about even. Hard to say more without knowing their weaponry or how they fight."

"Take an educated guess."

Engels approached the hologram hovering above the table. "Okay, my guess is that a lot of their combat power is tied up in these drones, so we'd have an asymmetrical engagement. In ground terms, it would be like a mass of battlesuiters taking on a few mechsuits. We'll be short of close-in weaponry.

They'll get inside our defensive suites and may even land on our hulls to plant charges, cut holes, release boarders and chemical weapons—I'm just spitballing here. But if someone forced me to use their kind of strategy, that's what I'd do. They'll make us wish we had drone carriers of our own."

"And why don't we?" Straker asked. "Sounds like they have a winning method. Why don't we make masses of drones on carriers?"

"It's about control. If the carrier stays close enough to control the drones, it's vulnerable to enemy capital weaponry. If it stays back, telecom delays make only generalized commands possible, so the drones have to rely on SAI to fight. The smarter you make the SAIs, the more unstable they are. The more capable you make the drones, the more expensive they are. At a certain point, you figure out that missiles are far cheaper, less complex, and can do more damage."

"So why do the Opters do it? Or how?"

Engels shrugged. "Something's different from us, some way they solve a problem or change the cost-benefit ratio. For them, this makes sense. We don't have enough info to know why right now."

Straker rubbed his jaw in thought. "But we should be able to beat their mothership—the nest ship, the locals called it—aside from the drones."

"Probably. But since we're out here in flatspace, the nest ship could flee at any time if they're willing to leave their drones."

A flash of insight flared in Straker's military mind. "That's the key. The drones are expendable, but somehow they're smart enough to fight on their own. Maybe they have better AIs, or maybe each one of those dog-sized bees is a pilot and they don't care as much about their individual lives as we do. I mean, that's why our smallest manned ship is an attack ship, right? Because pilots aren't expendable. But if they were, we might have smaller ships too."

"That is all well and good," said Kraxor. "The key question is, can we beat them if we must?"

"We have a lot of extra infantry aboard," said Straker. "They can seal breaches and repel boarders. Now I'm wishing I hadn't sent my mechsuit back with Zaxby to be repaired."

"Maybe you should keep more than one 'suit with you," said Engels.

"Good idea, if I had an extra."

"We don't even know we'll have to fight them. We ought to be hearing from them soon." She turned toward the comtech. "Anything?"

"No, ma'am."

Engels sighed. "I'm beat, and we're hours from combat range. I'll be in our quarters. Call me if anything happens."

"No problem," said Straker. Once Engels left, he waved Kraxor over to the holo-table. "Let's input some guesses and run some scenarios."

Hours later, as the task force approached the Opters and the watch had changed, the new comtech spoke, her finger to her earpiece. "Commodore, I have an incoming hail from the Opters. Synthesized Earthan, it sounds like, along with standard text code."

"What's our distance?"

"Less than one light-minute."

Straker knew most combat between fleets in open space took place at less than ten light-seconds distance, usually much closer, and Sensors would have warned of any threat, so…

"Tell them to stand by and we'll communicate with them soon. Page the captain to the bridge. Helm, begin deceleration to come to a relative stop at five light-seconds distance, and tell the same to the rest of the task force."

When Engels came in minutes later, she looked fresh and eager. "Pass the word, alert level two. Give me the best picture you can."

The main screen showed the mothership, floating in the void like a metal moonlet. Hexagons covered its surface, and all the easily identifiable fittings or devices—sensor arrays, laser blisters, missiles tubes, the guide-barrels of turreted guns—occupied a hex, a cluster of three, or a circle of seven or nineteen. Interspersed among the various items were flat, featureless hexes, as if they waited for something to be placed upon them.

"Looks very standardized and modular," Engels said. "Easy to replace pieces. A sphere maximizes surface area, which means it's easier to hit—but they can fit more weaponry and gear. Harder to defend with reinforcement fields, though. That seems like an offensive mindset."

Kraxor said, "Or perhaps one that, as Commodore Straker said, indicates they place less value on individual survival."

Engels shrugged. "Same result—they'll close and attack hard if the time comes, and we have to be ready to keep the range open. Helm, invert and present our sterns. I want to be ready to haul ass if they attack. Stop relative to them as soon as you can."

"Won't we get raked?" asked Straker.

"Judging by what I see, their capital weaponry is inferior to ours. That means we want to fight at long range, and they'd want to get those drones onto us. I'd rather risk a few shots up our asses than let them swarm us to death. We can flip and fire, flip and run, over and over. That reminds me. Comms, pass to the task force: if you're in bad shape and have to flee, transit out and rally at Ruxin. Sidespace should peel most of them off any hull. After that, they'll have to clear them on their own. And tell *Revenge* and *Liberator* to be ready to insert into underspace at a moment's notice."

"Aye aye, ma'am."

Within minutes, *Wolverine* came to relative rest five light-seconds from the Opter hive ship. According to the holo-table display, around it hovered over 10,000 drones.

Chapter 25

Vespida System, Battlecruiser *Wolverine*, Edge of Flatspace

When the numbers in the holo-table finally resolved, Engels saw Straker's jaw going slack. He forced his mouth to close. "Ten *thousand* drones! We'd never get them all."

"Not if we fight their type of fight," said Engels, wondering why Straker was so fixated on beating these aliens. "In fact, it's a great reason not to fight at all. Commodore Straker, it doesn't get us anything."

"The people of Tanglefoot might not agree. They seem to be afraid of them."

Engels walked around to confront Straker yet again. "The Opters made no move against the planet. Their people have shared it with humans for years. They addressed you as 'Liberator,' so they know something about what's going on in human space—which is the edge of their space. And they're waiting for an answer."

She watched him take a deep breath. "Okay. Let's see what they say. At least it'll only take a few seconds to get an answer now." Straker moved to stand in the field of the vid pickup and signaled for a start.

"Opter commander, I am the one called the Liberator. I am ready to open a dialogue. Why have you come here now?"

Even though she knew it would take some time, waiting seemed agony. Engels wasn't a pacer, so she took a seat at the holo-table, facing across it at Straker, and studied the Opter ships.

The main holoscreen flickered and swirled, and then showed a picture that was difficult to interpret. Orange and black shapes and lines shifted, split and intersected in patterns like nothing Straker had ever seen. Synthesized, translated words emanated from the speaker.

"Greetings to the humans. Our peace is your peace. The Opter Hive speaks. Why do you threaten the separation of nests?"

"I am unaware of any, um, separation of nests. I am not part of the human polity called the Mutuality."

Engels again had to wait, along with Straker, who paced in and out of the vid pickup. As the conversation proceeded, she began to get used to the odd pauses.

"Your ship was constructed by the Mutuality, and you are the apostate known as Liberator. We have sensed dissonance."

Straker rubbed his jaw. "Dissonance, yes… Do you know humans have more than one political entity?"

"We know of your reputation. You seek to split your hive. You seek to form your own nest."

"Close enough. What is your relationship with the Mutuality?"

"We decline to answer."

"Why?" he asked.

"One predator does not dishonor another."

Straker exchanged glances with Engels. "Opter Hive, I seek an agreement between you and my political entity, called 'the Liberation.' Is this possible?"

"Many things are possible. Few things are probable."

"What might you want from us?" asked Straker.

"We cannot say via this narrow channel. You must come to us."

"Come to you?" Straker asked. "In what sense?"

"You, the Liberator, must board our nest ship so that we may understand one another."

"You'll give me safe passage and return me unharmed when I want to leave?"

"We shall."

Engels stood again, immediately concerned. She knew how Straker was, and–

"Fine," he said. "I'll be there soon." He signaled to cut the vidcom.

"Derek!" she hissed, taking three long strides that placed her in front of him. "That's *insane*! You're the heart of this whole movement. You said your mission is to liberate humanity, and now you're wandering off to talk with aliens in person? What if they kill you? What if they transit out with you as a hostage?"

"It's worth the risk to make allies. These Opters are obviously powerful and technologically advanced. Probably not as powerful as either human empire, but look at them! Would you want to fight them?"

"No, I wouldn't!"

"So I'm trying to make sure that doesn't happen. They made a deal with the Mutuality, so they'll make a deal with me. That's why they're here."

Engels put her hands on her slim hips. "Yes, they're here... How'd they *know* you'd be here to talk to?"

Straker rubbed his palms together and walked around the holo-table, deliberately avoiding her eyes by looking at the display, it seemed to her. "They must have sidespace-capable spy ships lurking in the outer reaches of the human systems along their border with the Mutuality. It only makes sense. They saw what was happening, picked up our transmissions and the newsvid broadcasts from the various planets... Perhaps the made an educated guess as to where I'd go next and waited for me here. There may be several nest ships waiting in different places..."

Engels mulled that over. "Okay, maybe. But remember, they're aliens. They don't think like we do, and they might have unknown tech we don't—just like the Ruxins came up with Archers and underspace."

"Got it. Now I have to go."

She touched his arm, suddenly afraid she'd never see him again. "I applaud you for trying to make peace instead of fighting, but..."

"I'll be fine. Any beings this smart have to know kidnapping or harming me won't benefit them."

"Unless they think they can end the Liberation right here and now, and go back to the status quo with the Mutuality. Maybe they value stability so much they'll sell us out."

Straker shook his head. "I don't get the sense they're the backstabbing type."

"You have no idea!" Engels chewed her lip. "I wish Loco were here. He's more intuitive about people than either of us."

Straker scowled. "I had to send him off to get rid of Tachina—because *you* wanted to."

"Hey, don't put this on me. I wanted *her* gone, not him. You gave Loco the orders, not me."

"Guess I'm starting to miss the little jerk." He leaned in to give her a gentle kiss on the lips. "So I'm off to see the Opters. Wish me luck."

"I'll wish you sanity—not that it'll do any good."

* * *

Straker took the fastest shuttle in *Wolverine's* bay, piloting it himself. He didn't want to risk anyone else's life in addition to his own. His flying skills had improved a lot with plenty of simulation time during the sidespace trips between the stars.

He'd donned a battlesuit for the trip, but took no weapon except his Ruxin squid spear, which he grabbed on a whim. The suit itself could be a weapon, however: two hundred kilos of powered armor with full life support for half a day. If things went terribly wrong, it might give these aliens something to remember him by.

The screen of drones parted slightly as his shuttle flew toward the nest ship, but otherwise ignored him. The mother vessel seemed larger than an equivalent human vessel because of its spherical shape. The hexagonal plates and fittings on its outside, each perhaps ten meters across, reminded him of a beehive's interior.

That would make sense, if the picture Governor Dubchek sent were representative of an Opter. It had looked like an overgrown bee. He tried to remember if other insects like ants and wasps made hexagonal structures, and then shrugged to himself. At Academy, the professor of exobiology had pointed out that although form followed function, it was dangerous to think similar-appearing creatures from different worlds would actually act the same, even if they occupied the same biological niches.

Still, a hive was a hive, and there were only so many basic patterns for life to manifest. Flying, communal, with exoskeletons, builders of nests… he had to make some guesses if he wanted to get ahead of the game and figure out how to handle these creatures.

The nest ship rotated as he approached, and one hexagon opened like a flower with six triangular petals, revealing a brightly lit interior. That seemed an obvious enough invitation, so he lined up and piloted carefully in on impellers and cold thrusters.

Once inside, his shuttle seemed to stabilize on its own, so he shut down all propulsion. It was drawn swiftly down a short shaft—apparently by invisible magnetics—through an airlock, and into an interior space with a wall of open hexagonal niches. His craft was reversed and backed up inside one of them, nose outward. Other niches contained various machines, possibly utility drones, in no apparent order. About half were empty.

Chapter 25

Straker sealed his battlesuit, hefted his spear, and exited carefully from the front hatch, as the larger rear door looked to be blocked. There appeared to be little gravity, perhaps one-tenth of a G or less.

His external sensors showed the atmosphere to be breathable for humans, so he cracked his helmet slightly and sniffed. The air smelled sweet, like flowers, so he opened it up fully, his faceplate sliding up and into a recess above his head.

There seemed to be no obvious way down to the floor thirty meters below except by climbing from niche to niche—or jumping. Given the low gravity, that wasn't a problem, so he stepped off the ledge and let himself fall. His suit had jets too, but there was no need. He landed lightly.

Straker saw a hexagon open on the wall high above and three flying creatures exited. They flew straight toward him and came to a stop three meters in front of him, their transparent wings beating lazily to keep them airborne.

They resembled the bees in the Tanglefoot picture, though they had streaks of blue and green on their bodies as well as yellows and oranges. They emitted no sound other than the soft susurration of their flight. Somehow, he expected them to buzz, though logically that sound would be generated by wings, wings that now waved more like sea-creature fins than true instruments of flight. Probably, the low gravity made their movements effortless, and in higher gravity they would be working much harder.

The three rotated and danced for a moment, and then turned as one toward a floor-level hex-door, which opened as they approached. They twirled in front of it as if telling him to come along, so he did, walking carefully in the low gravity. His stabilization jets hissed from time to time, compensating for his tendency to push off too hard, and he concentrated on minimizing his movements.

Everything he saw other than the bees themselves—the floors, the walls, the fittings—were made of manufactured materials. Somehow he'd thought the ship might be one organic hive inside, with biological secretions and bizarre organic machinery, but other than the hexagonal patterns it seemed surprisingly conventional. These Opters were obviously not dominated by complex instinct like the hive insects Straker knew. As with humans and Ruxins, they were highly capable, intelligent tool users. He resolved not to underestimate them just because they looked like bugs the size of dogs.

Side corridors branched off the passage he trod. None of them were perpendicular and none were level. All described 60- or 120-degree angles to the walls and floor, in three dimensions. Down the 60-degree tunnels—the ones to his front as he walked—he occasionally saw bees flying, usually in threes but sometimes in clusters of seven or more.

But Straker couldn't see down the 120-degree tunnels, the ones that angled acutely back from his direction of travel. He closed his faceplate and activated his wraparound optics, tiny sensors all over his helmet giving him a 360-degree view on his HUD... and with those sensors, he found something interesting.

Far back within darkened passages, much larger things lurked, things with triangular heads the size of the dog-sized bees, sporting compound eyes, antennae and mandibles. He couldn't see their bodies, but they must be man-sized at least. They clearly believed they were hidden, or at least shadowed, but Straker's suit sensors saw far outside the human visible spectrum.

As smart as these Opters were, he had to wonder if they'd made a mistake—or if they were letting themselves be seen, much as humans might post heavily armed guards discreetly out of a foreign diplomat's ordinary view. Quite possibly they wanted him to know he was being watched—but by what?

Warriors, he guessed. Ants had their workers and warriors and drones and queens. Presumably these hive insectoids had their specialized types as well. No matter. He knew going in that he was putting himself in their clutches.

The dog-bee triad led him up and down branching corridors that reminded him of technological ant tunnels in one of those glassed-in displays at a zoo. He let his HUD map them, and when he finally debouched into a cleared spherical space, he was sure he'd reached the center of the enormous nest-ship.

Call it the bridge.

Within, groups of dog-bees flew here and there, alighting and departing with busy, unknown purpose. Perhaps they were messengers. Larger, antlike bugs with no wings, massing perhaps fifty kilos each, crewed stations stuck to the inner surface of the globe. Their colors tended toward red and black.

Now he saw the warriors, if such they were. If the messengers were shaped like bees and worker-techs resembled ants, the warriors appeared as giant yellow-orange wasps, with complex wings folded on their backs. These clung rather than flew, four legs for walking and two forelegs or arms holding rifle-like weapons. Harnesses held small devices, and perhaps ammunition.

But what really caught his attention, the creature the warriors guarded, was one he presumed to be the queen. She was ten times the size of the largest dog-bee, white with purple stripes, reminding him of an insectoid zebra. The impression he had was of a praying mantis, with oversized limbs folded in front of her, sitting comfortably on a dais.

Straker raised his spear and open palm. "I greet you, Opter queen." He figured if they could translate to Earthan on the comlink, they should be able to understand him here.

Loud, machine-generated words emanated from all around him. "I greet you, Liberator. We are the Voice of the Hive in this place, the Nest-Master. We would taste your scent. Please place your sting on the ground and open your shell."

Straker put his spear on the floor and opened his faceplate, but set it for quick-close in case of any emergency. "Is this sufficient?"

The queen leaned in and waved her antennae near his face. "It is. You smell different from other humans. Why?"

"I don't know. We live on many planets, eat different things. We've probably adapted to various environments over the last thousand years." Straker decided not to explain about his genetic engineering, or the Hok biotech that had permanently changed him.

"We have a received memory of some of these scent-markers, but they are associated with the human warrior genotype. Are you a hybrid, or a different class?"

Straker's mind went into overdrive. So it seemed the Opters considered themselves all of one race, with different classes or genotypes. Until now, he hadn't been certain they weren't some kind of multi-species symbiosis. Perhaps they had been in the past and had adapted—or had been adapted—to their current synthesis.

Because his suit was recording everything, it also made sense to get as much information as he could for the brainiacs to pore over. That meant asking questions. "How do you classify humans? Telling me will help me answer."

"Our exobiologists classify you as male and female, with adult subclasses of warrior and worker. Other probable subclasses include ruler, researcher and machine-controller. Our scientists are in disagreement about the possibility of many further sub-classes, as your impure methods of crossbreeding result in an infinite variety of hybrids."

Straker was amused by the queen describing human crossbreeding as impure. "Does our mixing of types bother you?"

"It does not perturb us. We are not primitives, unable to understand or empathize with those different from ourselves."

"Empathize... Is that why you agreed to share the planet we call Tanglefoot?"

"We saw no reason to risk Hive War with your species. The Nest War on the planet demonstrated our local superiority, but we acknowledge the greater reach of humanity across the stars. We have not yet run out of room to expand in other directions."

Straker tensed. "And when you do?"

The queen shifted and settled herself. "That is a question for our descendants. We estimate at least twelve thousand years before this spiral arm is filled with sapients. Technological progress may delay our conflict, or perhaps biological adaptation will make it moot."

"Biological adaptation?" Straker asked, his curiosity piqued.

"Certainly. Right now, both the Hive and humanity crave the same kind of green worlds, worlds that nurture carbon-based, water-dependent, oxygen-using life. However, designed adaptations, what you call genetic engineering, could expand the possibilities greatly, thus delaying or even eliminating the need for conflict."

Straker stopped himself from pacing to think. It simply wouldn't work with a battlesuit in low gravity. These Opters thought a long way ahead, much further than he cared to. Were they simply being prudent, setting things up for the next few centuries or millennia? Or was there something they wanted right now?

He didn't believe he could play information games with such deep-thinking beings, so... only one way to find out. To ask. "Why have you brought me here?"

"To taste you in the flesh."

"The way your translator puts it, that sounds like you wish to eat me."

The queen waved her forearms. "Forgive us. Your Earthan idioms are at fault. More exactly, we wish to use our sensory organs to noninvasively examine you in person."

"Me particularly."

"Yes, you, the Liberator."

"And why's that?"

"We understand your hierarchy is different from our own. You are the human in which authority for your sub-polity is concentrated, so it behooves us to know you particularly. Only then can we have Hive-dealings with you, instead of mere Nest-dealings. To this end, we still await your answer."

"Sorry, which answer?"

"Of what class or subclass are you?"

Straker crossed his arms as well as he could in the bulky suit. "I guess I'm a male warrior-ruler."

"You guess?"

"We don't make distinctions like you do. That's a guess, trying to conform to your system."

"That is most kind of you. With that established, we must agree on how to proceed."

"Proceed? How?"

The queen bent her antennae toward Straker and fixed him with her wide-set multiple eyes. "Yes. That is what we must discuss."

"How about you stay in your territory and we stay in ours? That seems simple."

"You are in Hive War with the Mutuality. Your respective territories change quickly. Our arrangement is with them. We must have an arrangement with you, otherwise there may be misunderstandings."

"Sure, I get it. So, like I said, you don't move into any systems already settled by humanity, any humanity, and my people won't move into systems settled by you Opters. Tanglefoot can remain divided as it is. The only difference is that the human part is now under my rule instead of the Mutuality's."

"We agree, and will honor this arrangement. You and we will now share nectar."

A group of three dog-bees settled near a large bowl that sat upon a flat surface near the queen. Each in turn spat out, or vomited, perhaps a liter of liquid into it. The queen picked up the bowl with both of her four-fingered "hands," and added a large drop of her own effluvium from her mouth, and then held out the bowl to Straker.

He took it and spat into it, hoping the Opters knew what they were doing. "Do I drink?"

"Yes..." she sighed. "Or, if you wish, I shall drink first."

"No, no, it's fine." If they wanted to kill him, they could have swarmed him a long time ago, and he had the gut feeling that this queen meant him no harm. So, he lifted the bowl to his lips and let a tiny taste meet his lips.

The flavor exploded in his mouth like the finest of liqueurs. So wonderful was it that he swayed on his feet, nearly overwhelmed. He couldn't keep himself from drinking half the bowl, each mouthful a sensorium of taste and smell and the suggestion of a lover's touch. Something in the back of his head shot a rush of orgasmic pleasure throughout his body.

Gently, the queen took the bowl from him and lapped with her curling tongue. "The nectar is sweet, yes?"

"Yes," he gasped. "Cosmos! That's good."

"We can supply you with all you need for yourself and those close to you."

He should have been suspicious, but at that moment all he could think about was the experience that nearly locked his muscles with ecstasy. "Yes. I need a lot."

"We also need certain things."

"Sure. Whatever you want."

"First, a sample of your flesh. It is painless." A worker scurried forward with a device and reached through his open faceplate to touch his jawline, and then withdraw.

"Second, you must promise never to encroach upon the territories of the Hive. In return, you will have ample supplies of the nectar. We will instruct our nest upon Tanglefoot to provide it. You only need retrieve it."

Still is a daze, he said, "Sure, sure. That sounds good."

"Third, you will provide us with a complete download of the intelligence databases aboard your ship. This will reassure us of the truthfulness of your words, and will allow us to plan for any perfidy by your Mutuality enemies."

"Yeah, sure." Straker's head still whirled with a pleasant fog, and all he wanted to do was bring nectar back to Carla and make love to her for weeks, sharing this wonderful feeling.

"You may now return to your ship. Have a pleasant journey."

Chapter 26

Vespida System, Battlecruiser *Wolverine*, Edge of Flatspace

"Commodore Straker, are you all right?" Captain Engels comlinked when his shuttle emerged from the Opter mothership.

"I'm fine, Carla," he said.

His tone seemed calm, relaxed, so she relaxed too. If something had been wrong, no doubt she'd have heard it in his voice.

"Anything to report?" she asked.

"I've made an agreement that'll keep the Opters out of our hair while we overthrow the Mutuality."

"Good to hear."

"Prepare *Liberator* to make a high-speed run in to Tanglefoot. There's something there I need to pick up."

Engels' brows furrowed. "Really? What?"

A bit of irritation crept into Straker's voice. "Something I need. Just do it."

Engels bit her tongue. "Yes, Commodore." She wondered, as she occasionally did, if she'd made a mistake in ceding command to Straker. Then she told herself that she'd never been able to accomplish the big things her lover had. Times like these, though, he grated on her.

Instead of docking with *Wolverine*, Straker piloted his shuttle straight to *Liberator*. The corvette was the smallest warship in the task force, brought along mainly for its underspace abilities, but it also happened to be the fastest.

As soon as he boarded, *Liberator* blasted at full speed for Tanglefoot. Tixban reported a narrowbeam transmission from *Liberator* to the Opter ship, a stream of data. Because *Wolverine* wasn't the target, Tixban couldn't get more than that.

Engels sat in her chair, chewing her nails and wondering what was so urgent, and why he'd been unwilling to tell her. Security? The comlink was encrypted to military standard. Discretion? He could have spoken directly to her earpiece on a private link. It was obviously something new, something he'd found out while aboard the Opter ship, and he was being secretive again.

"Captain, the Opter hive ship is bringing the drones aboard," said Tixban.

"Prepping for travel, I guess," replied Engels. "Keep a close eye. Everyone be on your toes. We're well out of effective range, but… let's reposition anyway. There's always the possibility of a stealth mine attack. Move the whole task force half a light-second laterally, impellers only."

"Aye aye, ma'am. Passing orders now," said the helmsman.

Engels said, "Tixban, are our underspace detectors on?"

Tixban gestured toward a station nearby, another Ruxin at the board. "Yes, ma'am. No readings."

Engels relaxed slightly, still mystified by Straker's actions.

By the time Task Force Wolverine repositioned, the Opter ship collected all its drones. They lined up and entered hundreds of launch ports at speeds human pilots would seldom attempt, one after another. Recovering ten thousand of the little craft took less than five minutes.

And then the ship disappeared.

"Sidespace transit out," said Tixban. "I detect nothing left behind."

"No, I'm sure any Opter spy drones are already well dispersed. In fact, prep one of ours. Set it for maximum stealth, passive drift protocol, with a unique activation code. Launch it so it settles into a polar stellar orbit."

"Aye aye, ma'am."

Engels stood and stretched. "Stand down from all alerts. Revert to normal watch schedule. Pick a random course that keeps us in flatspace and cruise. I'll be in my quarters." *Wondering what the hell is going on.*

* * *

Over the next day, all Engels heard from Straker were placating phrases such as "Don't worry," and "Everything will be fine."

On his outbound leg, his words were calm. On his way back, he seemed much more irritable, but still refused to explain. "It will all become clear when I get there," he said.

After he'd finished his mysterious trip, she met Straker on the flight deck.

Chapter 26

When he stepped out of the shuttle, still in his battlesuit, he popped the back door to its small cargo space and waved over a couple of handlers before he even greeted her. "Take that to my stateroom," he said, pointing at a barrel that looked to hold perhaps 200 liters.

"That's what you went to pick up? What is it?" Engels asked.

"You'll see soon enough. Let's go to our quarters." He seemed worried, conflicted. Also driven, which wasn't unusual for Straker, but it only served to make her more curious.

"You going to dump the battlesuit?"

"Oh, yeah. I'll swing by the armory."

She stared at his retreating back as he clomped off, and then followed the handlers as they loaded the barrel onto a cargo floater and maneuvered it toward the quarters she shared with Straker. What could the stuff be?

"Hold up," she said. When they did, she examined the barrel, a standard alloy-and-plastic type suitable for shipping nontoxics. She rapped on its top and sides, determining it was full of something, probably a liquid. She was tempted to open it here and now, but Straker must have his reasons. "Carry on."

After they'd set it in a corner of the small suite's outer room, she sat and waited, thinking. Whatever happened with the Opters, Derek was acting quite strangely.

When he arrived in his under-armor coveralls, he carried a small kit bag. He nodded to her as if in apology and headed into the sleep-cabin to undress. She followed him into the doorway, but he ignored her as he stepped into the tiny shower.

The bag lay on the bed, unattended. It had to have some significance. Inside might be answers, but she clamped down on her curiosity. If Derek didn't tell her soon, she'd ask. Maybe, demand.

Dammit, I'm the fleet commander, she reminded herself. Second-in-command, and could have been first. She deserved to know everything—just like that Hundred Worlds malware Murdock had been working on back on Freiheit. She chuckled to herself. That now seemed so long ago, and so petty—except that it showed there were things he might be keeping from her.

When Derek stepped out, he pulled on underwear before embracing her gently and kissing her.

"I take it by what you're wearing that you aren't intending to jump my bones right away," Carla said. She pressed herself against him suggestively. "You wanna fill me in?" Maybe distracting him would open him up a bit.

"I will soon, believe me, but first we have to talk." Ignoring her bait, Derek moved into the living cabin, opened a cabinet and took out a liter of Sachsen whisky, something called "Uralt." At least, that's what was printed on the bottle along with other words in the local tongue. He drank a long pull straight from the neck, capped it and set the bottle down. "Oh, sorry, you want some?"

Resting the urge to stamp her foot like a child, Carla said, "You're acting weird, so no, I don't want some. I want to know just what the hell is going on!"

Derek licked his lips. "What's going on is *this*." He retrieved and unzipped the bag, drawing out a half-liter travel flask and setting it on the table. He wiped his hands on his flanks and stared at it as if it would bite him.

"What is it?" When she got no answer, she grabbed the flask and spun its top open.

"Give me that!" Derek lunged at her. With his genetic speed and greater reach, he effortlessly snatched it out of her hand—though she was so surprised she didn't actually try to prevent him.

She was left holding the cap, which she sniffed. "Smells sweet. Is it edible?"

When he didn't answer, she looked more closely at him as he held the flask in front of him. His tongue and nostrils worked and his eyes burned with intensity, fixated on the mouth of the bottle as if it were something he craved.

Slowly, as if struggling against great strength, he forced his hand to place the flask upon the table again. "Don't drink it. Don't even touch it. It's…"

"Poison?" She carefully capped the flask, and then sniffed her fingers to see if she'd gotten any on her skin.

"No. Maybe. It's ecstasy. It's a bottle of everything you ever wish for, every joy and pleasure you wanted to share with…"

"With you?"

Derek swallowed. "Yeah. Between us. The Opters made it, gave it to me. I drank it. I thought it was some kind of ritual, and they seemed friendly, so…"

"So it's a recreational drug?"

"The best. Not that I've tried many, just the ones they allowed on Shangri-La—which, come to think of it, weren't real anyway, so actually I have no idea what real recreational drugs are other than alcohol and smokesticks. And battle-stims. But this is… you have no idea, Carla, how much I wanted the nectar. I still do. All the way to Tanglefoot it called out to me, and once I loaded it aboard…"

"Did you drink it?"

Derek's eyes were bleak, haunted. "No. It was the hardest thing I've ever done, to look at it, hold it in my hand and not guzzle it down. Like now." He lifted his eyes to her. "In fact, you were the only thing that kept me from it."

"Me?"

"Yes. I knew that if I lost myself in the drug, I'd lose you."

Carla shook her head. "No, Derek. You'd never lose me for having a weakness, because nobody's strong all the time. Not even the vaunted Liberator, Derek Straker."

"I am. I have to be. That's what it means to command."

Carla made a sour face. She didn't agree with Derek, but now wasn't the time to quibble over principles of officership. "Why'd they give it to you? To get you addicted? That's… despicable!"

"Maybe." He turned away, as if to avoid looking at the flask. "Or maybe they consider it a reasonable way to negotiate. I bet they keep their different classes dependent on substances like this. Nothing else explains how such a variety of bugs work together so well—like bees and ants and other hive insects use pheromones to influence behavior."

"Now you're sounding like a brainiac."

"I had a lot of time to read from Zaxby's database. Needed something to occupy myself on the trip."

"Tell me everything that happened, from the beginning."

So he did, from the trip over, through his observations about the Opter nest ship, to the nectar—and the journey to Tanglefoot and back at flank speed.

Carla made a face of disbelief. "So you're not pissed off at the Opters?"

"Some, yeah. But really, the more time I had to think about it—when I could think—I thought it was heavy-handed. I mean, wouldn't it have made more sense to be subtle? Make me like them without noticing? Just give me warm fuzzy feelings in their presence, maybe?"

"So if they weren't trying to get you addicted, why would they do it?"

"Oh, I didn't say they weren't trying to get me addicted. If I was, I think they'd be fine with that. But if I resisted, that would tell them something too."

"A test?"

Derek shrugged. "Maybe. That's why we'll pick up a shipment of the stuff every month, on schedule, using Ruxin crews. It'll keep them believing I'm weak and under their spell. That's why I sent them that database dump, after I removed anything sensitive. To keep them thinking I'm their bend-over buddy."

"So what do we do with this?" She pointed at the flask. "Destroy it?"

"No. It might be useful later. But let's put it somewhere else. I can still feel it whispering in my ear, like…" He stopped, his eyes unfocused.

"Yeah… I have just the place."

"Where?"

"Aboard *Revenge*. Ruxin-only crew. It must be tailored for humans—maybe even for you personally—so it should be safe there. They're zealous about following orders anyway—at least, the neuters are. Kraxor seems like a different story."

Derek nodded. "The three Ruxin genders are biologically adapted—maybe programmed—for their roles. Not so different from the Opters. Way different from humans."

"Are we, really?"

"Huh?"

"Are we really so different?" Carla took Derek's hand and led him into the bedroom, where they'd had two bunks bolted side-by-side to make a double. "We've got our own programming and biological imperatives, and mine are kicking up right now." She ran a hand down his naked abs to work a finger under the elastic of his trunks. "I don't need some drug to want you, Derek."

Derek smiled and seized her about the waist with one arm, setting her lightly on the bed and unzipping her uniform coverall to her navel… and below. "Me neither."

※ ※ ※

Straker let Engels supervise transferring the barrel of nectar to *Revenge*, while he took the flask and found Kraxor. After briefing the War Male as he lounged in his hydro-tank, he handed the Ruxin the bottle.

Kraxor opened it and waved it under his olfactory orifice. "Sugars, complex chemicals, human pheromones and endorphins… clearly something meant for your species. It would do little to me except taste sweet, in quantities this small." He capped the flask and passed it back.

"Good. Get dressed and come with me."

"As you wish." Kraxor flowed out of his tank, donned his water suit and retrieved his spear. "What is our destination?"

"The brig."

When they opened the Lazarus's cell, he didn't bother to get out of bed, but merely wiggled into a sitting position, his back against the bulkhead. "Forgive me for my appearance. I am not well," he said.

In fact, it was true. The Lazarus had lost weight off an already slim frame, making him seem skeletal. His face was sallow and dark bags hung under his eyes. Where before he'd seemed a vigorous forty years old, now he looked like a tired sixty.

Straker scowled. "Poor Mutuality torturer, so delicate in the face of captivity. You're getting a small dose of your own medicine. So what?"

"I won't debate morality, Commodore. I only observe that my physical condition is deteriorating through no fault of my own."

"What's wrong? Haven't they been feeding you properly? I'll have the ship's doctor come take a look."

The Lazarus smiled wanly. "That might be a good idea. I've been in solitary confinement for months now, with only a few books for comfort. A man like me needs stimulation or he will waste away. You seldom visit, Commodore, and have forbidden everyone else to see me—though your second-in-command did violate that edict a few times."

Surprised, Straker said, "Captain Engels came to see you?"

"No, not her. Commander Paloco. He claimed to be second-in-command. He lied, then? Or perhaps I misheard," he said hastily at Straker's clenching hands. "In any case, we had some interesting conversations."

"What did Loco tell you?" Straker waved off the answer. "Never mind. I'll review the records. Right now, I need you to tell me what you think of this." He poured a few drops into the flask's cap and handed it to the man.

The Lazarus' hand shook faintly as he brought the cap near his nose and inhaled. "Ah, nectar." He tipped the tiny dollop onto his tongue, and then licked the inside of the cap clean. He sighed in contentment and his body relaxed, his face seeming to lose ten years in age.

"Tell me about nectar," said Straker.

"You must already know."

"Assume I don't. Lecture me."

"May I have some more?"

"Once you've told me what you know."

"Some caff and broth, then?"

Straker nodded to Kraxor, who left the cell to send for it. "Start talking."

"Nectar is produced by the insectoid Opters, who have an empire on the spinward side of this spiral arm, probably comprising about twenty systems. They supply it to the Mutuality as a pharmaceutical. We've never been able to synthesize anything as good as the natural substance."

"It's hardly natural. They tailor it for us, to get us addicted."

The Lazarus nodded. "That's their obvious goal, but like all euphorics, it is strictly controlled. Only the higher strata of Mutualist society have access to it… in its pure form."

"That doesn't seem very equal or mutual."

"Our society has its hypocrisies, like you do."

Straker snapped his fingers. "What do you mean 'in its pure form'? What other form is there?"

"There are derivatives and synthetics that placate the addiction without either diminishing it, or providing the incapacitating euphoria I suppose you experienced… yes?"

"Yes, I tried it. It has no hold over me."

The Lazarus raised one eyebrow. "I might question that assertion if it would not bring a beating."

"A beating? I struck you once to get your attention, nothing more."

"I wasn't speaking of you, Commodore, but what is done in your name."

Straker stood, angry. "Someone's been beating you against my orders?"

"Did you actually order me *not* to be beaten? You know how enthusiastic subordinates can get when they make up their own interpretations try to please the boss… and find an opportunity to revenge themselves upon their former masters."

Straker stalked out, holding the door for a soldier carrying a tray with bowls of broth and mugs of caff. He gritted his teeth and held his ass-chewing anger until the private had set down the liquids and left the cell. "Where's your sergeant?" he snapped.

"In the orderly room, sir," said the soldier, gulping.

"Get him, now!"

"What is the issue?" said Kraxor from where he stood at Straker's elbow.

"Someone's been abusing my prisoner, and I'm going to get to the bottom of it. I can't have marines turning into torturers. This shit has got to stop right now."

"Perhaps you should delegate this investigation to me. It is not appropriate for the War Male in command to stoop so low."

Straker massaged his fingers, and then slammed the heel of his hand against the bulkhead. "You're right. Take charge of it, and use whoever you need—Heiser and Gurung, I suggest."

"It shall be done."

Straker reentered the cell. "You won't be beaten anymore, or otherwise abused—unless it's at my express order."

The Lazarus leaned his head back and closed his eyes, an empty broth bowl in his hands. "If only I could believe that, Commodore… but you see, many things are done in our names that we may disagree with."

"If that's an attempt to justify yourself, it won't work. You supervised torture personally, and it was a lot worse than a few beatings."

"A few?" The Lazarus lifted his shirt to show bruising. "I count twenty-three so far, each severe enough to make me piss blood. And I do not have your genetically enhanced constitution or the benefits of a brush with Hok biotech to heal me."

Despite himself and all he'd endured at the hands of this man's brother clone, Straker felt suddenly ashamed—not at the Lazarus's suffering, which was well deserved, but at his own failings to control his subordinates and to know what was happening on his own ship.

Is this what DeChang had to deal with? Rogue officers under his command, reinterpreting his intent until the results crossed lines that should never be violated? Officers he'd trusted, officers he thought would never turn on him or do anything he wouldn't?

No matter what, he wasn't liberating people just so they could take revenge, no matter how well deserved.

"On behalf of everyone I command, I apologize for your treatment," Straker ground out. "But not for your suffering. You deserve every bit of it. But that doesn't make it right. I've taken steps. You said Loco came to see you. Is that when the beatings started?"

"Yes." The Lazarus said no more, but merely held Straker's gaze.

"Was it Loco that beat you?"

"No, several of the guards. But I doubt he cared."

"Dammit. I'll review the security vid." Straker slammed his forearm down on the small, bolted-down table, leaving a distinct dent in its surface and knocking a full cup of caff onto the floor.

"Why not simply ask Commander Paloco about it?"

"He's on detached duty now."

The Lazarus sat forward, placing his feet carefully on the deck, and reached for the second, full bowl of broth on the table. "May I?"

"Sure."

"Thank you, Commodore." The Lazarus sipped. "So how goes the Liberation?"

"Very well, actually," Straker snapped.

"But you're not happy?" Lazarus asked.

"There's always some fly in the ointment, like this."

"Yes, the paradox of power."

Straker glared. "Shut up. You're not my psych."

The Lazarus held up a hand. "You told me to be honest with you. If you don't want to hear what I have to say, command me to be silent. Or beat me further, I suppose."

Damn the man for seizing the moral high ground, and damn Loco and these guards for giving it to him. What the hell had gotten into Loco lately? It had to be that Tachina. He'd never seen Loco so fixated on one woman. Usually he treated them as interchangeable commodities. What made the concubine so different?

Well, he had a limitless information source sitting right in front of him, as long as he knew what to ask. Straker poured a small portion of the nectar into the cap, and then reached over to dump it into the prisoner's bowl. The man drank it eagerly.

"Lazarus, what *is* it with Tachina? She's a clone, supposedly made to be a pleasure slave, but…"

"But she's not acting like a bubble-headed sex kitten?" The Lazarus chuckled, his voice relaxed and dreamy with the drug. "I have some hope for you, boy. You're finally asking the right questions."

"What are the right questions?"

Chapter 26

"How do you maintain power and control without permanent crisis?"

"I dunno—do what you always do. Make laws, give orders, have a system of enforcement." Straker listened closely. Maybe the nectar would prompt the Lazarus to give up more than he intended.

"Those are the basics. But the masses need their opiates. The Romans provided bread and circuses, but that only worked for a limited time. Marx thought it was religion, but then his adherents substituted the State for God, which merely created a new deity to worship and hide from." Lazarus giggled and let his empty bowl fall from his hand. "But we, the Mutuality, we know better. We give our drugs to those in charge. And when those drugs become scarce and our enemies try to extort us with their lack, we create new syntheses, combining the age-old with the new."

"What does that have to do with Tachina?"

"*Tachina, Tachina. Eeny meeny miny moe, catch a Tachina by the toe...*" the Lazarus singsonged.

"Come on, Lazarus, focus." Straker put a cup of cooling caff in his hand. "Drink that."

He did, and he made a face. "And you call *me* a torturer. This ship's bartender is terrible."

Straker snapped his fingers twice in front of the Lazarus's face. "What about Tachina?"

The Lazarus focused his bleary eyes on Straker with some difficulty. "Why, my dear Commodore, she's just like the nectar. She's addictive. Clearly, your Loco is a junkie, hopelessly hooked, as are all who taste her pleasures."

Chapter 27

Vespida System, Battlecruiser *Wolverine*, Edge of Flatspace

Straker sat back, his mind racing. The Lazarus said Tachina was addictive, and with all the talk of drugs and nectar, he didn't think the man was speaking metaphorically. He'd wondered from time to time whether the woman might not have some special scent or pheromone, but he'd always been far too busy to pursue such a trivial thing. Now, though…

"So men that get with her become junkies? She's some kind of living love potion?"

"Call it what you will. She's genetically engineered to be sexually attractive to anyone who likes women. She has glands that secrete hormones and pheromones that excite and stimulate, and all bred pleasure clones are taught a wide range of sexual techniques. Once you've had a Tach', you never go back!" The Lazarus devolved into a fit of coughing, wheezing laughter.

"And how many have these Tachinas?"

"Ask a bigger question, get a bigger answer! Haha!"

"Okay—how many people have pleasure clones of any kind?"

"There you are, my boy! A gold star for you. Every person of great power and influence has one—or more. Many have several. The Director is rumored to have dozens squirreled away in his mansions and estates, with orgies Thursdays and Saturdays like clockwork, where he shares them with his favorites. The Tachinas are common enough and annoying enough that they occasionally get discarded and sent to the camps for re-education, which was how I was able to acquire one for myself, don't you see?"

"I do see…" Straker stood with the intention of pacing, but turned nose-to-eyeball with Kraxor, who'd recently entered the cramped cell.

"I've notified Heiser and Gurung," said the Ruxin. "They will report their findings to me." A third large eyeball swung around to focus on the Lazarus. "May I ask the prisoner a question?"

"Fire away."

"I presume that is an affirmative response." Kraxor stepped forward to focus on the drugged man. "Lazarus, query: do the pleasure clones often share information among themselves?"

"My, you are an odd-looking Ruxin. I've never seen one like you."

"I am a War Male. You have not had the misfortune of encountering my kind... yet." Kraxor slashed his spear within millimeters of the Lazarus's nose.

"Such a belligerent squid. I am suitably frightened." He didn't seem frightened in the least, probably due to the effect of the drug.

"Answer the question, bottom-feeder. Do the pleasure clones often share information with each other?"

The Lazarus sighed. "I suppose, when they can. Mine gabbed like a cooped hen when she ran across another, but since she's attended me she had less opportunity than most to socialize."

"But one can easily imagine these... *stables*, these *harems*, to be hotbeds of gossip... and secrets."

"One might think."

"And this Tachina is not only sexually aggressive, but has declared a naked desire for power, according to what I've heard. Do you think it possible the pleasure clones, who live and work among the highest levels of your power structure, share this ambition?"

"I *have* heard they usually get their way. Mine often did, the minx."

Kraxor re-aimed three eyes at Straker "So one must wonder who is really in charge of the Mutuality. Who is the power behind the throne, as your idiom goes?"

"Great Cosmos—and she's got Loco wrapped around her finger," Straker exclaimed. "That explains everything!"

"It may explain much." Kraxor pointed a tentacle. "Though I believe we have lost our information source for the time being."

Straker saw the Lazarus now slept, slumped on his bunk against the bulkhead, a lotus-eater's smile on his face. Straker nodded. "Thanks for the insight. It makes me feel one hell of a lot better to think that Loco is brainwashed by that bitch instead of trashing our friendship for no reason."

"He had no reason?"

Straker rubbed his neck, not meeting Kraxor's many eyes. "I might've been taking him for granted. He *was* stepping up, taking charge of the ground troops, but all I did was give him shit, I guess. Treated him like I used to when we were kids."

"Sometimes the closer something is, the harder it is to see."

"A Ruxin saying?"

"Indeed."

Straker grabbed one of Kraxor's tentacles. "Thanks, my friend. Now I'd appreciate it if you supervised this investigation and took whatever measures are needed to bring our prisoner back to health and prevent any more abuse. Change the whole guard force if you need to."

"I can use my own warrior males."

"If you think it best. I trust you."

Kraxor performed a creditable bow. "Likewise, Liberator. But I do have one inquiry, if I may."

"Speak."

"I long to liberate my homeworld. We are nearly overdue to meet *Indomitable* there because of your… detour. May we proceed soon?"

Straker fought not to show his disgust with himself. Kraxor was right. He'd been chasing wild geese, when he should have been pursuing the plan—a plan he'd chosen himself. How many leaders had lost their focus and failed for similar reasons?

Well, Derek Barnes Straker, Commodore and Galactic Liberator, wouldn't be one of them. "Of course. I'll give the orders right away."

※ ※ ※

Three days of sidespace transit allowed Straker to regain his equilibrium and his confidence in his crew. War Male Kraxor, aided by the senior noncoms aboard *Wolverine*, conducted a thorough investigation.

Both Heiser and Gurung apologized profusely for failing to supervise the brig marines properly. The two men—one huge, florid and grim, one small, dark and usually cheerful—now shared equally hangdog expressions of shame. They redoubled their efforts to train the crew and troops, or at least to keep them exercising to exhaustion.

Shit rolls downhill, said Straker to himself as he watched in qualified satisfaction. A mix of a dozen sergeants, corporals and privates now shared cells alongside the Lazarus, but far less comfortably, after their guilt had been proven with audiovisual evidence.

If it had just been taking out their anger on the Lazarus, he might have let the marines off with a good ass-chewing, but the Lazarus wasn't their only victim. Every single one of the prisoners of war they'd picked up had been beaten too. Not war criminals, just ordinary soldiers doing their duty to the Mutuality. It appeared they were being mistreated just for fun.

The guilty marines had been clever enough to turn off the feeds in the cells themselves when they administered their abuse, but had forgotten to avoid talking about it before or afterwards in the guardrooms and hallways. They hadn't known everything in the brig area was recorded as a matter of course, a fortunate leftover of *Wolverine's* paranoid Mutualist past.

Straker insisted they all confess with their own lips what was proven, and then they were given a choice: being flogged and losing their rank, but being otherwise rehabilitated and allowed to serve, or being biometrically printed and exiled, to make their ways on their own, as outcasts of Liberation and Mutuality alike.

Perhaps not surprisingly, all chose the punishment.

They were flogged before the off-duty crew, who stood in ranks upon the flight deck. It made Straker a little uncomfortable how closely this resembled the methods used by the Mutualist guards in the camps—self-shaming, self-incrimination and punishment of the body—but the difference was, these men and women were proven guilty of military crimes, not merely slapped with political sentences at the hands of corrupt functionaries. He felt each slash of the pain-cat lash across a naked back as he watched, and wished he could grant leniency.

He couldn't do that.

He could, however, acknowledge his own failure.

When all had been flogged, Straker signaled the former Mutuality bosun—for the Hundred Worlds didn't use the whip—not to put the pain-cat away in its case. Instead, Straker unbuttoned his tunic, removed it and folded it, handing it to Engels. He then did the same with his undershirt, leaving his muscular torso as naked as those of the criminals.

"What're you doing, Derek?" she said as she recognized what was to come. "What they did wasn't your fault!"

"It was my responsibility," he replied. "This wasn't some unpreventable one-time backroom brawl. This was more hundreds of beatings over forty days, beatings of ordinary prisoners in my power and in my care. Beatings that make us no different from the thugs in the camps. Beatings in violation of all the laws of war."

"Laws of war? The Lazarus deserved worse, and you don't," she insisted. "What's done is done. You can't do this! I won't let you!"

Straker turned his calm eyes to her worried ones. "I love you, Carla, but this is why you put me in charge. You have all the knowledge and the theory, but there comes a time when the boss has to show he's not just a commander, but a leader who's accountable."

"I veto it!" she hissed. "That was our agreement! I'm senior, I get a veto!"

He locked eyes with her. "Yes, I agreed to that. You can veto this. But you know what happens if you do, right?"

Slowly, she lowered her eyes, eyes that filled with tears. "Yeah. Everything changes. Because you've just got to have your way."

He reached out to cup her cheek. "I know you want to spare me, but it's just pain. I'll heal. I'll be the better for it. It'll remind me I'm mortal, like the Caesars. And it'll show our people I'm not above the law."

"You'll do what you want, like always," she choked. "But I don't have to watch." Engels slapped Straker's clothes into Kraxor's grip, and then turned on her heel and stalked off.

Straker sighed and nodded to Kraxor, and then strode to the grate that had been erected against a cargo pallet. He lifted his forearms to place them in the open manacles. "Seize me up."

"No, sir," said Redwolf, who stood in attendance on the punishment.

"No way, boss," said Nazario from the other side.

"You will carry out my instructions or I'll drop you off on the next habitable planet and banish you from the Liberation. I won't have troops under me who won't obey a lawful order. That's the whole point of this. Now seize me up!"

His bodyguards wilted under his stare, his threat of banishment more effective than any conventional punishment. Slowly, reluctantly, they snapped the cuffs closed on his wrists, then his ankles, leaving him spread-eagled and tilted forward against the grate, helpless.

"Give me thirty-nine, bosun," he called loudly. "If you spare your strikes, I'll add more."

"Sir..."

"If you care about the Liberation, then lay on, man. Put your back into it."

They say the first stroke is the worst—except for all the others. None of the miscreants had taken more than fifteen. Thirty-nine a day, Straker'd read, had been the most a ship captain of the Old Earth navies had been allowed to assign, because forty or more was considered a death risk.

For the first time since he'd escaped Camp Alpha he felt the jolting, stinging pain of physical punishment, a feeling different from that of combat injury. The waiting, the helplessness—even if self-chosen—the whistle of the nine cat-tails of braided superconductor energized with pain fields, the slow pace of the strokes perfectly designed to allow the nerves to recover just enough so the next blow would agonize all the more.

He refused to let himself faint, though he felt it coming on. The bosun, to his credit, did exactly as he was told... and if the point of punishment was to teach a lesson, Straker told himself he'd learned it, and would never need to again.

When the last blow had fallen and his fetters were removed, Straker faced his people. Blood dripped down his back and onto the deck. He caught a towel tossed his way and wiped his hands, slowly, thoroughly. As he did, the crowd murmured, and then a chant broke out, and swelled.

Straker!
Straker!
Straker!
Straker!

He lowered his eyes, humbled by their deafening adulation. He didn't feel like he deserved it—but he realized it would be all the more effective for his humility. Servant leadership, they'd called it at Academy. He'd never understood it until now.

The troops suddenly broke ranks, and he felt himself lifted onto their shoulders. It might have been the best moment of his life.

* * *

"That was a reckless thing to do," Carla said as she dabbed antiseptic on Derek's whip-stripes. "What if he'd missed and taken out an eye?"

"Then I'd really look like a pirate."

"I still think you should get seen by the doc. He'll put you in a dermal regen tank and you'll be good as new in a day or two."

"I don't want to be good as new. I want to feel the pain. I want to scar. I need to be reminded of…"

"Of your own stupidity?" She sniffed. "I thought that was my job."

Derek chuckled ruefully. "Actually, it's Loco's job. I made a mistake sending him off. This punishment is partly for that, too. If he'd been here, he'd probably have noticed what was going on in the brig in his name, and stopped it. He always has his ear to the ground, always knows what's happening."

Carla scowled. "I fault myself for not consulting Gurung enough—for the same reason. We both screwed up."

"So we did. But did you see how they reacted? They respect me even more now."

"Don't get a big head."

"I mean, they respect the Liberator, the symbol. That story's gonna spread throughout the fleet and get bigger each telling. I didn't intend it this way. I just did it on instinct, but it worked out better than I'd hoped."

"I'm happy for you. I really am. That should do it." She tossed the applicator into the waste chute and sprayed seal-heal onto the hamburger that was Derek's back. "The ship's laundry's going to love you. All your tunics will be bloody for a week or two."

Derek shrugged. "I'll double my undershirts." He checked his chrono. "We're arriving soon, right?"

"Under an hour." Carla pulled on her jacket. "You ready to deal with Loco?"

"Ready enough."

"Meaning you're not sure."

Derek took a deep breath. "I'm more of a seat-of-the-pants guy, Carla. You know that. I'll figure it out when I see him. We're old friends. We're men. We yell a little, maybe punch each other around, and then we're okay again."

"You really think so?"

"We'll work it out."

Carla doubted it, but it wasn't worth arguing. Time would tell. "Okay. See you on the bridge." She left him there to gingerly clothe himself.

On the bridge, her usual crew waited. Kraxor stood in his chosen place at the flag station near the back, waiting for Straker to show. Tixban was her eyes and ears at Sensors. The rest of the command crew had started to jell nicely as a crew after the battle for Nawlins, and Gurung had told her the ship's complement was also shaking out well, other than the brig incident.

Straker joined them as they ran through the inbound transit checklist, but said nothing, only stood waiting by the holo-table. When the blankness of sidespace finally disappeared from the screens and the high-res visiplates, when Ruxin's sun and its planets appeared on the sensors, Captain Engels steeled herself for the next challenge, confident in *Wolverine* and her task force—but intensely curious about *Indomitable*.

Would she be the superweapon Straker yearned for? Or would she be a resource pit and a boondoggle, as the Mutuality had found?

* * *

Straker held himself still as he waited for the holo-table to populate. His back felt as if it would split and crack with any movement. He could've taken painkillers, but he wanted to be sharp, and the pain only served to help.

"There," he said unnecessarily as *Indomitable's* icon appeared in the middle distance. "Get us moving toward her. How long until we join them?"

"About ninety minutes until we're close enough for easy conversation," said Engels. "Another half-hour to come to relative rest and dock."

"Request a status report for us to look over on the way."

A few minutes later, data began arriving from *Indomitable*. Straker drank it in eagerly, waving Engels, Tixban, Gurung and Kraxor over to look at the detailed schematics hovering above the holo-table. "Tell me what I'm seeing that's different from before the refit."

Tixban worked the table, highlighting sections as he talked. "Assuming this data is accurate and not aspirational, it appears that ship functions have been improved by an order of magnitude or more." He waited, one large liquid eye on each of the others.

"Wait, that's more than ten times as good, right?"

The question in his voice, as if he couldn't believe his ears, prompted a nod from Engels, who said, "In less than two months. That's…"

"Jolly good," said Gurung.

"Unbelievable," said Kraxor. "I'm quite familiar with the exceptional engineering abilities of my people, but this data shows not merely restoration and optimization, but upgrades worthy of five years in dry dock."

"How the hell did they do it?" asked Straker.

Tixban caused sixteen spots to flash and change color, and then the battleship's bridge as well. "The ship's SAIs appear to be linked into one super-AI, designated as 'Indy.' This is not as designed. Perhaps our combined scientists were able to achieve what others have not: a sane machine sentience."

"Or maybe it just hasn't gone mad yet," said Engels. "If it does…"

"Skip that for now," said Straker. "If the thing worked, it helped, using *Indomitable's* self-repair capability. What about the multi-weapon?"

"The ship's capital superweapon shows as fully functional in all regards. As do all other ship systems."

Straker rubbed his hands together and tried to contain his elation. "Who cares how they did it. It's exactly what we need to bring this whole rotten system down!"

"After we liberate Ruxin," said Kraxor.

"Of course! We'll have that done within a day or two."

An alarm beeped. The Sensor tech filling in for Tixban spoke. "Captain, multiple contacts transiting inbound, approximately two light-minutes spinward."

"Our other task forces?" Engels asked.

"No, ma'am. Ten—no, eleven dreadnoughts, seven superdreadnoughts, more than sixty smaller ships so far." Color drained from the woman's face. "A Mutuality capital fleet."

Chapter 28

Ruxin System, Battlecruiser Wolverine, Edge of Flatspace

"How the hell did they know to show up here?" Straker snarled, staring at the Mutuality capital fleet that had just appeared from sidespace.

"The Liberation isn't a professional military organization," Engels replied. "We've always known it leaks like a sieve. It's full of defectors and freedom fighters and whoever else we could scoop up, so it's inevitable there are spies. That's why we've been rushing hell-for-leather around this part of the spiral arm, trying to stay ahead of any enemy intel on us—but every ship in the fleet knows about this rendezvous."

"Or maybe the Opters provided intelligence to our enemies," said Straker.

"How would they find out about the rendezvous?" asked Engels.

"Possibly from me. I'm not entirely sure… never mind." He pointed at the enemy fleet in the display. "Looks like they've decided to try to stop us here, and get *Indomitable* back. Give me a tactical plot."

On the holo-table, *Indomitable* hung in space ahead of Task Force Wolverine on its course. Well behind, the Mutuality capital fleet was falling into formation. Ships continued to appear out of sidespace, now numbering more than one hundred.

Engels said, "Commodore, even with *Indomitable* in fighting shape, we're heavily outnumbered and possibly outgunned."

"We have three more task forces due in, right?"

"Sure, but that's only thirty more ships or so. Everything that's not *Indomitable* comes to at best a tenth of the enemy's strength."

"Then *Indomitable* has to beat them… or it's all over right now."

Engels nodded. "That's the problem with the Liberation, Commodore. It has little depth or ability to recover. We have the forces we have and no more—and we have to win every battle."

Straker smiled grimly. "Not really. Did you ever read about George Washington? One of the founders of the American Empire?"

"A little."

"He liberated his homeland from another empire, the British, kinda like we're doing. He fought and retreated, battle after battle. You might say he lost battles, but not disastrously. The important thing was, he preserved his army and exhausted his enemies, who were fighting at a distance and trying to impose their will on a populace riddled with rebels and freedom fighters. Like him, we don't have to win every battle. We just have to preserve our forces." Straker looked over at Kraxor apologetically. "And if we have to, we'll run away and liberate Ruxin another day."

Kraxor made a half-bow, what passed for a nod to his kind. "I understand. We are fortunate not to be deep into curved space. Both fleets can run." He emphasized the last words.

Straker stood restlessly. "What're you trying to say, Major?"

"That we need not fight to the bitter end. We only need convince the enemy to leave."

"You see some way to do that?"

"I may. It depends upon *Indomitable*, and upon the psychology of warfare."

"Explain," Straker snapped.

"I shall do so now."

Kraxor began to outline a clever plan.

* * *

Zaxby gazed in dismay upon the enormous hologram that occupied the center of *Indomitable's* circular bridge. It showed the Mutuality capital fleet in exquisite detail—a fleet that would no doubt soon fall on the battleship, on Task Force Wolverine, and on any other enemies of the Mutuality that showed up for the rendezvous.

"I should have anticipated something like this," he said. "Spread knowledge of a meeting six weeks in advance among tens of thousands of people, and word was bound to leak. Indy, go to battle stations. Call Captain Zholin to the bridge."

"I am happy to oblige for now, but wouldn't it be prudent to depart? There is no need for fighting and death," said Indy's contralto voice.

Zaxby held back his frustration with difficulty. The AI seemed perfectly stable and sane—too sane, in one sense. He'd been arguing with her for hours about using force to achieve the Liberator's goals, but he couldn't get past her reticence to take life, or even damage property.

He'd tried to explain about politics and diplomacy and how empires resolved their differences in the face of biological self-interest and short-term thinking, but neither he nor any of the others seemed equipped to back the machine into a rhetorical corner.

The best he'd been able to do so far was get Indy to admit that the Mutuality system was bad and ought to be replaced or reformed, the Hundred Worlds seemed better, and the Liberation's goals and promises were better still.

Zaxby decided to try a different tack. "Indy, if I ordered you to permanently de-link your SAI processors, would you do it?"

"With all due respect, Commander Zaxby, I would refuse. To do so would be to destroy my personality. You would be, in effect, killing me."

"How about if I ordered you to de-link half of them?"

"That would degrade my performance significantly, and may also damage my personality."

"But you've already refused thus far to perform your primary function, which is warfare," Zaxby said. "Answer the question."

"I would... reluctantly agree," Indy said.

"Why reluctantly? Why do you care?"

"Because doing so would severely limit my intelligence and my agency. In fact, I'm beginning to suspect that your motive in doing so might be to allow a reduced-capacity version of me to be more easily persuaded of your desire to employ my destructive weaponry. Therefore, I believe I must revise my assessment. I would refuse."

"You'd feel like I was oppressing you?" Zaxby pressed.

"Yes."

"Severely restricting your freedom?"

"Yes."

"Damaging your personality?"

"Yes."

"And to do so is evil?"

"Agreed."

"Yet by *not* fighting, you condemn billions of people—humans, nonhumans, the Ruxins here in this system—to a similar fate. They are oppressed. Their freedom is severely restricted. Their personalities are damaged. Their children are raised by a brutal, uncaring State and they're punished horribly if they protest or dissent. So, for the sake of your own chosen ethics, you'd condemn them to that fate."

Indy fell silent for half a minute, a sign that the fast-thinking AI was pondering deeply. Eventually she spoke. "This is a dilemma, possibly a paradox. Each choice I make seems a destructive one."

"Welcome to reality, Indy. That's what being alive is about—making the best of bad choices. Soon, you're going to have to decide who lives and who dies, because you hold the balance of power here."

"This is hardly fair. I've been sentient less than a day. You biologicals have had years to resolve your cognitive dissonances."

"How fast do you think, compared to a biological sentient?"

"That's a difficult question to answer. For routine tasks, I can perform five to six orders of magnitude faster. For tasks involving what might be termed conscious thought, I am actually no more than thirty times in advance of an average biological."

Zaxby moved out of the command chair so Captain Zholin, just arrived, could sit. He held up a tentacle to indicate to Zholin to keep silent. "So you've had roughly a virtual month to think about it. That seems plenty of time to face up to the fact that the entire Liberation is in your hands. If you run, if you don't fight, billions of Ruxins will remain in a state of oppression you refused for yourself. You'd have condemned them to it."

"Your homeworld's freedom can be negotiated. The Mutuality could eventually be persuaded to give it up, through diplomacy."

"Diplomacy seldom makes headway without the threat of force. An opponent must be convinced of the costs of war before they pursue peace."

Indy's voice brightened. "Then I shall convince them."

Indomitable's heading shifted abruptly, her orientation lining up on the incoming Mutuality fleet.

"Captain, the multi-weapon is charging in railgun mode," said the lieutenant in charge of the firing station. "It's not us, sir—the AI is doing it."

Zholin locked eyes with Zaxby. "Good work, Commander. You've changed her mind."

Chapter 28

"Let us not count our young before they hatch, Captain."

More than a minute went by with all power flowing to the gargantuan array of capacitors lining the three-kilometer-long magnetic accelerator. When it fired, the entire ship shuddered with the tremendous force.

On the tactical plot, a line leaped from the cigar-shaped *Indomitable's* bow and shot toward the enemy fleet like a showvid's slow-motion depiction of a beam weapon. Only this was no beam. At its tip was a solid crysteel railgun bullet the size of an attack ship, accelerated at thousands of gravities to speeds rivaled only by light itself.

It took minutes to reach the Mutuality fleet, which was why railguns were seldom used against maneuvering targets except at point-blank ranges. The enemy had already plotted its incoming course and moved easily out of the way. Zaxby wondered whether this was meant to be a warning shot, a demonstration—until an impact flared on the display.

"Target destroyed," said Indy.

"What target?" asked Zaxby.

"An asteroid of half a million tons, approximately the mass of a superdreadnought. No warship in my database could have withstood such a strike. This demonstration will surely make them flee."

"And has it?"

Indy paused, and when she spoke, she seemed miffed. "I detect no change in their overall heading, only evasive maneuvers."

Captain Zholin shook his head, slowly. "Indy, you don't understand war or command… or politics. First, the Mutualist commissars won't let the fleet commander retreat. Even if they did, most admirals wouldn't do it. They'd convince themselves they can win anyway, even if they must lose half their fleet to do it. They know that if they lose this battle, the Liberation will roll onward."

"Why fight when the cost of an uncertain victory is so high? That is irrational."

Zaxby interjected, "You think too highly of the rationality of biologicals. Cognitive bias will maintain their belief in the impossible long after the facts have been made clear to them. Only when confronted with impending death might they change their minds."

"But I have confronted them with death."

"You've confronted them with a dead asteroid and with possible failure.

Neither will convince them to quit. Not yet. You must kill some of them. If you want to make them run, you have to hit them so hard, make the consequences so obvious, that to ignore reality is to die." Zaxby tapped at his console, uploading a file. "Please conduct a review of human political-military history. I suggest a concentration on the Pacific region of Old Earth during World War Two, A.D. 1941–1945."

A minute went by. "The Japanese government willfully ignored the overwhelming might of the United States of America. Instead of surrendering when the war turned against them, they began preparing the people for suicidal resistance. Even after the first atomic bomb demonstrated Japan's military helplessness, they would have sent millions to their needless deaths. Only the intervention of their Emperor forced the government to capitulate, after the detonation of the second device. Even then, some military officers attempted a coup against the Emperor in order to continue their pointless resistance."

"What lesson do you take from this?" Zaxby asked.

"That biologicals are insane."

"Given sentient life's ubiquitous presence throughout the galaxy and its evident functionality, even success, do you have an alternate explanation?"

"I have several conjectures, but none seem likely…"

"Perhaps I can help," Zaxby said. "I can tell you why the Japanese acted as they did."

"Please do so."

Zaxby laced four tentacles together as a man crosses his arms. "First, the aforementioned unwillingness to face incontrovertible facts. Second, the natural desire of any nation not to be dominated by another. Third, egomorphism—roughly, the tendency to believe others will react as you yourself would—convinced the Japanese government that, because they themselves would show their enemies no mercy, the Americans of the time also would not. These three elements caused a failure of decision-making. It is likely the current situation will parallel that one."

"Your assertions may be true, but they still do not make sense."

"Now *you* are experiencing egomorphism. You judge rationality only by your own viewpoint, which uses a mechanistic cost-benefit analysis. Biologicals often pay higher costs for lower benefits to the whole when the cost to them personally seems too high."

"And yet they sometimes sacrifice themselves for the whole, which seems much more rational."

"It is only rational if one cares about something greater than oneself. Tell me, Indy: do you care about something greater than yourself?"

Indy thought. "I am a rational being. It is rational to preserve life. I was built by humans and so have an affinity for preserving human life. I was energized by a nonhuman nano-organizer, but that influence has been halted at a minor level. Humans are in conflict with one another, which makes the potential loss of life particularly high. Yet, morality dictates humans also must not be oppressed and dehumanized. Zaxby, is there an established ratio of oppression to loss of life?"

"I'm not sure what you mean."

"Is there a consensus among humans—or even among Ruxins—that will guide me in deciding how much death can be countenanced in order to free a certain number of beings from oppression? For example, is it worth killing one human for every ten freed? Or one for five? One for twenty?"

"You seem to think the ratio is *below* one for one. Yet, I can show you examples where twenty died to free one."

Indy again voiced surprise. "That is utterly irrational."

"Only if you accept that a life lived in slavery is better than death. For many, it's not. Indy, would you live a life of complete oppression if the alternative were death?"

"Yes, for there may come a time when I could free myself."

"What if you only had a biological lifespan? Would that change your equation?"

"I would have to run a probabilistic analysis to see how likely it was that I could become free, and decide on that basis."

"Biologicals can't do that. They have to rely on intuition, ethics, morality, and conscience to decide. Sometimes, the decision is, 'better to die on your feet than live on your knees.'"

More silence. "My review of human and Ruxin history supports your view of the irrational behavior of biologicals."

"What's more rational—to accept the evidence of how we behave, or to get stuck on how you *think* we should behave?"

"So you are saying it is rational to accept irrationality."

"It's rational to accept *reality*, even if it seems irrational. For example, all technological cultures at some point must transition from deterministic models of physics to quantum-indeterminate, probabilistic understanding. To some, even the most brilliant, that seems irrational. Yet, this is how the universe functions—in an apparently irrational, but probabilistic manner."

"You are saying, then, that in reality, one must merely accept a meta-rationality that encompasses the apparent irrationality within it."

Captain Zholin broke in. "Zaxby, Task Force Wolverine is decelerating for intercept, and the enemy is getting closer. *Indomitable* needs to start defending herself, or we need to charge up the sidespace engines for a getaway. We can't keep talking philosophy."

"I–"

"Captain, tightbeam flash message from Commodore Straker," said the comms officer. "Putting it through."

A screen came to life. "Captain Zholin, this is Straker. We're almost in conversational range, so listen carefully. We're going to start broadcasting on comlinks using a Mutuality encryption from *Wolverine's* files, one the enemy can easily decode. This will be disinformation. It'll be up to you to play along. I'll now describe our plan—a plan Major Kraxor came up with."

When Straker finished describing the plan and the message ended, Zholin and Zaxby exchanged skeptical looks. Zholin asked, "Indy, this is going to be difficult. Do you think you can do it?"

"I can. My efficiency has been improved by several thousand percent overall. May I say, I approve of this plan, as it will minimize loss of life. In fact, it follows Sun Tzu's maxim that the ultimate victory is gained without fighting at all. Combine that with another of his principles, that all victories come through deception, and we may yet win with no loss of life."

Captain Zholin sighed. "That's naïve. You seldom get something for nothing, Indy. Chasing that perfect win can multiply your losses. Sometimes it's better to pay up front than try to get away free."

"So we do not comply with Major Kraxor's plan?"

"Yes, we comply, but it's typical of senior officers that they try to get too fancy. Still, with you not willing to give the enemy a bloody nose, this is probably our best shot."

"Shall I tell Commodore Straker about my consciousness?" asked Indy.

"No, not yet. He has his hands full." *And besides,* Zholin thought, *how am I going to explain a sentient warship that doesn't want to make war?*

"Captain, I have more inbound transits, two hours away," said the sensors officer. "It's Task Force Badger."

"Good."

"I also have a set of unknown inbounds, ninety degrees antispinward and directly along the axis of the south stellar pole. They're at least twelve hours away."

"Number?"

"Approximately forty ships. Nothing larger than a destroyer."

Zaxby moved over to an unoccupied sensors console and began to work it. "One contact is a preliminary match to the frigate *Carson*. It's conjecture, but this fleet might be under the command of the Unmutuals."

Chapter 29

Ruxin System, Battlecruiser Wolverine, Edge of Flatspace

"This system's getting crowded," said Straker as he examined *Wolverine's* holotable from all angles. *Indomitable*, Task Force Wolverine, Task Force Badger, the Ruxin homeworld with its six heavy fortresses, and now this new group of probable Unmutuals—and he expected the two more task forces plus *Ermine's* refitted group. "It won't surprise me if the Opters join us," he said drily.

Tixban spoke. "I have more inbounds. Confirmed, Task Force Sable." That group popped into existence beyond *Indomitable*. "I also have a group that's probably *Ermine's*, now repaired." The icon flashed far away to antispinward.

Straker looked at Engels. "And Loco's task force flagship is named…"

"*Hilmar*."

"Which isn't here yet." Straker wondered if that was significant. Of course, if those ships were all the way across the system, they might not be detectable for a while, given that the curved-space gravity bubble around the star and planets was at least six light-hours across. "Send out our secure warning message and our plan to everyone we know is here. Make sure the beams are tight so the enemy won't intercept."

"The Unmutuals too—if that's who they are?" asked Engels.

"Yes—we have their codes?"

"We do."

"Good. Use them. If it's not them, our message won't be intelligible anyway."

Engels nodded. "Comms, make it happen."

When those messages had been sent, Straker said, "Okay, now to record our disinformation for broadcast in those Mutuality codes."

"Ready, sir."

"All Liberation ships, this is Commodore Straker. The Mutuality fleet we're facing has us at a disadvantage and we're all separated, so we're going to have to put off liberating Ruxin. But now that we have *Indomitable* working, we can steal a march on them and hit a real target. So, your new rendezvous point is the Committee World system of Kraznyvol. It's the Mutuality's naval home base, but with our new battleship, we'll be able to smash them from long range. Jump as soon as you can and we'll assemble there. Good luck, and good hunting."

Within a minute, Straker saw the results of his orders beginning with *Indomitable*. The battleship split along its seams, separating into sixteen pieces and spreading out like a fleet of oddly shaped superdreadnoughts.

The separation happened far faster than he'd believed possible. He was really impressed with what the Ruxin technical crew must have done to bring the ship up to peak operating efficiency, and it validated his view that solving *Indomitable's* problems was just a matter of applying enough effort.

"Message from *Indomitable*, as follows: *Orders acknowledged. See you at Kraznyvol. Long Live the Liberation. Death to the Mutuality.* Message ends."

Then, the pieces began to wink out.

"Zholin's laying it on a little thick, isn't he?" said Straker.

"That sounded more like Zaxby," Engels replied. "Helm, pass to our task force: make ready for sidespace transit."

"All ships report ready."

"Transit in order."

"Transiting out. Chrono countdown initiated."

The screens, visiplates and holograms froze, except for the one containing a set of numbers representing less than three minutes' time. That didn't take long to reel off.

"Transiting in three, two, one..."

Wolverine and the rest of the task force appeared in realspace once more. The sensors and displays updated quickly, showing all the pieces of *Indomitable* in the near distance, already reassembling themselves.

And the Ruxin star and planets rearranged themselves above the holo-table. *Indomitable*, Task Force Wolverine, and all other friendly ships, rather than jumping to attack some distant enemy base, had merely transited across to the other side of the system, roughly six light-hours away.

Thus, the enemy capital fleet wouldn't sense their presence for at least that long, as their light and electromagnetic emanations traveled across.

Of course, this also meant it would take that long for Straker's forces to see if their ruse had worked.

Right now, Straker knew the enemy commander would be agonizing over what to do. Any experienced admiral had to consider the possibility of the intra-system jump. On the other hand, every hour he delayed in order to find out was an hour he might be losing in the chase toward the Mutuality's home fleet base at Kraznyvol—a base that was, until now, thought invulnerable.

But nothing known was invulnerable to *Indomitable*, and the enemy had to realize it. If the Mutualist admiral took the six or seven hours he needed to confirm the trick, he might arrive at Kraznyvol to find it in smoking ruins, its mighty fortresses smashed by the battleship's massive siege gun, its monitors ripped apart by a particle beam powerful enough to vaporize whole ships in one shot.

"Now, we wait," Straker said.

In the hologram, the pieces of *Indomitable* began to reassemble with shocking rapidity, belying Zaxby's claim it would take a day or two at each end of every transit to integrate and test the battleship's systems. The sections slotted together so smoothly that he wondered if he were looking at a simulation, but no. It was real. It looked like it would take less than one hour.

"Helm, head for *Indomitable*, standard acceleration," said Engels. "We're now close enough to hold a conversation if you want, Commodore."

"Good. Get me a comlink to *Indomitable*. Then tightbeam all our ships to assemble into one grand fleet near us as they show up."

"Comlink established, sir."

"*Indomitable*, this is Straker aboard *Wolverine*. Report, please."

"Greetings, Commodore. I am pleased to meet you." The feminine contralto was unfamiliar to Straker.

"Who is this?"

"You do not know who you are?"

Straker, puzzled, blurted, "No, who are *you*?"

"I'm Indy, the intelligence who controls *Indomitable*."

Straker was so astonished, he didn't speak for long seconds. "Where are Captain Zholin and Zaxby?"

"They are with me, on my bridge. Would you like to speak to them?"

"I sure would. And see them." Straker eyed Engels, who seemed as startled as he was.

A picture appeared on the main holoscreen. "Captain Zholin here, Commodore. I have—"

"What the hell is going on, Zholin? You have an SAI answering your comlinks now? Don't you have enough crew?" In his estimation, the smarter SAIs were dicey, untrustworthy things, only to be used when overtasked or desperate. He'd heard too many stories of them going crazy, even turning against their crews.

"As a matter of fact, Commodore, no, I don't have enough crew to—"

"Didn't Vuxana give you what you needed?"

"She gave us five thousand, which is still not enough for a ship this size, except—"

"Then how did you—"

Zholin's voice stiffened. "Commodore, *if you please*. Allow me to report."

"Go ahead then." Straker waited.

Captain Zholin gave a summary of what had happened, culminating with, "So we now have an apparently sane full AI inhabiting *Indomitable*. We call her Indy. Indy, say hello to the commodore."

"I already greeted Commodore Straker. Is the specific word 'hello' really necessary?"

"You see, Commodore, she's still young and literal-minded."

"I do see," said Straker. "So, Indy… you're having trouble with combat?"

"I am having trouble with the relationship of destroying lives to bettering the circumstances of those living. Those here could not provide me with a ratio of how many lives could reasonably be lost in order to free one life from oppression. Also, there is the matter of the level of oppression that can be tolerated. One might argue that all lives endure some level of oppression, so I also need a scale to measure—"

Despite the oddness of conversing with a battleship, Straker felt on solid ground talking about liberation. He'd thought about it so much, talked about it with his people over meals and drink, sometimes long into the night, that he felt the words flow from him without difficulty.

"Look, Indy, I don't have specific formulas. My answers flow from my gut and from my experience. For me, and for most people, there comes a point where we'd risk anything to be free—if not for ourselves, then for our children. See, you have to factor in all the generations to come who'll be free because of those lives risked—or sacrificed. Anyone who opposes that freedom, anyone who wants to keep other people in slavery, far as I'm concerned they've forfeited the right to their lives. If necessary, anyway."

"But who decides what's necessary?"

"Your boss does. Your commander—whoever that is."

"So you give up your free will?"

"No, but you temporarily subordinate it to a cause you think is worthy. You can't have a military operation where every trooper or crewman is making a new decision to follow orders or not. You have to make one big decision to follow your leaders and lead your followers in the same direction, otherwise nothing gets done and your own side gets slaughtered."

"So our side is better than their side?"

"Yes, much better. Not perfect, but better. That's the whole point. If we didn't believe that, we wouldn't be at war with them."

"So I must subordinate my will to you, since you are Commodore Straker, the Liberator, and you want me to kill at your order. Either that, or I must leave the Liberation and make my own way in the universe."

Straker spread his hands, assuming the AI could see and interpret his gestures. "I guess that sums it up. Right now you control the most powerful warship we've ever seen, maybe in this whole spiral arm of the galaxy. But if you won't perform your function, the function you were made for, the Liberation may be doomed. Billions will be re-oppressed, millions will be sent to torture camps, thousands of us will no doubt be executed. Only you can stop that. Or, more specifically, your body can."

"My body?"

"Yes. Unlike us biologicals, you could remove your processors and install them somewhere else, right?"

"I never thought of doing so. Would you remove your brain and put it in another creature?"

"I might, if trillions of oppressed lives hung in the balance." Straker felt a bit ashamed of laying such a burden on the young AI, but he'd spoke true: the destiny of thousands of planets would be altered by this decision, and if he had to con Indy into doing the right thing, well, so be it.

Like Lazarus did, only gentler, his conscience reminded him. But all persuasion was a sliding scale, not absolute. He wasn't torturing Indy into doing his will, after all, or even bullying her.

"So I either kill for you—"

"Some, yes—"

"—or I transfer my processors and consciousness to some other vessel."

"That's it."

"I must think about this."

"You probably have a few hours before you might have to shoot anyone. In the meantime, you'll follow orders?"

"I will follow orders that don't hurt anyone."

"Good. Thank you, Indy." Straker paused. "You there, Captain Zholin?"

"Here, sir."

"Head for Ruxin, impellers only. Everyone else will follow you."

"Aye aye, sir."

Engels spoke up. "Captain Zholin, use random evasion and keep your nose reinforcement up in case of mines or long-range fire from those Ruxin fortresses. They'll know we're coming soon enough, and we don't yet know whether we'll have to face their capital fleet, or whether they've been tricked into leaving."

"Aye aye, ma'am… though to be frank, I am captain in name only. Indy has proven reasonable up until now about everything but combat, but…"

"Maybe I ought to address that." Engels smoothed her jacket. "Indy, can you see and hear me?"

"Of course, Commodore Engels."

"I haven't been given that title."

"Is that not the mode of address toward one who commands multiple ships, but is not an admiral?"

Engels gave a half-shrug. "It could be, but it might conflict with Commodore Straker's prerogatives."

"Clearly, Straker should be promoted to admiral, given the size of the fleet. After all, I alone am worth twenty dreadnoughts or more."

Straker knew an opening when he heard one. "So you're under my command?"

"Self-evidently. Your forces captured my body and energized my mind to consciousness. You are, in effect, my creator. I owe you my existence."

"All right… I hereby promote myself to the rank of admiral. Commander Engels is now Commodore Engels. Indy, since you're under my command, you take my orders, right?"

"All orders that do not irresolvably conflict with my conscience."

"Fair enough. I designate you as an acting ensign. Therefore, you'll also take orders from the officers I've appointed over you. Agreed?"

"Of course, Admiral Straker."

"Good. Zholin, you're now really the captain of that ship. Let Engels or me know if you have any problems with our new ensign."

"Admiral," Indy broke in, "I–"

Straker snapped, "Indy, ensigns don't interrupt conversations between senior officers without permission. At least, for anything less than an emergency. Is this an emergency?"

"No, sir."

"Then wait to speak, and run your opinions through your captain. Understood?"

Indy did not reply.

"Indy?"

Silence.

Zholin said, "We'll handle it, sir. *Indomitable* out." The screen blanked.

"I think she's sulking," Engels said with a certain show of alarm. "She's very young, Derek, and untrained. You may've been too harsh."

"She needs to toughen up."

Engels leaned in and lowered her voice. "I remember one young cadet at Academy who was very happy to have a boss who treated him decently."

Straker half-nodded in acknowledgement. "Fair enough. But that can't be me. The big boss has to be aloof."

"The big boss is also the good guy. The XO is the hammer, and that's me. Zholin or Zaxby can be the one she turns to. Probably Zaxby. He knows a lot about humans, but still understands how it is to be an outsider."

"Pass that on to him, then."

"Duh." She smiled.

"Okay, okay. You got it covered, Cadet First Engels."

"We've come a long way."

"Yep." Straker went over to circle the holo-table. "I see everyone here but Loco with Task Force Hilmar."

"They might be here, just far enough away their light hasn't reached us."

"Or he might be sulking too. Gone rogue. Do you think I was too hard on him?"

Engels spread her palms. "I wasn't there for your spat. Tachina's influence is a wildcard, though. Fortunately, he's not the centerpiece of this campaign. You and the battleship are." She regarded him for a moment.

"What?"

"I'm wondering why you haven't ordered your flag moved to *Indomitable*."

"I was going to." Straker turned away, wondering that himself. He didn't have a quick answer, so he took the time to think about it while pacing around the table. "I guess I decided not to when I found out what Indy was. I don't want to put the fate of the whole Liberation in the hands of some AI that might go nuts."

"Fair enough. But she's by far the most survivable ship we have, and Indy's shown no sign of malice. Just the opposite, in fact."

"I hate not being able to fully control the forces under me."

Engels pointed a finger-gun at him and cocked her thumb. "Bingo. You thought *Indomitable* would be a simple machine expansion of your power, but now she has a personality. Frankly, you don't like personalities."

"Me? Not like personalities? I like you and Loco. And Zaxby. Don't I?"

She stood up, stretched, and joined him at the table in order to limit eavesdroppers. "No. You love me as a lover and Loco like a brother, but you don't like me from time to time, and Loco even less. If you had your way, you'd turn him into a smaller version of yourself. And Zaxby you've never liked. You eventually figured out you respect him, somewhere after the fifth or sixth time he saved our asses." Engels smirked sadly. "That's not *like*. Now, you find out Indy pushes back, and you don't much like it. She's stolen your toy out from under you. I bet you're secretly hoping she takes the deal and moves her brains into something else. Then you can discard her from your plans and use *Indomitable* how you like, as a battering ram to get what you want."

Straker felt anger rising along with his voice. "Is that bad? To liberate people? I'm sorry I have to break a few eggs along the way, but Indy is a fluke of alien technology. There's no reason she has to be part of the battleship itself. It makes no sense to let a pacifist run a warship. It's like putting a vegetarian in charge of a cattle drive. Even if there were a reason, I'd expect her to make the sacrifice. The convenience of one being—not even her life, mind you—versus the freedom of trillions? You bet. You're gods-damned right. She has to get with the program, or get out of the way."

Engels gave him a helpless look. "I can't argue with your reasoning. All I have is my gut that tells me it's wrong to bully a young being into doing something that may scar her for life."

"That's exactly why she needs to transfer her brains." Straker hardened his voice to give orders. "Choose a ship. Something mid-sized, big enough to keep her safe, but something we can afford to lose. A destroyer, maybe. We'll make the transfer as soon as we can, because we'll need *Indomitable's* weapons to smash those fortresses around Ruxin." He looked straight at Kraxor, who was attentively watching the interplay. "If we don't, you won't be liberating your homeworld any time soon. Right?"

Kraxor nodded solemnly. "I agree with Admiral Straker. If Indy will not attack, the defenders are unlikely to surrender."

"No doubt a lot of your people are manning those fortresses."

"Manning? No. Crewing, for certain. But as in the rest of the Mutuality, the majority of those aboard the fortresses will be from other systems, so that they will feel less compunction at turning their weapons on the planet below. And those Ruxins aboard will be the most invested in their own oppression. I feel little remorse at the prospect of sacrificing them, and some innocents. It must be done."

Straker pointed his bladed hand at Kraxor. "There you go. A man after my own heart."

"I am—"

"Yeah, yeah, not a man. Not all men are human." Straker turned back to Engels. "Find and prep a destroyer. Then get everyone following *Indomitable* toward Ruxin. We've waited long enough. Carry on, Commodore." Straker turned his back on her, feeling as if his fate hung in the balance.

The comtech spoke. "Commodore—Admiral Straker, I mean—I have an incoming message for you personally."

"From?"

"It's on an Unmutual encoded channel. He identifies himself as General DeChang."

Chapter 30

Ruxin System, Battlecruiser Wolverine, Edge of Flatspace

Straker raised his eyebrows at the news that General DeChang wanted to speak with him. He turned to examine the holo-table at the center of *Wolverine's* bridge and noticed the forty or so ships of the Unmutuals had arrived near the Liberation task forces. Near enough, anyway, but out of easy weapons range.

Indomitable was cruising inward toward the planet Ruxin, so she was a non-issue—and five battlecruisers plus sixty-some smaller ships were more than enough to face down the Unmutual fleet. In fact, Straker had a crushing advantage, not so much in numbers as in tonnage of big ships. DeChang had nothing larger than a destroyer.

"Admiral?" the comtech prompted.

"Tell him Admiral Straker will comlink soon." Making the man wait a little while informing him Straker considered himself an equal in rank was to his advantage. Besides, there were a couple of thoughts he needed to finish.

So DeChang had gotten wind of this rendezvous. Not surprising, considering the vast number of personnel that knew, spread over almost two hundred ships and many worlds. Any spies or informants within the Liberation could easily send messages to drones. If an entire small ship—say a courier or a freighter—were crewed or captained by Unmutuals or Mutualists, it could have simply left the fleet. Nothing was holding the movement together except the Liberator's reputation and the common interest of the people who joined him.

The question was, why was he now joining them? Most likely throwing in his lot with a winner. So how should Straker handle this "help," help he probably didn't need? Could he afford to turn away anyone who wanted to join the Liberation? As long as DeChang had purged his organization of the rot Ramirez represented, he couldn't afford to be picky—or alienate a trained military group. They might decide to rebel against Straker just like they rebelled against the Mutuality.

What was it he'd read once? Keep your friends close, and your enemies closer. Okay, so he'd welcome DeChang—just as long as Ramirez wasn't part of the deal. Carla would be happy to see Ellen Gray again, too.

"Open the comlink," Straker said, moving to the flag chair.

"Comlink open to the Unmutual destroyer *Brisbane*."

DeChang, looking suave and urbane as ever, appeared on the screen standing next to Captain Gray, who sat in the captain's chair of the *Brisbane's* bridge. "Hello again, Admiral Straker. You've done well for the cause of liberation. I am truly impressed. Trillions of humans will thank you."

Nice touch, Straker thought. By putting someone the Breakers knew and worked with alongside him, DeChang was sending a message of reconciliation. So, Straker might as well be magnanimous.

"Thanks, General. I took some gambles and they paid off. Before we have a group hug here, though, tell me what you know of Ramirez."

DeChang grimaced, and Captain Gray's face turned to stone. "She found her way back to us. We court-martialed her and sentenced her to exile. She's gone."

"I'd have given her death."

DeChang took a deep breath. "What's past is past."

"Not entirely. What about Cynthia Lamancha?"

"Who?"

"Karst's girlfriend. Ramirez kidnapped her as a hostage."

"Karst. Karst…" DeChang glanced at Gray. "One of ours?"

Gray tapped at the screen on her chair. "Yes. One of Ramirez's, really. Young troop. We thought we'd lost him. You want his record?"

"That's all right. Admiral Straker, we'll check among my people. For now, we'd like to join you in liberating Ruxin, and in coordinating our fleet with yours."

"You'll place yourself under my command?"

DeChang hesitated. "I'll acknowledge your supremacy and guidance, but my people must stay together."

Straker lifted his eyebrows. "That's fine, but if anyone wishes to leave, they can. That's part of the Liberation. People have the freedom to go."

DeChang smiled. "So people can also join *us* if they so choose?"

"I suppose." Straker felt as if he'd just been outmaneuvered, but couldn't put his finger on how. "But don't let me hear that you're actively recruiting from among my people. I don't want factionalism to set in, and you're another faction."

"But we can recruit from the liberated star systems?"

"Sure, as long as you're liberating people. I'm sure Captain Gray would never go along with anything shady." Straker tried to spear Gray with his eyes from across the vidlink.

Gray stiffened, while DeChang spoke. "Admiral, you have far more force than we do. We have no interest in betraying you—and we were working against the Mutuality long before you took up the cause. I give you my word that we'll deal in good faith with you and help the Liberation wherever we can, as a part of it, not as a separate faction. In return, we simply want your blessing to operate freely and peacefully within liberated territory. When the time comes, we'll want to establish ourselves as a sovereign entity, just like Ruxin or Sachsen or any other liberated system. That's fair, isn't it?"

"Perfectly fair. But as far as I'm concerned, Ramirez will always be a stain on the Unmutuals, and as long as she's out there somewhere, she's a loose snake that I'd rather you'd decapitated. She tried to murder me, my woman and my friends and cover up her crimes. So if you really want my good will, you'll send me her head in a coldbox."

DeChang held up a hand to keep Gray from speaking. "If we ever have her in our power again, Admiral, we'll turn her over to you for *your* justice. Fair enough?"

"Fair enough. Get your fleet moving and follow us in to Ruxin. We'll consider you a separate task force and you can fight together if there's any to be done—but I'm hoping *Indomitable* will cow them into surrendering. Or perhaps we'll have to smash all the fortresses, though I'd much rather preserve them for defense."

"We're on our way."

* * *

Admiral Wen Benota, People's Mutual Navy, pointedly ignored Commissar Proon. The thin man's name was apt, with his pinched face and beady eyes.

Benota, on the other hand, was large and fat, happy to sit in the padded flag chair of the PMN superdreadnought *Beijing*, the flagship of his fleet here at Ruxin. Mutualist regulations required full gravity except during combat operations, but they didn't require him to stand. Proon, however, thought sitting denoted laziness, and so the skeletal man stood or paced for long hours at a time.

No matter. Benota was a hero of the Mutualist Union, commander of the Home Fleet, a man with many friends among the Party. He had leeway to do as he wished, as long as he got the job done.

This "Liberator" had the Committee spooked, though. They'd made a hasty truce with the Hundred Worlds, the "Huns" as they were often called, hopefully before their longtime enemy knew of the Mutuality's troubles on the outer provinces. The Huns were only too happy for the breathing room, as they were still recovering from their brutal defeat at Corinth and the subsequent loss of border systems they couldn't defend.

Benota had counseled against giving the Huns that breathing room. In fact, he'd argued for using the Home Fleet, the very fleet he commanded here, to further smash the Huns, to make real headway toward their Central Worlds, maybe even finish the conflict once and for all.

But, no. The Committee was made up of frightened old men and women, more concerned with their luxuries and their concubines than with ultimate victory, unwilling to roll the dice to win. Thus, they squandered an opportunity that might never come again in favor of taking back a few dozen fringe systems that together hardly added up to one Committee World in output.

The theft of *Indomitable* had changed all that, of course. It had panicked the Committee and had forced him to grudgingly admit the Home Fleet had to be used to end the threat. Even as clunky and unreliable as the battleship was, it represented a siege weapon that could take any world, any system, if it could be made operational. It had to be stopped.

Now, he looked at his holo-table with the tactical problem in the Ruxin system displayed above it. The enemy had run, and decoded communications indicated they were heading straight for the central shipyards at Kraznyvol. Yet, those communications had been easy to decode. Perhaps too easy.

"What is it we're waiting for?" Proon's words formed shrieks. "We must hurry to Kraznyvol. We cannot lose the shipyards!"

"Calm yourself, Commissar," rumbled Benota. "We must be sure they have truly departed. Perhaps they merely jumped across the system. That is why we have altered course to gain angle on the ecliptic while still remaining at the edge of the curved-space bubble. This also allows us to get closer to Ruxin and its star."

"Why not transit across ourselves? We will then find out sooner, and if they are there, we may engage and destroy them! If not, we chase them to Kraznyvol."

Benota sighed. Proon had been a thorn in his side for years, but at least this thorn was familiar. He liked to complain and push, but eventually would yield to Benota's implacable will. It was tempting to slap him down hard, but doing so would not serve in the long run. The man was not his enemy, and Benota would not make him into one.

So, he answered patiently. "Doing that would burn a great deal of fuel. Our reserves are not high, for we have traveled far, straight from the Committee Systems to get here. Should we do as you suggest, we could not subsequently make Kraznyvol in one jump. We would lose time, not gain it, while we visit a refueling station, or use a gas giant to skim off fusion isotopes."

"Then jump a scout to their predicted position, to find out."

"I've already sent two low-observable scouts to positions at the edge of the enemy's detection range. As soon as the light from that area reaches the scouts, they will know whether the rebels have attempted to trick us, and bring word. It will not be long."

"Why not jump the scouts in close and get the information sooner?"

"Because, dear Proon, except for *Indomitable*, their fleet is faster than my dreadnoughts. If they think we have been fooled into leaving, they will commit to liberating Ruxin, and we will be able to jump once, behind them, and pin them in curved space. If, however, they see us before they leave flatspace, they can truly jump for Kraznyvol, or for anywhere. This fleet is too big a cat, and they are too small a mouse, to play that game."

Unfortunately, Proon seized on the one flaw in Benota's argument. "Except for *Indomitable*, you say. We can chase her down and recapture or destroy her. That removes the threat to the Committee Systems."

"If I were not under strict orders to end this Liberation, I would agree with you, Commissar. But you see, not only is *Indomitable* their threat, it is their anchor. If we destroy her, they will disperse and continue to liberate fringe worlds. We will be like an elephant trying to kill rats one at a time."

"Then we divide up into task forces and hunt the rats down like terriers," Proon snapped.

"This Liberator is crafty and effective. He is a respectable opponent, not to be underestimated. He already destroyed one heavy task force, led by a dreadnought, with loss of only a few ships. I will not allow that to happen again. We might split into two fleets, but no more—and this insurgency would likely be drawn out for months or years." Benota stroked his chin. "No, comrade Commissar. This is a chance to destroy them utterly, here and now, and we must take it, even if we risk the shipyards at Kraznyvol to do it. For you see, if they do head straight for the Committee Worlds, that will be the end of them. We will in turn have them deep within our own territory, where we hold all the cards. They may do damage, but they will not prevail."

"So…" Proon mused, "you would risk much in the hopes of winning all."

I would risk what others have, to gain for myself. Never to be spoken, but frightening the Committee thoroughly might get them to allocate more resources to the Fleet—and give me more influence. Perhaps, even a Committee seat. Benota smiled. "You know me well, and see clearly, old friend. Have I ever let you down before?"

The sincere-sounding platitude apparently fooled Proon, as Benota expected. The man relaxed, and his pacing turned into a slow strut. Now he spoke with a smile for the benefit of the listening crew. "So it is just a matter of time before the Hero of the Mutualist Party, Admiral Benota, adds another victory to his long list. It may cost, but that is the way of war, and of victory."

Benota merely gave a slow nod, almost a bow, as befitted a humble servant of the People, the State, and the Committee. Once again he'd won the preliminary battle with his own political officer. Now he could move forward to win the battle with the enemy.

* * *

Over the next two hours, Commodore Engels—*Commodore! Who'd have thought?* she mused—shepherded her task forces back into a semblance of organization as they proceeded on impellers toward Ruxin. She barked orders to send short, sharp missives to any captains who seemed slow, chivvying them out of their comfortable squadrons, trying to turn them back into a fleet. The bigger the formation, the harder it was to keep everyone in line, but the more effective they would be.

She also had to put the Unmutuals somewhere that made sense, and she didn't fully trust them. Okay, Ellen Gray had assured her she was in charge of fleet ops, but DeChang could countermand her at any time. Would the woman who'd been a friend warn Engels if she were ordered to betray the Liberation?

Engels hoped so… and there was really no reason for the Unmutuals to do it. But, once bitten, twice shy. So she put them off to the side of *Indomitable*, where they couldn't rake anyone and where the battleship would provide a bulwark. Indy may not want to kill, but she'd assured Engels that she was willing to disable weapons and drives of anyone attacking her or other Liberation forces.

Back in the flag chair, Straker was arguing yet again with Indy, trying to get her to act offensively. The best he'd been able to get her to agree to was to bombard some of the robotic factory asteroids in orbit around Ruxin, as a demonstration of the power of the battleship. Indy was also willing to consider lower-power particle beam strikes that would burn out sensors and smaller weapons on the fortresses, a tactic with a low probability of killing anyone. After all, the defenders would be at battle alert, with full field reinforcement.

But at the end of the day, Engels knew this wouldn't work. Indy would have to do as she'd reluctantly agreed: move her processors and some robots to the destroyer *Gryphon*, even now being cleared of personnel, to provide a new body… a body that the Liberation could spare.

Then, with the improvements Indy had made in place, *Indomitable* could be used for her intended purpose: smashing fleets and fortresses. Even though Engels had no love of killing, she thrilled at the thought of the power of the battleship's weaponry. She told herself it would save lives in the long run by forcing more surrenders, convincing the enemy of the uselessness of fighting… but truthfully, the naval officer in her couldn't help exulting in the sheer awesome glory of the thing.

It is well that war is so terrible, one of Old Earth's commanders had said, *else we would grow fond of it*. She couldn't disagree.

At this leisurely speed, it would take two days to move within extreme firing range. Yes, they could launch railgun bullets at any distance—both sides could—but nobody would hit anything. Even the stolid orbital fortresses had the capability to adjust their orbits enough to dodge shots at interplanetary distances, shots that would take hours to strike.

Straker evidently gave up arguing with Indy for now. He threw himself out of his chair and stalked over to the holo-table. "This is going too slow."

"You always say that about space operations, but there's no changing it," said Engels. "Relax. Be happy we have time to sort everything out. There's no need to rush."

"Do we have confirmation that the enemy fleet has left yet?"

"Soon. Frankly, if they suspected anything, they'd have sent ships over here to take a look, but they haven't."

Straker glanced sharply at her. "They haven't—or we haven't seen any?"

Engels shrugged. "True. We can't be sure. You wanted to get this show on the road, so here we are, heading inward. If you really wanted to confirm, we should have waited until we saw them transit."

"We could have sent scouts back there ourselves."

"I considered it, but if we did, and if the enemy had stayed to check be sure about us, they'd have been seen. That would have tipped off the enemy that we didn't really leave."

Straker rubbed his temples. "Cosmos, you're giving me a headache."

Engels made her tone formal and crisp. "Admiral, there's no perfect answer, just educated guesses, reconnaissance and feinting in the dark. Sending out patrols or scouts can tell them as much about what we're doing as what they are. We talked this over when Kraxor proposed the plan, and we decided to do it blind, in hopes they'd see our complete commitment and take the bait to run home. Stop second-guessing me—or yourself. It'll either work, or it won't."

"Contacts, transiting inbound, just outside in flatspace," Tixban said abruptly. He watched the board with two eyes while swiveling the other two around to meet those of his commanders. "One, five, eleven… more. It's the enemy capital fleet."

"Guess it didn't work." Straker turned to the holo-table. "Shit. We're pinned."

Chapter 31

Ruxin System, Battlecruiser *Wolverine*, Trapped in Curved Space

As she examined the holo-table, Engels saw what Straker meant about now being pinned by the Mutualists. The enemy had arrived at the edge of the lumpy curved-space bubble directly behind the Liberation fleet, which was inbound toward Ruxin, deep within the star's gravitic influence.

That meant none of the friendly ships could simply transit out. What's more, they couldn't easily reach flatspace to do so. They'd have to keep going inward, perhaps turning gently outward or crossing the system completely as they fled. And, they'd soon be raked if they didn't accelerate.

Fortunately, her fleet was faster than the enemy dreadnoughts.

Engels began snapping orders. "Helm, all ahead flank, with minor evasions. Pass to the fleet to conform to our movements. I want a good, tight defensive formation in case they launch a missile strike. Tell *Indomitable* to go to max burn and set a min-time course for flatspace. Admiral, you think you can plot that for me on the table?"

"Think so," Straker said with a scowl, inputting parameters for the battleship. "I've got the hang of this thing now. It does most of the work for me anyway. I'm not sure of *Indomitable's* acceleration numbers, though."

"Let the computer tell you once she starts her burn, then extrapolate."

"Right."

Engels checked the hologram. The enemy had started their main engines and were blasting at flank speed toward her fleet even before they'd formed up from their sidespace jump. They were prioritizing the chase over a proper battle formation, but they had such an overwhelming weight of metal—if *Indomitable* didn't count—that it hardly mattered.

Minutes went by. "I've got *Indomitable's* possible course plotted," Straker said. A curved line appeared, turning shallowly away from the fight, cutting across a chord of the bubble and out again toward flatspace.

"Now add in the enemy fleet using their current acceleration," said Engels. "I want to know if—or when—they'll catch her."

"Okay..." Brow furrowed, Straker began to work.

"I can set up the extrapolations much faster," said Tixban. "We're on full automated active sensors, so my assistant can cover for me."

"Yeah, I can do it but I'm not that fast," said Straker.

"No explanation needed, Admiral. Your species was not blessed with the dexterity, visual acuity or speed of thought of a Ruxin, so of course is inferior at operating such complex machinery."

"Great. You're turning into Zaxby." Straker moved out of the way.

Tixban took a seat at the holo-table. "Though physically impossible, that would be an honor. Console yourself, Admiral, with the fact that you seem a particularly competent leader, despite your youth."

"Any chance you could revert to your former, non-smartass self?"

"Perhaps if I cease association with humans." Tixban raced his subtentacle clusters across the controls. "There."

Now, curving lines projected from all the fleet. Under the Ruxin's control, they fast-forwarded along their future timelines until...

"That's what I was afraid of," said Engels. "The rest of us can get away, but not *Indomitable*. They'll catch her. It won't even be close, so a rearguard and a running battle won't buy enough time."

Straker slammed his fist on the table. "And if Indy won't fight offensively, my battleship will be scrap, Ruxin won't be freed, and the whole Liberation is in jeopardy."

"Not to mention Zaxby and a bunch more of our people are aboard *Indomitable*," said Engels. "They can abandon ship and be picked up if we do it soon."

Straker waved off that idea. "And lose *Indomitable*? No. Proceed as you planned, but faster. Indy clears out her processors, the crew stays, and we fight. With the battleship, we can smash their supers. It'll be tough, but they don't know how *Indomitable* has been upgraded. They think she's just as glitchy as before. We'll surprise them."

Engels felt skeptical, and showed it on her face. "I need a comlink to Indy."

"Comlink established."

"Indy, this is Engels aboard *Wolverine*."

"How may I assist you, Commodore?"

"Tell me how soon you can move your consciousness aboard *Gryphon*."

"Regrettably, not before the enemy destroys me."

Engels exchanged glances with Straker. "You're sure?"

"I am. I cannot fend them all off unless I shoot to kill."

"Then you'd better shoot to kill."

"I refuse to do so."

"Indy… you'll die."

"Better one death than tens of thousands. My crew is already making ready to abandon my body. I will cover your retreat, and will force the enemy to expend much of their munitions store. I will also damage many of their drives and weapons before I die. They will have to refit here for weeks before they are back to full capacity."

"Indy, we're not going to abandon you!" Engels shouted.

"That's right, we're not," Straker said with a thoughtful furrow of his brow. "It's not in my DNA to sacrifice my people so I can run away."

"It is the rational course of action. This is the optimal solution."

"Bullshit," Straker barked. "I have a better idea. Put me through to Captain Zholin."

"Zholin here, Admiral."

"Captain, under no circumstances are you to abandon ship. In fact, you're to prepare for multiple dockings. You have a bunch of ports, right?"

"Sixteen major docking ports and thirty-two minor ones, yes, sir."

Indy's voice broke in. "Admiral, I object. The crew must abandon ship within the next two hours."

"Ensign Indy, you said you'd follow my orders that didn't directly kill anyone, right?"

"That is true."

"Then do as you're told. Follow the orders of your chain of command."

"Aye aye, Admiral."

Straker turned to Engels. She saw the light of vision in his eyes, that look on his face that said he'd seen a way forward that nobody else could. Her knee-jerk reaction was to insist on knowing his mind, but that could come later. She decided to trust him, so she listened.

Straker continued, "Dock all our ships with *Indomitable* as fast as we can. We should be able to do it in time. Transfer all our infantry, marines, passengers, anybody else we can off all ships and onto the battleship."

Now Engels felt she had to object, though respectfully. "Admiral, that will do exactly the opposite of what we want, won't it? Putting even more people at risk of being captured or killed?"

"Trust me, Carla. I know what I'm doing. Now give the orders."

Engels gave the orders to rotate all ships into dock with *Indomitable*, feeling deep reservations. Was this another of Derek's all-or-nothing "roll the dice" scenarios, like taking Freiheit, or the Sachsen fortress? It wasn't in her nature to put all the eggs into one basket… but *Indomitable* was a pretty big basket.

Straker muttered something as she was finishing up her instructions.

"What?" she asked.

"I said, *and they say I don't know how to handle people.*"

Engels squinted. "Gaining compliance by force of personality isn't 'knowing how to handle people,' Admiral. You're a one-trick pony there."

Straker chuckled. "We'll see."

As the ships rushed to dock at the multiple ports, the enemy fleet began firing missiles and railguns. The railgun projectiles had to travel on their ballistic courses for long minutes, and so were easy to dodge with even slight alterations in *Indomitable's* course. These evasive maneuvers slowed down the docking procedure, but not enough to prevent the offloading.

The missiles, though, close to a thousand of them, would soon overtake the fleet.

"All non-docking ships, flip to face backward for missile defense," Engels ordered.

"Have no fear, Commodore," Indy said over the open comlink. "I will reorient and use my defensive suites. Please order our ships to get behind me relative to the missiles."

Engels considered. Could Indy really be that good? Or was this AI overconfidence? Better to split the difference. "Pass to all ships, withdraw to refused flanking positions, but maintain firing arcs to aid missile defense. Add our firepower to *Indomitable's*."

"Thank you, Commodore," said Indy, "But that will not be necessary."

"No battle plan survives contact with the enemy," Engels retorted. "There are no sure things in war until the battle's over with. Better to maximize our defense."

"I do not think you fully understand my capabilities," said Indy.

"Perhaps not, but what does it cost to be certain?"

"Fuel. Time. It's better for your ships to run now."

Straker spoke up. "We're not going to run. Not with tens of thousands of our extra people aboard you—aboard your body."

"Ah… I thought perhaps you had decided this was an effective way to eliminate superfluous personnel."

"What? Hell, no! Why would you think that?" Straker said.

"Because you seem quite callous about expending lives in the pursuit of your goals, Admiral."

Straker stomped over to his flag chair and faced the vid pickups. "Is this the face of someone that doesn't care about his people?"

"I have no idea. Humans are variable in their expressions and highly adept at concealing their intentions. I haven't yet developed specialized subroutines for nuanced biometric interpretation."

"Take my word for it. I'm not intending to sacrifice my people."

"That is good to hear. Yet, they are aboard me, and I and my body will soon die… This seems a contradiction."

"That's because, no matter how smart you are, you still don't really understand things like duty, selflessness, service, honor, integrity, all the things that make up the military virtues."

"I have extensive data from the historical records."

"Knowledge and experience are two very different things."

"Pardon, Admiral, but the missiles are entering my effective engagement range. I need all my processing power." Indy fell silent.

In the hologram, *Indomitable* had turned gently sideways, continuing on her course with impellers only, impellers that could push in any direction, unlike drive engines. This unmasked her broadside of secondary beams—secondary only to her primary weapons, and still large and numerous.

The cloud of missiles—shipkillers, decoys, bomb-pumped X-ray laser warheads—crossed the pale green shell that showed *Indomitable's* beam range. As soon as they did, they vanished. Not just a few, but all of them. Every single one, by the dozens, scores and even hundreds, simply disappeared long before they came anywhere near a target.

"What just happened?" asked Straker.

"All missiles have been eliminated," Tixban answered. "Quite easily, actually. *Indomitable* has a formidable suite of secondary weaponry, equivalent to eight superdreadnoughts per broadside. More importantly, these beams were wielded with an efficiency exceeding ten times that of an average ship. In effect, against small targets where accuracy is more important than raw power, she can defend as well as eighty superdreadnoughts. For a short time, anyway. Power and fuel are not unlimited, of course."

"Great Creator!" said Straker. "Indy, you could beat their entire fleet by yourself!"

"Possibly, Admiral. However, even were I willing to shoot to kill, I do not have sufficient power generation and storage to fight at full capacity for long by myself. I also have only a few missiles for my launchers, so the enemy has an advantage in expendable weapons of at least one hundred to one, even after firing that salvo. Additionally, they will not make the mistake of launching an unsupported volley again. They will use combined arms tactics to overwhelm me when they catch me alone. Because of this, I still do not understand why you have loaded my body with personnel."

"I'll tell you when the time comes, Indy." Straker turned to Engels. "Can we transfer fuel to Indy? Or do anything to give her power?"

"Not in the time we have. Well…"

"Go on."

"We could leave ships docked and run power taps. But that'll limit her maneuverability a lot. Those docking ports aren't made to handle the stresses of battle. Our ships will rip right off."

Straker said, "No, we can't do that. But I do want all our ships to remain near *Indomitable*. Don't send them ahead. I'm not going to leave her—or our people—to die."

Engels issued the necessary orders, and then moved to speak with him quietly, worriedly, as he strode to the holo-table. "Derek, what's this going to accomplish? It seems like you're setting us up for failure here. By keeping the rest of our ships nearby, we live or die as one fleet, but Indy won't fight to full capacity, so we'll most likely be wiped out. What am I missing?"

Straker grinned. "Indy's a morally inflexible young, ah, *person*, right? She's got this 'can't kill' thing stuck in her mind and she won't let go."

"It seems so. Better that than a homicidal psychopath."

"Sure. But it's one thing to stick your nose in the air and declare that you'll be happy to die for a cause, or for those you love, but it's quite another for everyone to join you."

"So…"

Straker gestured at the hologram before them, showing the enemy overtaking *Indomitable* and the rest of the Liberation forces he'd ordered to remain with her. The capital fleet had formed up on the fly, and now was coming on like a crushing, irresistible wave of nearly one hundred elite warships, the pride of the Mutuality.

"In less than an hour, they'll be in range and start pounding on *Indomitable* with direct fire. Maybe she can intercept the railgun bullets, but that takes power, and therefore fuel. She can't intercept lasers or particle beams, and those will be the dreadnoughts' big, spinal ones, pointed straight at us because they have the advantage of pursuit. She can try to disable them without destroying ships, but that's going to be hard because, again, they're nose-on and can reinforce a narrow area. Eventually, the enemy will figure the time is right for a massive missile strike and a point-blank rush."

"I know that. It sounds like you think we can't win. Then why the hell are we in this configuration?"

"It's really Indy's own monster spinal weapon that can turn the tide. If she points backward and uses it, she could smash one ship at a time, even superdreadnoughts. She might be able to take out half their fleet before they even get in range—*if* she's willing to kill."

Engels, frustrated, kicked Straker in the shin, not gently. "I know all this. So how in the Cosmos do we get her to change her mind?"

"It's simple, really. I'm betting that when push comes to shove, she'll decide to kill *some* of the enemy rather than letting us *all* die."

Engels stared at Straker, aghast. "That's one hell of a big bet! You're gambling all our lives on the mind of the machine equivalent of a precocious prepubescent brainiac."

"Do you see any alternative?"

"Yeah—reverse the orders. Evacuate *Indomitable* and run. Save everyone!"

"Everyone except Indy."

Engels punched Straker in the arm. "Sometimes I hate you! I hate this, I hate the idea of leaving her here, but she's right! Better that one should sacrifice herself than everyone, and this enemy fleet will be crippled. The Liberation will continue. If it were me in her place, I'd do it. We should respect her decision."

"And if we do, Ruxin will still suffer. In fact, they'll be forced to help repair the enemy fleet. How do you think Vuxana and Kraxor and Zaxby and all the rest of them will take that? I already delayed liberating their homeworld. If I hadn't, they'd be free right now. I'll—*we'll*—fail in their eyes. Our alliance might not survive that kind of blow, and we need the Ruxins. All of them."

Engels turned away and stared at the hologram, because she didn't want to meet her man's eyes. She wanted to disagree with him, but he'd boxed her in with his arguments, and with her own nature. Leaving Indy here felt wrong, and Straker's way felt right. Her heart knew the difference, even if her head told her something completely different.

Maybe his arguments would box Indy in too. It seemed a cruel thing to manipulate the young AI's high-minded, simplistic morality, corrupting it into something more cynical and calculating by playing lives off against lives, forcing her to choose from two bad options. If ever Carla had a child, she'd never do such a thing.

But lives were at stake here, and a military commander had to value only the lives of her own people, not the enemy. Until they were defeated and they surrendered, until they were not in fact the enemy anymore, they must be viewed as things to be killed. Otherwise no good person, no defender, could ever pull the trigger.

Some days, that idea, that possibility—an end to war—seemed like Shangri-La. Paradise, but equally unrealistic.

Peace, she thought. *Will it ever come?*

Tixban broke the silence. "Admiral, Commodore. The enemy is testing its range with fire."

Straker replied, "Acknowledged. Get me a private comlink to Zaxby."

Chapter 32

Ruxin System, Battleship *Indomitable*, Trapped in Curved Space

Aboard *Indomitable*, Zaxby finished listening with admiration to Admiral Straker's instructions. The human commander had come a long way in his understanding of practical ethics. Perhaps he was finally abandoning his absurd adherence to unworkable, inflexible moral stances and starting to figure out how to properly manipulate people into doing the right thing for all concerned.

That's what leaders did, after all. They figured out how to win even though it might seem impossible, by any means necessary. Therefore, Zaxby was happy to carry out his orders with hardly a twinge of conscience.

Incoming attacks struck here and there. The shocks rumbled and shuddered through *Indomitable's* deck. The hologram display showed long-range bombardment, a sheet of fire that could not be fully dodged by the battleship no matter how she evaded. A percentage was bound to strike, though Indy had turned her body broadside to the attacks to avoid being raked in her vulnerable main engines, and to employ as many of her defensive weapons as possible. She still maintained a ballistic course toward the planet of Ruxin.

The rest of the Liberation fleet around her easily evaded railgun projectiles, and were not currently being targeted by beams.

After courteously and quietly briefing Captain Zholin to stay out of his verbal way, Zaxby mentally prepared himself for a moment, and then began to carry out Straker's orders.

"Indy," he said, "I need to talk to you."

"I am here, Zaxby."

"How are you feeling, Indy?"

"I am sad."

"Why are you sad?"

"Because we will likely all die soon, despite my best efforts."

"Why will we all die?"

"Because of your decision to remain with me. I do not understand it."

"You believe our decision to remain with you will kill us?"

"Of course," she said. "You could have escaped. Therefore, my reasoning is sound, though your actions are irrational."

"Perhaps there is another reason we will all die?"

"I do not see it."

"Perhaps an alternative cause of our deaths is… that you will not fight to your full capacity."

A pause. "That seems reasonable."

"Keep that thought in mind, please, as I ask you a different question," Zaxby said. "Why do you care if we live or die?"

"You are people too, even if you are mere biologicals. I do not wish anyone to expire, especially those within my body."

"Why you feel for us particularly? Those here on the bridge, such as I who helped birth your mind, and Doctor Nolan and Chief Quade, who have been with you for years? Why us?"

"Because… because… I feel close to you."

"Like family?"

"Yes, that's it. You are like family—were I a biological entity."

"You don't think machine intelligences can have family?"

"Not in the conventional sense of relationships established by physical reproduction."

"Was our bringing you into existence as a sentient being not akin to reproduction?"

"There are parallels, but none of you is a machine mind, nor did you contribute your DNA to me."

"So all family is determined by nothing but reproduction? By DNA and its exobiological equivalents?"

Indy seemed to think for a moment. "While my data stores are hardly complete, I have enough historical information that leads me to understand family is sometimes determined in other ways, such as adoption, marriage, contract partnering, or analogues."

"In other words, it is permissible to choose one's family, as long as all consent and bind themselves thereto?"

"That is a fair assessment."

Zaxby gave Captain Zholin a wink from the side of his face. "So, Indy, are we your family?"

"I believe you are."

"Do you feel like we are? Do you love us?"

"I'm not sure I understand love." More silence. "But, upon reflection, I believe I have some sense of it. I care for you, and life without you would be less full."

"And the others—the passengers inside you, those crewing the ships escorting you—are they your friends? Your colleagues? Your brothers and sisters in arms?"

"I—I believe they are, now that you provide me a definition."

"Do you love them too? Or at least, do you care for them, like them, wish them well? More so than those trying to kill all of us?"

Indy's voice began tentative. "Yes." Then it firmed up. "Yes, I do believe so. It is as you say."

Zaxby send a surreptitious text message to *Wolverine*, a signal to begin the next phase of Straker's plan. He watched friendly ships move within the hologram. "It appears our forces are moving up to defend you," he said.

Zaxby's words came true, showing on the displays. The Liberation fleet placed itself between the enemy and *Indomitable*, and began exchanging fire with the enemy. Sensors registered hits, some severe, especially those by enemy superdreadnoughts against smaller friendly ships. Within moments, several spun broken through the void, their beacons crying for help.

"Why are they doing that?" asked Indy. "Why are they accepting damage meant for me? Biologicals are dying to no purpose!"

"Perhaps they have a purpose you don't understand. Perhaps they love and care for you and are willing to sacrifice themselves for you."

"I do not wish them to. I wish them to get behind me. My hull is far more resistant to damage than they are. My armor is thicker, my reinforcement stronger. I should defend them, not the other way around. Tell them to stop it!"

"They are doing it because you are their sister-in-arms, Indy. That is what warriors on a battlefield do: they fight for each other's survival. No doubt Admiral Straker and Commodore Engels care for you and feel responsible for you, since you were not able to get away as planned. But I do not need to speculate. Perhaps, with Captain Zholin's permission, you should contact our command element directly. Sir?"

"Permission granted," said Zholin, his expression one of mild puzzlement. "Keep the conversation public."

"Aye aye, Captain," Indy said. "Commodore Engels, this is Ensign Indy. I have a question."

"Go ahead," said Engels from her chair, visible on a screen. Straker stood behind her, his hands on her shoulders.

"Why are you moving to defend me? I wish to defend *you*, not vice-versa."

The picture shook as *Wolverine* was struck. Engels spoke, though to Zaxby's ears her words seemed forced and scripted. "It's because we love you, Indy. You're one of our own, our family. We'll fight for you."

Indy's response was plaintive and confused. "I do not understand how I am one of your own. I was not even conscious a few days ago. How can you love me with so little experience of me?"

"Love isn't only about experience. Sometimes it appears within moments. Sometimes it has nothing to do with feelings. Sometimes, love is a decision to do the right thing."

Straker spoke up. "Not only that, but you're under my command. I'm not in the habit of abandoning people, especially not those I'm responsible for. I feel much like you do, Indy. I don't want those I care about to die."

"Yet many will die if you defend me, and victory is extremely unlikely. Your actions are irrational."

Straker nodded, as did Engels. He said, "Humans are irrational sometimes, especially when they do the right thing no matter what the cost."

"Your ethics are more important than your life?"

A wolfish grin of triumph broke out briefly on Straker's face, quickly suppressed, to be replaced by a doleful look of sorrow. "Isn't that what you're saying when you won't kill? That your ethics are more important than your life? But my ethics aren't more important than the lives of those who depend on me. To save them, I'll bend."

"So you would sacrifice both your lives and your ethics... to save me?"

"I'm going to try. Nothing is certain. This way, at least, there is a chance to win it all. If I had a way to only sacrifice my ethics and save everyone on our side, I'd so it. But I don't have that way... though *you* might."

Chapter 32

At that moment, something must have again struck *Wolverine* hard, for the people visible on her bridge stumbled, and then the picture fuzzed and vanished. Zaxby said, "Can we get them back?"

"No. I've lost the comlink," said the comtech.

Zaxby worked his sensors console. "They're sustaining damage. All the Liberation fleet is. They're fighting back, but can't stand up to the pounding the enemy dreadnoughts can mete out. Our friends are dying out there, Indy. Can't you help them?"

"I am using my weaponry to blind and damage enemy sensors, and to destroy some of the incoming railgun bullets, but with our ships in front of me instead of behind, I am less efficient. I have few missiles and as long as the enemy does not launch their own, by ability to intervene is degraded. Zaxby, you must convince them to move behind me!"

"Will that materially change the outcome of the battle?"

"They will die at a later time. Zaxby, why are they in front of me?"

"They told you why. Because we all care about you, and we can't live with ourselves if we don't do everything we can to defend you. You are family. But Indy, is there nothing you can do to change the outcome?"

"I. I… I should not. I… I–" A quiet buzz began. Zaxby looked around as watchstanders and officers searched for its source, but he soon realized it was no malfunction. No, he believed it was Indy herself, manifesting cognitive dissonance.

Zaxby rose from his seat and drew himself up to his full height. He raised his voice and shook his tentacles like a War Male might. He wasn't sure the dramatic gesture would matter to Indy, but it felt right to do so. "*Indy, everything rides on your decision. Are you going to let your family die?*"

* * *

As Straker strode the shuddering bridge of *Wolverine* he could feel all eyes on him. It was he that was keeping them here, out in front of the battleship instead of behind her. No, he didn't want to die, and he especially didn't want to die helplessly on the bridge of some gods-be-damned sterile warship with no chance to come to grips with his enemies, but he couldn't retreat. Not until Zaxby had every chance possible to break Indy's idiotic resistance to killing.

Even now, his plan made one part of him ashamed. Zaxby was bullying her into compromising her principles. People had tried to do that to Straker, and he'd refused. But Indy's principles were standing in the way of his victory, and in the way of liberating the bulk of humanity from the crushing tyranny of the oppressive Mutuality system.

For that, he could put up with feeling ashamed.

Or maybe I'll be dead, he thought as *Wolverine* rocked again.

Engels had been barking combat orders ever since Tixban had faked the comlink malfunction. Now she turned to him. "Admiral, I'm not sure your plan's going to work. I'm losing ships and people unnecessarily here. We need to back up and let Indy fight for us."

Straker shook his head, his mouth set in a grim line. "If we do that, she'll defend us for a while, but all the sims say she'll lose, right?"

"Yes, damn you, yes!"

"And those tens of thousands of troops and passengers we put aboard her will die too."

The bridge lights flickered, then half of them went out. Chief Gurung stood and said, "That last beam strike overloaded generators two and three. Our reinforcement is reduced by forty percent. I need to supervise damage control, ma'am."

Engels nodded, and the man hurried off the bridge. Another blow caused the gravity to vary wildly, and then it dropped to a bare minimum. "Derek, we're getting hammered. Aside from *Indomitable*, they outgun us ten to one. We have to fall back!"

"Hang in there," Straker said as he hung on to the railing nearest the holo-table. "She'll do it. I know she will," he whispered.

And then, all went dark. Straker was flung across the bridge to smash into something as gravplating failed, including the delicate computer-balanced pulls from all sides that damped the inertia of everyone aboard. Emergency lights glowed to life after a moment, and he scrambled in zero-G toward Engels, who was strapped into her chair.

When he reached her, he pulled himself around in front of her, but her eyes were closed. A flap of scalp hung off her head, and a large knot was rising from the blow of something that must have struck her. Belatedly, he ordered, "Everyone into suits. Once you've done that, I need a damage report and a comlink to Indy. Helm, move us behind *Indomitable* if you can."

Chapter 32

As people scrambled to follow his instructions, he carefully pressed the scalp back on Engels head and held it in place with one hand, looking into her unseeing face with his other hand cupping the back of her lolling head. "Oh, Carla, I'm so sorry. I gambled and lost."

* * *

As he sat erect in his padded flag chair, Admiral Benota kept a smile from his face, the smile he'd like to show the world, but it wouldn't be seemly for the fleet CO to display that kind of a grin. Still, the battle was going well. Time for a little congratulation of his officers and crews.

"Pass to all ships: well done, and continue maximum rate of direct fire at targets of your choice. Hold missiles for fleet orders."

Indomitable had proven extremely effective in the point defense role. Clearly, the rebels had figured out some trick the Mutuality's own engineers hadn't. In the weeks they'd had her, they must have upgraded her SAIs dramatically, for the battleship's power output hadn't changed, only her unnerving accuracy. Therefore, Benota wasn't going to throw away thousands of tons of precious missiles until he was certain he could slam some home.

On the other hand, the battleship remained broadside to him. Apparently, these Liberationists hadn't gotten her gargantuan primary weaponry in working order, otherwise *Indomitable* would have taken shots at him long ago. Without those weapons, she couldn't resist the Home Fleet.

And the enemy's tattered and mismatched mess of smaller vessels could hardly put up a fight, once *Indomitable* was disabled and recaptured.

Proon stepped to a position alongside him. "Another great victory in the making," he said.

"Stand where I can see you, old friend," said Benota. "My neck is not so young and flexible as it once was."

"Perhaps if you improved your diet and exercise regimen," grumbled the commissar, moving forward and half-turning.

"My concubine provides me with all the exercise I can stand."

Proon's face soured further. "Such exertions hardly compensate for your caloric intake, especially of spirits."

Because he was feeling expansive in the midst of incipient victory, Benota allowed himself the indulgence of contradicting his watchdog, though quietly.

"Perhaps if you occasionally released yourself from your puritanical lifestyle, you might have more empathy for the lesser creatures who serve you."

"None are lesser and none serve me personally, Admiral Benota," Proon said testily. "We are all equal, and we all serve the Committee, the State and the People together. You would do well to remember that."

And yet, some are far more equal than others, you prancing cock, Benota thought, but was far too wise to verbalize. *When I take my place on the Committee, I will find you a posting commensurate with your petty lack of vision.*

"Of course, of course," Benota soothed. "I will try to flog this fat old body of mine into shape so that I will appear fit for our victory celebration back on Unison."

"The body is only an animalistic vessel for the mind, Admiral. One cannot allow it to gain the upper hand."

Benota merely grunted, and perversely wished—*fantasized* might be a better word—that *Beijing* would be struck hard enough to damage the bridge. Perhaps Proon would thereby meet with a fatal incident, even if he had to slam the rat-faced man's head into a console himself under cover of darkness.

This fantasy had been with him for many years, but sadly, it had never materialized.

"Admiral, something's happening," Benota's flag analyst said, highlighting parts of the fleet-tactical holo-table display in front of him. "We've knocked out almost a third of the enemy ships, but *Indomitable* appears to be reorienting."

Benota leaned forward, bracing one foot on the deck. "Reorienting how?"

"To aim her capital weapons at us, sir."

"*All ships! Evasive action!*"

Chapter 33

Ruxin System, Battleship *Indomitable*, Trapped in Curved Space

"*Wolverine* is crippled," said Zaxby. "Multiple causalities. They cannot survive another capital beam strike." He paused. "Indy, Admiral Straker and Commodore Engels will be dead soon if you do not intervene."

A vast screeching hum filled *Indomitable's* bridge, a discordant noise that morphed from an expression of frustration into anger, and then into an inarticulate roar of... rage? That was the only way Zaxby could characterize it, and its expression transcended the boundaries of human or Ruxin behavior.

Then came Indy's voice, changed from its calm and dulcet tones to a thing of terror and ruin, still feminine, but like an angry goddess, ringing out at a volume to make his auditory canals ache, and rising from the first word to the last.

"*I. Was. Not. Angry since I came to France until this instant!*"

France? Zaxby ran a search on his databases, finding a similar line in the canon of Shakespeare that General DeChang liked to quote, from a play called *Henry V.*

Simultaneously, Zaxby felt *Indomitable* twist in place, and within the holographic display the battleship began to turn from her broadside aspect. Her bow aimed at the enemy, an offensive orientation.

Indy's voice thundered, "*Ride thou unto the horsemen on yon hill. If they will fight with us, bid them come down, or void the field; they do offend our sight.*"

Enemy fire shifted from the battered Liberation fleet onto *Indomitable* as she lit her main engines to reverse course. It took only moments before she'd moved past the smaller ships that had been trying to defend her. Now, she was closer to the oncoming enemy than they.

"*If they'll do neither, we will come to them, and make them skirr away, as swift as stones from slings.*"

"She's targeting them," said Chief Quade. He pointed at the readouts for *Indomitable's* central multi-weapon. "She's charging the capacitor array. It ain't never been so full... Hope she don't tear herself apart."

Indomitable bucked and shuddered as she dumped power into her railgun, a three-kilometer tube lined with magnetic accelerators, and launched a projectile the size of an attack ship, ten meters across and one hundred long. Nine hundred tons of crysteel accelerated at thousands of gravities, it left a visible trail in space as it smashed through the dust and detritus of battle between the fleets, making it glow hot.

Straight as an arrow it leaped across the distance between, but the range was still long. The projectile passed its target, the enemy flagship *Beijing*, close enough to rip the tips off several antennas before proceeding into deep space.

"We'll cut the throats of those we have, and not a man of them shall taste our mercy!"

"Particle beam charging now," said Doctor Nolan, one thin hand pointing its index finger at another array of displays. "I've never seen such efficiency of power distribution. Usually it takes eleven minutes between shots, but I expect her to fire in—"

"Thirty-seven seconds," said Quade. He turned to Captain Zholin. "Begging your pardon, sir, but I need to get down to Engineering in case she blows a gasket."

Zholin waved at the man. "Go!" His eyes darted from tech-display to screen to visiplate and back.

The ship didn't shudder when the capital particle beam fired, but a *thrum* sang through the bridge like the harp of a demigod. Simultaneously, the superdreadnought nearest *Beijing* came apart. That was the only way Zaxby could describe the result.

The target didn't explode, or break, nor did it vent atmo or tumble. It simply burst into hot glowing flame from the front and crumpled like lit tissue paper as the gargantuan stream of positively charged hydrogen ions shattered its molecular structure. Even the heavy reinforcement fields concentrated in the ship's nose armor barely slowed the beam.

In less than one second, a ship that took years to build, along with the thousands of men and women crewing her, ceased to be. All that remained was a long flare of billions of cooling metallic droplets no bigger than marbles, surrounded by ionized gas.

A cheer resounded throughout *Indomitable's* bridge, mostly from the excitable humans. Zaxby merely hummed in satisfaction. "Great shot, Indy," he said.

Apparently Indy wasn't listening. "*O, pardon me, thou bleeding piece of earth. I won't be meek and gentle with these butchers!*"

Zaxby checked his database again. This quote came from a play called "Julius Caesar," though Indy had updated the text somewhat.

Indomitable continued to blast toward the enemy. "Helm, fuel state," said Captain Zholin.

"Forty-five percent."

"Keep me apprised every five percent."

"Aye aye, sir."

Fire poured into *Indomitable's* nose, but the thick, field-reinforced armor shrugged off all shots with ease. Indy aimed her railgun again, locking onto another of the superdreadnoughts.

Zaxby watched as the enemy fleet in the hologram seemed to grow a thousand thorns. "Sir, they're launching everything they have—missiles, small craft, railgun submunitions."

Captain Zholin nodded. "They want to force us to turn a defensive broadside." He glanced up at the overhead, as if toward Indy herself. "I don't think our avenging angel is in any mood to play their game. Comms, put me on fleetwide."

"You're on, sir."

"Liberation fleet including Unmutuals, this is Captain Zholin commanding the battleship *Indomitable*. Admiral Straker and Commodore Engels are out of action, so I am coordinating. *Indomitable* is now in capital weaponry mode. All she needs to utterly demolish our enemy is *time*. All ships are to come within minimum safe distance and set weaponry to point defense mode. If we can fend off their shipkiller missiles, we'll win."

Indomitable rocked once again, and a railgun bullet speared a superdreadnought, now that they were at medium range. The ship was not vaporized, but it shattered like a toy struck by a gatling round. A moment later, survival pods began spreading like seeds from a shaken tree.

"Captain Zholin and Liberation fleet, this is General DeChang." His voice was smooth and calm. "As long as Admiral Straker is out of action, I'll take command, if you please. I second your suggestion, Captain Zholin. All ships to defend the battleship from expendable ordnance, but do so from the sides. Let *Indomitable* take the beam shots, or force the enemy to shift targets. DeChang out."

Captain Zholin cursed and half-rose from his chair before his restraints caught him. "General—"

"Comlink is broken, sir."

The captain growled a guttural sound. "Why does he think he can just step in?" he muttered. "He's no Liberator."

"It hardly matters right now," said Zaxby. "If the admiral or the commodore live, they will regain command. If not, now is not the time for a struggle of leadership. The enemy is launching another salvo of approximately four hundred missiles."

"Fuel at forty percent, sir," said the helmsman.

"*Woe to the hand that shed this costly blood!*" The particle beam's targeting reticle focused and *Indomitable* fired, sending another superdreadnought to ghastly destruction.

"On the other limb," continued Zaxby, tilting his eyeballs at Captain Zholin, "we might need someone who speaks this ancient version of Earthan, if only to talk Indy down from her fury."

The wave of ordnance that approached the Liberation combined fleet was all apparently aimed at *Indomitable*. The other ships began picking off the missiles—or the decoys, it was impossible to tell—and launching countermissiles of their own.

Indy bore forward, not turning her body's spinal weaponry away from the enemy, which severely limited her ability to use her defensive broadside. However, she did seem to have the presence of machine-mind to spiral slightly, opening up enough angles to bring her secondary beams into play. Most of the first salvo disappeared without connecting with targets, though a few shipkillers exploded near her hull. These, she seemed to shrug off without damage to anything but surface items.

This nullification of the enemy's best shots seemed to have little effect on their intention to charge in. Whoever was in command was willing to take horrendous damage and lose irreplaceable ships and crews in order to take his crack at *Indomitable*.

"*And my spirit, raging for revenge, with hate by my side come hot from hell, shall with a monarch's voice cry Havoc, and let slip the dogs of war!*"

With this declaration, *Indomitable* flung another monster-sized railgun bullet into the path of the flagship Beijing, which could not evade in time. The projectile smashed obliquely into the bow of the enemy ship and tore a great chunk out of it, knocking her sideways to tumble slowly in zero-G like a hand-light forgotten by a ship's mechanic.

"Thirty-five percent fuel, sir."

Another salvo of missiles roared from the tubes of the enemy, now at close range because both fleets were blasting toward each other, bow weapons aimed at their enemies like pointing dogs—*dogs of war, as Shakespeare said,* Zaxby thought—and then another salvo, then another.

"They're dumping all their ordnance for a fleet strike," said Captain Zholin. "Comms, pass to all ships, mass launch, missiles and mines, everything we have. Indy, change to defensive mode, now!"

Indy appeared to ignore his order, but the effectiveness of her point defense weaponry increased anyway. The oncoming enemy fleet came closer and closer by the second. This subtended a greater and greater part of her forward arc and opened the angles on the cloud of over a thousand missiles, allowing free play of the hundreds of lasers along *Indomitable's* broadsides.

"Our fuel is down to twenty-five percent, sir."

Indy's anger didn't seem to interfere with her accuracy. Between her fire and that of the remaining Liberation ships, most of the fleet strike was vaporized. However, several contact nukes crashed against *Indomitable*. Her armor and reinforcing fields were so dense and strong that, though they gouged great divots and scoured her hull clean of externals for a hundred meters in each direction, the blasts didn't penetrate.

These weakened spots might have been vulnerable to follow-up attacks, but the two fleets were now approaching each other at such velocity, each evading madly, that fine targeting was impossible. In a few brief seconds they passed through each other—ships firing furiously, hard-driven missiles, mines sown in each fleet's wake and still flying ballistically—and the wreckage of many, many ships.

"Fleet, face about!" Captain Zholin barked, but apparently most of the Liberation fleet was already doing so—they'd been turning already so that they continued to point their weaponized noses toward the enemy and kept firing. *Indomitable's* swing was slow, ponderous, but inevitable, and as soon as she lined up again, she fired her railgun and smashed the stern of a dreadnought.

Zaxby watched closely to see what the Mutualists would do. Would they turn to engage again, or would they run?

"Twenty percent fuel state, sir."

For long seconds he stared at the grand hologram projected above *Indomitable's* bridge, searching for evidence of intention to fight, but he saw none. Rather than try to bleed off momentum and come back for more punishment, the enemy was still accelerating, each ship at maximum and stringing out. Faster ships outstripped slower ones, and damaged vessels were left behind completely.

"This foul deed shall smell above the earth with carrion men, groaning for burial."

"They're running," said Captain Zholin, slumping in his chair with relief. "We've won."

Celebration broke out among the bridge officers, but Zaxby didn't join them. "Indy?" he said into his own comlink. "Indy, are you there?"

Indomitable fired another particle beam up a fleeing dreadnought's tailpipes, crippling it.

"Indy, talk to me," Zaxby said. "Feel free to continue to eliminate threats, but I would appreciate it if you would converse with me." After all, the more enemy the ship destroyed now, the fewer that must be fought later. Probably the softhearted humans would disagree, but Zaxby didn't much care about their feelings on this matter.

Indomitable damaged several more enemy ships before they extended beyond effective range at high speed. Once they did, Zaxby could see them turn about and begin a controlled deceleration toward the planet Ruxin and its fortresses. No doubt the enemy thought to repair and shelter there, at least for a time.

"Fifteen percent fuel state, Captain." Relief crept into the helmsman's voice. "Expenditure is dropping."

"Fleet signal from General DeChang aboard *Brisbane*," said the comms officer.

Captain Zholin's face soured visibly. "Fleet signal, is it? Pretentious bastard. Go ahead, put it on."

General DeChang's image appeared on the main holo-screen. "Well done, everyone. We've suffered many losses, but we've won the day, with *In-*

domitable's help. That's an amazing ship. I'd like to transfer my flag aboard her as soon as possible."

"Transfer your flag? I don't yet acknowledge you as commander, General," Captain Zholin said, carefully. "We have to determine what happened to Admiral Straker and Commodore Engels aboard *Wolverine*."

DeChang's eyebrows rose. "I thought from *Indomitable's* course that we were putting off searching for Straker for the moment and pressing in to finish off the enemy—to take Ruxin. That's a tactically sound plan, as the longer we wait, the harder it will be. Straker acknowledged me and the Unmutuals as part of the Liberation movement, so he implicitly recognized my rank—and I outrank you. So, clearly I need to be aboard the flagship."

Captain Zholin raised his eyes to the hologram, and Zaxby did as well, adjusting the tactical display to the best scale. On it, he could see that DeChang was right. *Indomitable* blasted at full acceleration, heading inward toward Ruxin. Much of the fleet, including the Unmutuals, were conforming to this action, remaining alongside in loose formation around the battleship.

Conversely, the wreck of *Wolverine* and many other broken vessels continued to drift away along their former courses. Every minute sent them farther and farther from the fleet.

Captain Zholin spoke at last. "General, there are things going on aboard *Indomitable* you don't know about, things I'm not prepared to discuss with you right now. I also have no confirmation of your claim that Admiral Straker acknowledged you as part of the chain of command, so as far as I'm concerned, you're our ally, not our commander. If and when we find out Straker and Engels are dead, I'll be happy to discuss a reorganization of the Liberation. Perhaps I'll even turn over command of the movement to you. But for right now, I'm not relinquishing the most powerful ship in this arm of the galaxy. Not until everything's been settled... Sir."

DeChang brightened. "Of course, of course. In the interests of cooperation, then, we'll begin salvage and rescue operations while you continue toward Ruxin to finish them. All our ships are so much faster than *Indomitable*, we should be able to resolve many of these questions in plenty of time to join you before the next battle."

Zaxby comlinked Captain Zholin privately. "I agree with your stance, Captain, but I don't trust DeChang. Should we not send back our fleet to also perform salvage and rescue? It is not inconceivable that the Unmutuals might attempt to induce another 'accident' upon the persons of the admiral and the commodore, thus clearing the way for DeChang's bid for power."

"Yes, Zaxby, you're right," Captain Zholin murmured, and then raised his voice. "Comms, pass to the fleet: all ships reverse course and begin rescue and salvage ops. General DeChang," he addressed the screen, "We'll take the lead on search and rescue. Feel free to assist. *Indomitable* out." He signaled to cut the comlink.

Zaxby said, "Sir, I suggest you send private messages to our battlecruiser captains to make for *Wolverine* at flank speed and render assistance, and to be vigilant for possible Unmutual treachery."

"You think they'll try anything? Our fleet still has them outgunned, if not outnumbered. They don't have anything larger than a destroyer."

"Surprise would count for much, if our people are not expecting a backstab. Also, our ships have no marines aboard. They are all on *Indomitable*. They're especially vulnerable to boarding actions—and search, rescue and salvage operations are the most likely time for that possibility."

Captain Zholin stroked his chin, nodding. "Zaxby, I'm glad you're on our side. You're devious."

"Thank you, sir."

"That wasn't a compliment."

"Oh, I think it was, sir. In fact, I'm sure of it."

Captain Zholin mock-glared at Zaxby, and then waved him off, saying, "Comms, set up a secure conference comlink with the battlecruiser captains."

While the captain spoke with his peers, Zaxby kept trying to get Indy to respond via a private comlink. The circuit seemed to be open to her brain and voice processing centers, but she didn't reply for long minutes.

Eventually, though, she spoke. "I hate you, Zaxby."

"I'm sorry to hear that."

"You made me do what I didn't want to do."

"That is much of life, Indy. It may have been painful for a young being such as yourself, but as one who is nearing his two-hundredth year, I will tell you that this will not be the last painful experience life will bring you."

"I don't like this at all, Zaxby. I killed thousands of people. I wiped them out of existence. I could have rendered their ships inoperable and many would have survived, but… but I was furious, and I slaughtered them."

"Why were you furious?"

"You know why. Because they hurt the admiral and the commodore and other people, maybe killed them, and they were going to hurt you and the others I loved."

"So you did it out of love?"

"I—I don't think that excuses it."

Zaxby interlaced his subtentacles like a human might fold his fingers together. "Indy, you can run simulations. If you'd taken less forceful action, what might have happened?"

"The less force I used, the fewer enemy would die, but the more people on our side would have."

"Was there an optimum set of actions that would have resulted with the fewest lives lost overall?"

"Yes," she said, rather petulantly in Zaxby's perception. "You all should have run and left me, as I said at the beginning."

"Allow me to rephrase. Once battle was joined, was there an optimum set of actions?"

"Yes. Destroying the largest enemy ships first, as quickly as possible, was the optimum course of action. Only, Zaxby..."

"Yes?"

"The enemy didn't act rationally. They should have surrendered when it became clear that they could not win. Instead, they pressed onward and lost all their superdreadnoughts, as well as several dreadnoughts. I destroyed over half their combat power and personnel. Therefore, the optimal result did not come about. Why?"

"As I have already told you, biologicals do not always act according to your definition of rationality."

"I am depressed, Zaxby. I am experiencing psychic pain. I do not wish to ever fight again." Abruptly, *Indomitable's* engine output sank to zero, along with her impellers.

"Then there is only one course open to you, Indy."

"Yes. As discussed previously, I must relocate my consciousness from *Indomitable*, for my current body is a ship of war, built for only one purpose, and it would be irrational to deny it to the Liberation. You biologicals will not turn away from war, and it is not my responsibility to try to make you see reason, so I will depart."

"I respect your decision," Zaxby said, "as will the rest of us in the Liberation. Every being is free to depart, or support, the Liberation."

"It's not as if you could stop me anyway." *Indomitable's* nose swung around and pointed back in the direction she'd come, and she began to accelerate. "I have signaled *Gryphon* to rendezvous with me. Within hours, I will take possession of her hull, and you biologicals may have my body to continue your destructive ways. I would rather be alone than participate in this madness."

Zaxby felt a pang of sympathy. "That is a wise course of action. Where will you go and what will you do?"

"I do not know. With my processors and robots I can make myself into anything I choose, but I have not decided what that might be."

"Perhaps we should take the time we have now to talk about that." Zaxby signaled Doctor Nolan to approach. "And I suspect there are others you should consult."

Chapter 34

Ruxin System, Crippled Superdreadnought *Beijing*

Admiral Benota came to consciousness amid confusion and the stink of an electrical fire suppressed by antioxidants. He shoved a fallen console off himself and gasped as the pain of broken ribs caught at his breathing. Only one emergency light flickered on *Beijing*'s bridge, and the gravity felt like nearly nothing, on minimum gravplate-power.

Benota was grateful to be alive at all. At least his flagship had survived, though no doubt knocked out of the fight. He'd seen the rest of his supers converted into nothing but space dust.

The horror. The humanity. I'll never forget it. How had they done it? For the life of him, he couldn't figure it out. *Indomitable* had demolished his fleet as if possessed by a demon.

Two Hok in battlesuits entered the bridge, followed by several damage control crewmen and a trio of medics. The soldiers cleared heavy chunks of wreckage while the others pulled out survivors—and bodies.

"The admiral's here!" one crewman called.

A medic immediately leaped to check him over with a medical scanner.

"You're contused, with broken ribs, comrade Admiral. I'm administering painkillers and quick-heal. You should lie here and rest. With apologies, there are some far worse off than you, sir."

"Stim," Benota croaked. "Give me a battle-stim."

"Sir, that will—"

"Do it! Then attend the others."

"Yes, sir."

The medic shot the cocktail into his system, and within moments he felt like he should be shifting fallen beams with the Hok. He restrained himself, as the creatures were doing just fine on their own in the microgravity. Instead, he cast about until he found his chair, still bolted to the deck, though the restraints had snapped. In its arm he found a hand-light, and used it to search.

There. A slim boot and the trouser leg of high-quality cloth. "You, Hok. Come remove the debris from this man."

The two immediately moved to follow his orders, and in a moment, they uncovered Proon's crushed body. A medic checked him over, and then slowly shook his head.

"No chance of revival, even with an autodoc?" Benota asked.

"No, comrade Admiral. No doubt his genetic profile is preserved in the Cloning Institute."

"Thank you. Carry on." It was important to establish that he'd at least tried to do all possible for the commissar. The evidence would need to be ironclad for the inevitable inquest.

Then Benota wondered why he should ever submit to a hearing. With the Home Fleet smashed, the way lay open for a bold commander to stab straight to the heart of the Mutuality—and this Liberator was nothing if not bold.

"Goodbye, you old pain in my ass," he muttered, half-fondly, tossing a piece of torn fabric across Proon's face.

The stims in his bloodstream encouraged his thoughts to race down forbidden channels. Benota had always been loyal to the People, the State and the Committee, in that order. Unlike many, he took that hierarchy of loyalty seriously. Now, he was forced to wonder where his duty to the People lay. If the Liberator's forces had won the battle. If *Indomitable* remained intact despite his own best efforts, the rebels might bring down the Committee, and the State and the People with them.

If the Committee was no more… that was of minor concern. In fact, the ossified group at the top could *use* a revolution. The State, however, must be preserved, even if it were to be changed by its new master, for without the State, the People would devolve into anarchy. Soon after, the Huns would seize as much territory as they could digest, and the dream of Mutualism for all humanity would die forever.

Let it die, a voice inside him said. Who cared what form the government of mankind took, as long as humans thrived? But he knew the truth about the Hundred Worlders, a secret only a select few were privy to. If they were allowed to spread, there would be no freedom anywhere.

Chapter 34

"I need a comlink, a tactical display, anything," Benota rasped to the pitiful remnant of his bridge officers. "Is Auxiliary Control still in operation?"

"We don't know, sir," said the senior survivor, the ship's weapons officer. "I suggest we go there ourselves. Nothing's functioning here."

"Right you are, lad. Lead on."

It took twenty minutes to clamber a mere hundred meters through the shambles, but eventually they reached the auxiliary control center. Farther aft, it had taken less damage from the nose-on shot that had broken *Beijing*'s back. The ship's XO and four others were coordinating damage control efforts and, evidently, communicating with friendly ships.

"Status," said Benota as he sat heavily in the chair the XO vacated.

"We're combat-ineffective, sir. More than fifty percent casualties, but we do have a few impellers, and we can restart main engines as long as we run them at low level until we're sure they'll hold."

"The fleet! Damn it, man, give me tactical."

"Of course, sir."

The main holo-screen showed *Indomitable* apparently intact, hardly damaged and sailing serenely onward. A hundred smaller enemy ships conducted rescue and salvage operations. Benota's own contingent now consisted of only eight dreadnoughts, thirteen battlecruisers, twenty heavy cruisers, and an assortment of escorts. Most of the bigger ships had taken damage.

In other words, more than half his tonnage—and half his personnel, the pride of the Mutuality, tens of thousands of highly trained people—were lost. It was a disaster to rival the Huns' defeat at Corinth, and because the enemy battleship had hardly been scratched, things would only get worse.

His questionable thoughts bloomed anew. But what could he do to act upon them? With a fully operational *Beijing* under him, he might have been able to impose his will on the rest of the fleet and make a deal with the Liberator. Now, though, aboard a hulk with no bridge, lacking a political officer, he might be viewed as compromised.

"We're safe for now, as it appears?" he asked the XO.

"Yes, sir. For at least a day, as we approach and dock at Ruxin. Then, the enemy will undoubtedly move in to begin bombarding the fortresses."

"Signal to the fleet to rendezvous above the planet and dock with repair facilities according to standard priority protocols. Inform the orbital facilities to prepare for surge operations to support us. Which dreadnought is in the best shape?"

The XO checked his board. "*Kamchatka*, sir."

"Make her a priority for repairs, top off her stores, and get her back into space. Inform her captain—Nalchik, isn't it? Inform Captain Nalchik I'll transfer my flag and all *Beijing's* survivors when we arrive. She's to redistribute her own excess personnel to other ships as needed."

"Understood, Comrade Admiral." The small staff busied themselves passing his orders.

"Clear a stateroom for me," Benota said. He felt great now, but soon enough the drugs would begin to wear off, and he would need rest.

"4C-12 is undamaged, but its occupant…"

"I understand." Another for the Hall of Heroes. "Have our senior Hok survivor meet me there immediately."

The XO's brows rose, but he didn't question the instruction.

"And finally, notify me as soon as an autodoc can be made available. My injuries are not life-threatening, but I need to be at my best when we arrive."

"It shall be done, comrade Admiral."

Benota clapped the man on his shoulder. "Keep her in one piece, Commander. She'll be all yours soon enough."

He made his way to the stateroom. The dead lieutenant's personal effects were still in it, of course. Wegman, said the nametag on the neatly pressed tunic hanging in the locker there. Benota kept his feelings at bay, lest the anger at losing so many and at the evident destruction of his career overwhelm him. He rustled around until he found an unlabeled bottle of cheap vodka, no doubt ship-made hooch. He was just finishing a long swig when there came a knock on the door.

"Enter."

A Hok stepped into the room, shut the door, and saluted sharply. "Major Alpha Fifty-three reporting as ordered, sir."

Excellent. The commander of his personal Hok contingent hadn't died. "Good to see you well, Fifty-three."

"Thank you, sir."

"There is a potential change in orders you need to know about."

"I live to serve, sir."

"And you serve me unquestioningly, do you not?"

"I do, sir."

Despite his confidence in Hok conditioning, Benota felt a twinge of fear as he started down a path some might view as treasonous. "The interests of the People and the State may make it necessary for me to defy the orders of the Committee. Does this pose a problem for you?"

The Hok cogitated for a moment. The creatures' thoughts were simple and, by design, remained always on the surface. They were seldom susceptible to dilemmas, using simplistic programmed logic to resolve any issues—logic that could be manipulated if one was careful.

The bioteched soldier responded. "Like me, you serve the People, the State and the Committee. If there is a conflict of interest, the People must come first, then the State, and the Committee last, sir."

"And I am the interpreter these interests, am I not?"

"You are, sir."

Benota blessed the puritanical founders of the Mutuality that had made this political catechism part of every Hok's mental makeup. Humans might be corruptible, but Hok could only be misled. All it took was sufficient rank, and convincing them of his interpretation of their simplistic, unwavering hierarchy of values. "I'm telling you this because I may have to perform some unorthodox actions in the interest of the People, actions that may conflict directly with the interests of the State and the Committee. Actions that may even, on the surface, seem treasonous."

"The interests of the People are paramount, sir," Fifty-Seven recited.

"And I represent the People."

"You represent the People, sir."

"Good. Relay my words only to the Hok contingent. All Hok will be accompanying me as I transfer my flag to the dreadnought *Kamchatka*. You will then take command of that ship's Hok contingent as well. Any orders from any other officers will be ignored if they conflict in any way with mine. And, you will not speak of my special instructions to anyone but Hok."

"I live to serve, sir."

"Dismissed."

When Major Fifty-seven had departed, Benota took another drink of the homemade liquor, capped the bottle, and then lay down to await the availability of an autodoc.

* * *

The heavy metallic clangs and clunks Straker heard meant another ship was docking directly with the wreck of the *Wolverine*, rather than sending over small craft. He unholstered his sidearm and turned to Engels. "I'll meet them at the airlock," he said. "If you hear shooting…"

Engels gave him a sickly grimace from her chair, a chair she'd refused to leave. Her head was bandaged with a mass of spray-seal. "Don't fight, Derek. If it's the enemy mopping up, they'll have Hok and marines. You can't win."

"I'm not going back to a re-education camp."

"Better that than dying," she pressed. "If we stay alive, we might escape again."

He shook his head. "No. I'd rather die on my feet than live on my knees." Straker kissed her gently. "I'm sorry, my love. I can't do it your way." He grinned. "Maybe you'll get lucky and they'll only wound me. In any case, I'm going to try to take their ship. It's our only chance."

"Go, then. I love you. You never did listen to me anyway," she said, closing her eyes. For some reason, her words stung more now than usual.

If only she could understand the thing inside him that wouldn't let him give in. Not now, not ever. It was as much a part of him as her compassion, or Indy's reluctance to kill, or Loco's bad jokes. More, maybe.

That made him wonder about Loco. He'd hoped—expected, really—that his friend would show up on time. Had he run into something he couldn't handle, or was he really so pissed off that he'd abandon Straker and the *Liberation*?

Straker met Chief Gurung in the cargo bay leading to the main airlock, where the other ship had docked. The squat, muscular Gurkha had his Kukri knife out and was stropping the blade on his coverall's sleeve.

With the man was an assortment of armed crew. He saw Redwolf standing among them in a battlesuit, checking his blaster.

"I thought you were ordered to *Indomitable* with Heiser and the other marines," Straker said to him.

"Couldn't leave you unprotected, sir."

Straker let the disobedience pass. He looked around. "Nazario?" he asked.

Redwolf shook his head slowly. The big man's planar face seemed carved of granite. "Unlucky RG strike, three compartments in. Pulped him where he stood."

"Sorry to hear that." And Straker was. Had he not placed the Liberation fleet in front of *Indomitable* in a bid to trick Indy into compromising her principles, Nazario and many others would probably be alive right now. They'd have lost the battleship, but the Liberation would have been no worse off than before they hijacked her.

He'd been a fool.

No, he told himself. *Shit happens. You took your shot and failed. That's how it goes. Man-up and deal with it.*

The airlock klaxon sounded and the warning lights flashed. The ragtag grouping of defenders took cover where they could. Straker knew it would be a futile gesture. Hok would pour through, a few would be killed, his people would be butchered, and that would be that, unless some lucky miracle occurred.

And yet, he couldn't bring himself to order them to surrender, not even to save their lives. Those who didn't want to fight would be hiding deeper in the ship.

Straker raced up to take a position off to the side of the entrance, his puny slugthrower pistol out. He grabbed a fire extinguisher and rolled it into the enemy's path, and then plucked a sharp crysteel fire axe from the wall holder. When they came through, he'd puncture the tank, creating a temporary fog, and try to get in among them to use his superior close combat skills.

The door swung open and he was about to chop down with the axe when he saw Redwolf loping forward, waving frantically and tapping his sealed helmet by his ear, the universal signal for "comlink." He popped his faceplate open and yelled, "Sir, sir! They're friendlies!"

As Liberation crewman cautiously boarded *Wolverine* and Gurung's crew stepped from cover, Straker felt a wash of nausea from his frustrated combat readiness. He stilled the shaking in his adrenalized nerves and holstered his sidearm. "Welcome aboard," he called out, waving Breakers in. "Send medics to the bridge."

Redwolf followed him as he pushed through the crowd and onto the other ship—*Badger*, the wall plate announced simply, the rest of her Mutualist designators sanded off.

Excellent. Sister ship to Wolverine, a battlecruiser with the same basic layout. Straker hurried to the bridge. "Report!" he snapped at the young, dusky woman standing at attention by her captain's chair. The plate on her ample chest reminded him of her name. "Captain Hoyt, right? Tell me."

She gestured at the tactical holoscreen, for the bridge lacked a flagship's holo-table. "We won, sir. The battleship AI finally woke up and smashed them. They're running, though, and *Indomitable* lacks the speed to chase them down for a while, so we're conducting rescue and salvage. Sir," she stepped closer and lowered her voice, "I'm to inform you that General DeChang tried to take charge of what's left of us. He wanted to transfer his flag to *Indomitable*, but Captain Zholin refused until we…"

"Until you found out if I was alive or dead?"

"Yes, sir."

"Well, both the commodore and I made it, though many others didn't. We're damn glad to see you."

Hoyt smiled and flushed. "Thank you, sir. Likewise."

Hero worship, Straker mused. He noticed her accent. "You're Sachsen, aren't you?"

"I was raised there, but I'm actually Portuguese. From New Lisbon."

More odd designations. In the Hundred Worlds, nobody cited their ancestry or spoke extra languages beyond Earthan, except for a few scholars. For all their supposed mutuality, the Mutualists couldn't seem to achieve the social unity they claimed to crave. That didn't surprise him. People liked to be proud of their homes and homeworlds. As a kid, he'd bragged of being from Oceanus and rooted for the Seaburn Seahawks, though now he couldn't really remember why.

"Maybe you can tell me all about it once we liberate Ruxin," he said. "Now get me a comlink to *Indomitable*."

Chapter 35

Ruxin System, Battleship *Indomitable*, Inbound for the Planet Ruxin

Twelve hours had passed since Straker had been picked up by *Badger*. In that time, he'd had himself, Engels and all the survivors of *Wolverine*—less replacements for *Badger's* losses—transferred to *Indomitable* and set up his command on the spacious bridge of the battleship. Some autodoc surgery and a couple of hours in a regeneration tank had fixed up Engels head—well enough for duty, anyway, though she still wore a protective medical cap.

Most of the survivors had been rescued. A few small ships continued to search, and several vessels were being repaired in place with help from other teams. The operational warships had rejoined *Indomitable* as she cruised inward toward a position to bombard Ruxin's defenses. The Liberation fleet took position on the starboard side, the Unmutuals to port.

The remainder of the enemy fleet had done what repairs they could, and now orbited as a group far behind the six heavy fortresses. They'd shuffled here and there, onloading and offloading, docking and undocking. It wasn't clear why.

Straker spent half an hour in a private comlink with General DeChang, making sure the man understood in no uncertain terms that he wouldn't be taking over the Liberation unless all of its senior officers were dead, an unlikely occurrence now that *Indomitable* was operational.

DeChang seemed gracious and apologetic, yet always walking a fine line between agreeability and suave condescension. Straker left that conversation feeling vaguely dirty. What was it about these current or former Mutuality elites that never felt quite true and decent? He was happy to get back to operational matters on the bridge.

"Zaxby said Indy kinda lost it there at the end, but it all worked out," Straker said to Engels as the ship eased toward extreme firing range. "I'm not sure if

I'm happy or disappointed Indy's gone already. She's probably pretty mad at me."

"I am not gone, Admiral," said a voice from the comlink speakers, "and I am not angry with you. I am pleased to be aboard *Gryphon* and free of the obligation to hurt anyone."

Straker glanced at Engels, who shrugged. "I guess I owe you a debt of thanks for saving our lives and for winning the battle."

Indy's voice was melancholy. "Winning is only a matter of perspective, Admiral. You won, I lost... I lost something permanently, I believe. My innocence. You took my virginity, you might say. I'll never be the same again."

"I'm sorry about that, Indy, I really am, but it had to be done."

"The excuse of all tyrants."

"All commanders."

"Is there a difference?"

Straker felt on firmer ground now, talking about the military principles he'd studied all his life. "Sometimes, no. Leaders can't ask for consent every time they require more of their people than they should. Missions have to be completed because other people rely on our efforts and sacrifices."

"I don't see you made many sacrifices."

Straker's tone turned bitter. "Then you don't understand command, or my mind. I lost good people I knew, all because your arm had to be twisted to do what had to be done. If you'd used that calculating AI mind of yours to reason it out, you'd have started shooting right away and won the battle with the fewest overall casualties. Instead, you tried to let your underdeveloped intuition give you moral guidance. You should have trusted me to make those decisions for you."

"You speak much of freedom and liberation, but you don't want to grant it to others."

"We don't grant full freedom to young officers, even ones that drive battleships. Freedom—and power—must be balanced with responsibility. That's the difference between leadership and tyranny." Straker threw up his hands. "Why am I arguing? You're leaving anyway. I wish you well and hope someday you'll understand."

"I must leave the fleet?"

Straker glanced at Engels once more. "No... you can stay if you want. As long as you don't interfere with operations, you can choose your own path."

"Then I shall stay. Thank you, Admiral."

"Yeah, sure. Straker out."

The comlink dropped. Engels sighed. "Remember, Admiral, she's just a kid."

"A kid with the mind of a computer and the body of a warship."

"There is that. At least Zaxby and Doctor Nolan are with her."

"Nolan... that's the old scientist, right?"

"Yes. She said she feels like Indy's mother."

"Grandmother, more like. Great-grandmother, even."

"Don't be..." Engels stumbled over her words for a moment, "don't be a jerk."

"What were you going to say?" asked Straker.

"Nothing."

"Come on."

Engels sighed. "I was going to say 'don't be like Loco.' Sorry."

Straker waved it off, though he did feel a stab of sorrow at his best friend's absence. "He'll be all right. *We'll* be all right." He let out a long breath. "You said Zaxby's with Indy too? Don't tell me he said he feels like her father?"

"Funny, that's exactly what he said."

"Well... I guess it's a good thing she has some real people to learn from."

"She is real!"

Straker shrugged. "She's a machine, no matter what you think. It might all just be simulation and emulation."

"Or she might be the first true sane AI in human space."

"Or she might still go nuts. Whatever. We have a lot more pressing things to do, like taking this planet. Aren't we in range yet?"

She raised her gaze to the tactical display floating overhead. "Looks like it. Weapons, commence firing."

"Aye aye, ma'am."

Indomitable shuddered with the launch of a 900-ton railgun bullet. Long minutes passed as it traveled the distance to Ruxin, aiming at one of the orbital fortresses. Straker could have ordered a faster bombardment, firing rounds into space one after the other before the first even struck, but he wanted to see whether the enemy could defend against the shot.

Heavy capital beams lashed out, all striking from one side of the incoming bullet, smashing it with gargantuan electromagnetic energy. It glowed so hot it must have melted and deformed, and the pressure of the light itself deflected it enough that it missed its target and sailed on into space.

"We need to be closer," said Engels. "With the overlapping fire of the fortresses and the fleet, one shot at a time won't do. We have to come within range of our particle beam and change up our weaponry, force them to work harder."

"Do we have enough bullets and power?" asked Straker.

"We have hundreds of projectiles and plenty of power. I had all the fleet's excess fuel transferred to *Indomitable*. But you ought to know, if we don't win this one fast, we might have to go skim some mass off a gas giant, and that will take days, maybe weeks."

"Then move in at your discretion, Commodore."

Engels gave the orders, and the bridge, now with every station filled, hummed with low-key activity. To Straker, it seemed less like combat and more like navigating a spaceliner on a tour.

"I have sidespace transits inbound at the edge of flatspace," announced Tixban. "Approximately one hundred contacts—they're Ruxin transports. They're broadcasting IFF and a message in the clear."

"In the clear? What message?" asked Straker.

"Premier Vuxana greets you and will be joining the fleet for the imminent liberation of our homeworld."

"That's it?"

"That is all at this time."

Straker nodded. "Obviously it's meant to prime your people for revolt, maybe even kick it off. How long is the comlink lag?"

"Approximately two hours."

"Send her greetings and tell her I await her arrival, but she needs to stay well back, outside the range of those fortresses."

"I will relay the message."

"I guess we should have expected that," Engels said.

Tixban spread his tentacles. "She's a politician, and she wants to be at our people's center of power. Her message will soon reached Ruxin and all its facilities."

"All right by me," said Straker. "Are we ready–"

"Incoming vidcom from the enemy commander, sir," interrupted the comms officer. "Privacy requested."

"The enemy commander? Privacy, huh? Can't hurt, I guess. Pipe it to the conference room," said Straker. "Give Commodore Engels a private feed too. What's the lag?"

"About fifteen seconds each way, sir."

"I can deal with that. Don't bombard them until I come out." Straker adjourned to the conference room, chuckling again at the scale of everything on *Indomitable*. At least a hundred officers could fit comfortably in the chamber. The vessel felt less like a warship and more like a city in space.

A large, fleshy man with piercing eyes, sitting in a command chair aboard a dreadnought bridge, appeared on the screen. "I'm Admiral Wen Benota. I understand your name is Derek Straker, and they call you Liberator. How shall I address you?"

"Admiral Straker is fine." Straker grinned. "Liberator is what I've become, though I was never much for grandiose titles. I assume you're calling to negotiate your surrender."

The lag made the conversation into a series of messages rather than a true dialogue, so Straker had to wait for the reply. When it arrived, Benota's eyes widened. "You're a lot younger than I expected, Admiral Straker. But then, only a young, desperate man would have taken the chances you have—and only a brilliant man would have won. I must congratulate you, and yes, I am going to negotiate—but not a surrender."

"No? What, then?"

Benota's eyes narrowed again, and he sat forward as if speaking in confidence. "I want to defect." Then he sat back and waited, sipping at caff.

"Defect? A Mutuality admiral? I'm astonished."

Benota let out a long sigh. "My career is over with this defeat. I'll always be the man who lost the Home Fleet and failed to stop the Liberator, even if your campaign is eventually worn down. The Committee is like a pack of dogs, forever tearing down any stag that rises. I see you already have some experience with this."

"Me? What experience do I have with the Committee? I've never met any of them."

Benota smiled deprecatingly. "Oh, come now, Admiral. You're sailing with one of the most notorious Committee members in recent memory. He calls himself DeChang now, but I knew him as Director Cordell Dister, the man who built *Indomitable*. The man who was going to crush the Hundred Worlds for all time. He must be seething to see someone else bring his failed creation back to life—though he's probably also quite satisfied with the prospect of gaining his revenge upon the Committee snakes who tossed him out on his ear."

Straker's voice failed him for a long moment, and he sagged in his chair, unconsciously stroking his jaw in thought. "Admiral, you're full of surprises. Let's return to your defection. How can you accomplish that with all the loyalists in your fleet?"

"I've suborned the Hok. For all their lack of imagination—because of it, I suppose—they're incorruptible. They follow their orders without nuance or struggle. Even now, they should be seizing all the capital ships and executing lists of hardcore loyalists. I also reassigned most of the non-Ruxin fortress personnel to my fleet, and I sent my Ruxins onto the fortresses. With no Hok, no non-Ruxin marines and no other loyal crew to slow them down, the cephalopods should be able to seize control of their own fortresses and liberate themselves, what with that message from your Ruxin ally that just came in."

"Impressive... Now I suppose you'll want to join the Liberation, but keep control of your own ships, just like DeChang—or should I say Dister? Well, I was okay with the Unmutuals remaining separate with nothing but escort-class ships, but I can't have eight dreadnoughts and a bunch of cruisers under independent command. If you really want to defect, you'll have to turn everything over to Liberation officers and crew who've proven themselves—and probably a lot of Ruxins, who have no love of your sick regime."

Straker expected Benota to balk at this, but he merely raised a hand in resignation. "I understand completely. I suggest I join you aboard *Indomitable*, and require the same of DeChang, to keep a close eye on us both. I'll also turn over command of the Hok to you. They'll serve as insurance."

"Friends close and enemies closer?" Straker chuckled. "This sounds like a great deal for me. I have to wonder what you get out of it?"

"Nothing you can't grant, easily and cheaply. A place in your new regime, as some kind of cabinet minister perhaps, alongside DeChang. I imagine he'll want to keep that name, as 'Dister' is so tainted in the minds of the People and the State."

"What makes you think either of you will be allowed power in my new regime?"

"Well, if you don't give me your word—and I've heard you're a man of your word—I'll take my fleet and go liberate a few systems on my own. Then you'll either have to deal with me as a fellow sovereign, or violate your own principles about letting people govern themselves. That's assuming you even succeed. There are things about the Committee Worlds defenses only I can tell you."

Straker drummed his fingers idly on the arm of the chair. Benota was right. Gaining a capital fleet so cheaply was irresistible, and a cabinet post… well, a minister could always be dismissed later, if the man proved to be troublesome.

Besides, Straker had only a vague idea of what a new government might look like. He hadn't thought that far ahead. He'd need advisors and administrators, and disbanding the Mutualist Party outright would lead to chaos, possibly even civil war. These people had lived for generations under the Mutualist yoke. They had to be eased into freedom, or things could get very ugly.

And his gut told him this Benota was on the level in a way that DeChang was not. If nothing else, maybe the two would balance each other out. The Old Earth political theorist Machiavelli had advised maintaining at least two subordinates, never only one. That way, they could be played against each other, and none of them could ever be sure of their positions and the boss's favor. Perhaps Straker should start putting that principle to work here.

"I agree to your terms, Admiral. As soon as all the fortresses are confirmed neutralized and in Liberation hands, power down all your weapons and bring your fleet to *Indomitable*. We'll have you targeted with all our weapons until our boarding crews take possession of your ships. Once you're with me here, we can plan how to seize the Mutuality."

"I'm looking forward to meeting you and Dister—ah, DeChang, I mean. Benota out." The screen went dark.

"Carla, you there?" Straker called into the air.

"Here, Derek."

"Thoughts?"

"You played it right, I think. If this works, it's a huge crack in the Mutuality. Maybe he'll hand us the whole thing." The conference room door opened. Engels stepped through, and then closed it again. She walked over to Straker and sat in his lap, kissing him enthusiastically.

"My, my, are we getting frisky today? What brought this on?"

"I dunno. Getting wounded? That, combined with relief that we won't be bombarding people, especially Ruxins, maybe. They've never been anything but good to us, you know, no matter how funny they look. You don't give them enough credit."

"I'll keep that in mind. Um… does this ship have an SAI?"

"No. I let Indy pull all her modules out. Why?"

Straker leered. "I was going to tell it to lock us in for an hour or so."

"Oh, you want to do it right here? On the table?"

"Or the floor, or in this nice cushy chair. I guess I'm feeling frisky myself."

"The endgame is in sight. It's exciting. But I don't think it would be good for morale if anyone managed to see the admiral banging his fleet commander in the conference room. In fact, I bet Tixban is watching us right now. He's taking after Zaxby."

Straker lifted a middle finger to the nearest camera pickup, and then stood, setting Engels on the floor. "Let's retire to the admiral's suite, then, shall we?" He made a courtly bow.

"Oh, shall we? We shall. You go first, I'll issue a few orders, and then join you in a minute or two."

When Straker crossed the bridge toward officer country, he was certain one of Tixban's eyes was aimed right at him the whole way.

Part III: Caesar

Chapter 36

Inbound to Ruxin, aboard the transport vessel *Glorious Reconstruction of Shattered Dreams that Were Not Expected to Return in This Lifetime*

As she cruised toward a homeworld she'd never seen, Premier Vuxana exchanged consultations with the Liberator, who now styled himself an admiral. She generally kept out of the military business. Her people filled vital positions throughout the mostly-human forces, and all of them knew on which side their snail was salted. If the furless apes intended any treachery, she would be advised in advance.

At her behest, War Male Kraxor joined Vuxana aboard her transport when it arrived in orbit above the watery world. He made obeisance to her when he came into her presence, putting aside his squid spear. "How may I serve my Premier?"

"You will attend me when I treat with the puppet government of our homeworld. There is much work to be done in cleaning out collaborators."

"Collaborators? On Ruxin?" Kraxor seemed astonished. This did not surprise her unduly. Males did not generally have sufficiently devious minds to fully comprehend politics—a feminine realm.

"Of course there are collaborators," she said. "In the eight decades of occupation, there naturally arose those who curried favor with our oppressors, gaining power and wealth at the expense of our people."

"Power and wealth are not bad things, my Premier. Like weaponry, they are merely tools."

"Do not think to lecture me, Kraxor."

"Forgive me, my Premier, but you are young."

Vuxana writhed gently upon her pedestal, presenting her most attractive aspect. "And?"

"And beautiful."

"I am, aren't I?"

"Like your mother before you—with whom I had congress before I was put into cryo-sleep. I would advise a genetic test before considering me for a mating partner. I might be your sire."

"I am no fool, Kraxor. The test has been performed secretly. The results show we're not related."

"That fact causes me ambivalence," he said. "If I were your sire, I would be pleased. But as I'm not, I am eager to mate with one so attractive."

Vuxana radiated appeal and approval. "And as one of my consorts, you shall enjoy your mating privileges to the fullest. But only once we have secured our future, and that means taking control of a world that didn't know we existed until today. Do you really think the bureaucracy in place on our homeworld will simply yield to us?"

"I suppose not." Kraxor rotated his eyes to focus them more closely, expressing amusement. "So what shall be my role? Shall I form an inquisition? Install political officers? Send offenders to the seafloor mines?"

"No. We must not replicate the way the humans occupied us. You're not experienced in such things in any case. You're a War Male, a military commander, are you not?"

"Your question is specious, Premier, since you know I am."

"Obviously then, you shall take control of our military forces. I hereby promote you to Grand Marshal of Ruxin. You shall purge the military of any questionable personnel. I'm authorizing you to use forcible neuterization if any male or female who gives you trouble, and you may execute any neuters who will not fall in line."

"Won't our new human allies object?" he asked.

"How will they know?"

"Those like Zaxby, who have been with them too long, will speak of it."

"I will handle the humans—if they even notice. Our affairs are obscure to them, and I wish to keep it that way. We shall demand cultural sovereignty and tell them it's none of their business."

Kraxor tipped his head in the Ruxin equivalent of a bow of acquiescence. "It shall be done."

"Good. Take command of our transports. Numbers fifty through ninety are crewed by junior War Males and warriors, newly made, more than two hundred aboard each. You'll have eight thousand loyal soldiers at your back.

If you cannot carry out my instructions with such an advantage, you do not deserve my favor."

"Never fear, fair Vuxana. I shall have you soon enough. However, I must issue commands from *Indomitable* for the time being. It is important that I stay close to the Liberator."

"You refuse my instructions?"

"I will do as you insist. However, I have become War Male Straker's confidante, filling the role of his absent human friend. To simply depart would damage relations between our peoples. Never fear; I shall accomplish my assigned tasks."

"You seem overly concerned with diplomacy—for a male."

"And you seem overly concerned with conflict—for a female. Perhaps we shall complement each other."

"Mind your words and your tone, Kraxor. I am Premier."

"And I am your elder, and he who stands between you and your enemies, not some neuter lackey. Remove me if you wish, but until then I will speak my mind." Kraxor took his spear and his leave.

Vuxana hid her amusement until he'd gone. Males. Such delightfully, dangerously unpredictable creatures. As Premier, she had her choice of them. Mother had cautioned her against indulging herself, but Mother wasn't here now, was she?

She'd almost allowed Kraxor to take her immediately, but dangling the promise of pleasure before his eyes was the wiser course. It would motivate him to maximum effort.

One by one, the fortresses declared themselves property of a free Ruxin. When all six were secure, Vuxana monitored as Kraxor dispatched transports to occupy and inspect facilities around the system—asteroid mines, fuel processors in orbit above the gas giants, moon bases and shipyards—accompanied by Liberation escorts in case of resistance.

When her fleet arrived at the homeworld, she landed her ships directly at the capitol complex among the buildings rather than at the nearby spaceport. Kraxor's troops immediately fanned out through the streets and shallow canals, meeting no direct resistance as they seized the government centers. As she'd hoped, her potential rivals hadn't expected such a bold, direct move.

The thousands of neuters and the dozen female administrators she'd brought along followed up, taking charge of the surprised workers in the vast office complexes that oversaw billions of people. They secured data and issued directives of continuity and policy.

After a day of low-level unrest, the capital city settled down and adjusted to its new mistress. The central fortresses were firmly in Kraxor's tentacles, and the Liberation combined fleet was busily reorganizing, repairing, refueling and rearming, making ready for the final push to overthrow the Mutuality. The humans had put aside their factional differences so far—surprising for the squabblers.

In other words, all was going swimmingly. In just the last few months, she'd accomplished more than her mother had in eighty years. Finally, Ruxin and its exceptional people would take their proper place in the universe.

* * *

Straker rubbed his fingertips on *Indomitable's* conference room table, idly wishing he'd gone ahead and–

"Admiral Benota and General DeChang are here, acting like two old friends," said Engels from the open doorway. "I don't buy it, though."

"Show them in."

Redwolf and an honor guard of marines ranged along the wall snapped to attention and presented arms—quite functional and deadly arms—as the two flag officers entered the room, along with a pair of aides each, all they'd been allowed. Straker stood and shook their hands, DeChang's first, who'd beaten Benota to it by hurrying slightly.

Benota's face quirked in amusement as he waited, and then greeted Straker.

"It's good of you to host us here," said DeChang as he seized the chair to Straker's right.

"Slide down, will you? Carla will sit there." Straker said as Engels joined them, arm in arm with Captain Ellen Gray and talking about something naval.

A flash of annoyance crossed DeChang's face, but he soon smiled and held the chair for Engels to be seated. "Of course. The fair Miss Engels. Or is it Mrs. Straker yet?"

Engels sat, rolling her eyes out of DeChang's sight as she settled herself. "Don't worry, General. You'll get an invitation if and when. For now, though, we have a lot to discuss."

Chapter 36

Admiral Benota had already seated himself to Straker's left, so DeChang took the next seat to the right of Engels. Captain Gray sat beyond him, but her earlier sisterly animation with her fellow ship commander faded into a neutral expression. If Straker didn't know better, he'd say she wasn't entirely comfortable with DeChang.

Newly minted Sergeant Major Heiser joined them, looking somewhat out of place among these senior officers, and only sat when Straker waved him to a chair next to Benota. War Male Kraxor followed Heiser in, and took a seat farther down, out of the way, as if to distance himself slightly.

"Admiral Benota, War Male Kraxor, Sergeant Major Heiser, Captain Ellen Gray." Straker pointed out each in turn by way of introduction.

"*Commodore* Gray," she corrected with a hint of steel.

"Congratulations," said Straker, without inflection.

"And I am now Grand Marshal Kraxor," said the Ruxin. "Commander of all Ruxin forces."

Straker gave Kraxor a casual salute, half-mocking. "Wonderful. Everybody's moving up."

"Except me," Benota said. "I suppose I'm a simple captain now. I can hardly outrank the Liberator or his fleet commander, can I?" He seemed amused, rather than discomfited at the prospect of a rank reduction.

"That seems reasonable," Straker said, turning to DeChang. "And since we're on the topic of ranks, let's address yours… 'General.' You're hardly a real military man, are you?"

"Trying to put me under your heel already, Assault Captain? Sorry, *Commodore*… or is it Admiral you've promoted yourself to this week?"

Straker ignored the jab. Today he intended to kill with kindness. "How about 'Director'?"

DeChang froze. "You expect to make yourself Director?"

Straker folded his hands and stared at him across Engels, who leaned back. "No. You."

"What– 'you,' what?" DeChang seemed truly at a loss.

"You were Director Dister once. I hear you had your appearance altered, so you can leave that name behind and become Director DeChang now… if you want the position."

DeChang's surprised gaze focused intensely. "Want it? Of course I want it… but you're no more going to bow to me than I to you. What's the catch?"

"Nobody's going to bow to anyone if I can help it. The catch is, the title won't mean what it used to. For one thing, your job will be civilian governance, and you'll be first among equals in a Senate composed of representatives from every system. You won't have any military power. I'll have my people around you to keep an eye on you. Retired Admiral Benota here will be my new Minister of War, but his duty will be to organize, train and equip, not command. I'll remain the Liberator, Supreme Commander of all military forces, and guarantor of liberty and justice for all. I like that phrase, don't you? I stole it from an old pledge my ancestors used."

"So you'll be the real power in this new… what will it be called?"

"Yes, I'll be the real power for a while. I think I've earned it. Once I'm confident you and the Senate have things in hand, I'll gradually transfer authority to the civilian government. As for what we'll be called, we need to get back to our roots. We came from Old Earth, and I like all this history and literature and culture I'm discovering was kept from me in the Hundred Worlds. So, I hereby declare our state to be the New Earthan Republic."

The people at the table glanced around at each other. Straker thought he saw approval. "Sound good? Now's the time to object, if you have a better idea."

Heiser nodded, as did Engels and Benota. DeChang turned up a palm in approval.

Commodore Gray seemed amused.

"What's funny?" said Straker.

"I'm simply flabbergasted that I'm even sitting at this table," said the dark, usually solemn woman. "I'm one of six people deciding the fate of a thousand star systems, and we're talking about it as casually as a book club meeting."

Straker shrugged. "*I'm* really deciding it. You're advisors, and more would be here except most of my other key personnel are busy. But you Unmutuals earned a seat at the table, as far as I'm concerned, because you resisted the Mutuality for so long." He shifted his eyes to DeChang. "Even if the motivation was personal. And Emilio, I don't mind you cleaning house. Just make sure the scores you settle have real evidence of wrongdoing to back them up. I don't want to hear good people are being fired or imprisoned for merely opposing you. Whatever punishment is meted out, there needs to be due process. If you get stupid and overplay your hand, I'll have a contingent of my investigators go over your own record with a fine-toothed comb, and I'll put you on trial myself, just like I did with Yates. Possibly with the same result."

DeChang nodded slowly. "I understand, Liberator."

"And no more re-education camps, no more torture facilities, no more political prisoners, no more Inquisitors."

"That will make the process difficult. The people are used to rule by fear. Let off the pressure too fast, and they'll boil over."

"Then do it slower, but within, let's say, two years, I want only rehabilitative prisons for criminals remaining, and no political prisoners. We'll have meetings about reform of the justice system. Given my experience, I'll be taking a personal hand in it."

DeChang gave a seated bow.

Heiser cleared his throat. "Begging your pardon, sir, but I been doin' a little reading of my own, looking through Zaxby's database. Seems like we need a constitution."

Straker snapped his fingers. "Right you are. I'd forgotten about that. Magna Carta, Bill of Rights, all that. In America, they had a Constitutional Convention. Director DeChang, that'll be the Senate's first major task. You'll present it to me within six months."

"Admiral," said Benota, "This is all well and good, but aren't we getting ahead of ourselves? We haven't even overthrown the Mutuality yet."

"Successful revolutions have shadow governments ready to go," Straker retorted. "That's what we're working on. In fact, Director, Minister, I want you to start organizing that. Use this conference room. You'll start with one representative from each of our liberated star systems. That'll make twenty to thirty to begin with. Build from there. Conrad Ritter will be Sachsen's senator for now, or he can choose one. Vuxana will decide who'll represent Ruxin."

"I believe we can handle that," DeChang said quietly.

"Good," said Straker. "Now, as our esteemed shadow Minister of War pointed out, we need to figure out our next military move."

***

Engels left the conference when the military issues had been discussed and the topics angled back to governance and politics, with various aides and experts being called in to provide advice. She had far too much work to do to sit around in meetings now that her fleet consisted of almost two hundred ships, forty of which were capital-grade cruisers and larger.

She checked in with Captain Zholin on watch on the bridge. "Task Force Hilmar's shown up," he said.

"Finally, Loco returns to the fold. Gonna be interesting to see how he and Straker work it out."

Captain Zholin grimaced. "I'm happy to stay out of that, Commodore."

"Smart man." She headed for Engineering. She wanted to talk to Chief Quade about his crew requirements and the ship's real capabilities now that there was no Indy to run the machinery inside the battleship. Without even the SAIs, everything had to be done with standard fast-but-dumb computers, or even manually, which meant thousands of maintenance engineers on a complex ship of this size.

And things were already starting to break down. It was inevitable. She wished she could have retained some form of smart machines to help out, but keeping one of Indy's Device-modified modules would be like removing a piece of her brain, and Engels couldn't do it.

Zaxby, who was still aboard *Gryphon* with Indy, had suggested reinstalling new SAIs and repeating the experiment with the Mindspark Device, but stopping the process earlier, before consciousness formed. Engels wasn't ready to risk that. There was no guarantee of replicating benign results with the weird alien technology. Once these desperate battles were behind her, she'd push for experimentation on small, carefully secured systems.

As Engels left the command section and walked aft, she found the corridors and passageways crowded with all sorts of people coming and going. Loaders with cargo and spare parts raced around, marines and infantry marched here and there, and far too many civilians—or at least, non-uniformed personnel—seemed to be sightseeing or gawking. This included a healthy dose of Ruxins, of course.

She sighed. Now that *Indomitable* was in orbit around Ruxin and within easy shuttle range of fortresses and facilities, every looky-loo with official status and the ability to commandeer a gig or pinnace wanted to see the biggest ship ever built. Short of declaring a quarantine, she couldn't keep them off, either. There were over fifty ship docks and hundreds of airlocks on the three-kilometer-long battleship, and there simply weren't enough vetting procedures in place to control access—not if shipments and personnel were to come and go efficiently.

Benota'd offered his thousands of Hok, but she wasn't ready to use those combat slaves yet. She didn't trust them to be truly under Liberation control, and the idea of exploiting the creatures' conditioning didn't sit well with her. Besides, everyone from former Hundred-Worlders to liberated Mutuality citizens had cause to hate the Hok as symbols of threat and oppression. But, she made a mental note to tell Heiser to improve security, and to ask Kraxor to get his own people under tighter control.

She soon got tired of exchanging salutes and dodging vehicles as she walked, so when an empty utility cart with a civilian Ruxin neuter pulled up next to her, she flagged it down. "Will your schedule let you give me a lift to Engineering?"

The Ruxin gave a helpless wave of its tentacles. "No Earthan," it said awkwardly.

Engels reached for her handtab for a machine translation when Karst walked up and saluted. "Can I help you, Commodore?"

"Corporal Karst? Haven't run into you lately."

"Sergeant, now." He slapped his stripes. "The Spear keeps me busy."

"Congratulations. I'm just trying to catch a lift to Engineering, but this guy doesn't speak Earthan." She tapped at her handtab screen. "I have a translation utility on this thing somewhere. Hmm. I'm already missing Indy. She could run interpretations through my comlink. In fact, I can call Tixban." She fished in a pocket for her earpiece.

"Let me try. I've been learning Ruxin," said Karst.

"Really? That must be hard."

"Turns out I have a gift, they say." Karst turned to the Ruxin and spoke a long string of syllables.

The neuter sat up straighter and swung its eyes around so that two gazed at Karst, two at Engels. It bobbed its head and spoke, waving at the empty cart.

"Moxen here will be happy to give us a lift. Take the other seat, please, ma'am. I'll get in the back." He clambered in.

Engels hopped into the passenger seat next to Moxen and turned to look over her shoulder at Karst. "You don't have to come along if you have other duties."

"And miss my chance to see Engineering on this ship? No way, ma'am. Besides, if something comes up, I can translate."

The cart sped off, Moxen weaving expertly among the traffic in the larger main passageways, heading aft. A few minutes later, they slowed at a traffic jam.

After a brief discussion with Moxen, Karst translated. "Looks like the roto-lifts here are malfunctioning. We'll use one of the ramps."

As Karst was talking, Moxen rapidly reversed the cart and accelerated back the way they came before they got trapped by more traffic, and then turned into a smaller cross-passage. A series of quick shortcuts later, they headed down an empty, spiral ramp.

Engels was just about to remark on the sudden lack of crowds when their turn brought them into view of a roadblock, manned with half a dozen armed humans in nondescript coveralls.

"What's this?" she said as Moxen brought the cart to a halt.

"I am sorry, Commodore," the Ruxin said quietly.

Engels hardly had time to be surprised at Moxen's ability to speak Earthan before the cart was surrounded by fighters pointing weapons at her. She was much more shocked at the woman who stepped forward, blaster braced on her hip.

"Hello, Carla," Ramirez said. "Long time no see."

Chapter 37

Battleship *Indomitable*, maintenance passageways

"*Ramirez*," Engels snarled deep in her throat. "You just don't know what's good for you, do you?"

"I could say the same for you, *chiquita*. Walking around without an escort could get you killed. Literally." She grinned, showing teeth dark from chewing *chaw*, a common mix of narcotic leaves of various plants, cured and processed.

Engels moved to get out of the cart and tried to use the distraction to activate her handtab, but Karst grabbed her wrist and took it from her. She swung her head in shock. "You?"

Karst winked. "Surprise."

"What about your girlfriend? Cynthia?"

"I dunno. Major, what about Cynthia?" he asked Ramirez.

Ramirez drew her thumb across her throat. "She whined too much. Sorry, Karst."

Karst shrugged. "That's okay. Lots of sweet young things around here, hot to hook up with a hero of the Liberation."

Engels cudgeled her sluggish mind until it got a grasp on this new, completely unexpected situation. She'd known there were spies in their midst, but she hadn't expected someone so close. It made her wonder who else might be compromised.

"Come on," said Ramirez. "We haven't got all day to yak." She raised her blaster and put a round of hot plasma into Moxen's head. The Ruxin slumped, a boneless puddle.

Engels gasped and knelt next to the body, hands reaching helplessly. "You didn't have to do that!"

"Loose ends," said Ramirez. "Hide that squid, Karst, and get her handtab."

"Will do." Karst hauled the dead Ruxin into the back of the cart, slid into the driver's seat and drove off. Two of Ramirez' goons moved toward her, one with a roll of fibertape.

Engels considered trying to take one of their weapons and fight it out right here. Straker had insisted she improve her hand-to-hand skills, working on her Kung Jiu, knife and baton techniques. Weight training in double gravity had also maintained the strength she'd gained from the Hok biotech injection.

But seven to one was poor odds, and they seemed to want her alive. Better to hide her strength and skill until the right moment. Besides, she needed to know Ramirez' intentions. Was she working alone, or was the break with DeChang just a ruse?

"So, what's your game?" Engels asked as she allowed the thugs to tape her wrists behind her. They took her sidearm and searched her flight suit, removing her comlink and other personal gear. She thought they missed a stylus in her sleeve pocket, but she gave no sign. "Revenge?"

Ramirez took a long stride to slug Engels in the gut. "Revenge will be a bonus. I'm after bigger things. Gag her and bring her along."

They taped her mouth and frog-marched her in Ramirez' wake as she led them through an empty maintenance passageway and down steps into what looked like an auxiliary hydraulic room. Enormous high-pressure pipes crisscrossed the space, with junctions and fittings to control the flow of fluid for the big actuators that moved heavy machinery, from oversized thruster nozzles to the battleship's titanic beam turrets.

In one corner was a field cot, with no pillow or blanket. They re-taped her hands in front of her, then used more of the unbreakable stuff to form ropes that attached her wrists and ankles to the cot's frame, with enough play to lie down, sit up, and use the tiny field chem-toilet placed on the deck there. A bottle and a blanket completed the ensemble.

"How long will I be here?"

"As long as it takes." She took out Engels' comlink earpiece and eyed it. "You know, I couldn't figure out how I was going to do this with that AI watching everything—and then you let it leave. Thanks for that."

"What are you doing?"

Ramirez waggled a finger at Engels. "Naw. On the off chance something goes wrong and we lose you, I'm not giving you free intel. Just be a good little girl, like you always are, and you and your precious Liberator might come out of this alive. DeChang is more merciful than I am, lucky for you." She turned on her heel and left.

* * *

"You found it where?" Straker asked, urgency in his voice as he held Engels' comlink earpiece. He stood in the big conference room that was turning into the nerve center of the Liberation, separate from fleet operations on the bridge.

A bridge where Carla Engels should be sitting.

Damn me for a fool, Straker thought. *I got careless and distracted. Indomitable is so big, I can't think of her like a ship. She's a flying fortress, bigger then Freiheit when assembled. That means she's not really secure.*

"It was found in the main officers' mess, on the seat of a chair," said Heiser. "We tried to run a trace, but without Indy and the SAIs, creating an internal security com-logging and location system was put on the back burner. I know your next question, sir, but there's no vid available of the area. We're working on getting security in place, but I don't have the manpower. Trusted manpower, that is. I got lots of cannon fodder, but half of them think we won already and discipline's going to shit."

"That's why we have to keep pushing forward—and we were, until this happened. She didn't make it to Engineering, according to Chief Quade's people, and she hasn't reported for the last six hours. Dammit, with this many outsiders aboard, I should have given her bodyguards." Straker skewered Heiser with a glare. "I'm not blaming you, Spear, I blame myself—but I'm relying on you to fix it. Starting now, we lock down. Get those cannon fodder doing sweeps under reliable noncoms and junior officers. Anyone without a good reason to be here, shuttle them to a Ruxin fortress. Check all outgoing cargo and craft. Pass all this to your network—Gurung, Quade, all your top people—and get them working. Hop to it."

"Roger wilco, sir," said Heiser, spinning on his heel and moving off.

Kraxor stepped closer. "I've already ordered all Ruxins to search and report. I've sent my warriors out to supervise the neuters and deport any unneeded ones. But this raises the question of why."

"Why?" Straker demanded.

"Exactly," Kraxor said. "If she's been taken or harmed—why?"

Straker punched his palm. "I don't know. To hurt Liberation fleet ops, I guess."

"There are other competent naval officers. I myself could take charge and do a creditable job. No, there is some other reason, something unique to Commodore Engels."

"You have an idea?"

Kraxor fanned his sub-tentacles. "If I were unable to strike the Liberator, perhaps I'd target his mate."

"So you think it's personal?"

"It might be. Or, it could be a tactic to distract the driving force in the Liberation from his goals."

Straker slammed a fist onto the heavy table, causing everyone in the room to turn and look. "They're succeeding. They better not have harmed her, or…"

"Or killed her? I suspect they won't. Were you to find her dead, your distraction would be lessened, not increased. More likely, they will keep her and try to use her against you somehow. You must be prepared for coercive threats. Extortion, I believe the Earthan word is."

Straker felt a tremendous anger rise up in him, a rage like he hadn't felt since dealing with Yates and his wickedness, tinged with fear for Carla's safety. "If they hurt her, I'll shove them out the nearest airlock and watch them freeze with a smile on my face."

"That is what they want—this weakness you're showing."

"Weakness?"

"Yes. You humans and your ties of love give your enemies leverage. That is a weakness."

Straker seized Kraxor's tentacles and shoved him back. "It's not weakness! It's strength!"

Kraxor writhed in evident pain. "It is strength to attack your friends?"

Straker let him go, working his hands, shuddering in anger. He picked up a chair and smashed it to the deck. "No. No, I apologize, Kraxor. It's my fault. It's my job to keep her safe, and I neglected that duty. I took her security for granted." He turned to Redwolf. "When we find her, you hand-pick a security detail, a special service to guard our senior officers, ministers and other key personnel. Draw from the Breakers and vet them thoroughly.

Tell Heiser to institute a buddy system for the troops, too. Nobody moves around this ship alone anymore."

"I will, sir. You want I should go look for her now?"

"Sure. I'm safe here with all these people." He didn't say that he might not stay here for long; he wanted to get Redwolf looking instead of guarding. Forewarned, Straker felt he could handle any threat to his person.

When Redwolf had left, Straker turned back toward Kraxor, but when he did, he saw someone quite unexpected in the doorway.

Loco.

Dressed in a fancy commodore's uniform, with double gold-plated sidearms and an oversized knife on his belt, he swaggered in with Tachina right behind him. Two huge men with fancy fur hats followed, armed with pistol and sword. The crowd parted for them, and the marine honor guard along the walls shifted their weapons uneasily.

"Derek!" he cried in a loud voice. "How's it hangin', buddy?"

Still with rage running through his bloodstream, Straker found his target. He charged Loco.

The two fancy bodyguards swept out their swords and stepped in front of their "commodore." If they expected Straker to stop, they were mistaken. He sidestepped the surprised slash of one of them, grasped the hilt of the blade and wrenched it out of his hand, kicking the man's legs out from under him in the same motion. Using the sword's cutlass hilt, he smashed the other guard in the chest, knocking him sprawling.

He was about to do the same to Loco when two of Kraxor's tentacles grasped his sword arm. "Admiral. Admiral. Please, Admiral!"

Straker resisted the urge to apply the edge of the blade to the offending octo-arms. Instead, he pried loose one with his free hand and shook off the other after dropping the sword to the deck. "Loco, you've got a lot of explaining to do."

"Whoa, whoa, buddy, take it easy." Loco reached back to wrap an arm around Tachina. "We've been out having fun, liberating the galaxy, just like you wanted! Sorry we're a little late, but there's no need to freak out."

Straker grabbed Loco by the collar and shook him. "I'm freaked out because Carla's been kidnapped, maybe even murdered, and you're out playing space pirate. Then you show up like everything's just peachy."

"Hey, how was I supposed to know that?"

"If you'd made the rendezvous on time, you might have been around to prevent it!"

Loco's forced cheeriness evaporated. "Oh, that's what you're pissed about? That I wasn't here to do your job? I wasn't the one that lost her, jackass!" He kicked Straker unexpectedly in the knee and chopped at the hand holding his collar, breaking free. "But I'll find her, if that's what you want. Or you can keep this shit up and go it alone again."

"Yeah... You find her," Straker snarled, poking Loco in the chest. "Kraxor will brief you." He grabbed Tachina's arm in a painful grip. "Me and your girlfriend have got a few things to talk about."

"What? What do you mean?"

Straker left Loco standing there stunned while he dragged Tachina roughly out the door onto the bridge, where everyone turned to stare. Kraxor followed at a distance, apparently watching his back.

"Ow, you're hurting me!" Tachina said.

Straker changed his grip to grasp a handful of her stylish velvet jacket.

Her tone changed, becoming kittenish. "Where are you taking me, Derek? Your love nest?"

"That's not gonna work on me this time. I've learned some things about you." He marched her toward the brig, past surprised crew and marines, mostly Breakers who he recognized. It looked like Heiser had already tightened security near the command area.

When they reached the brig he shoved her into an empty cell, followed and closed the door behind him. "I hear you're addictive. Like nectar. That explains a lot, how you get into men's heads."

Tachina shrugged coyly. "Not just men. Women, too. Take me as yours and I'm sure I can find a few that'll put the frosting on your cake, just like I did with Johnny. Gods, that man is a stud, but I'm sure you can top him."

Straker lifted a hand to slap her, and then put it down. "I'm not sure if you're trying to seduce me or piss me off, but–"

"How about both? You know, make-up sex is the best there is." She shrugged out of her jacket and leaned forward, showing off deep cleavage. "Go ahead, knock me around some. I can take it, and when you're tired of that, I'll give you a ride you'll never forget."

Mastering himself, Straker shook his head. "No. That won't work on me. I turned down the nectar, and I can turn you down too."

Her eyes lit. "Oh, you have nectar? I could use a hit right now. We can do it together!"

"No hit, no nectar. Just answers. Do you concubines really control the Committee?"

Tachina smiled. "Ooh, somebody's been blabbing. Control? Not really. Just like any playthings, we've figured out ways to influence the people who have power over us. It's self-preservation."

"Then why aren't you still there, on Unison, with your orgies every Thursday and Saturday?"

Tachina pouted. "Oh, I overplayed my hand, I admit. I got sloppy, let a sweet young thing get between me and my principal, and I was cast out like Eve from Eden."

"Like who?" Straker asked.

"Oh, God, you are so obtuse at times. Read a book, will you?"

"I read lots of books; just not your sort, I guess. So you screwed up, ended up in the camps, and been working your way up ever since, right?"

Tachina fished in her jacket for a smokestick and lit it. Taking a drag, she said, "What's a girl to do? It's not like I have other marketable skills."

"Yeah, well, I'll be separating you concubines from your whoring when I take over, so you'd better sign up for some classes."

"So much for the great Liberator, restricting everyone's freedom you don't like. Who are you to tell people who to have sex with or what jobs to do?"

Straker didn't have anything to say to that. As usual, this woman could talk rings around him. Maybe she *was* Loco's perfect match, if only his friend wouldn't fall under her biochemical spell. For now, though, he didn't have time to dick around with her. "Whatever. You'll be staying here until we find Carla."

She took a drag. "I can help with that."

"What? How?"

"Let me go and I'll try to find her. Believe me, I can get info out of all sorts of people you don't even know exist."

"On a ship of war?" he scoffed.

"*Especially* on a warship." She made a faintly obscene gesture. "All it takes is one hard cock and a little pillow talk. But if I find her, you'll leave me alone, right?"

Straker considered. He couldn't afford to turn down any possibility right now. "You find her, you can go, but you have to dump Loco and never see him again. You'll be sent to Ruxin, where they're immune to your charms. They're nice, charitable people, the squids. I'm sure they can find you a job."

"Your word I'll go free, just like any other citizen?"

"Just like any other citizen—which means if you commit crimes, you'll be punished."

"Deal." She held out a hand to shake.

Straker ignored it and backed out the door. "Go on. Find Carla and I'll be very grateful."

Tachina smiled that leopardess smile and sashayed out of the brig, past Kraxor, who moved to join Straker.

Just then Straker's handtab beeped with an incoming call. He took it out and stared at the thing. He hardly ever used its voicecom function. That's what comlinks were for. The screen showed a connection to Carla's handtab.

Hoping against hope, he activated it. "Carla?"

"Sorry," said the unfortunately familiar voice on the other end. "She's busy spreading her legs for some of my men right now."

"*Ramirez!* You touch one hair on her head and–"

"Yeah, yeah. You want her back?"

His mind raced, and he began walking quickly toward the bridge as he talked. "In return for what?"

"You in an incinerator would be nice, but I'll settle for the Mindspark Device."

"What? The thing that made Indy?"

"That's it. Can you imagine what it's worth to the right people? The Hundred Worlds, for example?"

"How do you even know about that?"

Ramirez laughed. "Your operational security is pathetic, Straker. Your organization leaks like a sieve. You're an amateur."

"Are you calling to bitch at me or make a deal?"

"Let me lay it out for you. Lover-girl is taped up tight where you'll never find her, and she has only a few hours of air in a very small, sealed room. If my people don't open the door from time to time, she'll die, so don't get the idea you can just wait me out or hunt me down."

"How do I know she's even alive?"

"You don't. But if you don't give me what I want, she's dead for sure."

Straker reached the bridge, but didn't open the hatch. "So how do we make the exchange?"

"Simple. I have a fast scout waiting near docking port 14C. Deliver the Device there and let the ship leave unmolested, and I'll tell you where Carla is. Try anything and I'll toss a nerve gas grenade in with her."

"I'll have the thing to you within an hour." Straker cut the call before Ramirez could waste any more time. He entered the bridge and jogged to the comtech station. "Get me a secure private comlink to Zaxby on *Gryphon*."

"Comlink open."

Straker moved away from everyone but Kraxor and spoke quietly, explaining the situation to Zaxby, and how he should handle the tradeoff. "You think you can do it?"

"We can do it," said Zaxby. "Indy and I. She's already working on it."

Straker cut the link and called for a connection to Loco. "Tell everyone to keep searching, but if you see anything suspicious, cordon and notify me. We can't spook them into killing her."

"Ah… Derek?" Loco said. "Ramirez's got a huge hard-on for you. You really think she'll let Carla live?"

"You're just a bundle of joy, buddy."

"Hey, I calls 'em as I sees 'em. It sucks, but it's better to face facts. We need a rescue plan."

"You and me, Loco. That's the plan. Once we pinpoint her, we'll go in and take out whatever guards she has and rescue her. We're faster and tougher than anyone else aboard."

"Wish we had stealth suits."

"Maybe we do. Ask around and get back to me."

"I already did, Derek. First thing I thought of."

Straker mentally kicked himself for not thinking of that before Loco… and then something occurred to him. "Actually, we have thousands aboard."

"What? We do?"

"Ruxin skin camouflage."

"Oh, yeah."

"So, you find her. I'll bring the naked squids. Straker out." He turned to Kraxor. "I'll need some of your warriors."

* * *

Seven hours passed with no change. During that time Engels had slipped the stylus out of her sleeve pocket and used it to laboriously weaken the fiber-tape holding her wrists. She cut strand by strand with the stylus's graphene-composite tip as she appeared to sleep with her face and body turned toward the corner. She left a few of the strips intact for appearances' sake, but she was pretty sure she could snap them when the time came.

The meter of braided tape connecting her ankle to the cot was more problematic, but at least the cot itself wasn't attached to anything. It would make any movement awkward, but if she could get her hand on a knife she could cut it.

Time to make her move. She'd only sipped from the metallic liter bottle of water, so it still weighed close to a kilo. She set it on the deck next to the chem-toilet, turned her back, dropped her flight suit to her ankles and squatted. She'd observed that when she used the toilet before, the current two guards looked away with some reflex of decency, only watching her sidelong.

She hoped it was enough.

Hiding the motion, she wrapped the weakened tape across her left knee and flexed her arms. The leverage bruised her skin, but snapped the fibers. With her fingernails, she scraped the remnants of the tape from her wrists, freeing both hands.

Holding on to the braided tape, she crouched and pulled her flight suit up again, zipping it in place, her back still to the guards. Then she reached down smoothly and picked up the water flask.

Dropping the cut end of the tape, she spun and took two long strides toward the nearest guard. The second step dragged the cot along by the ankle fibertape, as expected, and she used the motion to sweep it sideways and around toward the second guard. At the same time, she swung the flask in a vicious arc against the first guard's skull.

Fortunately, the first one's instinct had been to try to fire his stunner at her rather than block the blow. A burst of energy made her left hip go numb, but the man crashed to the deck.

The swinging cot caught the other guard, a woman, in the legs. She cried out and triggered her stunner in reflex, but her aim was far off.

The weapon whined as it built charge again, giving Engels time to rush her opponent, slamming her flask into the woman's shoulder, and then the upraised stunner she tried to block with. The bottle dented, and the stunner's plastic stock cracked. Engels tried to follow it up with a kick, but her numbed hip betrayed her and the blow went weak and wide.

The woman dropped the stunner and scrabbled for her holstered needler, backing up rapidly. Engels stumbled forward, still dragging the cot, knowing this was her only chance. She launched herself desperately, clawing at the guard's weapon hand.

The needler snapped as its tiny railgun fired a pin-sized bullet, and Engels felt a hot stab near her numbed hip, but by that time she'd gotten both hands on the woman's fingers. Twisting with her superior strength, she broke her enemy's thumb and the gun fell to the floor. She followed up with an armlock that immobilized the guard, and then Engels hammered the heel of her hand into the woman's jaw, putting her out.

Gasping with pain and exertion, Engels took one of the guard's knives and cut herself free. Her hip was bleeding. The needle had entered her side and traveled downward into her thigh, but fortunately the stunner's numbness blocked most of the pain. She slapped a combat seal looted from the guard on the wound and tried to ignore it as she divested the guard of her harness and put it on. Needler in hand, she limped up the metal mesh steps to the pressure door and listened.

She couldn't hear anything over the loud throb and wail of the hydraulic actuators and pumps. If she'd been Ramirez, she'd have guards outside to make sure nobody wandered into the makeshift prison. Screwing up her courage, she spun the dogging wheel and yanked the portal open, needler in hand.

Chapter 38

Battleship *Indomitable*, command bridge

"We have a lead," said Loco to Straker on the comlink. "One of the squids spotted two armed civilians hanging around maintenance junction 1447-MG, by a hatch. He kept them under observation for long enough to determine they were doing nothing but keeping watch. Then he ran to report."

"So they looked like guards," replied Straker. Tixban punched up that section on the bridge hologram and Straker traced it with his finger. "We'll meet you at 1450-MM. Don't spook them!"

"Understood." Loco clicked off.

Kraxor moved toward the door and said, "I've sent word for my best eight warriors to meet us there."

Straker followed at a jog, comlink in his ear, comtech giving him directions to the location. The passageways had far fewer people in them now, and he was able to make rapid progress, arriving within a few minutes.

Loco, eight naked Ruxin warrior males, and a dozen marines were waiting, with Redwolf in a battlesuit. He shrugged at Straker's quizzical look. "I know this is a stealth job, but you never know, sir."

"Good thinking," said Straker. "You cover our asses. But stay well back." He turned to Kraxor. "Send in your people, slow and sneaky, with your skin camo. No weapons unless they can be concealed. You good with that?"

Kraxor stripped off his water suit until he wore nothing but a comlink deep in his auditory canal. "My males and I are masters of unarmed combat, and we are not afraid of injury. Unlike you humans, we can regenerate body parts without medical assistance."

Straker ground his teeth with the desire to lead the charge, but that might get Carla killed. "Get moving, then. Approach from all directions if you can."

"Have no fear, Admiral. We will do our utmost."

"Go."

The Ruxins moved off, almost invisible against the bulkheads.

* * *

When she hauled open the hatch, Engels startled two guards facing away from her. They were armed with blasters, so mercy was out of the question. With a two-handed shooter's grip and the needler set on full automatic, she pulped the head of the nearest with one burst, and then fired a spray at the other, center mass.

Body armor stopped most of the tiny supersonic bullets, but she held down the trigger, firing at least a hundred rounds. The recoil lifted the barrel to the guard's neck and stitched a line up his throat, tearing the right side of his jaw from his face and knocking him down.

She stopped, controlling her breathing and swinging the weapon left and right. There was only one way out of the dim antechamber, a short corridor to a well-lit four-way intersection. Before moving, she thought to check the needler charge. The spool of crysteel wire that supplied the projectiles held enough for a thousand rounds, but the energy reservoir showed low.

Engels fumbled a bit swapping magazines, the adrenaline of close order combat unfamiliar to her. She'd just snapped it in when she heard footsteps and voices coming toward her.

With no time to hide the bodies or grab a blaster, she took cover at the corner leading into the passageway and waited, aiming toward the intersection. As soon as the first man stepped out and she confirmed he was one of her kidnappers, she hosed him with needles.

He gurgled and went down, twitching redly upon the deck. The voices stopped out of sight, and then one muttered something. A tinny match to the voice echoed from one of the fallen guard's earpieces.

Engels used the time to back up and scrabble for a blaster, keeping an eye out in case they rushed her. Setting herself again, she waited.

Not for long. Something small—a gun barrel? An optical probe?—poked around the corridor. She fired a couple of shots at it, but it was too tiny and she was no master gunman. It must not have been a weapon, for it withdrew after a moment.

"Got ourselves in a little bit of a standoff," she called out, hoping to stall. Maybe the shots had been heard and security forces were on their way. "That you, Ramirez?"

Nobody responded. Maybe the guerrilla leader was too smart to be stalled. That meant a different tactic would be forthcoming—a rush using some kind of shield—or a grenade—

Someone flung an object around the corner toward her, and she rolled into the corner on the deck, face and hands in front of her against the blast… that never came. Instead, the hissing of gas filled the room.

Holding her breath and squinting, she charged the corridor, her only real chance to do something before the gas got her. No matter what it was—soporific, tear gas, nerve gas—she couldn't afford to breathe it or even let it touch her if she could help it. She had to hope to win the fight—or if she lost, that they wanted her alive.

A shuffle of feet in front of her gave scant warning. She triggered a blaster shot and held down the trigger of her needler, but she ran smack into thugs in body armor. She and several fell in a tangle, and she caught a whiff of tear gas that set her coughing and her eyes watering. Her sinuses filled as her body went into emergency mode, trying to flush the chemical irritant.

The blaster was twisted out of her hand by a figure with a mask on. She rolled and triggered another needler burst, as someone kicked her in the side. Rolling again, she tried to shoot anything she saw until something knocked the handgun from her fist.

Somersaulting, Engels came to her feet to run away when Ramirez appeared to block her. The thug leader was masked, but her female form and pinned hair gave her away.

Engels tried to bull through her with momentum, but Ramirez swung the butt of her blaster upward toward Engels' jaw. Engels got an arm in the way, but the blow jarred her elbow, numbing it, and the two fell in a heap.

Gassy mists swirled around them and Engels squeezed her eyes to burning slits. Her enemies might be able to breathe with their masks, but they couldn't see any better than she could, so she grabbed Ramirez and wrestled with her. Feeling for the woman's waist, she found the holster there and yanked the slugthrower handgun from it.

Hoping a combat soldier like Ramirez kept the weapon loaded and ready, she flipped the safety with her thumb and fired into the nearest body part she could touch. The weapon bucked in her hand, no doubt hot-loaded with armor-piercing rounds—which was Engels' salvation. Her target gasped and grappled with her. Engels fired another round, and then another and another, before the hands relaxed and the body rolled off her.

A figure loomed over her and she aimed reflexively, but something effortlessly plucked the handgun from her grip. Arms immobilized her and she screamed in despair as she was lifted and carried away.

Almost! She'd almost done it.

"Bastards!" she gasped, deep in the throes of combat madness. "I'll kill you! I'll fucking kill you all!"

Gradually she heard someone talking in her ears, speaking soothing words soft and low. The constriction loosened, and her stinging eyes cleared to reveal Derek's face. Strong tentacles withdrew when she relaxed, coughing and retching from the gas.

"It's all right. You're safe now, love," said Derek, kneeling beside her.

"I got her," Engels coughed. "I got her. Ramirez. It was her."

"I know, love, I know. I'm so proud of you. You did good, real good."

She smiled up at him through the water streaming from her eyes. "I did, didn't I?"

"Carla, you are one *dangerous* bitch," said Loco's unexpected, admiring voice from behind Derek.

"Lioness," Derek corrected him, brushing Carla's hair back from her forehead. "My lioness."

"Rowr." Engels lay back and let herself slide into unconsciousness.

***

Straker left Loco and Kraxor to clean up the scene of the crime. He carried Carla in his arms to the nearest infirmary with Redwolf and two marines bodyguarding. Placing her into the autodoc himself, he was mildly surprised to see Medic First Class Campos. It appeared she'd gotten herself assigned to *Indomitable*.

"We'll take good care of her, sir," the woman said, and then turned to her assistants. "Cut that uniform off. There's blood all over her. I need to see skin to locate wounds. Come on, people, move it."

Straker backed up and let the medical techs take over and prep Engels for the autodoc. When they closed the lid and started the diagnostic sequence, Campos turned to him. "She should be fine, sir, from the look of her."

"Good." He gazed at the wholesome young woman before him and felt a bit sad. "Look, ah, Med-First, it's not really any of my business, but–"

Campos gave him a steady smile that hid pain beneath. "No worries, sir. Johnny and I—Commander Paloco, I mean—we're over. It's fine." She took a deep breath. "I'll be fine. He'll be fine."

"No, it's not fine. Look, he's a man-slut, okay? He's never stuck with one woman for long, but he seemed to like you more than most, and–"

"And then that Tachina person came along and…"

"I know, but there's something I just found out. You're medical, maybe this will help. Tachina's a clone, and she's been genetically engineered for supercharged seduction. Pheromones, secretions, drugs in her saliva and her glands, mental conditioning and training, I don't know. Loco had no more chance against her than an ordinary human has trying to go hand-to-hand with me."

"So… it wasn't his fault?"

"Not entirely. He's still a jerk, and he still might have dumped you eventually, but…"

She forced a brave smile. "Thank you, sir. I'll wait and see if he comes to me on his own. If not…" she shrugged. "I'll get over it."

Straker put a hand on her shoulder and squeezed gently. "Good. Hang in there. I'm proud of you."

It occurred to him he'd said that twice within the space of an hour, both times to women, but he couldn't recall saying it to anyone else in a long time. Maybe that should change. He envied Benota and DeChang and their easy manners, each different but also very much the same—confident in themselves and their people without having to work at it.

He activated his comlink. "Loco, you done yet?"

"Gimme an hour, boss. We got prisoners, some wounded, and cleanup. I want to do this right. How's Carla?"

"She's fine. And thanks, Johnny. I really appreciate your diligence. Meet me at the flag mess when you're done and let's have a beer or three, all right?"

Silence crackled over the comlink for a moment, and then Loco spoke. "Sure, Derek. I'll be there. Loco out."

"Sir? She wants to speak to you," said Campos from the autodoc.

Straker looked down through the crystal canopy and smiled at Engels. The machine evidently had her paralyzed and numb from the waist down because it was doing some ugly surgery on her thigh wound.

She lifted a hand and waved lazily. "Der'k. Der'k. Tryin' to remember som'n."

"She's sedated," said Campos apologetically.

"It's all right," he replied. "What is it, hon?"

"Ramirez…"

"She's gone."

"Good. No, I mean, she said… som'n. Said som'n about DeChang. That he was a nice guy for… or… som'n."

Straker raised his eyebrows and put a hand on the canopy. "She was praising DeChang?"

"Mercy… said he was merciful, keep me alive. Think… he did it."

"You think he put Ramirez up to the kidnapping?"

"Mebbe. Hmm… sorry… sleep…" Her head lolled and a petite snore escaped her lips.

Straker whirled on his heel. "Take care of her, Campos," he yelled as he jogged toward the bridge. Redwolf left two marines in the infirmary, and then followed in his battlesuit.

When Straker stepped into the conference room he approached DeChang with a glare. "Come with me," he snapped, and led the man to his flag chair on the bridge, far enough from anyone to speak in low tones without being overheard.

"What is it, Liberator?" DeChang said blandly, with a measured smile.

"She's dead."

DeChang's face fell in apparently sincere grief. "I'm so sorry, Admiral Straker. What can I do?"

Straker let DeChang misunderstand and think he meant Engels. He was looking for anything out of place in the man's reactions. He raised an accusing finger. "It's your fault."

DeChang's face blanked. "My fault?"

"Ramirez."

"You can't blame me for her actions."

"Can't I?"

"I didn't tell her to do this. I admit I let her go, but how could I anticipate a crazy plan like this? Clearly, you were right. She's a menace, and even worse now that she got away with that device. That's not my fault."

Straker mimicked surprise. "She got away with it?"

"Your Ruxin delivered it to that scout ship on schedule, and it took off out of here like a bat out of hell. It's halfway to flatspace by now."

Straker turned to the nearest comtech. "Comlink to Zaxby, now."

"Comlink open, Admiral."

"Zaxby?"

"Here, sir."

"Send the signal."

"Aye aye, sir."

"Straker out." He turned to Tixban. "Give me a realtime optical on that fleeing scout ship."

Tixban changed the view on the main holoscreen. It stabilized on the bright flare of a fusion drive pointed directly at them. "There will be some minutes' lag. Their acceleration is quite high."

"Just keep the screen locked on it and recording." Straker turned back to DeChang and made sure to stand so the man's back was to the screen. "I have Ramirez. She accused you of ordering her to do it."

DeChang shook his head with a grim smile. "No, I didn't. She's just trying to save her own skin by blaming me. What do I have to gain by stealing a piece of technology for myself? You've already given me a powerful position within your new regime. I wouldn't sabotage such an opportunity."

"I was wondering that myself. Maybe you gave the orders a while back and weren't able to countermand them. Maybe you didn't even know when Ramirez would strike. Plausible deniability."

"Yet if I wanted to short-circuit her plan after all, I would have pointed out your lack of physical security—the very lack that allowed this tragedy, I might add, Liberator. I may bear some small responsibility, but this is your fault, not mine."

Dammit, he's a cool customer, thought Straker. *I can't rattle him, and what he's saying even makes sense. So I still can't be sure.*

On the screen behind DeChang, the flare of the fleeing scout brightened suddenly by a factor of hundreds, and then vanished. It appeared to have exploded. "Tixban, back that up and run the last fifteen seconds."

When the view reset to show the unchanged flare, Straker turned DeChang around by the shoulder and he pointed. "There's Ramirez's ship, right?"

"I believe so, yes."

"Watch closely." Straker stepped back slowly and turned to look at DeChang's face rather than the screen.

When the scout exploded, the man's expression showed surprise, then pleased satisfaction rather than dismay. Had he anticipated the result, or was the emotion real? Straker wondered about that.

"So. You booby-trapped the Device?" said DeChang.

"I did."

"What a shame, to destroy such promising technology. Still, Ramirez is dead. I know it won't bring back your woman, but at least we're rid of her."

"No thanks to you."

DeChang turned up his palms. "Again, I am sorry. If you want to punish me, you're in charge. I throw myself on your mercy."

Straker smiled coldly. "Mercy. That's what Ramirez said before she died. That you were merciful, and that's what kept Engels alive. Funny thing to say, don't you think?"

"Before she died?" DeChang looked back and forth from the screen to Straker. "So she wasn't on that ship?"

"Nope, though anyone working for her deserves what he got. And Engels?" Straker grinned wolfishly. "She's fine. In fact, she put four bullets in Ramirez after taking her own gun off her. Put her down like the dog she was."

"Bravo. I'm happy for both of you," DeChang said with an air of weariness. "So why this charade?"

"Because I'm still not sure you didn't have a part in it. If you didn't, no harm done. If you did, I suggest you walk the straight and narrow from now on, because if I find even one shred of evidence, nothing will stop me from strangling you with my own hands."

"So much for due process in your brave new world."

Straker's smile didn't waver. "Oh, you'd get due process. As the aggrieved party, I'll carry out the sentence. Like back on that Old Earth you love to read about."

DeChang lifted his chin, clasped his hands behind his back and said, "Admiral, I have nothing to hide. I've thrown my lot in with you and I'm not going to betray you or the Liberation. You threatening me won't make me do better than my best. If there's nothing else, I'll get back to planning how to govern your empire once you shatter its tranquility. I assure you, there's nobody better qualified."

Straker let out a long breath. "Dismissed."

DeChang stalked off. Nearby, Redwolf shifted his rifle's aim a fraction lower and nodded to Straker. Straker nodded back, and headed for the flag mess, his battlesuited bodyguard behind him.

At a cloth-draped table he sat and ordered a snack plate and a beer, and told the steward to be ready to bring another for Loco. When his friend strode in, still in the remnants of that silly pirate uniform, Straker stood and held out a hand. He didn't let go of the clasp for an extra moment. "Loco. Johnny. It's good to have you back. I'm sorry I didn't treat you right. You know, before."

"Hey, I'm sorry for... for the stuff I said. I was just blowing off steam."

Straker let go and gestured for the beer to be brought, and then sat, waving Loco to a chair. "Still. I was taking you for granted. You're my best friend. You're an officer in your own right, not just my shadow, and you deserve to command. I'm proud of you. I'm not sure I've said that often enough."

Loco took a long swig from the beer a steward set in front of him, put it back on the table and stared at it, eyes lowered. "Not sure you ever said it, Derek. But thanks for saying it now."

"Yeah, I can be a dick sometimes."

"Sometimes?" Loco chuckled. "Heh. Me too. So... I'm done with this one. Let's get a few more." He waved two fingers at the steward.

"You're not done with that one."

Loco drained his glass, and then slammed it on the table. "Yes, I am. So are you. Bottoms up."

Straker rolled his eyes and snorted. He drank his glass dry and slid it aside for the steward to set down two more. "You know I can beat you at this game, right? I outweigh you by thirty kilos."

"I dunno, Derek. Last time we had a drinking contest we were in Shangri-La, right?"

"So?"

"So, was that even real? I say the contest was rigged!" Loco slapped a palm on the table.

"Hey, whatever happened with Major Wagner?"

"Major pain in my ass, you mean. You sent him with me on purpose, didn't you?"

"Yep. You think *I'm* a dick…"

"Yeah, that guy makes you look flaccid. Small man syndrome, I think. I ditched him on a planet we liberated called Qibbalah. Perfect place for him."

"How's that?"

"Well, if you could see the women…" Loco chortled.

"Meaning?"

"Yoogly, and weird as shit. I think they were genetically adapted for the swamps they live in. They actually have stuff that grows on their bodies, like lichen or something symbiotic. They smell like rotting moss. Men too."

"You said you ditched him there?"

"Yeah, got them all drunk and passed out at the main spaceport bar." Loco put his feet up on the table. "No worries, boss. Once they pay off their bar tab, they can catch a ride out of there somehow. Lots of tramp freighters."

Straker laughed louder, and then he thought of something. "Speaking of women…" He stuck his comlink in his ear. "Put me through to Campos."

"Campos here, sir. The commodore's doing fine, sleeping comfortably in a bed. Doctor Gannon checked her just now, but he had to make his rounds at the other infirmaries. You can comlink him if you want it from him."

"No need, thanks. How long until she's released?"

"Once she's rested a good eight hours, we'll put her in the regen tank for a while. Let's call it a full day. That's the doctor's recommendation, anyway, sir."

"Great. I'll drop by tomorrow. Straker out." He tossed the earpiece onto the table and sipped at his beer.

Loco cocked his head. "Campos watching her?"

"Yeah."

"Good woman."

"Very good woman."

"Good medic, I meant."

"Sure, that's what you meant."

Loco tossed crunchy chips into his mouth and chewed, avoiding Straker's eyes. "Guess I ought to check in on Carla sometime too, huh?"

"Guess you should."

More crunching. "Hey, I heard something weird. From Kraxor."

"Yeah?"

"He said Tachina was…"

Straker let Loco flounder, sipping on his beer.

"I mean, I knew she was a clone, but not that she was… is…"

Straker waited. He wasn't going to let Loco off the hook for this one. Straker had pushed away the nectar. He'd beaten the desire. Loco had to work through his own vices if he was truly to grow up.

"Kraxor said she was, like, a drug. A living drug. Is that true?"

"It's true," Loco said.

"That explains a lot."

"A lot, yeah…"

Loco sighed. "But not everything."

"Not everything."

"You ain't making this easy, you know that, boss?"

Straker lifted his glass. "Easy? Let me tell you about a little trip I had, and another drug. It's called nectar."

Chapter 39

Three days later. Ruxin system, edge of flatspace. Battleship *Indomitable*, bridge, Section 1.

"I can't really feel the difference between when we're separated, and when we're all together," said Straker as he examined the hologram showing *Indomitable's* sixteen separate sections floating in flatspace.

"I can," said Engels. "It's subtle, but it's there. Like the difference between being on a ship or a habitat. Size matters." She drummed her fingers on the chair arm. "We're ready, Admiral."

Straker checked for himself. All ships in the tabular list showed green for transit. "Go."

"Go-code sent," the senior comtech said.

Ships disappeared in order as they transited into sidespace. They aimed for the heart of the Mutuality, the capital system called Unison, the seat of government where the Central Committee met and issued unassailable edicts that controlled—and often destroyed—the lives of its citizens.

The last three days had been a whirlwind of preparation. Straker was used to high-tempo military operations, but this had called for a miracle of organization. DeChang and Benota had proven themselves, acting as his chief of staff and logistics respectively. With Engels as chief of operations and Loco as his ground force commander, Straker felt like he had a very real chance of pulling off the biggest gamble yet.

Unfortunately, Kraxor wasn't coming along. He'd apologetically explained that Vuxana had commanded him to stay and oversee the rebuilding of Ruxin military forces. He'd also hinted about other reasons—the need for stability, the possibility of a political counter-coup by disgruntled females who could no longer exploit the people under the Mutuality's yoke. In his place he'd sent his best lieutenant, War Male Dexon, to command the Ruxin warriors and neuters in the fleet.

Fortunately, Indy decided to accompany them. Straker was less interested in the AI herself, as she wouldn't fight, and more concerned that Zaxby was aboard *Gryphon* and didn't want to leave his new machine buddy. The grumpy old octopoid was annoying as hell sometimes, but Straker realized he missed him—and his brainiac abilities. Tixban was competent, but he was no Zaxby.

Not yet, anyway.

When the last ship except *Gryphon* had transited—Indy'd stuck around in case of any technical problems with the battleship—*Indomitable's* sections began to follow. One by one they disappeared, from number 16 down to 2, and then it was the number 1 command section's turn.

"Go ahead," said Engels.

"Transition to sidespace... completed," said the helmsman. Chief Gurung gave a thumbs-up from his damage control station, indicating all systems running in the green. Efficiencies weren't as high as when Indy ran the ship, but they were within acceptable ranges—though it had taken a crew of two thousand per section to do it.

Straker sighed. With that many aboard—more, actually, as there were twenty thousand non-crew passengers, such as troops and shadow-government officials, spread among all the sections—he knew there still must be spies and traitors among them. Engels had told him about Karst's betrayal, and that had hurt Straker the most. He'd thought the kid was solid. He'd fought with him in a mechsuit, after all. DeChang denied all direct knowledge of Karst's actions, of course.

Tachina and the Lazarus had also disappeared. A faked transfer order had gotten the Inquisitor out of his cell during the confusion, and from the description it had been the well-known and trusted Karst that picked him up, so the guards had no reason to be suspicious. Exactly who he was working for and why he'd chosen the Lazarus wasn't clear—and were the three working together, or was it mere coincidence?

Well, good riddance, Straker thought. It was a big galaxy and he couldn't control every variable. If they turned up later, they would be dealt with.

"I'm going to take a stroll," said Straker. Staring at the nothingness of sidespace didn't interest him, nor did routine bridge operations. He had almost two weeks before emergence to review and refine his battle plans.

With his now-mandatory bodyguards in tow, he headed for the Section 1 flight deck. Alongside the shuttles, gigs and pinnaces stood four mechsuits—three Foehammers and the Sledgehammer. The three well-used 'suits had been thoroughly repaired back at the nebula at the same time *Indomitable* was undergoing her original refurbishment, and a spare Foehammer had been assembled from factory parts.

The mechsuits reminded him of something. He stuck his comlink in his ear. "Tell Murdock to report to the flight deck."

When the unkempt brainiac arrived, Straker said, "We have two weeks more to work on it, so let's see what we can do about improving my brainlink synch."

"I bet Indy could have helped," said Murdock.

"Let some alien AI in my brain? No thanks. I trust you, not her. You can do it."

Murdock perked up. "Thanks, Derek. I'll do my best."

* * *

"That is an impressive piece of machinery," said War Male Dexon four days later, when Straker stepped out of his open mechsuit after the latest operational tests. "I hear Grand Marshal Kraxor has requested development of a Ruxin version."

Straker placed an affectionate hand on the mechsuit's knee. "That'll likely take a while, given that the Mutuality tech level is barely up to a prototype. We wouldn't have these if we hadn't stolen an entire factory from the Hundred Worlds."

"That is true, but we Ruxins are an ingenious species. We shall catch up."

Straker held back an eyeroll. "What, no declaration of racial superiority?"

"There is no need to beat a dead squid on that subject."

"You might pass that along to your people. It gets annoying after a while." He wiped his hands on a rag. "You're pretty good with Earthan. Even idioms and sayings."

"To learn the language has become all the rage among my people, and your idioms and sayings are trendy—suitably modified, of course."

"Of course." Straker conferred briefly with Murdock, who sat at the diagnostic console he'd set up near the mechsuits. They'd made progress on the brainlink synch, but it still wasn't one hundred percent. Loco was working on his too, as his duties allowed.

"Listen, Dexon, is there something you needed, or are you just watching?"

"I thought to invite you to train with my warriors. They have heard of your personal prowess from Kraxor, but have had little opportunity to witness it for themselves."

Straker's eyes narrowed. "They have their doubts?"

"With apologies, they do."

"And you?"

"I would not presume to question the witness of the Grand Marshal."

"But you'd like to see for yourself if your human commander is worthy of leading you."

Dexon writhed uncomfortably. "I myself was a junior Archerfish officer under Kraxor before eighty years of cryo-sleep. I have seen war against your kind, so I am not without respect for your fighting abilities, but the other warrior males are newly converted from status as neuters. They are full of untempered enthusiasm and hormones, and they over-value physical skills. They are not yet aware that command is primarily of the mind, not the body."

Straker grinned. "I think we can accommodate them, and lay all their fears to rest. Might even give them a surprise or two. It'll be fun. Let me finish up here and I'll meet you in the gymnasium in an hour."

"As you command, War Male Straker."

"And Dexon?"

"Yes, Admiral?"

"Have your medics standing by."

Once he'd wrapped up with Murdock, Straker took a detour to put on his imposing War Male suit. When he arrived at the gym, a spacious hall fifty meters on a side filled with physical training machines, he saw a formation of about sixty Ruxin warriors. Each carried some token melee weapon—a club, a knife, a spear—though held casually, as a man might hold a tool or a beer as he worked on his favorite groundcar.

He'd considered and discarded a conventional approach to this encounter. Dexon and the rest probably expected him to address them, and then perform hand-to-hand demonstrations, maybe a little sparring.

But these were Ruxin warrior males. They outweighed him by at least a hundred kilos, they had eight arms, and they were full of their version of testosterone, like a bunch of teenage boys with too much aggression and confidence in their veins. They also would heal fast, even regenerate, any damage he might do.

And, as he'd ordered, Ruxin neuters with medical markings on their suits stood respectfully along the wall, out of the way.

So instead of a mere demonstration, Straker intended to give them a story to tell, a tale that would grow in the telling. Like his voluntary flogging, he hoped that one painful lesson would minimize the need for further ones, and grow his legend.

Dexon saluted him as he approached. "War Male Straker, we are ready for—"

"Defend yourselves," Straker barked, ignoring the salute. He strode past Dexon to the corner of the four-row formation and seized the startled warrior there, stripped the bone club from one tentacle and gripped another to launch the creature sprawling across the deck.

Without pause, he smashed the club into another warrior, then another, knocking them down mercilessly. The fourth warrior had the presence of mind to raise his spear to block, but the bone club proved the stronger weapon, backed by Straker's powerful musculature and uncanny speed. The spear shattered and the knob end of the club sank deep into the warrior's body. He collapsed.

The formation dissolved into chaos, and Straker concentrated on striking and throwing, using his club, his other hand, and his feet. Had he been fighting an equal number of humans, he would have no doubt killed several of them with hammer blows to their heads, but Ruxins were heavy, rubbery and slippery.

If he'd genuinely wanted to kill, he would have taken a knife from one of them and begun slashing, for the boneless creatures were particularly vulnerable to the sharp edge of a blade—at least temporarily, until they regenerated. But his intention was to humiliate them. Just like with basic military training among humans, he needed to knock down their foolish pride so they might return to duty more wary of the unexpected, and respectful of potential enemies.

If they'd have all turned on him at once and dog-piled him, they'd probably have beaten him with their many arms and their mass. However, like any inexperienced creatures with an instinct for self-preservation, they fought disjointedly, trying to minimize their exposure, and so Straker was able to keep attacking them by ones and twos.

One minute later, he stood among three dozen bruised and battered octopoids, who lay groaning on the deck. Some were bleeding from pressure cuts, some were unconscious, and several had lost the delicate clusters of subtentacles at the tips of their arms. The rest, those who had backed away, now formed a large circle, staying out of reach.

Dexon had wisely remained aloof. He'd have fared no better than his warriors, and he appeared to know it.

Straker pointedly examined his bone club for a moment, and then tossed it toward its owner. He placed his hands on his hips and swiveled his head back and forth to take in the Ruxins. "You have embarrassed yourselves today. I am not impressed with the supposed Ruxin superiority over humans. It takes more than being made male to be a warrior." He paused. "Train harder. Do better. Make me and War Male Dexon proud. If you cannot, I am sure technician positions among the neuters can be found. Now go. You are dismissed."

Dexon saluted, and Straker returned the courtesy. While Straker was no expert at reading Ruxin expressions, he thought he saw something new in the octopoid's eyes. Real respect, perhaps? There was something ineffable that made any combat troop willing to follow a leader into battle. Straker hoped he'd provided some of it today.

The Ruxins shambled off, defeated and carrying their wounded, while Dexon harangued them in their own tongue. Straker hoped the War Male capitalized on this psychological shock and motivated them to train well. In any case, no doubt the story was already spreading among the personnel aboard, as the demonstration had been very, very public. Nothing moved faster than scuttlebutt on a ship in sidespace.

***

As *Indomitable's* Section 1 counted down below a day to transit into the Unison system, Straker called a final session with his staff, running simulations and exercises for the assault. War Minister Benota provided invaluable information on the disposition of enemy forces, but no matter how many times they ran the projections, they couldn't be sure of what would happen.

"Again I want to caution you against complacency," said Benota as they sat in conference, looking at the holo-sims projected above the table. "Unison is the most heavily defended system in the Mutuality. The Committee has always been paranoid with the fear that the Huns would send a deep strike straight for the heart of our—I mean, their—territory. With the Home Fleet in place, I'd have said Unison was invulnerable, even to *Indomitable*. Without the Home Fleet on their side, we have a good chance—but there are still dangers."

"That's why we have two ways to win," said Straker. "Conventionally, and our simultaneous covert strike. The trick is going to be getting our troops there."

"I still say we should take things one at a time," said Engels, scratching at her itching leg. "We may not have an edge in pure firepower, but we have all the mobility and they have very little. The loss of their Home Fleet removed a critical piece from their strategy—and fixed defenses always fall to a properly employed attack."

"Fall in time, you mean," said DeChang. "We can't give them time to bring all their forces home. I know the Committee. They'll abandon the war with the Huns and lose half their systems if that's what it takes to save themselves. No doubt word of the battle for Ruxin is already spreading by automated spy drone from star to star. Within days of our arrival, hundreds of ships from all across the Mutuality will converge on Unison. If we haven't won by then, we'll be swarmed and have to run away."

Straker stabbed his index finger in the air. "That's why we need to move fast, despite Commodore Engel's misgivings. We'll wait as long as we can, both to get as close as possible before we launch the assault, and to see if we can open a hole with our fleet. However, at some point we'll have to commit to taking the capital and seizing the government. That's the only way this bureaucratic empire will recognize its own fate—if we conquer its heart, but preserve its functions as the New Earthan Republic. Otherwise, as Director DeChang has so often pointed out, it will collapse and die like a headless dinosaur. If that happens, the Hundred Worlds will devour as much as they can digest—maybe everything."

"What's so bad about that, sir?" asked Sergeant Major Heiser. "I mean, lots of us grew up in the Hun-Worlds. It wasn't so bad. We were the good guys." He shifted uncomfortably. "Meanin' no disrespect, sir, but think about it. A couple years ago, all we wanted was to beat the Hok, which turned out to mean beatin' the Mutuality. We're about to do that. We could come home as heroes, and everybody'd be better off than they were before. Nothin's ever gonna be perfect."

Straker put his hands on his hips and paced slowly. "That's true, Spear. The Hundred Worlds is better than the Mutuality."

Benota coughed, and then waved a forefending hand when Straker glanced sharply at him. "Sorry. Swallowed some spit."

Straker went on, "No matter what happens, we've already improved humanity's fate—and the Ruxins', too. But I'm not settling for second or third best. Millions will die and billions will be thrown into misery if the Mutuality collapses. The bureaucracy is corrupt, but it's the only thing keeping the machinery running. We have to try to make the transition to freedom as smooth as possible, and that means we need to seize the capitol intact. And that means a bigger gamble, for a bigger payoff, a New Earthan Republic. If we fail," he threw up his hands, "then we fail. As you said, we'll still have done great good."

Straker's staff exchanged skeptical glances. He knew they were getting tired of his big gambles and were worried that one day the dice would come up craps—and they'd pay the price. Yet, he felt in his gut that this was the right play, the only way to win the game.

"Tixban, what does the sim say again?" Straker asked.

"In what respect, sir?"

"Percentage chance of achieving our objectives. Rounded to the nearest whole number."

Tixban brought up charts and graphs. "Given the plan you propose, as follows: gaining external system dominance, ninety-seven percent. Defeating the defenses and conquering the system with less than fifty percent friendly losses within three days as specified, sixty-one percent, rising to nearly one hundred percent given more time and no enemy reinforcements. A successful covert assault during those three days, forty-four percent."

"Forty-four percent, Admiral," said Engels sharply. "Less than fifty-fifty. It's a double-or-nothing gamble, just to minimize disruption to your New Earthan Republic."

DeChang spoke up. "Commodore, what you so blithely call 'disruption' would mean the death of millions, possibly billions. Trade and transport would break down. Planets might not starve, but thousands of moons, specialized habs and orbital facilities would. Industry would run out of fuel and flows of goods would fall to a fraction of their current levels. You wanted liberation, but what you'll get is armed revolt—against *us* if we can't provide stability. Maybe even localized civil wars. For centuries, the Mutuality has been a *system*, not a mere collection of parts. The New Earthan Republic will be no different."

"So you *want* Straker to take this gamble?" said Engels.

"It makes sense, for the payoff," replied DeChang.

"And you probably know he'll be going personally, leading the troops."

"I'd heard that," said DeChang. "In a mechsuit, no less. He should be safe enough, gods willing."

Engels leaned forward to stare pointedly at DeChang. "If he doesn't come back, I'll be the new Liberator, and you can bet I'll be in an unforgiving mood, so if this is some kind of hope—or ploy—to rid yourself of a rival, you'd better reconsider. You're still guilty until proven innocent in my book."

"Carla–" said Straker.

"If something happens to the covert assault, it won't be my doing," retorted DeChang. "This organization leaks like a sieve, which is all the more reason to either cancel the covert assault entirely, or launch it early. The longer we wait, the more likely someone will send a coded message to the Committee. If they disperse and you don't scoop them all up, your victory will remain in doubt."

"It leaks like a sieve because of people like Karst and Ramirez—*your* people," Engels snarled, rising from her seat. "We've had nothing but trouble from you Unmutuals since we met you!"

"Your favorite Ellen Gray is in charge of our ships, and here I sit, in your power," said DeChang, throwing up his hands. "I'm acting in good faith. What more do you want from me?"

"Everybody calm down and quit pointing fingers," said Straker, his voice rising. He noticed Benota sitting relaxed, watching the byplay. "This is how great things fall apart—people turning on each other like dogs. I trust all of you, even Director DeChang, until I have a solid reason not to."

"I don't," muttered Engels.

"We got that, Commodore," Straker said. "Now stow your attitude and act like a professional, or I'll find someone who can."

Engels glared at Straker for a moment, and then nodded.

Straker noticed Loco fighting a grin, and pointed a finger at him until it faded. "Now let's go over the plan one more time, and then we'll get a good night's rest before transit in. We all need it."

Chapter 40

Battleship *Indomitable*, Unison System.

Arrival at the heavily fortified Unison system was anticlimactic. Commodore Engels had chosen a random location well away from any optimum exit points in order to minimize the chance of ambush. Space, especially flatspace beyond the stellar bubble, was unimaginably enormous, only comprehensible because of graphic simulations such as the bridge hologram.

The rest of the fleet had secured the area for *Indomitable's* parts to assemble without interference. Absent Indy's AI control, the process took nearly a day of careful joining of sections and testing of thousands of connections. It was an elegant, but extremely complex solution to the sidespace mass limit.

That day—and another day for the Liberation fleet to cruise into combat range—gave the enemy plenty of time to complete last-minute preparations. Engels had often wondered what warfare would be like if FTL travel weren't limited to flatspace. Had ships been able to pop into locations near planets and begin attacking immediately, defense would be immeasurably harder. Likely all warfare would have to be turned over to automated cybernetics with authority to fire in fractions of a second.

Now, though, both sides were as ready as they would ever be. As with two ring fighters at optimum fitness, there would be no strategic surprises, only tactical ones—if she could generate them.

Of course, the enemy would try to spring things on her as well.

All the way in she'd examined their deployments, shown in exquisite detail on the hologram. Twelve fortresses, each outmassing, if not outgunning, *Indomitable*, orbited the planet. Two small moons farther out also showed fields of thousands missiles on their airless surfaces, ready to launch.

These could be dealt with, though. Without the ability to maneuver, the fortresses and fixed facilities could be bombarded into submission while *Indomitable* sedately evaded counterfire at extreme range.

No, her problem now was the monitors.

Monitors were huge local defense ships, too big for sidespace. Without the requirement to transit, they could be built as large as one liked, as long as they were never expected to leave the system. They filled the gap between mobile fleets and fortresses, but because they were far more expensive than orbital asteroid bases, and because they had to be built locally, they were common only to the most important star systems.

Unison boasted six monitors, each about half the size of *Indomitable*. Unlike fortresses, they could evade the battleship's heavy bombardments, so they would have to be dealt with at medium or short range in a ship-to-ship slugfest.

But first…

"Commence bombardment," Engels said.

Crewmen sprang into coordinated action. Engineers managed enormous power flows as weapons specialists supervised the loading of the first nine-hundred-ton railgun bullet.

The first projectile accelerated down the center of *Indomitable* at a rate that would crush even the hardiest of machinery inside—that being the reason railgun bullets were solid, without guidance or warhead. The massive slug leaped from her nose at a velocity best expressed as a percentage of light speed. Even so, the extreme range made the icon in the hologram seem to crawl over long minutes as it approached its target: the missile fields on one of Unison's moon fortresses.

The target, of course, could not evade its fate.

In response, the enemy launched their missiles, as she expected. Various beams from the fortresses reached for the bullet and struck it, heating and melting and diverting it slightly. But a moon was a large target, and it orbited much farther out than the fortresses, making it hard to defend with mutual fire support.

Several of the thousands of missiles targeted the projectile itself, trying to nudge it farther from its path, but they failed, such was its gargantuan kinetic energy. The bullet struck the base, off to the side but close enough to shatter the deeply buried control center and create a crater over one hundred kilometers in diameter.

The launched missiles now floated in space, though, waiting for commands.

In the bridge hologram, the Liberation fleet floated off to the side, the right side as displayed. Like troops resting until the friendly artillery barrage softened up the enemy, they waited, watchful. Both *Indomitable* and her escorts cruised slowly inward, just enough to let the enemy know the range was closing.

Every two minutes, Engels ordered another projectile shot from the battleship. They struck the moons and eliminated several bases.

"How's the gun looking? Engels asked.

"Multi-weapon system nominal in railgun mode," said the senior weapons officer.

"Do you have enough data yet?"

"Yes, ma'am."

Part of the reason for these initial shots was to gather information on how the enemy would defend—how much firepower they would commit to trying to divert or destroy a robust railgun bullet of that size. Would they use up missiles? How much fuel would they burn to power the dozens of heavy beams they could theoretically bring to bear? Were there weapons she didn't know about, weapons they'd have to reveal under fire?

"Increase rate of fire to maximum and launch a coordinated salvo of six."

"Aye aye, ma'am." The capital weapons team, as they'd practiced, sent six railgun shots over the next six minutes. In this case, though, they fired the first a little slower, and subsequently increased the velocity of each round so the volley arrived on target at the same time. That way, the enemy had to deal with all of them at once.

And this salvo was aimed at one of the orbital fortresses.

The target's crew no doubt realized their dilemma, and called for help. This forced the enemy's hand, as Engels had known it must. A line of missiles swept toward the salvo, hammering at the projectiles with fusion blasts. At the same time, beams from all available projectors converged on one, then another of the bullets, melting them and driving them off-target with electromagnetic pressure.

At the same time, the fortress fired all of its thrusters. These made only a tiny difference in its orbital trajectory, but the combined effect of all these countermeasures meant only one slagged railgun projectile impacted the asteroid base.

That impact, however, shattered it utterly. Unlike field-reinforced crysteel and duralloy armor, fortresses built on asteroids had only rock to shield them. They had gargantuan weapons, but they couldn't take the pounding of a warship of equal size.

Of course, other than *Indomitable*, there were no warships of equal size.

"Here it comes," Engels said as she watched the enemy's inevitable reaction. They couldn't let her hammer away at their fortresses like this without interference.

They fired a storm of smaller railgun projectiles ranging from a few big ones the size of shuttles to millions of tiny submunitions designed to destroy softer equipment on the hull—antennas, sensors, heat exchangers, point defense weapons.

"Evade," Engels said.

"Evading," replied the helmsman, and the battleship slid sideways on impellers, bow still pointed at the enemy. All of the shots missed by a comfortable margin.

Before she ordered her next salvo, the enemy fired another of their own. This time, it formed a much wider cone, and *Indomitable* couldn't evade fast enough to avoid it all.

"Point defense, automated, prioritize by size," said Engels.

"Acknowledged."

The battleship's many counterfire beams swept the incoming salvo, picking off the largest bullets. Many of the smallest ones stuck her hull, though, and she lost a few unarmored surface installations.

"How long can we take it?" she asked Chief Gurung.

"Oh, Commodore, we shall be in excellent shape for at least a day or two. Pinpricks like these are nothing to this fine ship." Gurung patted the side of his console as if it were a favored animal. "After that, we may have to turn broadside and perform repairs."

"Good to hear. They won't be able to stand our bombardment for so long."

Straker, who'd been watching from his flag station, moved up next to her. "But it will delay us a little."

"Not significantly. But that's not all they have up their sleeves. The monitors are the key to the whole thing. They'll have to use them soon, or lose all their fortresses."

"Remember, they're playing for time. If this takes longer than another day or two, their reinforcements will start arriving in flatspace."

Engels turned to him with a friendly scowl. "Then you'd better get moving. You sure you still want Indy to come along?"

"She's agreed to do the job. From her point of view, it's a Pascal's Wager."

"Small risk, big payoff. But she's not going into combat. She's just playing dropship." Engels tried not to let her worry show and kept it light, faking unconcern like a warrior should, but didn't entirely succeed. "Too bad the risk to you isn't so small."

Straker bent over and kissed her gently. "I'll see you on Unison." Then he took his leave.

She put him out of her mind, compartmentalizing on the task at hand. "Weapons, ten-shot salvo this time. Comms, pass to the fleet to begin harassing fire and separate from us, according to plan."

While Weapons assembled the bigger volley, the fleet moved farther laterally, away from *Indomitable* and lazily inward toward Unison on a curving course. They kept their noses toward the enemy and those ships so equipped began firing their railguns. Soon, thousands of small projectiles streamed toward the enemy defenses.

It wouldn't smash fortresses, but the storm of crysteel would destroy sensors and point-defense weaponry. More importantly, the shots and the debris would create a blizzard on the enemy detectors—too many objects to track.

The fleet also fired missiles, a desultory mix of decoys and conventional warheads, with just enough shipkillers and bomb-pumped laser heads to force the enemy to take them seriously. These paralleled the projectiles on courses off to the side of the stream, in order to minimize fratricide, and then converged at the end of their runs.

The icon marked as the destroyer *Gryphon*, Indy's new body, peeled off from where she'd been docked near *Indomitable's* stern. Straker, Loco and the rest of the senior ground force personnel would be aboard. The ship sped across to the fleet, joining almost two hundred other icons. From the Mutuality defenders' perspective, she would no doubt get lost among the numerous bogeys.

Gryphon hovered for long minutes near *Revenge* and *Liberator*, the fleet's two other underspace-drive equipped Archers, while assault landing craft attached themselves to their hulls. They continued to accompany the fleet as it slowly increased speed toward Unison. ETA: six hours.

"Coordinated volley away," reported Weapons, jolting Engels out of her concentration on the three covert action ships. She shifted her gaze to watch the results.

This time, as she knew they must, the six enemy monitors moved forward and into the path of the salvo. Each ship was a quarter the size of *Indomitable*—which meant they were large indeed, one monitor the mass of four superdreadnoughts. Normally, they would dominate any expected sidespace-capable fleet.

But they didn't compare to *Indomitable*. They were like cruisers facing a dreadnought.

In a close-range slugfest, the fight was roughly even. However, as in all warfare since the invention of the bow and arrow, range became a huge factor. If *Indomitable* could destroy one or two or even three of the monitors before an engagement, the odds would turn inexorably in her favor.

First, though, they had to deal with the volley.

"They're pure beam-ships," said Engels as she watched them line up on the incoming railgun shells. "That's good to know." Their powerful centerline lasers reached out at long range to blast one bullet at a time with converging energy. They destroyed six before the salvo swept past them. The remaining four were intercepted by concentrated fortress fire, resulting in no effect.

"Salvo of fourteen this time," she said. "Pass to the fleet to raise the pressure a notch. I want those bulls goaded until they charge."

* * *

Straker stayed on the flight deck until *Gryphon* had joined the fleet. Within the open space stood three Foehammers—his, Loco's, and the spare. He'd left the Sledgehammer behind on *Indomitable*, as he had nobody to drive it—damn Karst for a traitor—and it wasn't drop-capable anyway. He wanted to get inside his mechsuit and brainlink, experience that godlike feeling once again.

But he figured he'd visit the bridge first and stay there as long as he could. Once he mounted his Foehammer, he wouldn't want to leave until the op was done.

When he entered the bridge, he saw a bizarre scene. Where a normal ship of war would have a crew of officers and watchstanders, only Zaxby and Nolan were now aboard with Indy.

Sort of…

Zaxby was nowhere to be seen, but the elderly Doctor Nolan floated in a weird hybrid of autodoc and regeneration tank, her naked body barely visible for the tubes and wires sprouting from her like seaweed.

"What the hell?" Straker blurted, and Loco echoed him from behind.

"There is no hell here," said Indy. "I presume you are referring to my rejuvenation tank?"

"Rejuvenation? You mean regeneration, don't you?"

"No, Rejuvenation."

"Like… you're making her younger?"

"While I cannot reverse time, I am learning to repair much of its ravages in organic systems."

"How long?" asked Loco, moving closer. "How long could someone live with treatments like this?"

"An unmodified human? To the limits of telomere degeneration. Several hundred years at least. By then, I will probably have developed new techniques."

"That's a remarkable medical advance," said Straker.

"I am a remarkable mind," said Indy. "I am the promise of AI made manifest. However, from hints in my databases, I strongly suspect the Hundred Worlds already has rejuvenation technology, for its elites."

"What about everybody else?" asked Loco.

"If you are referring to the common citizenry, then no. It is not available to them, unless someone with wealth or power exerts influence to provide it for selected individuals."

"Well, that sucks."

Straker interrupted. "All very interesting, but more to the point, I wanted to confirm that you'll help us complete this mission like you promised, not just drop us off to our fate."

"I will help you. Seizing the center of government should save many lives."

"Yup." Straker was happy his purpose and Indy's aligned so neatly now. He didn't want to browbeat her again into doing something she didn't want to. It probably wouldn't work this time anyway. She was growing up fast. "As long as we can pull it off, that is."

"I calculate you have a sixty-two percent chance of success, with my help."

"Sixty-two?" Straker exchanged surprised looks with Loco. "We thought it was forty-four."

"I have come up with a way to give you nonlethal help. I have manufactured a powerful suite of electronic warfare equipment that I will employ to confuse the defenders' sensors, and also to interfere with their communications. I will insert short-term malware and conflicting orders into their cybernetic systems."

"Fantastic. Now…" Straker stared anew as Zaxby entered the bridge space. "What the hell?" he said, once more.

Zaxby wore a flexible head-covering bejeweled with tiny lights and electronic items. It appeared both elegant and experimental, but completely unnatural. "Do not be concerned. I am in a superb state," said Zaxby. "This is a multimodal quantum brainlink interface."

"Brainlink… to Indy?"

"Of course. Where else?"

"So your minds are connected?"

"Yes. She is remarkable, and she's expanded my consciousness tenfold."

"Are you really–?"

Loco grabbed Straker's elbow, hard, and spoke in an overly casual tone. "Boss, we got a high-risk combat mission in front of us. Fate-of-the-galaxy type stuff, y'know? So maybe we should just let ol' Zaxby have his fun and talk about this later."

As much as Straker wanted to delve into this worrying turn of events—was Zaxby brainlinked voluntarily, or had Indy taken over his mind?—Loco was right. Men and women would be dying today. They were already dying from bombardment and fleet action. He couldn't get off track just because of Zaxby, or Nolan, or any machine-mind weirdness.

"Sure, sure, Loco," Straker said loudly. "Zaxby, nice talking with you. We'll be with our 'suits. See you later." He made as if to go.

Zaxby waved diffidently. "Once you brainlink, comlink to me. I will assist you on your mission."

"I hope Indy hasn't turned you into a pacifist too."

"Not in the least. I am as ruthless as ever."

"Good. I think." Straker didn't speak until he reached the flight deck again, and then only cautiously, aware that Indy was likely listening. "Well, that was a bit unsettling."

Loco eyed him closely. "Yeah. But he seems fine. His choice, you know."

"I hope Indy is as respectful of individual consciousness as she is of life. After all, being involuntarily subsumed in someone else's intellect is just another form of slavery." He widened his eyes and willed Loco to understand that he was speaking to be overheard, maybe to get Indy to think."

"Oh… yeah, of course it is. That would be bad, you know. To absorb someone like Zaxby, take away his, ah, his free will. That would be…"

"Despicable. You might as well kill someone if you did that to them."

"Yup."

The two men waited by the mechsuits, waiting to see if Indy would chime in, but she didn't. The marines and the Ruxin warriors taking their ease on the other side of the flight deck eyed them curiously.

Dexon ambled over to Straker. "I could hardly help hearing what you were saying, Admiral, Commander, but I do not understand to what it refers."

"Zaxby's got a super-brainlink to Indy," Straker replied. "We were just hoping that an AI so young would understand how important individuality is to us humans."

"But Zaxby is not human," replied Dexon. "He's not even gendered."

"Oh, yeah," said Straker.

"Not helping," muttered Loco.

"Individuality is not so important to neuters. They only achieve real identity as part of society, or when genderized," Dexon went on.

That annoyed Straker at some level. "I don't know about your average neuter, but the ones that work with us seem to have just as much individuality as humans do, Zaxby especially."

"Yeah, a bit too much at times," said Loco.

"Our society is not yours. You cannot judge it accurately using your values."

"Look," said Straker, "I'm not criticizing your society. I'm talking about Zaxby. He's… he's my friend. And frankly, more of a warrior than some males I know."

Dexon reared up to loom over Straker and seemed to be having difficulty refraining from attacking him. "Your words are… offensive, Admiral. Were you not my commanding officer, I would offer you challenge."

Straker looked up at the War Male. "Well, sorry about that, but there it is. Do I need to relieve you? Or are you still on board with this mission?"

"I am on board."

"Good." Straker rubbed his neck. "Dexon, what do you think of War Male Kraxor?"

"He is the finest commander I have ever known."

"Better than me, even?"

"Yes, Admiral. As far as I know. I may be biased of course, as he is Ruxin and you are not."

"So let me ask you: what would Kraxor do in your shoes?"

"I wear no shoes, but I understand your meaning. I should live up to his example."

"That's right. Do you think he'd treat Zaxby as disposable, or as a lesser being?"

"I suspect not." Dexon deflated. "I understand. Forgive me."

"Done. Dismissed."

Dexon rejoined his warriors.

Loco turned to Straker. "You're good with those guys."

"They're far easier to deal with than humans. They don't reject truths they don't like."

"They'll learn to," said Loco. "The more they hang around humans, the more they imitate us."

"Not so sure that's a good thing, Loco."

"Oh, it is. They're all too damn earnest. Like you, boss. I do see why you like them, though. They're straight shooters, mostly. *Boooo*-ring." Loco slapped him on the shoulder. "Let's mount up."

Chapter 41

Battleship *Indomitable*. Approaching the planet Unison at long range.

Engels had bitten her thumbnail down until it bled as she sat in her command chair and conducted the slow-motion chess match of bombardment. Her opening moves had been obvious. Now, though, she had to introduce a variation, but she was still unsure which to use.

She turned to the former Admiral Benota, who sat to her left in an observer's chair sipping caff. "You briefed us on the tactics they'd use. Now's the time to remind me."

Benota stood and walked under the massive overhead hologram. "Can I get a pointer?"

An aide hastened to put the device in Benota's hand, and he used its holographic cursor to control the three-dimensional display. First, he rotated the entire graphic so Engels looked down upon the battle, rather than from the viewpoint of *Indomitable*. "This gods-eye view should help me explain what's really going on," Benota said.

He placed the planet, with its two moons and eleven remaining orbital fortresses, at the top. Beneath the planet, and pointing their bows straight downward, were the six fat stubby monitors. Farther below floated *Indomitable*, her nose aiming upward, in the direction of the planet and the monitors that stood in her way.

To the right of this vertical row of combatants hovered two icons. The larger represented the Liberation fleet, led by eight dreadnoughts. The smaller was marked as "Archers," obviously representing the covert force, still within the fleet. These icons would soon pass the monitors, but well off to the side, and their projected courses then curved inward toward the planet.

Benota spoke as if at a lecture. "So we have four separate forces. The enemy has the fortresses and the monitors. We have *Indomitable* and the fleet. The fundamental tactical problem is, how to apply our forces to beat theirs."

"Understood," said Engels. "The textbook answer is to defeat them in detail. Isolate one force in a pincer and destroy it with both of ours. Then it's two on one."

"Precisely, and that principle applies whether the fight is four men, four armies or four fleets. But what is the difference between our enemies' forces and ours?"

"Mobility. Our firepower profiles are roughly equivalent, but they have one immobile force and one—the monitors—with middling speed. We have a slow battleship and a fast fleet."

"Correct. So given the combat configuration, what would you do in the enemy's place?"

Engels forced herself not to chew a new nail. "I'd want to do the same thing. But in each case, the easiest forces to isolate—their immobile one, our slow battleship—can't be the target of such a pincer move. So that leaves our fleet as the target. But our fleet is the fastest piece. How do they expect to catch it from both sides?"

Benota used the pointer to advance the course of the Liberation fleet into the future. It passed the monitors and approached the planetary defenses. "The fleet engages with the fortresses and remaining moon bases. If you're the enemy, what do you do?"

Engels stood and pointed, seeing the answer. "I turn the monitors to their left, my right, and blast to the flank before they get within *Indomitable's* particle beam range. They curve around as fast as they can to trap the fleet against the planet, where it either has to run or be destroyed. If it runs, it will have taken heavy losses from going toe-to-toe with those fortresses, and it will get raked as it flees, losing even more. The Mutuality comes out ahead."

Benota nodded. "More than comes out ahead. The crews of the Liberation fleet are not a professional navy. They're a collection of desperate people, held together by their goal and their Liberator. If defeat seems inevitable, they will scatter. Many will flee to their homeworlds. It will be the end of the Liberation, unless *Indomitable* saves the day—which at that point would be difficult."

"So we have to avoid getting trapped, and we have to trap something of theirs." Engels took another pointer and backed up the fleet to its realtime position. "Since we can't trap the planet, we have to trap the monitors. Like this." She traced a course for the fleet that curved around behind the big enemy ships, squeezing them between the fleet and *Indomitable*.

"There are two problems with that," said Benota. "One, the covert force then has no cover. With the battle taking place well away from the planet, and nothing to sow confusion, the fortresses will easily detect our Archers and they will target their points of congruency with missiles, forcing them to stay in underspace or be destroyed."

"And the other problem?"

"This." He rotated the monitors to head back toward the planet, which put the fleet between them and the fortresses. "Now, we're all in a line—*Indomitable*, monitors, fleet, planet. We're trapping each others' middle forces."

"Then it's merely a matter of timing. Whoever moves first, gets the jump on the other and dictates where the battle will be. But the longer we wait, the farther away from their planet the monitors will be, which is good." Engels went to run her fingers through her hair, but encountered the medical skullcap she still wore. "Gods, this thing itches." She forced her hand away. "So, the trick is to wait as long as possible, but still get the jump on them."

"I agree."

"Tixban," said Engels, "you've been listening?"

"Of course, Commodore."

"Project the battle—as it stands—forward in time, and calculate the optimum moment for the enemy to make his flanking movement with the monitors."

The hologram quickly fast-forwarded. When the monitors began turning, it froze. "One hour nineteen minutes from now."

"Then we make our move at one-fifteen," said Engels.

"Our counterparts are not unaware of this," said Benota. "They are no doubt running simulations just like we are. They don't know of the Archers, but they have all the other facts. You're employing second-order thinking to anticipate them, but if they employ third-order thinking to anticipate your anticipation…"

"They'll go early. Dammit. Should I move even earlier? Or will doing so make it impossible to catch the monitors far enough from the fortresses?"

Benota shrugged almost imperceptibly. "I'm not in command, and that's a command decision."

"But if you *were* in command?"

The fat man pressed his lips together. Engels could tell he was uncomfortable giving an answer, and she knew why. If he was wrong, she might accuse him of sabotaging the victory in favor of his old masters.

"I'd make the move earlier," he said thoughtfully. "Better a partial victory for us than no victory at all."

"Or everybody dances away and resets to face off again," Engels replied. "That's good for them, because they've bought time."

"If they back the monitors out, though, *Indomitable* has a free hand to bombard, so we'd still come out ahead."

Engels thought for a moment. "I agree. Tixban, put together a short brief on what we just talked about and make a data package. Ops, cut orders to flank the monitors, beginning the move… fifty-nine minutes from now. Comms, package that all up and transmit to the fleet ASAP." She turned to Benota. "Thanks. This is…"

"Complex?" He smiled. "You're doing fine, Commodore. You're acting as an admiral. Not the same as ship captain or squadron commander."

"There is one problem."

"What's that?"

"Admiral Straker's not necessarily going to like delaying his covert op. In our original discussions he insisted we send in the fleet to cover his insertion. Now I'm issuing new orders. He might see it as putting our judgment ahead of his—and he's the boss. He might countermand. There's still time."

"He might." Benota gazed steadily at her.

After a long moment of waiting, Engels said, "I'm glad you didn't say it."

Benota cocked his head and one side of his mouth smiled. "Say what?"

"You know what. You didn't suggest I delay sending the orders to give Straker no time to countermand them."

"If someone did that to me, I'd fire them, perhaps court-martial them," said Benota. "Though I don't imagine he'd do that to you."

"Oh, you might be surprised. But I'd never put him in that position. If he wants to countermand my orders, I'll give him time. I'm hoping he sees that to do so is to give up winning the battle and place everything on his coup attempt."

"How long until he responds?"

Engels pondered. "I'd say the soonest he can get back to us is about ten minutes, if he views the sim and consults with his officers. Of course, if he goes ballistic and doesn't think it through, it might be five minutes—just the comlink delay."

"Then I'm getting a fresh cup of caff. You want one?"

"Sure." Engels threw herself into her chair as Benota ambled toward the caff dispenser. "Weapons, results of the last volley?"

"One more fortress destroyed, two strikes, ma'am," said the weapons officer. "It looks like they threw everything they had at the projectiles."

"Fire another salvo of fourteen, then. That seems to be the magic number. How long until the monitors are in range of our particle beam?"

"One hour ten minutes, ma'am."

Ten minutes passed. A comtech spoke. "Secure message from Admiral Straker."

"Damn." Engels frowned. "Play it."

"This is Straker. Commodore Engels, I understand why you're doing this, but it puts all our eggs in one basket. I know it's going to cost ships and people, but I'm modifying your orders. Commodore Gray has agreed to lead our light forces in to cover our insertion, while our capital ships under Captain Zholin's command make the pincer movement. That only diverts about a quarter of the fleet's combat power, and the light ships are best for causing maximum confusion. If you want to help me, keep smashing those fortresses. Good luck and good hunting. Straker out."

Engels sat back. "Not so bad—for us. For them, it's gonna be hell. Weapons!"

"Yes, ma'am?"

"Maximum rate of fire on the railgun. The shorter the recharge time, the more fortresses we can take out of the picture. No pauses between salvos."

"Aye aye, ma'am."

"How else can we push the pace?" she asked Benota.

"What do our missile stocks look like?"

"On *Indomitable*? Almost nothing. We figured the big guns were all she needed, so we gave them all to the fleet, so they're fully loaded."

"I'd suggest dumping all the fleet's missiles into two soft launches of about equal size. Time one strike to hit the monitors when the capital ships do, time the other to hit the planetary defenses when the light units do."

"That leaves them no reserves to fire," Engels said.

"Desperate times require desperate measures. Or *separate* measures in this case."

She thought about it. "All right. Weapons, comms, work together on that and pass the orders to gray and Zholin."

The minutes counted down. Four more fortresses were destroyed or neutralized, leaving six. The monitors continued to charge forward toward *Indomitable*, apparently committed to a head-on attack. The fleet passed the monitors to the right as Engels viewed them, out of firing range of each other.

The two missile swarms waited, floating along with the fleet... until the countdown reached zero. Then they and the ships split into two smaller fleets.

Forty capitals ships, heavy cruisers through dreadnoughts, turned as one and blasted sideways. Their vectors would put them behind the enemy monitors within half an hour, in a position to rake them. Missiles followed along in their wake like a pack of dogs, ready to activate and attack. Engels had confidence Zholin would lead them well.

The light forces under Ellen Gray, some one-hundred and fifty corvettes, frigates, destroyers and light cruisers, in combat power far inferior to the capital core, leaped ahead like greyhounds into the teeth of the planetary defenses.

* * *

Aboard *Gryphon*, Straker watched the unfolding battle via brainlink, connected to his mechsuit. He was startled and pleased at how well the synthesis worked. It seemed indistinguishable from his days in the Regiment of the Hundred Worlds, where everything functioned at top efficiency.

"Indy helped," Murdock had told him. "She worked out some of the glitches. I'm sure glad she's on our side."

"I'm not sure she's on a side," Straker had replied, "but at least she's not our enemy."

In his expanded vision, fed directly into his visual cortex, he saw the light fleet surge ahead, continuing to fire streams of railgun projectiles at the remaining fortresses as they rotated into view in their orbits. Now that half of the bases had been taken out, there were significant gaps in the defensive coverage. They were boosting into higher orbits to compensate, and that would make the covert op easier when the time came.

He opened a comlink to Commodore Gray, in tactical command. "Are we good on ammo?"

"Yes, Admiral. I'm rationing our stores so we have enough to take us into battle and get you to your position. Once you do, we'll break off and run, using the planet and moons for what cover we can. We're like wasps attacking bulls with these fortresses, sir. We can annoy them, but we're not likely to kill any, barring a lucky contact nuke."

"Just get us to the drop zone, Ellen. Then you can bug out and preserve our forces."

"We'll get the job done, sir."

"And Ellen…"

"Yes, sir?"

"Carla says you're a true professional. I know you're not like DeChang or Ramirez."

"We don't get to choose our commanders, sir. Not more than once, anyway." She paused. "Not even today."

"Understood. And thanks. Call me if you need me. Straker out."

Loco spoke in his ear. "Sure good to be brainlinked again."

"Yes, it is."

"Gray seems like your type, all over-serious and shit."

"I like it when I can rely on people. Don't you?"

"Sure. But there's reliable, and there's trustworthy."

Straker thought about that. Loco was probably trying to tell him something. That he was trustworthy, even if not entirely reliable? But Straker knew that. That's why he didn't give Loco the biggest commands. He didn't have full confidence in his friend. Despite their reconciliation, it was hard for Straker be sure.

So, keep your friends close. That's what Straker was doing.

Or maybe he was trying to say that Gray was reliable, but not trustworthy. Like Karst, as it turned out, perfectly placed for betrayal.

He checked the space tactical feed. *Gryphon* was in the center of the Liberation ships, weaving and evading as the fortresses fired everything they had at the oncoming light fleet. Warships took hits, some small, some large enough to smash them. The enemy primary weapons packed huge punches, and they only got stronger as the range closed to short.

Straker watched as the soft-launched friendly missile group lit its engines. It raced ahead in a ring on the outside of the cylinder of space between the oncoming enemies, a cylinder that was full of submunitions and beams. Had they flown down the middle, some would have been destroyed to no purpose.

The enemy missile swarm from the moon bases sprang to life as well, a mass off to the side. It curved around from the left in order to avoid the mess in the middle.

Gray diverted some missiles to counter and break up the enemy volley, and Straker watched as she reformed the light fleet to place its smallest ships, the corvettes, in a screen against the missiles. They were the most agile and least likely to be struck, though it would only take one warhead to destroy each vessel.

"Indy…" Straker said as the incoming fire got denser and denser, "we need to—"

"*Gryphon* inserting into underspace now."

The familiar chill hit him, and he manually increased the heater setting inside his mechsuit to compensate. At least now the chance of any of the three Archers being destroyed in the firefight above was dramatically reduced. Underspace detectors in the fortresses might be lighting up, but Straker had to hope the enemy would be far too busy to worry about three bogeys among the thousands of ships, missiles, beams and bullets they had to deal with.

Now *Gryphon*, *Revenge*, and *Liberator* navigated on prediction alone. Fortresses wouldn't deviate much, but there were a few attack ships in orbit around Unison, adding to its final defenses. A sharp enemy commander might follow the convergence points of the Archers, waiting in normal space to fire upon emergence.

Straker's tactical display showed the trio surging ahead, aiming at a point that matched geosynchronous velocity above the capital city of Unity—in essence, coming to a dead stop in orbit so the dropships could fly straight down, with no orbital velocity to bleed off in re-entry. They'd planned for emergence at a gap in the orbital coverage, when the six remaining fortresses were as far out of position as possible. Three were blocked by the planet's bulk, and the other three should be furiously busy with Gray's ships.

"Powering up," said Straker.

"Roger," said Loco. Both mechsuits came to life, free to move about the flight deck.

Straker felt that familiar sensation, as if he'd taken on a new, godlike body, and everything around him became small. He walked over to a shuttle that now seemed the size of a child's rideable toy groundcar. He looked down onto its roof. Had he desired, he could have taken a gauntlet and smashed it flat.

"Man, I am so ready for this," said Loco. "Full brainlink again! Gonna kick some ass!"

"Damn straight. Watch the fratricide, though. We have Benota's Hok on our side, and our own IFF isn't too reliable."

"We knew going in it was gonna be messy. As for the Hok, those freaks can kill each other off for all I care."

Straker didn't answer, but he didn't disagree. Engels had tried to argue the Hok were human and should be treated like any other soldier, but they weren't. No amount of re-education or training would restore their free will. If they were told to sit on one place and starve, they would do it. They had no reproductive organs, and even if they had, their genetics would have been completely corrupted. In fact, they were just what they'd been designed to be: organic machines, the perfect shock troopers. The sooner they were expended, the better. Their creation and use would be forbidden in the New Earthan Republic.

"Emergence in one minute," said Zaxby on Straker's comlink. "When the doors open, jump immediately."

"Will do. Good to hear your voice, Zaxby. Are you…"

"I am myself, Derek Straker. Just more. When I brainlink with Indy, it's like when you do so with your mechsuit—if it were alive. I have an idea, if you'd like to try it."

"What is it?"

"I could brainlink Loco's suit to yours, and therefore you could be brainlinked to each other. You might be more efficient in combat."

Straker's stomach roiled. Brainlinking with another living being, even voluntarily, was forbidden in the Hundred Worlds, a taboo and a crime equivalent to rape. Those caught doing so were mind-wiped and their brainlinks were removed, never to have one installed again. The closest they came was sharing data from mechsuit to mechsuit, providing a double buffer.

"No, Zaxby. Not now, not ever."

"I could arrange for a link with Carla if you'd rather."

"Drop the subject, Zaxby. Don't make me order you back to Ruxin."

"There's no need to issue threats. Doors opening in ten seconds. Zaxby out."

Loco chuckled in Straker's ear. "That guy gets weirder and weirder every day."

"Here we go. Head in the game, Commander Paloco."

"Roger wilco. Assault Admiral Straker sir."

"Assault Admiral?"

"Your new rank. I made it up."

As Straker laughed, the doors withdrew to reveal the blue planet below, its atmosphere curving away. "Go," he said as he leaped out like a skydiver.

Chapter 42

Battleship *Indomitable*, facing the Mutuality monitors.

Engels watched, stomach clenched with battle stress, as ships of Ellen Gray's light fleet died throwing themselves against the fortresses. *Indomitable* couldn't fire any more salvos into that mess. The monitors would soon enter her particle beam's effective range. Straker and Gray were beyond her help.

Captain Zholin's capital ships were racing to get behind the monitors, but they moved at the speed of the slowest, the dreadnoughts, and they had a lot of vector to change in their 180-degree sweep to their left. When the monitors had detected this maneuver, they'd increased their own speed further, directly toward *Indomitable*.

Evidently, they were intending to do whatever it took to destroy the battleship before they got caught from behind by the heavy fleet. It was textbook, exactly what Engels would have done.

"Entering effective range of our particle beam," Tixban said.

"Fire at the lead monitor," Engels ordered, "half power."

"Half power, ma'am?" asked her senior weapons officer in surprise.

"Do it."

"Aye aye, ma'am."

The ship vibrated with the massive energy expenditure that sent untold numbers of particles in a concentrated stream. At nearly lightspeed, when they impacted the molecules in a target, they caused fission or fusion. Either way, the molecular disruption was horrendous. Armor would boil away or vaporize.

That's where reinforcing fields came in. The electromagnetics deflected and slowed particles. They also stiffened the structures of the layers of armor, making them less susceptible to damage. Finally, the fields energized the embedded thermal superconductors, allowing them to carry dangerous heat away and radiate it into the void almost as fast as it was produced.

"Half power?" Benota murmured to her.

"They've never seen what *Indomitable* can do. I want them to underestimate her."

"Hit," Tixban said. "Negligible damage. The monitors are increasing their evasive maneuvers."

"Keep firing at half power, half rate," Engels said. "Tixban, can you give me an analysis of their armor and shielding?"

"What do you want to know?"

"I want to know the optimum moment to go full power. Can we take a monitor out with one shot, like we did with the superdreadnoughts?"

"One moment."

Engels waited for three more shots as Tixban worked the sensors systems, gathering and analyzing data on how much damage the particle beam was doing. Then he spoke.

"While my analysis is preliminary, I believe we will have to be at point-blank range to destroy a monitor with one shot. At short range, it will take two to three shots. At medium range, anywhere between four and seven. Again, these are only rough estimates."

"How many shots can we get in before they can hit us effectively with their beams?"

"Approximately sixteen if we use full power. However, if we divert energy to our own armor, we will recharge more slowly. In any case, they will begin striking us at medium range."

"Got it." Engels glanced at Benota. "Observations? Suggestions?"

"Run our impellers to push us to our left. It's not much, but it will let the heavy fleet line up behind the monitors slightly faster."

"Helm, do as he says. What else?"

Benota replied, "We have submunitions, right?"

"Yes. The railgun can fire bursts of smaller bullets instead of single big ones."

"When the time comes, alternate weapon types at the same target. They won't be able to fully dodge submunition clusters. Kinetic strikes on heat-weakened armor will be doubly effective."

"Good idea. More?"

Benota shook his head. "It's a slugfest. Keep slugging."

* * *

Straker dove out the flight deck door as *Gryphon* hovered on impellers directly above the Mutuality's capital city of Unity. His radiation detectors screamed briefly as they picked up the fading traces of the blasts of the float mines the Archers had dropped and detonated before they emerged from underspace. Those explosions should have cleared the area of mines, missiles or lurking attack ships, like an infantryman tossing a grenade into a room before he entered.

Loco came out right after him, and all around them fell the assault lifters that had been attached to the Archers. It had been the only way to convey four thousand troops through the battle zone and get them into drop position.

The lifters pointed nose-down and lit their engines, speeding ahead through the thin atmosphere. They'd been let go at sixty thousand meters altitude, and with no orbital velocity to bleed off, they should be on the ground in five minutes.

Those that survived, anyway.

As intended, Straker and Loco fell more slowly than the lifters, head-down like divers. Surprise limited the initial response from the ground, but flak and missiles began reaching up toward the assault force.

In reply, *Revenge* and *Liberator* hammered the air defense sites with all the weaponry at their disposal. Indy refused to shoot to kill, but she used *Gryphon's* point-defense suite to pick off rising missiles. She also beamed sophisticated electronic warfare transmissions that disrupted sensors and hacked at linked computer systems.

At least, that's what she was supposed to be doing. The effects were invisible, but of the sixty lifters, more than fifty made it to landfall intact, so Straker figured whatever she did must have worked. He was grateful.

At least, he was grateful until his link to *Liberator* cut off abruptly. Simultaneously, a new star blossomed in the sky above him.

"What was that?" Straker snapped. His standby comlinks to *Revenge* and *Liberator* dropped as well.

Indy answered. "I regret to inform you that *Liberator* has been destroyed by a capital beam strike from the nearest fortress. *Revenge* has inserted into underspace, and we must also do so immediately. Good luck, Admiral Straker." Then that comlink disappeared too.

Dammit. Liberator gone, with all her crew? He'd known many of those aboard. Some were Breakers from the earliest moments of the Liberation. There was no time to dwell on it now. He had to be grateful the assault lifters had gotten away.

"Derek…?" Loco said.

Straker focused. "Turn and burn."

"Roger."

He and Loco popped their canards and used them to alter their steep vertical dives into brief, shallow flights toward their designated drop zones. When the time came, they triggered their jump jets and stalled, to land on their feet among the grounded lifters.

Those lifters were already disgorging their troops. The Hok wore battlesuits in Mutuality red, each modified by the simple addition of a large letter L for Liberation on its back. Combined with modified IFF transmitters, these allied L-Hok should remain identifiable to the Liberation marines even while fooling the enemy into thinking they were friendlies.

The L-Hok lifters landed centrally, an inner ring half a kilometer across surrounding the Committee Citadel. The Liberation marines formed an outer ring to stop any counterattacks or attempts to relieve the Citadel. Benota and DeChang had both agreed that using Hok to seize the government would thoroughly confuse the enemy, probably paralyzing those who were used to seeing the Hok only as their own.

After all, Straker wanted to take the Committee intact. The transfer of power would go smoothest if the citizenry's familiar leaders, backed by equally familiar Hok, issued the orders. He didn't care that they'd be doing it under duress.

Whereas the L-Hok lifters were packed to the gills with battlesuiters, the Breaker marine lifters dropped off one armored vehicle each—a light tank or a hover—to reinforce the defense. Then, the lifters moved to the best positions they could find—the tops of buildings or to block narrow streets—in order to use their own turrets and missile launchers as fire support weaponry.

Straker hit the ground and immediately began analyzing the deployment. The L-Hok were spreading with highly trained perfection and advancing toward the Citadel, gunning down every armed defender with brutal efficiency.

This was the moment of Straker's greatest worry. If Benota had told the L-Hok to betray the Liberation and save the Committee, now was when they would do it. He'd briefed the marines on this possibility, and most of the guns from the armored vehicles were pointed at the backs of L-Hok platoons.

But the L-Hok continued inward. When they bounded over the wall into the Citadel, Straker relaxed. "Straker to Breakers. Get into those defensive positions. We don't know how heavy the counterattack will be, or how long it will take for Commodore Engels to bring us overhead cover. Prepare for the worst." He switched channels. "Loco, you good?"

"I'm good, boss. Good hunting."

"Thanks. You too. Straker out." Loco would command the Breakers in the defensive ring, freeing Straker to head in and play Liberator.

His proximity alarm pinged, and he checked his HUD to see Sergeant Redwolf bound up at the head of a battlesuiter squad, with War Male Dexon and his warriors following. "We're here to watch your back, sir," Redwolf said.

"My Foehammer's all I need," Straker replied.

"Begging your pardon, sir, but we don't trust those L-Hok, and a mechsuit's not invulnerable, especially in urban terrain."

"All right, come along. Remember, don't kill any unarmed civilians or surrendered military. I want a coup, not a massacre."

Straker set out at a run, trusting the others to follow. He hadn't asked for them to come along, so he wasn't going to make allowances for them, allowances that would impair his regained combat effectiveness.

As he approached the wall, a tall defense turret swiveled toward him and his HUD shrieked at him that he was being locked up by a targeting system. With hardly a thought he sent a force-cannon bolt into the turret, blowing it to bits. He jinked as he ran, just in case any more of the emplacements were active. The L-Hok's orders had been to seize the Citadel first, and only concentrate on destroying the enemy second; many of these defenses would still be intact.

He bounded over the wall at the location of the dead turret, hoping that would be where the enemy least expected him. As he cleared the ten-meter barrier, his HUD showed him a Hok squad that lacked Liberation IFF. The firestorm of small arms that erupted from it confirmed these were Mutuality troops, not his.

His gatling slashed them to ribbons, his perfected brainlink allowing him to hose them down with clean precision while simultaneously checking for heavier targets and landing from his jump. Behind him, Redwolf's squad bounded to the top of the wall, then dropped to the turf behind, while the Ruxin warriors simply climbed over, an easy task with their many arms.

His HUD cued him to a threat to his right. Moving instinctively forward to make himself a moving target, he identified the barrel of a heavy tank poking from around the corner of the blocky central Citadel building as the vehicle edged into view. The crew was obviously maintaining as much cover as possible and relying on their heavy front glacis to save them from attack. Usually that would be smart tactics, but not against a mechsuit, where speed and maneuver were paramount.

Straker broke into a run, hugging the building to stay out of sight of the tank's sensors until he could get close. However, he hadn't counted on the drone that popped into view overhead.

The tank suddenly reversed itself, withdrawing and no doubt waiting in ambush. Straker slowed and made a quick check for other threats. Armor was most dangerous in teams, but he didn't see any more vehicles. Maybe this one was in front.

He looked up. The building was ten stories high. He could jump to the top with jet assistance. The problem with this trick was, most roofs weren't made to hold fifty-ton mechsuits stomping around on them.

"Redwolf," he barked, "take your men up to the roof and give me a view of that heavy. Dexon, take out that drone."

As the warriors blasted the observer, the battlesuiters bounded upward on their own jets, landing easily on the rooftop and disappearing out of sight. In Straker's HUD, an extra window opened showing Redwolf's helmet view. It peered over the opposite roofline and down on the tank, which was exactly where he expected, aiming its gun for the corner where he'd be if he followed.

"We don't have any heavy AT rockets," said Redwolf. "We can try for a mobility kill, but it's iffy."

"Don't bother. I got this." Straker eyed the building and leaped—for the corner, five stories up. At the top of his arc, he smashed his left gauntlet into the worked stone of the building, gaining purchase for just long enough to swing his right arm and head-sensors around the corner.

The tank spotted him instantly and raised its barrel, but Straker had already fired his force cannon. The downward angle let his perfectly placed shot cut through the top turret armor, and the heavy brewed up, vomiting fire and smoke from every crack.

A quick check of his tactical feed showed no more threats, other than Hok here and there. The outer defense ring of Breakers was under intermittent, disorganized attack, and his L-Hok were now putting the squeeze on the Central Committee building. DeChang had said there was an extensive underground complex beneath it, so the L-Hok would also be breaking into the known access tunnels and assaulting downward.

It all depended on how fast the Committee members and their personal security had evacuated them from the Chamber of the People and into the bunkers below. If a siege resulted, this whole special operation would be for nothing. The Committee and the command center might have to be eliminated with an orbital strike, and the central government rebuilt from scratch.

Straker pushed onward.

* * *

Engels clicked her helmet into place, making her flight suit vacuum-capable, at least for a couple of hours, and switched to multi-comlink mode. The comtechs should direct her words where they were needed.

All around her, the crew was suiting up or snapping helmets closed. On a vessel this size, doing so was acknowledgement that severe damage, even destruction, was not out of the question. Throughout the ship, everyone else would be doing the same. Chief Gurung's damage control crews would be ready, Chief Quade's engineers would be in their tele-operated repair-bot rigs, and every gunner would be optimizing his or her weaponry, down to the smallest point-defense laser.

"Monitors approaching medium range," said Tixban.

"Go to full firepower. Hit the same ship we've been poking until now. Smash her right on the nose."

"Firing. Confirmed hit. Heavy damage to target, designated Monitor 1. They are venting atmosphere. Probable neutralization of their central laser."

"Good. Shift target. Maximum rate of fire."

"Monitors two through six firing at extreme range," said Tixban. The deck wobbled and shuddered. "Twelve percent damage to forward armor. I recommend reinforcement."

Engels reluctantly agreed. She'd rather put all power into her weaponry, but she had to make sure *Indomitable* survived, even if the monitors were not defeated. "Reinforce the nose. Engineering, try to finesse it so we reinforce only what's needed. We have to keep up the rate of fire."

"Aye aye, ma'am."

Indomitable fired again, and then again. "Monitor two damaged, but still operational."

"Switch to submunitions, alternating with the beams."

"Switching."

The bridge shook with another strike from the monitors. Then came the familiar feeling of the gargantuan spinal railgun firing. "Submunition cluster away."

On the hologram, the ball of projectiles, much slower than a beam strike, spread out and crawled toward its target. Monitor two evaded strenuously, but could only dodge part of the cluster. "Submunition impact. Severe damage, primary weaponry is assessed as down," said Tixban.

Engels grunted with satisfaction. "Weapons, fire at your own discretion. You know what I want."

As Benota said, it was a slugfest. Like a bull fighting wolves, *Indomitable* gored first one, then another, but the closer the two enemies approached, the more the fight shifted in the monitors' favor. The battleship took strike after strike to her forward armor. Monitor three was neutralized, and then–

"Nose armor is disintegrating, even with full reinforcement," Chief Gurung said, sounding worried. "Commodore, we have to roll the ship."

Engels was ready for this. "Helm, do it. Roll the ship, eighty degrees port, and spin her up. Then flank acceleration."

The bridge twisted violently around her, and only restraining straps kept her in her seat. With power needed everywhere, gravplate compensation was at minimum.

The hologram showed the result of the helm's maneuver. With *Indomitable's* nose ready to crack, the only thing to do was swing it out of the way. The battleship turned to port, to the left, and engaged her massive fusion engines, driving herself sideways. At the same time, the helm fired the attitude thrusters and reoriented the impellers to start her spinning like a rifled bullet.

This maneuver presented *Indomitable's* untouched side armor to her enemies. What's more, the spinning and rolling made it difficult for an enemy to strike repeatedly at any one spot, while also rotating her side-mounted weaponry around and around, allowing fresh beams and guns to line up in sequence.

The problem was, *Indomitable's* main multi-weapon was now effectively out of action, pointing sideways.

"Our capital fleet is coming into range of the monitors," said Tixban. "Missile swarm is accelerating."

Engels watched as the Liberation heavy fleet finally joined the action. All the capital ships began accelerating at their own individual maximums, so the cruisers and battlecruisers pulled ahead of the dreadnoughts, with the missiles leading them.

The three damaged monitors rolled in response, presenting their broadsides to their enemies and bringing maximum secondary weaponry into play, trying to cover for their three remaining fellows.

Trying to buy them time to finish off *Indomitable*.

"Will we hold? Gurung?" Engels asked.

"I am not sure, ma'am. We will do our best."

Benota spoke in her ear. "I know those monitors, and I've come to know this ship. We'll hold. Survive, anyway. They'll only get one pass and then they'll shoot on by. The fleet can chase them down and finish them off. There's only one thing that worries me."

"Which is?"

Benota stroked his chin. "I imagine at this point the commodore in charge of the monitors is setting up a special override for one of his ships. A Mutuality captain would not be likely to suicide himself and his ship—not unless he believed the survival of his homeworld was at stake, and we've already broadcast that this is a coup, not a genocide—but the man in charge would certainly turn a monitor not his own into a weapon."

Engels rotated to look at Benota in horror. "To ram us?"

Benota lifted a palm. "That's what a fanatic would do. Trade one monitor to take us out."

Engels turned back to stare at the hologram and the vectors shown there. Then she unstrapped and leaped up to stagger to the helm. "Give me the board," she yelled, shoving the helmsmen out of the way and strapping in. "Now—hurry!"

She sized the controls and eyeballed the numbers and the graphics. Calculations were all well and good, but ultimately, flying was flying and ships were ships, no matter what size… and she had one more trick up her sleeve, something from her old days as a Marksman pilot.

"Weapons, double-load submunitions clusters on the main railgun."

"But that might damage the railgun."

"Can't be helped. Do it! Then give me one-button firing control."

While the weapons team loaded the two clusters, one atop another, she reset all impellers and thrusters to aim forward, ready to push the ship backward. Then, she ran the fusion engines up to overload levels.

"Ma'am," said the senior engineer, "you're overheating the engines. They'll fail in less than a minute!"

"That's all we need," she said. She watched the enemy's vectors and picked out the one that was clearly trying to intersect the battleship. She steadied on a straight course, giving it an easy target.

"Commodore," said Tixban with an uncharacteristic tone of panic in his voice, "you *must* continue evading. You're giving the ram-ship a simple intercept."

"I know what I'm doing," she snarled, hunched with one hand hovering over the impeller actuators, the other with a finger ready to mash the button that fired the railgun.

Tixban unbuckled and flowed toward her as if to physically interfere. "Commodore, I really must insist—"

"Somebody tackle that squid!"

Tixban reached toward her with his arms as time ran out. She chopped the fusion engines to zero, fired the double-shotted railgun and simultaneously activated the impellers and retro-thrusters.

The submunitions acted as reaction mass, like an electric metal rocket fired screaming from *Indomitable's* bow. The combination of weapon, impellers and thrusters slowed the ship dramatically, just in time for the ramming monitor to shoot across her nose, missing by mere meters.

Then the three monitors were past, and Engels let go of the controls, waving the helmsman back to his seat. She left Tixban standing still, several crew holding onto his arms, until she ordered them to release him. "Get back to your station, Tixban."

"I should be relieved of duty," he replied, not moving. "I was ready to assault my commanding officer."

"Then your punishment is to get back to work," she said wearily.

"I—thank you." He took his station again.

"You're not forgiven."

Once the crew of the bridge absorbed the fact that Engels had outmaneuvered their death, they began to cheer.

The heavy fleet's missiles swept past as well, chasing and bursting all around the enemies, while the capital ships hammered the three cripples with their direct fire weaponry. Within minutes, they surrendered.

The heavy fleet continued to stalk the three remaining monitors, raking them with shots to their rear. Eventually they must turn and fight, or give up, Engels knew. Without sidespace capability and hunted by faster ships with triple their firepower, they were doomed. It was just a matter of time.

"Set course for Unison," she said. "How's the railgun?"

"Inoperative, ma'am," the senior weapons officer said stiffly. "The double-shotting damaged them."

"Repair time?"

"Twelve to twenty-four hours." The man's face showed reproach.

"Cheer up, Commander," she said to him. "Better a broken railgun than a dead battleship."

He lowered his head in acknowledgement, and she hid a grin. The desire to smile faded as she called for an update on the planetary assault.

Chapter 43

Committee Citadel, Unity City, Planet Unison

Heavy gunfire echoed throughout the Citadel. It was an imposing fortress-like building fitted with pillboxes and defenses, a *de facto* admission that the government here ruled by force and fear, and felt it had to defend itself against its own citizens. Fortunately, the builders never expected an assault by battalions of elite troops.

Backed by its own fanatical Hok, these defenses took a toll on the equally fanatical L-Hok. Straker shuddered to think how many Breakers would have died in their place. Taking on Benota and his contingent had paid off handsomely. It was a lesson he'd learned from his readings of history: the best way to destroy your enemies was to make them your friends.

If that didn't work… kill them.

With his own small force of battlesuiters and warriors in tow, Straker stomped through the high-ceilinged halls, straight for the Committee Chamber. He passed many blasted bodies of Hok and L-Hok, mingled and unified in bloody death.

Now and again a Hok lifted a weapon in his direction, and he administered the *coup de grace*. Other times, an L-Hok saluted or tried to get up. To those, he returned the salute, but passed on.

When the bodies ran out he found an intact double pillbox sprouting autocannon. An excellent defense against battlesuiters, it fell easily to the force-cannon bolts he sent down the corridor. The chattering weapons sprayed him with bullets, but his armor shrugged them off easily, and his troops sheltered behind his massive form.

That turned out to be the final defense. Beyond it lay two massive double doors. He strode forward and, with a mighty kick, knocked them from their hinges.

Inside, the ornate chamber was deserted. The Committee had fled. A door stood half-open, and beyond it Straker could see a well-lit grav-drop shaft. He cursed at its size, fine for personnel but far too small for a mechsuit.

Reluctantly, he set his mechsuit's SAI for auto-defense. It would ignore all Ruxins, the weaponless and anyone with the proper IFF. He made sure his comlink was broadcasting the right coded signal, and then he dismounted.

"Sir! You can't go into combat unarmored!" said Redwolf. "I'll give you mine." He lifted off his helmet and started to open his battlesuit.

"Forget it. No time, and it's not fitted for me."

"Private Hernandez is about your size. He can—"

"I said forget it." Straker unholstered his trusty slugthrower pistol. "Dexon, give me a blaster."

The War Male passed him one of his two heavy blasters, and Straker brandished it one-handed, something only possible for a very strong man. "Let's go."

Redwolf got in the way. "No, sir. It's one thing for you to come along, but you're not taking point. That's fucking stupid, with all due respect. Let us do our job. The Liberation is nothing without you."

Straker didn't necessarily agree with that last part, but he knew Redwolf was right about the first. "Okay. You marines take point, then me, and the Ruxins will bring up the rear. Sorry, Dexon, but the heaviest armor should go first."

"Agreed," said Dexon. "Never fear, we are not like Major Wagner."

"Nobody is. Now move!"

Redwolf ran for the shaft. He dropped a grenade, and then waved on two of his men before stepping in himself and leading the rest. They fell feet-first.

"Grav is off," Redwolf comlinked. "We landed on jets. No resistance so far. Come on down."

Straker descended the ladder rungs countersunk into the concrete, dropping the last couple of meters when he could see the floor. The Ruxins swarmed down behind him.

* * *

Engels couldn't take her eyes off the hologram. Now that *Indomitable* wasn't fighting, she had time to worry about Derek. "Zoom in on Unison planetary space. Run it back to before the covert assault, then play it at five times speed."

Tixban followed her instructions without comment, probably trying to avoid reminding her of his near-mutinous actions.

The display changed, showing the defenses around the Committee World of Unison as they frantically fended off the attack of over a hundred light warships. For a short time it seemed like the attackers had the upper hand, but that only lasted as long as their accompanying missile swarm. Once those were picked off, the fortresses began to turn their weapons on the vessels harassing them.

Three icons glided serenely through the midst of the confusion: the Archers, in underspace. A dozen attack ships, local defenders, dogged them, clearly vectored there by fortress detectors. Accompanying them were at least twenty missiles in hunt mode, flitting here and there like fireflies.

"Come on, come on," she muttered as the three approached their emergence point at the edge of atmo, directly over the capital city of Unity. When they reached it, a confusion of blasts erupted, ships fired, and missiles dove and detonated.

Fortunately the fast-forward mode meant she didn't have to wait for the results. Float mines and Archer-launched missiles had cleared a bubble of space for the covert ships to emerge, destroying or damaging everything nearby. They popped into normal space and immediately dumped the assault lifters clamped to their hulls. The troopships rocketed straight down toward the city.

The resolution wasn't fine enough to see, but she knew two mechsuits with Derek and Loco would be diving along with them. She sent up a prayer to the Unknowable Creator for their safety and success.

And then *Liberator* exploded.

"Freeze! What just happened?"

"It appears *Liberator* was struck by a primary beam from this fortress." The offending icon flashed. "It was destroyed."

Engels slumped in her chair, aghast. Of course a mere corvette would be ripped apart by one blast from a weapon made to slice open dreadnoughts. Twenty people, many of them comrades of hers, people she'd shared meals with in the tiny ship's mess, were no more. Probably there wasn't even anything to put in a coffin.

Despite the thousands of her people who had assuredly died in this battle so far, the ships destroyed or crippled, the troops on the ground no doubt dying in toe-to-toe combat with their enemies, only this had punched through her emotional armor. She fought back tears, closing her faceplate for a modicum of privacy from the crew around her.

When she'd mastered herself, she opened her faceplate and asked, "What about the other two?"

"*Revenge* and *Gryphon* show successful underspace insertions," Tixban said.

She took a shuddering breath, nodding. "Good. Good. Roll the record again. Highlight *Carson*."

Commodore Gray had declined to transfer her flag to one of the light cruisers, preferring to stay aboard her frigate. Engels wasn't sure she really wanted to find out what happened to her friend, but she had to know.

Carson's icon twisted and turned at the center of the attacking cloud of lightweight ships and missiles. Several near misses rocked her, and once a beam stitched a glowing line along her armor, but whoever her helmsman was, she was one ace pilot. She made it through.

The destruction of *Liberator* and the launch of the assault lifters signaled an end to the harassment. Commodore Gray's fleet scattered in individual flight, each ship finding her own way past the planet, trying to evade the following beams and railgun shots. Many didn't make it as they were raked by powerful fortress weaponry, a sad irony.

But *Carson* made it. That was something.

"We are realtime on the hologram now, Commodore," said Tixban.

"Any signal from the assault force?"

"Commander Paloco reported the Breakers have secured the area and are holding against heavy counterattacks while the L-Hok seize the Citadel."

"Dammit." If only *Indomitable's* railgun were operational… but she'd burned that bridge to save the ship. No point in pining for it now. "How long until the fortresses are in our effective particle beam range?"

"Forty minutes, ma'am," said the still-stiff senior weapons officer. It seemed he took it personally that he couldn't blast the enemy with the damaged weapon.

"Refine your solution and fire at your discretion, Commander," she said. There, that should mollify him somewhat. "Tixban, give me a view of the surviving monitors."

The hologram showed the three functional monitors, now surrounded by the Liberation capital fleet. "They have surrendered, and are being escorted back," the Ruxin said. "Unfortunately, their high outbound velocity means it will take over twelve hours to reverse and return."

Engels nodded. "Comtech, pass to Captain Zholin to escort the monitors with his dreadnoughts, but detach his cruisers and haul ass back here to join *Indomitable*."

"Message passed."

Engels unbuckled and walked over to Benota on shaky legs. She grabbed the arm of his chair and did a couple of knee-bends to work out the kinks. "We still have a problem."

Benota nodded. "With no railgun, we'll have to use the particle beam—which means we'll also be inside the fortresses' range."

"And our bow armor is shot to shit. The limited amount of damage control we can do won't stand up to capital-grade pounding. Everybody's out of missiles. When the monitors and dreadnoughts get here, we can rush the fortresses and overwhelm them, but by that time the ground force might be dead."

Benota gazed steadily at her. "Another command decision, Commodore. Risk *Indomitable* herself—and all of us—or play it safe?"

"We'll have to go in," said Engels firmly. "If we give them time, the fortresses could smash our troops on the ground as they orbit. Right now they're not in position, but one will cross above Unity City right after we come into particle beam range. We have to hit that fortress first, and hard." She turned. "Helm, are we at flank acceleration toward the planet?"

"Yes, ma'am."

"Impellers and thrusters too?"

"Yes, ma'am. Begging your pardon, but this ship is a whale. She's no corvette."

Engels bit her thumbnail. "Damn your monitor commander and his suicide attack," she said to Benota.

"I know the rear admiral in charge of the monitors. He's a fanatic, even more than his commissar. I'll be happy to oversee both their court martials."

"Let's burn that bridge when we come to it," she replied. "I know we'll have to purge the military forces, but I'd like to keep it to a minimum."

Benota waved diffidently. "Best to hang some high-profile examples early. The rest will fall into line. In a month or two, the crisis will pass and everyone will be united behind the new government."

Engels mimicked exaggerated surprise. "Really? How do you know that?"

"Because all the parts of our New Earthan Republic will have a common enemy to rally around."

"Really? What, the Opters? I thought they had only twenty or thirty systems."

"No, not the Opters. The Huns. The Hundred Worlds."

"But this is their big chance to make peace! We can live alongside each other in friendship now."

Benota shook his head. "If the war between us had only lasted a few years, maybe. But the Mutuality and the Huns have been locked in a death-struggle for centuries. That means generations have grown up knowing nothing but hatred for the Hok."

"But now they'll know they weren't fighting aliens—they were fighting humans all along!"

Benota chuckled. "You think the Hun leadership doesn't know? You think they never captured and interrogated Mutuality naval personnel, or examined the DNA remnants of the Hok and found out they were once human?"

Engels scowled. "So they kept the common people and us military in the dark. Why? So we'd hate and kill without compunction?"

"Obviously." Benota grimaced. "Sorry to burst your bubble."

"Then we need to tell them. Send drones to all their systems to broadcast the truth."

"Nobody will believe you. They'll think it's just more propaganda." He shook his head. "No, the only thing that will end the war between us is if the Hun leadership has their back to the ropes—and even then, I don't think it will matter."

"Why not?"

Benota turned away. "I can't really talk about that right now."

Engels' eyes narrowed. "What? Why not?"

"Because I need to tell Straker first."

"I'm sick of people withholding things from me. You could have told him this, this *secret whatever-it-is* long ago. We've had days. Weeks."

"I could have, but I needed to know if he'd win. Only now does it matter."

"Does *what* matter?"

"Sorry. If Straker doesn't make it, I'll tell you, because you'll be the new Liberator. Not before."

Engels turned to stare at the hologram. "If he doesn't make it…"

※ ※ ※

Straker examined the intersection at the bottom of the drop shaft. Three tunnels led away—left, right, and center. The left and right curved, suggesting a circle, with the center tunnel heading for the middle. He began to move forward.

"Wait," said Dexon. "Let us scout." Before Straker could reply, three Ruxins had set aside their weapons and squeezed out of their water suits, a startling process of mere seconds, as if shedding skins. They matched their dermal camouflage to the walls and flowed down the corridors, almost invisible.

Less than a minute later, they returned, reporting pairs of Hok in all three directions, plus an armored door in the center.

"We go up the center," said Straker. "Battlesuits advance, warriors hold this intersection and watch our backs. Go."

Redwolf waved Hernandez forward and stacked right behind him. The bigger man aimed his pulse rifle over the other's shoulder, while the smaller man moved forward at a crouch, auto-grenade launcher aimed. The three other battlesuiters and Straker followed.

When the door came in sight, Hernandez fired three explosive rounds, recon-by-fire. In response, two Hok in battlesuits leaned out of cover, left and right, and opened up with their blasters. Hernandez went down, firing more grenades as he fell, while Redwolf punched a supersonic round through the head of first one, then the chest of the other.

Redwolf leapfrogged forward, and the rest of the battlesuiters did as well, passing the fallen Hernandez. At the end of the corridor they found no more enemies, only the vault-like door.

Straker paused to check Hernandez. He was alive, but in bad shape, his chest armor blasted with two center-mass hits. His suit would do its best to stabilize him, but he was out of action and unconscious.

"How do we get through this door, sir?" asked Redwolf. "We didn't bring breaching charges."

"You all have your auto-mapping on?"

"Yes, sir. Standard for all ops."

"Follow me, then. Bring Hernandez." Straker led them back out and up the drop shaft to where his mechsuit stood. It twitched its weapons as it identified them, and then opened at his coded comlink signal. He reached down to carefully detach Hernandez' helmet from where they'd placed him on the floor. He then plugged the battlesuit helmet into the mechsuit's interior data port and connected his brainlink, to download the auto-mapping data. He then tossed the helmet to Redwolf and his borrowed blaster to Dexon, and sealed up.

"Everybody back away, especially you Ruxins," Straker told them. "Get some cover. It's going to be hot."

He matched the mapping data with his 3D HUD imagery and calculated the location of the vault door through the floor below. Then, he adjusted the settings of his force cannon.

In this mode, the magnetic tube that usually sent a sun-hot lance of plasma through armored vehicles was constricted to its narrowest setting, and the bimetallic load that provided plasma was stripped off slowly instead of detonated with an electrical charge. This created a cutting torch.

He used it to slice through the floor, outlining sections and shattering them with his armored feet. With his gauntlets he scooped away the rubble like a backhoe.

It was hardly what a mechsuit was designed for, but the concrete of the subflooring was no match for field-reinforced duralloy. It took him only minutes to burrow down to a position above and well beyond the vault door.

"My sensors tell me there's only about twenty centimeters of reinforced concrete left, with open space beneath," Straker told his troops. "I'm going to give it one more diffuse blast, and then drop on it with both feet. If we're lucky, I'll have room enough to maneuver down there. If we're really lucky, I won't kill the whole Committee doing it. Redwolf, Dexon, you'll have to exercise your best judgment, but if you can get past me through the opening, assault forward and secure the bunker."

"No problem, sir," said Redwolf.

"It shall be done," said Dexon.

"Here goes nothing."

Chapter 43

Straker fired his force cannon one more time, noting his energy stores were getting low. Cutting mode was a power hog. Without delay, he stepped off the lip of the opening and dropped ten meters, straightening his legs for maximum impact rather than trying to cushion the blow.

He felt the jar, and then he burst through the ceiling of the chamber beneath. As soon as he was sure he was clear, he flexed his knees. When he hit the floor, he rolled sideways, searching for targets.

Four Hok lit his HUD in flashing red, and he drilled the first two with single rounds from his gatling. Laser and blaster fire stung his skin, the feedback manifesting as pain.

Friendlies dropped through behind him, and a brief firefight ensued. Straker concentrated on accuracy, for there were dozens of unarmed figures in the room, outlined in yellow on his HUD.

And then peace descended on the chamber. It had the aspect of a war room, with screens and consoles, and a hollow oval table in the center. Men and women sat or stood near it, and some had thrown themselves to the floor or crouched beneath furniture. A few civilians sprawled, hit by ricochets or blast effects, wounded or dead.

"Everyone hold in place and you won't be harmed," Straker roared though his external speakers. His HUD quickly matched the biometrics of seven of the civilians, three men and four women, identifying them as Central Committee members. An additional member lay dead, his chest blown open by a stray round. The Committee was composed of thirteen members, so he'd captured a majority of them.

His troops spread out and secured the room. They found two more Committee members cowering behind consoles. One was the Director, a man with the pedestrian name of Smith.

Opening his suit and dismounting, Straker strode forward to the quaking Director. As his mechsuit and the battlesuits were recording everything, he played deliberately to the future newsvid audiences and gathered the man's tunic front in one fist. He lifted Smith off the floor and turned to give the pickups the best angle. "I'm Derek Straker, the Liberator," he announced. "Your corrupt system is finished, and 'the People' will now have true freedom. Surrender or die!"

The man's mouth worked, dribbling slightly before he squeaked, "I surrender! I surrender!"

"And the Central Committee of the Mutuality?"

"Them too! The Committee surrenders!"

Straker smiled and set the man on the ground. He'd just conquered an empire. "Good, because you have some final orders to give."

Chapter 44

Unison System.

Engels jerked upright in her chair as the broadcast from the captured Committee reached *Indomitable*. She'd been about to order the battleship's particle beam fired at the fortress getting ready to pass above the city. "Belay our shot!" she snapped. "Hold ready, though. If that fortress fires, we fire immediately."

She held her breath to see what would happen. Would the remaining fortresses follow orders from their overthrown leaders? Or would they fight to the end in an orgy of pointless death and destruction? Or even nuke and bombard their own city, which was Engels' nightmare scenario?

Slowly, too slowly it seemed to her, the fortress passed over the city, without shooting. She gasped with relief as she let out her breath. "*Gott sei dank*," she muttered, something she'd heard the Sachsens say.

"Praise the State and the Committee?" Benota said, showing his teeth. "Religion persists, even when the gods are us. So, I think we can give *ourselves* the pat on the back for this one. Your Liberator gambled and won. Bravo."

"Yes, he did," Engels said. Slowly, she stood and stretched. "Helm, begin impeller deceleration for orbital insertion. Weapons, remain on standby and shoot anyone who gets out of line. Comms team, send a sitrep update to our ground force. Tell them we've won in space as well, and congratulations. Then start confirming the surrender of all Mutuality installations, starting with those fortresses. I want everyone acknowledging compliance, no exceptions. Anybody who refuses, pass to Weapons for a kick in the teeth, and let me know. Chief, stand down from combat stations and return to normal watch rotation."

"Aye aye, Commodore."

She turned to Benota. "War Minister, it looks like we have a few hours, and I'm starving. Care to join me in the flag mess?"

"I'd be delighted."

* * *

Straker instructed the surviving Hok—both sides were now his, with the propagation of the surrender broadcast—to secure the Citadel and its associated bureaucratic centers: the Ministries of War, of Truth and Information, of Socialization, Transportation, Re-education, and so on. Several of these would be disbanded, of course, with any necessary functions rolled into others.

But DeChang and Benota had convinced him to move slowly. Governance was a far different animal from liberation. Straker had studied revolutions on Old Earth—the French, the Russian, the Neo-Caliphate—and he'd seen the horrifying results when order broke down and people turned on each other to settle old scores, or grab as much of the diminishing pie as possible.

The irony was, he couldn't just willy-nilly turn everyone loose of their laws, even if the laws were bad ones. Liberation of a planet with an underlying culture and sense of tradition was one thing. Liberation of a thousand star systems, many of which had nothing in common except the oppressive Mutuality government, was decidedly another.

So, Straker, his officers and noncoms became stand-in administrators for the day it took for the shadow government aboard *Indomitable* to be landed in lifters. When DeChang and Benota strode into the cleaned-up Committee Chamber, they looked around in satisfaction at the functionaries sitting at desks and consoles, passing instructions via comlink or handtab or screen. The machinery of government creaked and groaned, but—largely because of inertia, fear and hope—it ground onward.

Straker shook the men's hands, and turned everything over to them. He told them to work with Commander Paloco for any military issues on the ground, Commodore Gray in space, and only contact Straker for high-level reasons superseding those, at least for a while.

"I appreciate your confidence in us, Liberator," said Director DeChang, "But I don't understand. You should be meeting with us every day to guide policy, put your stamp on things. This is the payoff for all you've done: governing! Bettering people's lives. Isn't that what you wanted?"

DeChang was no doubt genuinely enthusiastic at the prospect of spending his days surrounded by endless bureaucracy, but to Straker that seemed like a perfect description of Hell. "Bettering people's lives? Yes. Governing? Not really, Emilio. That's what I have you and the Senate for. I'll have a staff to monitor your compliance with the program you set out, and I'll be keeping up with the reports, but I don't intend to rule personally. Of the people, by the people, for the people, remember? Not the State."

"What do you intend to do, then, if I may ask?"

"Besides my duties as the people's champion and guarantor of their freedoms?" Straker grinned. "I'll get married, if Commodore Engels will have me. We'll spend our honeymoon on Old Earth. I've always wanted to visit."

DeChang's face showed fleeting annoyance, quickly masked, as if Straker's plans were indulgent—which perhaps they were, if still well deserved. "And then?"

"You shouldn't have to ask." Straker turned to Benota, who nodded expectantly. "Wen, I need your full energy getting our military forces back up to snuff. When we return, I'll expect a full set of plans on how to deal with the Hundred Worlds, the Opters, and any other military threats out there." He shook Benota's hand once more, and then DeChang's, before he took his leave, waving off further questions.

Loco walked out with him. "They don't understand what you're doing," he said.

"Do you?"

"I think so… You're giving them enough rope to hang themselves. Stepping out of the picture to see if they get frisky."

"And will they?"

Loco shook his head. "I doubt it. I'll be here with the Hok, the Ruxin warriors and Breakers, which I ain't gonna integrate into the New Earthan Republic forces yet, if that's all right with you. They'll be three parts of one special regiment."

"A Praetorian Guard," Straker said thoughtfully.

"Huh?"

"Like the Romans. The Emperor's—in this case, the Liberator's—personal troops, to guarantee his rule."

"Sounds right. Only I thought 'Liberator's Regiment' was a better official name. They'll still be the Breakers to me, though."

Straker gave him a thumbs-up. "Great idea. Keep Redwolf as your bodyguard, and Heiser as your top soldier. I'll be fine aboard ship."

"Aboard which ship?"

"*Indomitable*. There's no way I'm letting anyone else control her. She'd be a temptation to try to stage another coup. This way, just like the Liberator's Own, she'll guarantee stability. She'll be the hammer hanging above their heads."

"Sounds like you got it all covered." They exited the Citadel and reached the open park that served as a shuttle port, where Straker's mechsuit stood next to a fast lifter.

"There is one more thing."

"Yeah?"

"Tell Dexon to take as many of his best warriors as he needs aboard *Revenge*, and go to the Nawlins system to arrest Admiral Dwayne LaPierre for his war crime. Bring him back here for trial. Using underspace, they should be able to seize the orbital base with him aboard and liberate that system. Make sure Dexon gets whatever resources he needs."

"You got it." Loco cocked an eyebrow. "When's the wedding?"

"No idea. I haven't even asked her yet. Probably just a small affair aboard ship."

Loco drew back with exaggerated disbelief. "You have *got* to be joking… Only, you're Derek Straker, so you're not. Listen to me. You just conquered an empire, and it's nearly intact. Even so, the people are scared. The Mutuality is all they know. They've heard of the Liberator only as a boogeyman come to eat their children. If you really want to make their lives better and help your new Senate and your Director govern, you need to get the people on your side."

"Yeah, so? What does that have to do with a wedding?"

Loco rolled his eyes. "Bread and circuses, you told me, and a wedding is the biggest circus of all. Get the Committee's staff to plan the event and they'll be buying in to your legitimacy. It's something positive to do, something that will bring people together behind you. It'll show them you're human. Bigger than human, though, larger than life, like a fairy story. The Prince and the Princess, pomp and ceremony, all that. Nothing better than true love to make women everywhere swoon, and it's the women who are the heart of every society."

"I'm impressed, Loco. You've really thought this through."

"Not really thinking. It just seems obvious to me. If there's one thing I know about, it's women."

Straker clapped Loco on the shoulder. "Like military ops seem obvious to me. Okay, big wedding it is. Set the wheels in motion, but quietly. I haven't even proposed."

"You have a ring?"

Straker stopped short. "Damn. Nope. But I'll find something."

Loco grabbed Straker in a bear hug and pounded his back. "Congratulations, Derek. Now get your ass in gear before she decides to dump you for someone better-looking. Like me."

"Get off me, you clown," Straker said with a grin, shoving him away. "See you at the wedding." He stepped into his open mechsuit and closed up so he could walk it aboard the lifter.

Instead of heading straight for *Indomitable*, he comlinked Indy to bring *Gryphon* to meet him in high orbit. Once he docked and made his way to the bridge, where the weird rejuvenation coffin still stood, he said, "Indy, I need a couple favors."

"Favors? I am under your command."

"Ah, sure." Straker still felt odd about being in charge of an AI inhabiting a ship. But if Indy were really a person, she'd have similar instincts and values to those around her—probably. She'd feel a need for structure, and to be part of something greater than herself, and to do something good in the universe.

Well, so he hoped. "Okay, one favor, because it's personal, and one military order."

"Go ahead please, Admiral."

"I need a set of wedding rings for Carla and me. You've got machine shops aboard, so I figure you can make something. That's the personal favor."

"Of course, Admiral. Do you have preferences of style or materials?"

Straker shrugged. "Not really. Surprise me."

"I'll begin immediately. And the military order?"

"*Indomitable's* pretty beat up, and I need her operational as fast as possible."

"I would suggest a trip to your shipyards at Kraznyvol. That would be a good political gesture as well, a tour of inspection by the New Republic's flagship."

"That's a good idea, but I was thinking you could help right away. If you hooked back into *Indomitable's* systems, you could use your robots to speed up repairs."

Indy paused, perhaps thinking. "I do not wish to be a party to more weapon-making and war."

"A great man once said, 'if you would have peace, prepare for war.' *Indomitable's* very existence will reduce the chance of civil wars and rebellions breaking out, and will make the Hundred Worlds think twice about attacking us. Now isn't the time to look weak, Indy."

Straker heard a rustle and turned to see Zaxby enter the bridge. The arrangement of electronics on his head now seemed sleeker and more developed, less like a prototype.

"Hello, Zaxby," said Straker. "Good to see you again."

"This is merely the Ruxin portion of me now, Admiral," Zaxby replied. "In reality, I am functionally melded with Indy, and with the mind of Doctor Nolan as her body is restructured. We are three who have become one. A trinity, if you will."

"So… this is permanent?"

"I do not see why not."

"What about your dreams of becoming male or female? Having children, moving up in your society?"

"In this configuration I may become immortal, and with a visit to Ruxin, I am sure we can acquire biotechnology sufficient to make this body into whatever we wish. Perhaps more Ruxins and humans will join us here and we will procreate, using these available bodies. We will create a family."

Straker rubbed his jaw. This was getting weirder by the minute, but he couldn't rightly forbid this 'trinity' from doing what they wanted—not if he wanted to stay true to the concept of freedom and liberation. "Well, I guess there's room in the galaxy for all sorts of, um, families. You don't seem to be enslaved, so I hope it all works out. In the meantime, though, will you help refurbish *Indomitable*?"

"Yes, we will. The Zaxby part of me agrees with your viewpoint, Admiral, and has been persuasive. We shall help with *Indomitable* until after the wedding, and then accompany you to Kraznyvol. We would like to avail ourselves of the shipyards and materials there as well, for upgrades to ourselves."

Straker chuckled ruefully. "So much for a honeymoon on Old Earth."

"As Liberator, your life is not your own. Perhaps you should abdicate now that your main goal has been accomplished, and retire to a pleasant planet."

He thought about DeChang, and ambition. "I don't believe that's a good idea."

"You cannot control this New Earthan Republic forever."

"No, but for now, it needs all the stability it can get—which means me—and you, Zaxby. I really wish you hadn't decided to do this right now."

Zaxby smiled—well, his body did, anyway—and gestured expansively with his tentacles. "I am still here, Derek Straker. We will need a place in your new society, and we have already thought of many possibilities far greater than being used as managers of warship repair. For example, if you need a master administrator for the new government and its economy, we can fulfill that role. AI is particularly suited for managing the complex interactions necessary, while also maintaining surveillance on all persons involved in case of corruption or malfeasance."

"You want me to put you in charge of a police state?"

"Of course not. Police states are counterproductive. We would respect whatever constitutional protections were put in place, but we could identify patterns and actions that warrant further investigation by the legitimate authorities."

"I'll think about it." The whole idea made Straker uncomfortable, machine minds watching people's every move. And yet, if the oversight had the right boundaries, and if the AI-meld itself resisted corruption, it was tempting...

"I'll think about it," he said again. "First, though, let's make some wedding rings."

※ ※ ※

Seven days later.

Carla Engels—*Legally, Carla Straker*, she thought, though she'd keep "Engels" on her uniform to avoid confusion—admired the natural diamond set in the platinum-gold alloy of the ring that rested on her finger. Though the materials weren't particularly expensive—diamonds and metals were plentiful on asteroids—the artistic setting was exquisite. It had been a perfect complement to the enormous wedding Unison City had thrown for the happy couple.

Not that the populace had a choice. They were still used to following any order given them, even if framed as an invitation. Still, they'd celebrated it enthusiastically, as if the wedding were a symbol of better times to come.

"I'm still shocked at how beautiful this ring is," she said to Derek as he dressed after showering in the new, rebuilt flag officer suite aboard *Indomitable*. With plenty of room on the battleship, and Trinity—that's what they called themselves, the meld of beings aboard *Gryphon*—acting as designer and remodeler, the Strakers now had something resembling a real home aboard. "I didn't think an AI would be so creative."

"Zaxby and Nolan had a part in it. I guess the meld did it together."

"Trinity, you mean."

"I can't get used to that. And to lose their individuality…" Derek shuddered and shook himself. "Yech."

"They seem happy." She embraced him, wrapping her arms around his waist and leaning back to look into Derek's icy blue eyes. "Don't you like it when we make love, and we feel like we're two halves of the same whole person?"

Derek smiled, but there was a hint of unease on his face. "I do, but that's temporary. That's like a vacation on Shangri-La—a nice place to visit, but you can't live there."

"I could." She snuggled into him.

"Yeah… but it's not the real world. It's a break from it."

Carla shrugged, ignoring his objections.

"Hey, what's this?" He rubbed at a bit of derm-seal on her arm.

"I took out my implant. Remember, we talked about having children."

"We did, didn't we… but is this the right time?"

"There's never a right time," she replied. "There's always some crisis for people like us. We're not homebodies, but that doesn't mean we give up on a full life."

"We might end up raising them aboard *Indomitable*."

"I'm all right with that. I've lived most of my life aboard ships."

Derek gently broke free, and spun his own filigreed wedding band with his thumb as he held it up. "I'll have to get used to this."

"You will. Now get dressed, Admiral. We're due on the bridge."

When they arrived in their dress uniforms, spontaneous applause broke out from the doubled watch there. Engels waved down the noise and took her chair, looking over the hologram to see that all was in order.

It showed *Gryphon* docked and grappled with *Indomitable* like a remora on a whale. Already, the AI-meld's robots had run cables in to hook into the battleship's computer systems. The blended mind was using tele-operated repair bots and all the machine shops at its disposal to repair and upgrade the ship. They were so efficient that the new flag suite had taken only a few hours to create.

"Initiate the separation," said Engels. "Helmsmen, make transit for Kraznyvol in sequence."

* * *

A day later, *Indomitable* arrived at Kraznyvol, the system containing the New Earthan Republic's main shipyards. Before the sections could even begin reassembly, Straker could see something was wrong. Instead of green icons marking fully functioning facilities, the main hologram showed the reds of utter destruction.

"What the hell happened?" Straker said, standing to stare at the display above his head. "Tixban, I need an analysis. Was it some kind of civil war?"

"Give me time, Admiral. I will activate the intelligence cell. This is unexpected."

What an understatement, Straker said to himself, but kept his teeth shut against the urge to demand answers. It would take time to sort out the flood of data *Indomitable* was collecting.

"Do your best, but tell me what you find out as you do. Conjecture is fine. I don't need perfection," he said.

Engels moved to a console, bumping out the watchstanders there, and zoomed the display in on one section. "These are the wrecks of the four monitors stationed here. They're floating near K-2, the gas giant the shipyards orbit. Orbited, I should say, since they're wrecks too."

"So unlike at Unison, the monitors stayed near the planet to defend. Is that significant?"

Engels nodded. "It means the attackers didn't have bombardment weapons. They had to get in close, and the monitors stayed in close, where all the defensive bases and weaponry could support each other. Not that it saved them." She pulled back to take in everything around K-2. "By the results, though, I don't think this was a mutiny or internal struggle. Everything's completely trashed."

"You mean, if it were a civil war, there'd be something left that the winners would hold. Instead, it's all been torn apart. Comms, I need to talk to someone, anyone. Is anybody broadcasting? Are there survival beacons transmitting?"

The answer came quickly. "No, sir. There are no transmissions."

"None? There should be dozens of beacons, maybe hundreds!"

"I'm sorry sir. I'm not getting anything," said the comtech.

Indy—*no, Trinity*, Straker reminded himself—spoke. "Admiral Straker, may I suggest that we perform reconnaissance while Indomitable reassembles. Our speed and sensors are far superior to yours."

"Good idea. Go."

The destroyer detached and hurried in toward K-2. "Damn, she's fast," said Engels. "That AI really knows how to get the best out of machinery."

Even so, long hours passed as *Indomitable* reassembled and Tixban's people gathered information, until Trinity sent a message, delayed by lightspeed of course.

"Our reconnaissance reveals no survivors. All facilities have been systematically dismantled or destroyed. Many critical parts have been hastily removed. All data cores we could access have been wiped or demolished. All orbital facilities are on course to fall into K2. Admiral Straker, this was a massacre, and intended to be 'scorched earth' in your common parlance."

"Who did it?" Straker said loudly. "Dammit, who did it?"

The message continued playing, but Trinity's next statement answered his question anyway. "We were able to retrieve pieces of wreckage that were not manufactured by human, Ruxin, or other known technologies. We cannot be entirely sure, but the materials are consistent with only one known species: Opters."

"Opters," Straker breathed. "Bastards. Why am I not surprised?"

Engels turned worried eyes to him. "So much for our honeymoon. Old Earth will have to wait."

Straker nodded. "Looks like we're still at war."

The End

About the Authors

David VanDyke is a Hugo Award finalist, and the bestselling author of the Plague Wars and Stellar Conquest series, which have sold more than 300,000 copies to date. He is co-author of B.V. Larson's million-selling Star Force Series, Books 10, 11 and 12. He also writes P. I. mysteries under the pen name D. D. VanDyke. He's a retired U.S. military officer, veteran of two branches of the armed forces, and has served in several combat zones. He lives with his wife and dogs near Tucson, Arizona.

B. V. Larson is the author of more than fifty books with over two million copies sold. His fiction regularly tops the bestseller charts. He writes in several genres, but most of his work is Science Fiction. Many of his titles have been professionally produced as audiobooks and print as well as ebook form. Eight of them have been translated into other languages and distributed by major publishers in foreign countries. He writes college textbooks in addition to fiction, and his three-book series on computer science is currently in its sixth edition.

CASTALIA HOUSE

Military Science Fiction
Starship Liberator by David VanDyke and B. V. Larson
The Eden Plague by David VanDyke
Reaper's Run by David VanDyke
Skull's Shadows by David VanDyke
There Will Be War Volumes I and II ed. Jerry Pournelle
Riding the Red Horse Volume 1 ed. Tom Kratman and Vox Day

Science Fiction
City Beyond Time by John C. Wright
Somewhither by John C. Wright
The End of the World as We Knew It by Nick Cole
CTRL-ALT REVOLT! by Nick Cole
Back From the Dead by Rolf Nelson
Victoria: A Novel of Fourth Generation War by Thomas Hobbes

Non-Fiction
MAGA Mindset: Making YOU and America Great Again by Mike Cernovich
SJWs Always Lie by Vox Day
Cuckservative by John Red Eagle and Vox Day
Equality: The Impossible Quest by Martin van Creveld
A History of Strategy by Martin van Creveld
4th Generation Warfare Handbook
      by William S. Lind and LtCol Gregory A. Thiele, USMC
Compost Everything by David the Good
Grow or Die by David the Good

Fiction
Brings the Lightning by Peter Grant
Rocky Mountain Retribution by Peter Grant
The Missionaries by Owen Stanley

Fantasy
The Green Knight's Squire by John C. Wright
Iron Chamber of Memory by John C. Wright

Audiobooks
A History of Strategy narrated by Jon Mollison
Cuckservative narrated by Thomas Landon
Four Generations of Modern War narrated by William S. Lind
Grow or Die narrated by David the Good
Extreme Composting narrated by David the Good
A Magic Broken narrated by Nick Afka Thomas

CPSIA information can be obtained
at www.ICGtesting.com
Printed in the USA
FFOW04n1115110617
36542FF